Curse
of the
chosen one

The storyline was seamless. I was turning pages and found myself becoming one with the tale and loved every word. I knew the characters. I couldn't turn the pages fast enough. I thoroughly enjoyed all of it. The imagery was beautiful. I could see it all in my mind's eye, and feel the sadness in my heart when intended. This first book in the *Mark of the Faerie* series has the makings of a masterpiece. I can't wait to read Book two!

—Author Michele Ethier Anderson (Misha) *Dolphins A Wing*

Such a perfect time for another mystic series that offers a breath of freshness and a take on the other magical places we have heard of. The author does a wonderful job writing colorful and textured images for our imagination to visualize. Offering a sense of adventure, romance, and mystery all woven together I couldn't put this book down. Eagerly anticipating the release of the remaining book series. There is so much to offer and satisfy my inquiring mind. Such a beautiful story with rich characters, highly recommend if you are looking for another great series and magical world to get lost in.

—Amy Fortner

Curse
OF THE
CHOSEN ONE

Book I of *Mark of the Faerie*

Patricia Rae

RaeDiance Productions

Books may be ordered through booksellers or from the publisher's website:

www.MarkoftheFaerie.com

Hard Cover ISBN: 978-1-7345528-0-5
Paperback ISBN: 978-1-7345528-1-2
E-book ISBN: 978-1-7345528-2-9
Library of Congress Control Number: 2020901795

Cover and book design by Longfeather Book Design

I dedicate this book to my brother, Ron.
He was one of the bravest men I ever knew.

SCOTLAND
WESTERN
ISLES
(HEBRIDES)
CAITHNESS
SUTHERLAND
Kirkwall
ROSS
Faireshire
Dornoch
Torres
Elgin
Cawdor Castle
NAIRN
ELGIN
Inverness
BANFF
ABERDEEN
INVERNESS
KINCARDINE
FORFAR
Glamis
Dundee
Birnam Wood
Dunsinane Hill
PERTH
Scone
ARGYLE
COLMEKILL
(IONA)
FIFE
Macduff's Castle
Inchcolm
STIRLING
Edinburgh
HADDINGTON
Glasgow
EDINBURGH
RENFREW
BERWICK
LANARK
PEEBLES
AYR
SELKIRK
ROXBURGH
DUMFRIES
NORTHUMBER
KIRKCUDBRIGHT
WIGTOWN
CUMBERLAND
ATLANTIC OCEAN
IRELAND
NORTH
ENGLAND

chapters

&

ꜰꜱʏ

Pronounced /ˈfā/ Meaning:
Short name for a race of beings known as Faeries.

People disappear all the time.

We don't often know where they've gone. Sometimes they return on their own, and sometimes they are found by others who help them discover their way back.

But some people don't ever make it back, and those who are left behind wonder if it was a choice, or if foul play was involved in preventing the return of their loved ones.

We can never be certain what fate has in store for us, or what our destiny holds. And if we think we have some sort of control over the outcome of our future, then we are forgetting that we are not alone in this world.

To live a full life is a common desire of all living beings. If we lose sight of how humanity needs to strive for the betterment of all creatures, we face the reality of a bleak future, and very possibly, our own destruction.

It is when we are most content that we need to carefully watch for and respect the waves of change. Be prepared and be ready. It behooves us all to remember that we do not live on this Earth alone and that not all beings are visible.

People disappear all the time, so be sure to watch your step.

CHAPTER 1

THE PROTECTOR

Braden MacPherson picked up a piece of broken stone and scratched on the wall, marking the passing of another day in hell. The small, barred window was too high for him to see out, but it cast daylight onto the floor of his cell. This was his only indicator of day and night, though both held the same unchanging reality. Time had lost all meaning. Day slipped into night, night into day, repeating itself until the inevitable finally came—his anticipated execution.

The rancid smell of filth and decay had become a permanent part of him. Distinction between his prison cell and the man he once was no longer existed. Only a few days before, he had been stripped to the waist and hung by his wrists as a British warden slashed his back with the lash, asking the same questions over and over again: "Where are the other rebels? Who's hiding them? Give us names!" But he refused to provide the information they wanted. "Take him back to his cell," the warden spat after he had done his worst. "We'll let those wounds fester for a few days." Standing in front of his captive, the greasy man grabbed a handful of hair and lifted Braden's head. Through eyes blurred by tears and sweat, the forlorn prisoner looked into the warden's face, still flushed from the effort of swinging the cat o' nine tails. "When the lash meets your back again, you'll be ready to talk."

The pain from the flesh being ripped from his back caused Braden to clench his jaw so hard he thought his teeth would surely break, but he would not betray his comrades or the few Jacobite rebels who hadn't been captured or killed at Culloden. And Lord knew there were very few still alive. He could still see the battlefield littered with bloodied and dismembered bodies, his brothers-in-arms fighting for Scotland's freedom from the British tyranny. Now that the courageous band of Jacobite rebels, led by the Bonnie Prince Charles lay in bloodied defeat, Braden knew that in the eyes of his captors his life had no value whether he talked or not. Soon there would be no point in keeping him alive.

According to his lines on the wall, Braden had been in his stone cell for only fourteen days, but it felt so much longer. Except for his barred window, the only other opening in his confinement was a narrow slider at the bottom of the cell door. Once a day it opened, and something that vaguely resembled food was poured into his metal bowl. On some days, his body so weakened from torture and malnourishment, it was a struggle even to put his bowl in front of the door, much less eat. With each passing day, he began to accept that death would be his only escape from the monotony and torture. He knew he couldn't take much more and prayed that he would just fall asleep and not wake up.

As he started to slip away one evening, hoping it would be the last time he would ever have to face the stone walls or the lash again, Braden was startled back to reality by a biting pain in his ribs. He rolled onto this back to see a dark figure looming over him.

"Get yer arse up, now! Come wi' me and dinnae say a word." The guard grabbed Braden by the arm and yanked him to his feet like a rag doll. Imprisonment had drained the strength from the defiant rebel, who had once been a strong and vibrant warrior. In days past, no one could have snuck up on Braden without him already having drawn his dirk and holding it at the intruder's neck within two pulses of a heartbeat. But not on this day.

The guard pushed the prisoner out of his cell and down the hall, not the way he had been taken before, but in a new direction. *Maybe today it will all be over and this is the way to the end.* Though death was what he thought he wanted, an instinctual need to live quickened Braden's heartbeat. There was still a part of him deep inside that was not ready to die. Believing his death was at hand, a sick feeling grew in his belly at the thought of what lay ahead.

The two men, one with a knife and the other with his ankles in shackles, stumbled down the dark stone hallway. When they came to a cross-corridor, Braden shuffled to a stop. "To yer left," whispered the guard. "Come on, move faster."

The thick odor of oil-soaked torches filled the air, and their light created eerie, misshapen shadows of the men as they made their way through the corridors. At the top of a stair well, the desperate prisoner stopped abruptly, dreading what waited for him at the bottom, but a stabbing pain against his open wounds almost brought him to his knees.

"Keep going, down the stairs," the guard ordered. The shackles were just long enough for Braden to take one step at a time, and he had to catch himself more than once as the guard pushed him forward. Upon reaching the last step, they entered a large room that at one time had held many prisoners. Rusted metal wrist cuffs hung from the wall just below the ceiling. The smell and the presence of men who had hung and died here still hovered in the stagnant air.

"That door over there, move," the guard growled under his breath as he pushed his prisoner across the room. Struggling to get his feet under him, Braden stumbled and then fell hard against a large wooden door with rusty metal hinges and a round metal pull.

Terrified at what might be waiting for him on the other side, Braden backed away from the door. "Pull that bar back, slow and quiet like." The guard pointed to a long rod that slid across the top of the door, bolting it closed.

Feeling his mortality slipping away, Braden stared at the door until pain from the knife in his already wounded flesh impelled him into movement. Reaching up with both hands, he pulled back on the bar, creating a resounding c*lang* that echoed off the walls. "Damn it, man! Push the door open, move!" The guard once again used his knife to punctuate his order.

With what little strength he had left, Braden leaned his weak body up against the door and began to push. As the door creaked open, he felt a cool breeze across his face. Another quick push from the guard sent the shaking prisoner flying through the opening. After tumbling to the ground, Braden eased himself up on to his hands and knees. Though the night was near pitch dark, he could feel grass and dirt between his fingers and knew he was outside the prison walls.

"It's up to ye now, maggot. Dinnae know why anyone would want to save the likes of ye, but good riddance." As the guard spit out his words, Braden heard the sound of the bolt sliding back into place, locking the door from the inside. He stayed on his hands and knees, waiting to be dragged off and killed, but nothing happened. Small creatures of the night were the only sounds he heard over his rapidly beating heart and the ragged breath burning at his throat.

As his eyes adjusted to the dim light of the night sky, Braden scanned his new surroundings, which seemed to be an empty courtyard. Cautiously, he stood up and took a deep breath of the cool night air, something he thought he would never do again. But why? Why was he brought here in the middle of the night? What did the guard mean when he said that someone wanted to save him?

Braden took in his surroundings, but with no moon or outside lighting, there was little to see. His senses on alert, he shuffled his way along until his outstretched hand encountered a wall. Turning his back against the wall, he winced as his open wounds touched the rough surface. It was cold and wet, covered with slimy moss. Slowly, Braden felt his way along the rock wall, one small step at a time, as wide as his shackles would allow. His eyes on alert for any movement, he came to a corner, then another wall. After stumbling over a large rock, he steadied himself and continued on. Survival mode had kicked in. His only instinct was to keep moving.

As he continued making his way along the slimy stone surface, Braden's hand butted up against a large rock sticking out abruptly from the wall. He felt a slight breeze coming through a thin crack in the wall, an opening! Pushing his fingers into the crevice between the two stone walls, he pulled back with all the force his weakened body could muster. Slowly, a door leading out of the courtyard swung free. It had been left slightly ajar, but why?

Braden looked nervously over his shoulder, and half expected to see guards running up to drag him back to his cell where they would beat him senseless. But he heard nothing except the chirping of the crickets, the repeating bellow of a bull frog, and the rustling of the wind through the trees. Pulling the opening wide enough for his body to pass through, he looked out into a forest. Dark and secluded, it beckoned to him, *Run! Run as fast as your shackles will allow!*

Again, the nagging question ate at him. Why did the guard bring him here in the middle of the night knowing there was a way to escape? His mind raced frantically in a hundred directions while the trees called to him. *Run before it's too late, run!*

After quickly scanning the outer perimeter, Braden began moving as fast as the chains would allow. With his heart pounding in his ears and his rapid breath burning in his lungs, he shuffled out the door and escaped the prison walls. Though the shackles cut into his ankles with every stride, he pushed himself forward, ignoring the pain. At first, the forest didn't look that far away, but now as he ran for his life, it seemed like miles. What he had imagined would take only minutes now seemed like an eternity. As his weakened body struggled to move faster, Braden's mind commanded. *Have to keep going, almost there, don't quit moving!* More than once, he stumbled and fell, tumbling across the ground, but each time he pushed himself back up and kept going.

After finally reaching the safety of the trees, Braden stopped to catch his breath. Gasping for air, he leaned up against a large tree trunk and took one last look at the prison. He watched for any movement, but saw nothing. Planning to go deeper into the forest, he pushed away from the tree, but as soon as he moved, a heavy hood was thrown over his head, and a pain cracked like lightning through his skull. As he dropped to his knees, everything went black.

CHAPTER 2

FAIRESHIRE

The sweet scent of laurel blended naturally with the earthy smell of moss as the sun's warming rays converted the previous night's rain into a lazy steam rising up from the ground, completing the quaintness of the small village of Faireshire on a warm summer's day.

Isaboe McKinnon hung her wet laundry to dry in the afternoon breeze, pondering just how different Faireshire was from what she'd left behind in Glasgow. In the big city, she had hired help to assist with the daily duties of keeping a home. There, her life had been centered around dinner parties and social events. Glascow was a seaport with bustling docks, filled with ships coming and going at all times of the year, and it boasted to be one of the country's largest shipyards. This major trading port was a busy city, full of life as cargo ships brought strange people from faraway lands. A constant stream of traders brought fresh spices, strange foods, colorful clothing, and intriguing trinkets from around the globe.

Just the opposite, Faireshire was a sleepy little town tucked among the lush, rolling hillsides of the Scottish Highlands. Moss-covered rocks lined the banks of the lazy Glochshire River, where giant oak trees stood tall and majestic, as though trying to reach the heavens. The air was sweet with the scent of lavender. Beautiful fields of purple heather grew in abundance, accented by the bright yellow flowers of the Scottish gorse. Nestled in a valley, with the Tory Mountains to the east and the Lowery Hills to the west, this fairy-tale town sat just outside the aspen tree line of Lowery Forest.

Though Isaboe enjoyed the slower pace, she had found the people to be reserved, sometimes to the point of aloofness. And it didn't take long for her to confirm that Faireshire held its own little secrets. Even in Glasgow, she'd heard myths and superstitious stories of the town's entanglement with the faerie, and she wondered if that was why the people here were so wary of strangers. But Isaboe didn't give much thought to the myths; her primary focus had always been on the needs of her family.

Her husband, Nathan, had been hired by the city to engineer and oversee the building of a bridge across the Glochshire River. The district constable placed in Faireshire by the British Parliament had been ordered to create a new avenue of commerce through the Highlands for the Empire's trade. This bridge would create a direct route to Dornach, a growing port town and a rest point on the road to Inverness, the largest market town in the Northern Highlands.

Most of the Highland natives were small farmers, planting crops or raising cattle and sheep. The British government, however, was confident that the new road would encourage businessmen from the cities to move north. The English had secured their hold in the Highlands when they defeated the Jacobite stronghold at the Battle of Culloden, and most Highlanders scoffed at the idea that the new bridge would do much to encourage trade. It was, they whispered, just a way to ensure that the British army had another route across Scotland. But whatever the cause, Nathan jumped at the offer and moved his young family to the mysterious little town.

Though washing clothes was a humbling job, in her attempt to fit in with the Faireshire community, she opted to do her own laundry and not hire help with her daily chores. Besides, the day had turned warm and pleasant, a rare treat in the narrow valley, and she enjoyed the warmth of the sun. Clouds usually hovered over the sleepy little village, so a bright and sunny afternoon made any chore outside more enjoyable.

When a gust of wind loosened the comb from her long auburn hair, Isaboe pulled it out. Brushing the hair away from her face, she started to put it back in place, but then stopped and looked closely at the comb in her hand. It was a thing of beauty, this anniversary gift Nathan had just given her. The threaded glass beads wrapped around the end sparkled like diamonds in the sunlight, and a smile crossed her lips at the thought of this man who loved her, who made her feel so secure. Having just celebrated six years of marriage and two children later, she knew she was fortunate. Isaboe looked forward to watching her two beautiful children grow and blossom in this place, so far from the big city.

Leaving the bustling life of Glasgow hadn't been terribly difficult, nor was moving further away from a family she hadn't seen in nearly twelve years. Three sisters and a mother, who still lived in Edinburgh as far as she knew, were Isaboe's only living relatives. Henry and Marta Cameron, respected community leaders and long-standing members of the Greyfriars Kirk, had taken her in as an infant at the request of the very insistent deaconess, Sister Miriam. Though the Camerons already had three girls—Deidra, Cecilia, and Saschel—they were one of the most affluent families in Edinburgh, and surely they would not find it difficult to feed one more. So, against Marta's wishes, Isaboe was adopted and became their fourth daughter.

As a child, Isaboe didn't understand why the only mother she had ever known seemed so burdened and reluctant to show any kindness toward her, much less love. Marta Cameron was a stately woman, slender and always proper in her appearance, but her heart was cold. As Isaboe grew, she learned to guard her heart against Marta's stinging words and lack of affection. Fortunately, her adoptive father, Henry Cameron—a well-educated and successful business man who always wore a guarded smile—had shown genuine love for her. But that was taken away when he died. At only twelve-years-old, Isaboe felt she had lost the only person who truly cared for her.

Shortly thereafter, she was sent to Larbaness Boarding School for Girls in Glasgow, which was just fine with her. If Marta thought her action was not only a reprieve for herself, but a punishment for her daughter, she was sorely mistaken. For Isaboe, it was a Godsend to be among other young girls, who for the most part came from very similar backgrounds—wealthy, but ignored.

The years at Larbaness went quickly, and Isaboe grew to be a confident and lovely young lady, or so she was told. Groomed for a refined lifestyle, she was prepared for the opportunities provided to someone of her status, and the moment was presented at a school dance shortly after she turned sixteen.

Nathan McKinnon was among a group of young men who'd come to the dance from the Boys School of Beacon Hill. The dark-haired, brown-eyed engineering student was immediately smitten by Isaboe's slender, graceful body, flowing auburn hair, and captivating green eyes. He vowed that she would be his partner for every dance that night, and for the rest of his life, if she would have him.

During the following year, the young couple spent as much time together as they could. After receiving his degree, Nathan wasted no time in asking for Isaboe's hand in marriage. With a promising career ahead of him, he knew there was only one thing missing for an ideal beginning—a beautiful and engaging bride. Though Isaboe was still young, and her exposure to life outside of school had been limited, Nathan made her feel wanted and loved. He was ambitious, hardworking, and came from a good family. Though maybe not the most handsome man she had ever known, he would provide her with the lifestyle she was accustomed to.

Isaboe recalled the day she had solidified in her heart she was making the right choice. It was the same day she received word that her mother wouldn't be attending her wedding.

"Elsa Randolph…Lidia March…Isaboe Cameron," the head mistress read off the names as she held the letters in her hands.

Isaboe walked briskly to the front of the room to take the letter. A fortnight before she had written to her family informing them of her engagement. She also asked, rather boldly if she did say so herself, about the state of her dowry. During her years at Larbaness, Marta had never written to her, nor had she ever visited. So Isaboe was apprehensive about the response she would receive.

"Is it from your mother?" Jenny St. Clair was well aware of her roommate's anxiety in regard to Marta's reply. But Isaboe only nodded and slipped back into her seat, giving her friend an uneasy look.

"That's all the mail this week, ladies. You are dismissed," announced the head mistress as the sound of scooting chairs and girls conversing immediately filled the hall.

"I'll read it back in our room. Nathan's coming by in half an hour and I want to change before he arrives," Isaboe whispered to Jenny as they walked out into the foyer. "Hopefully, I'll have some good news to share with him about my dowry." She couldn't help her nervous smile.

But the letter didn't hold the news she was hoping for—not even close. "This bit of money, that's it? This is an embarrassment! I saw what my sister Deidra had in her dowry. Mother had a whole chest of linens, dishes, *and* family heirlooms when she married." Sprawling across her bed, Isaboe moaned loudly. "Five hundred pounds is the money Father put away for me before he died. Mother is giving me nothing! How can I present Nathan with only this?"

"Five hundred pounds is a lot of money, Isaboe." Jenny frowned at her. "It will help you to afford all those things you'll need to start your own home. Anyway, Nathan won't care. He's crazy about you, regardless of what your dowry holds." Jenny sat on her own bed listening quietly as her roommate sobbed. "Who knows, maybe when your mother comes to the wedding, she'll bring your chest with her."

Giving Jenny a sorrowful expression, Isaboe sat up. "Mother's not coming," she said, handing the letter to her friend. "Neither are my sisters. It's my wedding, but I'll have no family in attendance, and no dowry to speak of. This is horrible! I'm certain Nathan's parents won't agree to the marriage now." Picking up a small porcelain vase from the table next to her bed, she threw it across the room. As it shattered on the floor, Isaboe dropped her head onto her pillow, pounded her fist into the mattress, and screamed, "I hate her!"

But just as Jenny had predicted, Nathan didn't care, nor did his parents. Instead of the big wedding Isaboe had hoped for, just to show Marta she didn't need her family or their heirlooms, the young couple agreed to have a small ceremony at his parent's home. He had waited long enough to be with the woman he loved, and they were married that summer.

Nathan had taken a job working for the City of Glasgow, and soon became a respected engineer, specializing in bridge construction. Just three months after their marriage, Isaboe discovered she was carrying their first child. The thrill and fear of becoming a mother was unsettling, but more than anything, she wanted to have a child she could love with all the passion and devotion she had never known from Marta or her own birth mother.

The months passed quickly and the day finally arrived. A baby boy was born. As Isaboe held the precious bundle in her arms and looked into the face of this beautiful gift from God, she knew there was no limit, in Heaven or Earth, to the love a mother can have for her child.

Having been raised in an unloving environment, she now had what she always desired—a loving family. She vowed that her son would know how much he was wanted and loved every day of his life, and she would do whatever was needed to make sure he knew that. They named the boy Benjamin, after Nathan's father, and he was the pride and joy of their little family.

For Isaboe, her life finally felt complete. With the promise of memories to be made and love to be shared, it was a life she looked forward to with great anticipation. She hoped the years ahead would be filled with happiness, sprinkled with many moments of joy. But whatever her future brought, Isaboe looked forward to experiencing it all—the good and the bad—with all the bits of life that come in between.

CHAPTER 3

A NEW LIFE

Braden awoke to a throbbing pain in his head that pounded with such intensity he couldn't open his eyes. He reached up to stop the assault and felt an agonizing lump protruding from the top of his head. It was pumping searing heat and pain through his entire skull. As he gradually became aware of his surroundings and the soft bed he was lying on, Braden opened his eyes and slowly sat up. The world spun around him, and his stomach instantly rebelled. He began to vomit violently, but since he hadn't eaten in days, it was only dry heaves.

Sitting hunched on the side of the bed, Braden took long, deep breaths in an attempt to stop the whirling. It took a few more minutes before he could raise his head to look around. Though his vision was out of focus, the former prisoner knew he was in an unfamiliar room. It was definitely not his prison cell. An oil lamp sitting on a table next to the bed cast a warm light about the small room. Against the opposite wall, he could make out a jug and a plate of bread on top of another table. When Braden looked down, he didn't recognize his clothing. The shirt and pants were clean and fresh; there were no rips or ragged tears, no filth or blood stains. Leaning slightly forward, he expected to see his feet still in shackles, but they too were gone. No metal rings dug into his ankles, only the nasty gashes of where they had been.

Certain he was no longer in prison, the unsettling question of *why* gnawed at him. Not that he was unhappy with being free of that hell on Earth, but Braden needed to know what was next. He slowly stood up, but after one small step, the spinning started again. Losing his balance, he stumbled around the small room trying to get his feet under him before falling into a bookshelf. As the books tumbled off the shelf, he fell against the table holding his food and drink, crashing them to the floor. Darkness once again rimmed the edges of his consciousness. Just before hitting the floor, he heard a faint voice and felt a strong grip leading him back to the bed.

The simple attempt to stand had exhausted him. His breathing was labored, and Braden lay on the bed covered with beads of perspiration. Behind closed eyes he slowly came back to a place of stillness, and the spinning room eventually came to a stop.

"You can't be up yet, man. You took one hell of a whack on the head. And you were weak *before* Ox took a crack at you. 'Tis lucky he didn't kill you. The stupid man doesn't know his own strength."

Braden opened his eyes slightly and looked up at a stranger standing next to his bed, but his eyes refused to focus on the man's features. "Who are ye? Where am I?" Braden tried to put words together, but found it difficult to speak.

"Just get some rest. The master will be in to see you shortly," the stranger said, before turning to leave the room. It was the last thing Braden remembered before slipping back into darkness.

Sometime later, he woke again, and this time felt the warmth of sunlight coming in through a small window. It was the first direct sunlight Braden had felt in more days than he cared to count. After he was able to sit up, and the room safely remained stationary, he looked around. There was a new plate of food and a jug on the table he had previously knocked over. The floor had been mopped clean, and the books were replaced on the shelf from his first clumsy waking. Taking a moment to check the strength in his legs, Braden managed to stand, but he could still feel the edge of dizziness. His head continued to pound as he leaned against the wall for support and made his way to the window. With his vision out of focus, it took a few moments for his eyes to adjust to the light.

The window overlooked a small, well-manicured courtyard with an inviting cobblestone walking path that led into a large garden. A handful of people were working the grounds, unaware they were being observed. Braden again had the unsettling feeling of not knowing why he was here, wherever *here* was.

As if he had known that his guest was awake and looking for answers, the door to Braden's small room opened and an elderly man entered. "Good day to you, young man. How is your head this morning? Still a bit tender, I should say." The tall, dignified looking man had long, white hair pulled back and tied. He had a white beard to match, with bushy, white eyebrows that protruded over his dark, deep-set eyes, giving him a scholarly appearance. Above his dark blue robe, tied with a white sash, a tranquil smile filled his aged face.

Walking over to the plate of food on the table and seeing it untouched, the man glanced at Braden, who was still leaning up against the wall. With sweat beading on his brow and upper lip, the rebel watched the older man's every move.

"Not much of an appetite yet, aye? Well, that will come back in time." Taking a chair next to the table, the man crossed his legs and folded his hands in his lap, then looked at Braden with an understanding smile. "I'm sure you must have many questions, so, if you feel strong enough, let's be about it."

"Who are ye? Where am I? Why am I here?" Braden's voice was strained, and his rubbery legs felt like they could give out at any moment. His breath was labored, and just standing was difficult, but he gave a twisted smile, "How about just startin' with the basics?"

"Why don't you sit down first, maybe have a bite to eat. That might make you feel a bit stronger." The older man seemed genuinely concerned for Braden's condition.

Though he waved off anything to eat, Braden decided that sitting back down was good advice. Never taking his eyes off his mysterious host, he made his way back to the bed.

Apparently convinced that his guest was not going to collapse on him, the white-haired gentleman offered answers to Braden's questions. "My name is Demetrick, and you are in my home. I had my men bring you here upon your release from prison, though I have to say, I never intended for you to be struck with such a blow to the head. I must apologize for Samuel. He tends to be all brawn and very little brain."

"So....ye made arrangements for my release? Why? I dinnae even know who ye are."

"No, you don't. But I know who *you* are, and I need a man just like you. So I paid the guard to make sure you could find your way out."

"What do ye mean, a man like me? What do ye want?" Though Braden was grateful to be out of prison, he was uncertain what his release was going to cost him.

"I need a man to take on a task of great importance. Not just any man, mind you, but a man with loyalty and conviction, a man who holds true to his word, regardless of the cost. He must be brave, a leader, and a strong warrior who can defend not only himself, but those he is sworn to protect. I know all about you, Braden MacPherson. You led a regiment against King George's army, and even against all odds, you never backed down. You never claimed defeat or surrender. You would have fought to your death before turning your back on a cause you believe in, however insufficient your means were in waging such a war. Your men trusted you, looked up to you, and knew they could count on you. I need all these attributes in a man that no one will miss. Your execution was already scheduled. As far as anyone who might have known you, well, they all think you're a dead man."

Braden struggled to understand what the older man was trying to tell him. "So, ye saved my life for some kind' o mission, but what? And the Brits obviously know that I am no longer in their prison. What about them? Are they not gonna be lookin' for me?"

"You won't need to worry about the British. They'll soon forget about Braden MacPherson."

It started out as a light chuckle, but then gradually built into outright laughter. Unfortunately, however, Braden's momentary lapse into frivolity caused the pain in his skull to reignite. Trying to stop the agony and regain his composure, he held his head before finally looking back at Demetrick. "What, did ye pay off the entire British army as well? Ye're a mad man if ye think the Brits are gonna forget about me! Ye said it yerself, ye know who I am and what I did. The Brits dinnae take lightly to that kind of rebellion. It is just a matter of time before they find me and the rest of the Jacobites. We're all finished. It's over. The English want us all wiped off the face of the Earth. Do ye not understand what I'm telling ye man?"

"Oh, yes, *I* completely understand. What *you* don't understand is that after completing the task I have assigned, the British Army will have forgotten all about you. But just in case there might be a few diehards, we'll provide you with a new identity."

"And just what is the task ye have assigned for me?" Braden asked as he looked at Demetrick under a heavily furrowed brow. He wasn't certain he wanted to know.

Demetrick stood and headed for the door before turning to reply. "I'll tell you the rest when the time is right. You first need to regain your strength and heal your wounds. Alex will send a nurse around daily to check on your recovery. Your health is the first order of business."

After opening the door, Demetrick turned around. "Oh, and Braden, there is one more thing. You are a guest in my home and shall be treated as such. If I were you, I wouldn't get any ideas about running off or doing anything rash. Just as easy as it was to get you out of prison, it would be just as easy to put you back. You may be right, and the British may be looking for you as we speak. It would so ruin all my plans if I had to hand you over. So know this—I offer you a second chance at life, a new identity, and in return, all I ask is that you fulfill a request. Though it is not a simple one, it is one of great honor. That is why I chose you, Braden MacPherson. I hope I have chosen correctly. I do so hate to be wrong." Demetrick flashed a warm smile before walking out and closing the door.

Chapter 4

The Myth

The sharp, demanding cry of her second child brought Isaboe back from her moment of nostalgia. Two-year-old Anna was awake and hungry. Brushing back her hair and replacing the comb, Isaboe picked up her basket of laundry and went into her comfortable little home to rescue her screaming child. "There, there, my wee one, don't cry. Mama's here." The moment she scooped up little Anna, all crying ceased. As Isaboe rocked gently and hummed to the child, now cradled in her protective arms, a happy and contented smile broke across the porcelain face of the beautiful baby girl.

While warming up a bowl of creamed potatoes, Isaboe noticed the sunlight captured in the golden strands of Anna's hair. She wondered if the color would match the sunset glow of her own. The baby's eyes had already turned to resemble her mother's, with the exception of the speckled bits of gold that floated in the deep green irises of Isaboe's enchanting eyes. They were missing from her child's, but other than that, it appeared that little Anna was going to be a duplicate image of her mother. As she stroked the soft curls of her daughter's fine hair, Isaboe couldn't help but wonder if these characteristics had been passed on from her birth mother. She had always wondered if the star-shaped birthmark on the inside of her right arm, a mark also shared by her daughter, had been passed down from the ambiguous woman who had birthed her. It all added to the mystery. Her birth mother was someone she thought about often. Who was she? What was she like? But more importantly, why had she felt it necessary to give her baby away? Was she unmarried, too young, too poor, or perhaps too selfish to love anyone but herself? After giving birth to Benjamin and then three years later to baby Anna, Isaboe couldn't comprehend how anyone could forfeit the love of a child.

Benjamin was only two when Isaboe discovered that she was expecting again. He also had begun to take on a parent's features, but it was his father's dark hair and deep-brown eyes that made it so obvious just whose son he was.

When Anna Isabella McKinnon made her screaming debut into the world, Isaboe had no doubt of the endless capacity of a mother's love. This helped to heal her own deep wounds, and the reality of her own loveless mother didn't seem to matter anymore.

"Good day, my lady. Mind if I join you?" Young Margaret MacDougal stood at the open door of Isaboe's kitchen, peering in and waiting for an invitation. The spunky twelve-year-old was the daughter of Fredrick and Edna MacDougal, who lived just down the road. The girl had a face full of freckles, a head full of curly, fire-red hair, and a passion for the McKinnon children. The MacDougals were one of the oldest families in Faireshire, and their heritage in the quaint, little town went back as far as anyone could remember.

"Well, good day to you Margaret. Yes, please come in. I'm just trying to get Anna to finish her afternoon meal, but I'm afraid that most of it is on her, rather than inside her."

At the sight of Margaret, a huge smile broke out across the baby's face, accompanied by a squeal of delight. Having spent a good deal of time with Margaret since their arrival in Faireshire, both Benjamin and Anna adored her. The fresh summer day had filled Anna with a bit of the Irish, and she apparently didn't care much for creamed potatoes. They were smeared across her forehead, down the side of her face, and squished between her pudgy little fingers.

Margaret laughed as she squatted down next to the child. "Just look at you now, you silly little lass. You'll be a fine mess to be cleaning." She gently stroked the top of the baby's head before untying the soiled cloth from around her neck.

"Oh Margaret, you needn't bother, I'll clean her up. I'm sure you didn't come over to wash up our little piggy Anna."

But when Isaboe brought a clean damp cloth, Margaret extended her hand and took it with a smile, making it clear that was exactly what she'd come for. "Really, I don't mind. I know you have your hands full caring for your home, Mr. McKinnon, and both little ones," she said, wiping potatoes off the baby's face. "After I clean up Anna, I'll take her outside. We're gonna take off our shoes so we can feel the grass between our toes and chase after butterflies. On a fine day like today, I do believe we'll have no trouble finding butterflies."

The truth was that Isaboe still had a few chores left undone. With Nathan and Benjamin on an outing, this would be the opportune time to catch up on things she wanted to accomplish before the evening's special event.

"Margaret, tell me what the festival is like. Last week I went to the town meeting and offered to help, but the women told me everything had already been taken care of." Isaboe knew she was still considered an outsider, and the majority of the townspeople hadn't accepted her yet, save the MacDougal's. Though most of the men seemed to be friendly, she had received a cool reception from the female community.

"Well, the festival is always held on the first full moon of mid-summer," Margaret began, "and everyone gathers in the square to thank Mother Earth for the upcoming harvest. There is a Summer Queen chosen from all the girls, and she sits on a tall seat called a tavell. Mrs. Frasier has sewn a beautiful white gown for her to wear, *and* she gets to keep it! The rest of us will dance around her and throw flower petals into the air. Then the mothers and fathers take colored ribbons and wrap them around the tavell while they chant, asking the spirits for a good harvest and for blessings in the coming year. Then there are games, music and dancing. Everyone brings lots of delicious food. That's my favorite part!"

"It sounds like a good bit of fun," Isaboe said with a smile, as she regarded the young red-haired girl. "About this Summer Queen, how is she chosen? Is there a particular age the girl must be? Could you be the Summer Queen?"

Margaret dropped her eyes, and the smile disappeared from her freckled face. "No, it won't be me. I'm not pretty enough," she replied quietly.

Isaboe saw the hurt look cross Margaret's face as she stared into her lap. "Well, that's just nonsense, you certainly are pretty enough. Anyway, it doesn't really sound all that great—sitting way up on a tall seat while everyone else is singing, dancing, and eating good food."

As she looked up at Isaboe, the smile returned to Margaret's face, and she even began to chuckle. "I never thought of it like that before. You're right. It doesn't sound that great at all!"

"Anna is very fond of you," Isaboe said as Margaret hefted the child into her arms.

"And I of her, Ma'am! And of you, too, of course!"

There were few girls Margaret's age in Faireshire, and she had felt welcomed in Isaboe's home. The women in town may have murmured jealously over their attractive neighbor, but their pettiness apparently didn't matter to Margaret. On the contrary, the young girl's face lit up whenever she was around, and Isaboe, too, enjoyed spending time together as their bond of friendship grew.

Carrying the baby on her hip as she headed out to the sunshine, Margaret didn't get far before Isaboe drew her attention. "I'd be grateful if you could watch Anna for a bit. I'm going to gather some mushrooms for a dish I'm making for the festival."

"Sure I can," Margaret replied. "Just don't go into the forest," she added, turning to head out with Anna in her arms.

"Why? Why shouldn't I go into the forest?" A curious look accompanied Isaboe's question.

Margaret stopped and turned around. "Because, it's midsummer's eve, of course. Nobody goes into the forest on midsummer's eve," she replied bluntly.

"I don't understand. What does midsummer's eve have to do with not going into the forest?"

"The faeries could get you and take you into the realm of the fey. Don't you know the stories?" Her eyes grew wide and solemn.

"No, I'm afraid I don't. Why don't you tell me?" Isaboe humored the girl and the myths she'd grown up believing, but wanted to hear more.

Margaret shifted Anna to her other hip before continuing. "Alright, well this is what my mum told me. If you go into the forest on midsummer's eve, you could fall into a hobble. If you do, you'll be taken into the faerie world and be gone for years, and years, and years! My auntie told us about a woman who was gone for a hundred years, but it seemed like only one day to her. So you should never go into the forest on midsummer's eve. No one ever does, just in case."

"Just in case what? That it might be true? Margaret, you don't really believe that do you? It's just a myth, a tale someone made up a long time ago."

"I just know that no one ever goes into the forest on midsummer's eve, and you shouldn't either."

Margaret seemed so serious about the topic and by the look on her face Isaboe thought it best not to debate the issue anymore and just agreed with her. "Alright, fine, I'll stay out of the woods. But what, my dear, is a *hobble?*"

The young girl sighed deeply as she rolled her eyes. "It's a circle of stones, or flowers, or toadstools, or just about anything that's in a perfect circle. It's also called a faerie ring, and if you step into one," Margaret's voice lowered, "you can fall into the realm of the fairies and not even know it." Her words were laced with mystery, matched by the look on her face.

Now Isaboe really felt like an outsider in this town. "Alright, I'll make sure to stay clear of any faerie rings today. Anything else I should know?"

"No. That's it. Just stay out of the forest," Margaret repeated.

"Fine. I'll stay out of the forest." Now it was Isaboe who was rolling her eyes, feeling rather foolish at making such a commitment based on a ridiculous myth.

Seeming satisfied with Isaboe's response, Margaret offered up a smile before walking out the door with Anna still on her hip.

Isaboe reached for the basket she used to gather herbs and followed the girls out. "I won't be long. If Nathan and Benjamin return before I do, you'll be sure to tell them I'll be back shortly, aye?"

Restless and wanting down, Anna squirmed in Margaret's arms. "Aye, you can always count on me, Mrs. McKinnon. And I'll take good care of little Anna," Margaret called over her shoulder as she skipped in the opposite direction, chasing the giggling two-year-old.

Isaboe smiled as she strolled down the path behind her home. "Everyone should have a friend like you Margaret," she said quietly to herself.

The search for the right mushrooms proved to be a greater challenge than Isaboe had expected. Though she found small ones here and there, she knew that the biggest would be found at the base of large trees where it was cool and moist. She looked carefully at the curtain of oak trees just a few yards away. With her basket hung on her arm, Isaboe glanced back over her shoulder to see if anyone was watching. Feeling silly she'd allowed a child's mythical story to make her pause, she shrugged as she started into the forest. She thought briefly about Margaret's warning, but that didn't stop her progress. "Sorry Margaret, but myths don't gather mushrooms."

Following the path she had always taken with the children, Isaboe headed into the shadows of the trees. She'd been in the forest many times, but never had the huge fungi appeared so bountiful. She would have no trouble filling her basket, be back in plenty of time to start her stew, and still find something pretty to wear for the festival. Needing only a few more, Isaboe spotted a group of perfect mushrooms at the base of a large old oak. As she walked toward them, not paying sufficient attention to her footing, she stumbled over a tree root that was twisting up out of the ground.

Falling forward, Isaboe sprawled onto the forest floor with a thud, and the basket went flying, along with all of its contents. Though the impact was slightly painful, she wasn't seriously hurt.

Frustrated and annoyed with her clumsiness, she pushed up from the ground, brushed the hair back from her face and the dirt from her dress. She'd just begun to recover the scattered collection of mushrooms when she noticed a row of beautiful blue irises shooting up through the organic matter. Thinking that they would make a lovely arrangement to take to the festival, she shifted her thoughts and walked over to the flowers; but her breath caught when she noticed that the row continued around her in a circle. Beautiful blue irises were growing side by side in a perfect ring… *and she was standing in the middle of them!*

Abruptly, and in unison, the irises sprayed out a delicate mist that shot into the air and settled on her like fine dust. A jolt of panic warned Isaboe to leave the circle, but she was quickly overcome by dizziness. Placing her hands on the sides of her head, she tried to stop the spinning, but lost her balance and found herself sitting on the forest floor. As the spinning increased, she felt both nauseous and sleepy at the same time, so she decided to lie down, just for a moment, to let the feeling pass before making her way back home.

In the middle of a perfect circle of beautiful blue irises, on a soft carpet of fallen leaves and velvet moss, Isaboe laid down under the shade of the ancient oak tree and fell into a deep sleep.

CHAPTER 5

RECOVERY

As days became weeks and turned into months, Braden slowly regained his pre-prison strength. He seldom saw Demetrick and spoke with him even less, but just as promised, every accommodation was made to make him comfortable and well attended.

Summer lengthened the days, and on warm afternoons, strolls through the compound surrounding Demetrick's spacious home became commonplace. Braden was seldom alone on these walks. His nearly constant companion was a tall, spry youth named Alexander, who insisted that Braden call him Alex. Only the boy's mother and Demetrick called him by his full name.

Alex had resided at the compound for two years while being tutored by Demetrick. The boy was bright, if a touch overly-enthusiastic. His large, happy brown eyes matched a smile that seemed too big for his face. His long legs and gangly arms made him appear clumsy. But what Alex lacked in physical attributes, he made up with a sharp mind and a desire to learn from the master.

Master Demetrick, as Braden soon learned, was not only his liberator, but was apparently a powerful wizard. When Alex shared this information, Braden decided neither to comment nor to think on it. Magic, he knew, was dangerous by nature, and could as easily help and heal as it could befuddle, or even kill. Grateful for his rescue and Demetrick's hospitality, Braden opted to just accept the information for now, and did not ask further on the matter of wizardry.

Demetrick's compound was strategically surrounded by multiple outbuildings; a large barn filled with livestock and feed, sheds for storing supplies, and, of course, an abundant garden. The garden was split into two sections, one where vegetables and fruit trees grew, and in the other, ornamentals, herbs, and fragrant flowers filled a well-manicured courtyard. All these areas were within the compound and accessible to Braden. However, the smaller huts tucked deeper into the surrounding forest were unofficially off limits.

"What's back there?" Braden asked as he nodded toward the restricted area.

"Oh, just some storage sheds. Master Demetrick keeps a number of peculiar and very interesting items tucked away back there." Alex's vague answer was not unusual. He gave Braden one of his quirky smiles and kept walking. "Hey, guess what? I made a mouse disappear today!" he exclaimed.

"What's so special 'bout that? I've made lots of mice disappear," Braden said coldly.

"I didn't kill it. I made it *disappear!*" Alex said with a sweeping gesture and a gleam in his wide, brown eyes. "You know, like vanish before your eyes!"

"Disappearing mice? Hmm," Braden regarded his companion. "That's what ye've been learning from a wizard all these years, how to get rid of rodents?" He shook his head. "So, where'd it go?"

"Well, I don't actually know. I was only able to accomplish the first half of the spell, making the mouse disappear. I wasn't able to make it reappear. So, unfortunately, the poor little creature I fear is lost in limbo somewhere."

Braden thought the mouse's demise had an interesting irony to it. "Sounds like a terrible fate, even for a rodent." Feeling the familiar knot of unease in his gut, he caught Alex by the arm and turned the lad toward him. "Alex, I ken I've asked ye before, but, what's my fate? I feel much like yer missing vermin. I'm not dead, but I also feel like I dinnae exist. How long is Demetrick gonna keep me in the dark? Not that I'm ungrateful for all he's done, but what's this great task he has in store for me?"

"Even if I knew, it's not my place to tell. When the time is right, the master will let you know," said the young apprentice with reverence.

For all of the boy's faults, Braden was impressed by his loyalty. Though he was sure that Alex was meant to keep watch over him, he couldn't imagine that the clumsy youth would be much of a physical challenge if he chose to escape. "So, how is it that every time I take a turn about the grounds, ye show up? An' dinnae tell me ye use magic keep track of me," Braden growled. "Ye're not that good a wizard."

"What? Can't a friend join you for a walk?"

"Oh, we're friends now, aye?"

"I'd like to think we are."

"So, the reason ye shadow me is because of my charming personality? It has nothing to do with keeping an eye on me, making sure I dinnae run off? If I wanted to run, does Demetrick really think ye could stop me?" Looking every bit the warrior, Braden stood with his hands on his hips, glaring at the boy, aware that he was physically intimidating,

"Well, physically, no." Alex took a few steps backward. "But there are other ways I could stop you, if I had to. I don't have to worry about that, do I?" the young wizard-in-training asked nervously. "Because, I really would rather not use those skills, especially on someone who has such a charming personality," he said with a wide grin.

Though he tried, Braden couldn't stop the grin that crossed his face. "Dinnae worry. I won't make ye use yer skills," he said, slapping Alex on the back, jolting the young man into step beside him. "Ye can let Demetrick know I'm not running. But I'd prefer to know what he has in store for me. The stronger I get, the more anxious I am 'bout the unknown, and I dinnae care much for surprises."

The two men continued their walk as Alex rattled on about this and that, though Braden wasn't paying much attention. Passing a stone building filled with drying herbs, the tantalizing fragrance of the harvested plants floated out of the open door. Glancing inside, Braden could see the tied bundles of herbs hanging from the rafters. He also saw shelves stacked with glass jars. Some of the jars were filled with what looked like colored stones. Others contained what seemed to be distorted animals floating in a brown liquid. He opted not to ask what those were used for.

"Ho there!" The deep voice announced the arrival of Demetrick's other resident in training; Samuel. A stout, strong man, Samuel was a bit slow, or "touched in the head" as Alex would say. Unfortunately for Braden, his introduction to Samuel's strength had come by the way of an overly aggressive blow to the head following his escape from prison. Though no young wizard, Samuel proved his worth with more menial tasks, and his loyalty to Demetrick matched that of young Alex.

"Hello lads," Samuel said with a nod. His dark, greasy hair was combed to one side, and his pants, which were held up by suspenders, only reached down to the top of his ankles. A dirty shirt covered an upper body that bespoke years of hard labor, with thick arms and a neck to match. "I'm on my way to the hen house," he said rather slowly. "The cook wants me to fetch a fat hen. If ye're headed that way, we could walk together."

It had begun pleasantly enough—the three men strolling through the grounds—but it didn't take long before Alex challenged the bigger man. "Oh come on, Ox!" he taunted. "You never know what you're talking about."

"My name is Samuel!" the large man roared.

"You're a big, dumb ox. The name suits you."

Samuel lashed out with a large meaty arm, but Alex was far too quick. He ran circles around the slower man and used Braden as a shield while continuing his taunts.

Refusing to intervene, Braden turned around and started back toward the compound just as Demetrick appeared on the path. All it took was one stern look from the old man for his two apprentices to stop their quarrel, looking like a pair of scolded puppies.

"That's quite enough. Samuel, I believe the cook sent you on a task. Alexander, if I recall, you have a spell that needs perfecting." Demetrick's voice was low and soft, but it saw the two miscreants scrambling. With a satisfied grin, he looked back to Braden. "Won't you finish your walk with me? There is someone I would like you to meet."

As they walked back toward the house, a silence fell between them. Braden hated to admit it, but when he was with Demetrick, he felt transparent, as if the old man knew his deepest thoughts. He assumed it was another aspect of being a wizard, the ability to make people believe in the power of magic, without ever seeing it in action.

"Braden, what was your livelihood prior to joining Prince Charles' campaign?" Demetrick asked, breaking the silence.

"Farming."

"And what was your weapon of choice on the battlefield?"

Giving Demetrick a curious look, Braden paused before answering. "I preferred an ax, but I could kill with a scythe just as well. What's behind the questions?"

Demetrick only smiled as they entered the courtyard. Waiting there was a well-dressed gentleman by the name of Archie Ferrell, a friend of Demetrick's, and as Braden would soon learn, an expert swordsman.

"I think it's time to see what you can do," Demetrick said, as Archie held out a Claymore basket sword, hilt first.

Braden looked with anxious reserve at the hilt of the sword dangling in front of him. "I told ye; my weapon of choice was an ax, not a sword," he said, glaring at Demetrick.

"Then it's time to make the sword your weapon of choice," Archie interjected, his voice revealing the bold pomp of the affluent.

Demetrick stepped back and took a seat on a nearby bench. Crossing his legs and arms, he made a small gesture, indicating he was ready for the demonstration to begin.

Rubbing a hand across the stubble on his jaw, Braden took a deep breath and slowly let it out before grasping the offered sword. He swung it a few times, testing its weight, and took a stance he had seen other swordsmen take before. It felt awkward, and he knew he was out of his element.

Touching the tip of his sword to Braden's, Archie gave a nod, and the dance was underway. At first, the casual sparring was simple and un-aggressive, an obvious ploy on Archie's part. Braden had little difficulty blocking Archie's novice moves, and it didn't take long for him to become overly-confident and let his guard down.

After a few more minutes of easy swordplay, the tempo started to change. Archie's moves became sharper, quicker, and his sword seemed to snap through the air. Even his foot speed increased as he danced around Braden easily while holding one hand behind his back.

To the contrary, Braden held the sword with both hands, and swung it as if he was swinging his ax. But its lightness made his swings reckless. He attempted to keep up with Archie, turning in a circle while blocking blows and ducking from the sword swinging toward his head. The sound of steel clashed through the courtyard, with Braden dancing backward as the men continued their mismatched exhibition.

That was until Archie quickly swung his blade, catching Braden off guard, as well as off balance. Unable to stop from falling, he found himself on his back, his weapon ripped from his hand, and the tip of Archie's sword at his throat.

"A true warrior should have mastery over all his weapons," Archie said smugly, standing over his fallen opponent.

When the swordsman finally withdrew his weapon, he turned and picked up the other sword. As he sauntered across the courtyard, he didn't see Braden rise to his feet.

"Archie," Braden called out, causing the other man to turn. The impact happened so fast that Archie didn't see it coming. When he landed on the ground, holding a hand over his bleeding nose, the shock in his eyes told Braden that the blow had given the impression he was looking for.

"Mastery isn't necessary in war, only survival," Braden growled, standing over Archie with a clinched fist. Moments before the man had bested him, but that hadn't stopped Braden from getting in the last word, or the last swing.

"Braden!" Demetrick was immediately on his feet, shocked at the warrior's obvious lack of a gentleman's protocol.

"No, no. It's alright Demetrick. No harm done," Archie said as he stood and retrieved a handkerchief from inside his vest, pressing it to his nose. "I may have had that coming."

"What was this about?" Braden turned his furrowed brow on Demetrick. "I'm sure ye were expecting a better performance, but I wasna prepared to put on a show!"

The old wizard looked pleased. "Oh, on the contrary. You reacted exactly as I expected you would." He then turned to Archie, who was dabbing away the last traces of blood. "Though I must say, I didn't expect to see you on your back. Impressive," Demetrick said with a satisfied smile. "I believe the cook has prepared a special lunch today. Would you gentlemen care to join me?"

As Demetrick led the way, Archie followed, but paused to look back at Braden who hadn't yet moved. Gingerly touching his nose, he gave Braden a grin. "I'd say you do have mastery over that fist. But if we could start over, I'd like to teach you the art of the sword. Why don't you join us, and we can discuss it over lunch," he said with a sweeping gesture of his arm and a genuine smile.

Somewhat tentative, Braden stepped up beside Archie. "Sorry 'bout the cheap shot. Old habits."

Archie placed a hand on Braden's shoulder and fell into step with him, "No apologies necessary, my good man. It's been a while since I've found myself on the receiving end of a blow. It's good to be reminded of what that's like, so I never let it happen again."

The summer afternoon found the three men caught up in conversation as they dined outdoors. Enjoying pleasant company and good food, they sat peacefully together. It had been a long time since Braden could remember feeling so at ease, and he relished in the comfort of it. He listened intently as Demetrick and Archie swapped stories, and he learned much about his host that day. This was a good man, a man to be trusted, but a very powerful one as well. There were forces around him that were not easily explained or understood, but were definitely to be respected.

"As I remember, my wife and I were at the market," Archie replied when Braden asked how he and Demetrick had met. "I noticed a group of boys taunting a stout, simple-minded chap. Samuel, if I'm correct," he said, looking at Demetrick, who only nodded. "At first, I didn't give it much thought, until this old man stepped in and attempted to stop it. 'Alright boys, that'll be enough,' you said. Two of the rag-a-muffins went running, but one fella stood his ground. The brave, stupid lad said, 'What are you going to do about it, old man?'

"It was such a small gesture that if I hadn't been looking directly, I would have missed it. You don't find many as subtle as Demetrick here. But in the moment after the mouthy boy issued his challenge, his breeches fell down around his ankles. Of course, he was immediately the center of attention. When the red-faced lad attempted to pull up his trousers, he found them stuck to the ground around his feet. But it was when he called out for help that things got really entertaining." Archie couldn't help laughing. "Every time the lad opened his mouth, it wasn't words that came out, but instead, the sound of a jackass. So the boy is shuffling along with his pants down around his ankles, baying like a bloody mule. Now he's the one being taunted," Archie concluded with a satisfied smile. "I walked over to Demetrick and said; 'I have two boys at home. Can you teach me that trick?' And we've been friends ever since."

"How long did ye leave the boy baying like a jackass?" Braden asked, amused with the story.

"Only a few minutes," Demetrick answered, "but long enough for him to learn some humility."

Entertaining though the stories were, Braden felt a growing sense of unease. Demetrick was powerful, and he had his own sense of justice. If he resorted to public embarrassment to teach children, what would Braden's lesson be?

As the days passed, Braden continued to grow stronger. But his real strength training began one warm summer morning when Alex bounded into his room. "Good morning, sir. I trust you've had a good night's sleep," the boy said in his normal upbeat tone. "Have you had a bite to eat yet on this beautiful day?"

"Aye, just came back from the cookhouse. What can I do for ye?" Braden asked.

"Master Demetrick would like you to meet him at the blacksmith's forge."

"Why?"

"He did not tell me, nor did I ask. I'm just delivering the message."

"When?"

"Just as soon as you can; he'll be waiting for you there. So, if you'll excuse me, I have other errands to run today. Best of luck to you." Alex then turned and scurried out.

Demetrick only addressed Braden directly when there was a task to be learned or a challenge to be undertaken. Anything less would be left for Alex to relay. Braden knew that whatever awaited him at the forge would be part of his preparation, though preparation for what, his months in the compound had not yet revealed.

When Braden arrived at the forge, Samuel was hammering on a glowing hot rod of metal balanced on top of an anvil while he held it in place with a large pair of tongs. It was not uncommon to see the large man at work in the forge; the difference this time was that Demetrick stood to one side of the fire, observing his strength and precision. The heavy hammer tapped methodically on the glowing metal before Samuel turned the rod and repeated the action as the sound of hammered iron rang throughout the compound.

"Welcome, Braden," Demetrick said quietly. His smile and handshake were warm. "Thank you for not keeping me waiting. I trust that your training with Archie is going well. He tells me that you are quickly picking up the nuances of swordplay, says that you'll be quite skilled in no time."

"Archie gives me too much credit, but I do enjoy our sparring, and the challenge. Thank ye for arranging my training," Braden said before nodding in Samuel's direction. "What's going on here?"

"I've decided to replace the decaying wooden gate that leads to the gardens with an iron one. We've lost many crops over the years to the red deer, so I've asked Samuel to start on it." The wizard casually clasped his hands behind his back. "We hope to have it up before harvest."

"Harvest isn't far off. Wouldn't it be more efficient to replace it with another wooden gate?" Braden asked.

"We already have, more than once, but the iron gate will last."

Braden nodded as he watched Samuel tapping the iron ore with the large hammer until the metal no longer glowed, then returned it to the coals. "How many rods do ye need for this gate?"

"By my calculations, we will need one hundred and fifty-four rods, plus hinges and latches."

"How many has he done so far?"

Demetrick counted the small pile of rods cooling in the morning air. "Counting these, Samuel has completed twenty."

"And ye need a hundred and fifty-four? I dinnae think yer gonna make it before harvest," Braden said with a chuckle.

"Not if Samuel has to do it by himself, most likely not. That's why you are here. Samuel will be teaching you the skill of the blacksmith."

The humor completely disappeared from Braden's face. The thought of spending a gorgeous summer day sweating over a hot fire and beating the bloody hell out of a piece of iron did not sound appealing.

"Every day after breakfast you'll meet Samuel here, and he will teach you the craft."

"Every day? What about my training with Archie? How am I to pick up a sword if ye have me swinging a hammer all day long?"

"I don't think all day will be necessary. Let's start with three or four hours in the morning, say until lunch. In a week or so, I'll check back to see how the two of you are progressing. Depending on how many rods you've completed, we will adjust your schedule accordingly. As you said, harvest will be here before we know it, but if you put some effort into it, the two of you should be able to accomplish this task easily."

"Demetrick," Braden called out as the wizard began to turn away. "Please don't tell me that learning the skill of a blacksmith is the great task ye have chosen me for. Not that I am ungrateful for all ye have done, but I expected something a little more grand than learning to be a smithy."

Demetrick turned to look back at Braden and held his gaze for a moment before replying. "It's always good to learn a new skill. Be thankful for it. You'll never know when it might come in handy," he said with a smile and a nod before turning away.

Swinging the hammer for four hours straight took a toll on Braden. He hadn't recovered his strength as much as he thought. When he woke up the following morning, he felt like he'd been run over by a herd of horses. Every muscle in his arms and back ached. But without fail, Samuel showed up at his door early each day, eager to teach his new student the next lesson.

Samuel was a skilled blacksmith, and though he may have been a bit lacking in common sense, he knew the hammer and the forge. Working the metal was something he did very well. The work didn't require much communication or instruction, and Samuel did most of his teaching by example. It wasn't long before Braden had forged his own pieces from the chunks of iron ore. After a few hard weeks, the hammer—that at first seemed heavy and awkward—swung through the air with an authority that resembled a skilled blacksmith.

As Braden's strength increased and the muscles in his chest and arms continue to build, his body gradually sculpted back into the man he used to be. But as he sweated in the forge, he couldn't help wondering if he was like the prize pig being fattened for slaughter. Obviously, Demetrick was grooming him for something physical.

In the afternoons, he was always able to find the energy when Archie came for another round of fencing. The swordsman returned frequently over the next few weeks to test Braden, hone his skills, and improve his footwork. As midsummer approached, and having fully recovered, Braden had an uneasy feeling that this retreat would soon come to an end. Though he grew increasingly apprehensive about the task Demetrick had in store for him, Braden never asked for details. He knew that when the time was right, the old man would tell him.

On the morning of midsummer's eve, Demetrick sent a message asking Braden to join him on a stroll. As they walked off the grounds, Braden had a feeling that this was the day he would learn what was expected of him, and he followed the wizard with renewed anxiety.

CHAPTER 6

REALM OF THE FAERIES

The enticing music seemed to be traveling a far distance across a wide abyss to reach her senses, and Isaboe felt it before she heard it. As the music became louder and closer, the sleep that hung on her like a dense fog gradually began to lift. With concentrated effort, she finally managed to open her eyes, and through an edge of dizziness, mentally pulled herself into awareness. When her other senses awoke, the smell of moss and wet leaves filled her nostrils, and she realized she was lying on the forest floor.

As Isaboe pushed herself up off the ground, she rubbed her eyes to clear the remnants of her mental fog. Now she could hear the music more clearly and realized there were singing voices as well. She looked in the direction the music seemed to be floating from and could see a clearing where people were dancing around a tall pile of wood, as if stacked for a bonfire that hadn't yet been lit.

Thinking that the festival must have started without her, Isaboe was at once confused and angry. She'd been told that the festival was being held in the town square, not in the forest among the trees. She also wondered why no one had bothered to stop and wake her. Surely they must have seen her lying here, yet they had all walked right by her to enter the clearing. Not willing to be ignored and left out of the festivities, Isaboe rose to her feet, but was startled by the sound of a woman's voice behind her. "Welcome home, dear. It is so good to see you again."

Turning around, Isaboe met an elegant young woman with long golden hair, wearing a flowing white gown. She had smooth, delicate features and a smile that instantly melted Isaboe's anger. "I'm sorry. I don't think I know you. Have we met before?" Isaboe asked, as her manners took over for her mind, which she seemed to have left on the forest floor.

The fair-haired woman gently took Isaboe's hand and led her towards the clearing. "You must be very thirsty from your journey. Come, my dear, join the party and have some sweet wine."

As the two women entered the clearing, children carrying small baskets filled with herbs and flower petals encircled them. The young girls were adorned in richly-colored dresses, and ribbons of flowers were entwined in their hair. The boys wore leggings and embroidered tunics in various colors of the earth. Sweet sounds filled the air as the children sang, skipping and dancing around them while tossing delicately scented flower petals.

Isaboe was surprised when the entire congregation began greeting her with warm smiles and hugs. As pleasant as this all was, it was also confusing. In the short time she'd lived in Faireshire, she had never felt welcomed, always an outsider. Now, everyone seemed so happy to see her. Isaboe returned the greetings and hugs with a hidden reserve, but as her head cleared, she heard something unusual and disconcerting.

"Welcome home Mother Alaina. Alaina of the moor has returned to us. The Mother has returned to renew our birth. Let us celebrate and welcome her home."

She heard these words from everyone who greeted her, even though Isaboe didn't recognize a single one. But that didn't make sense. Faireshire was a small community, and though she had lived there only a short while, she assumed she would know most of the people at the festival. Yet, none of these faces looked familiar. Even their clothing looked foreign. Most women in town wore the common attire: a dark smock with a fully-laced bodice and a full skirt of petticoats. However, these strangers wore soft, flowing gowns, clothing she would have donned for bed. The men all had the same leggings and tunics. Other than the children, all the adults looked to be about the same age, no older than thirty winters. As she looked around, hoping to recognize at least one face, an uncomfortable feeling began to grow. Isaboe turned toward the woman standing next to her, and said; "Excuse me. Where is my husband, Nathan? And my children?"

The woman didn't answer, only smiled and directed her to sit on a large cushion covered in animal hide. The cushion sat on a small wooden platform overlooking the unlit bonfire in the middle of the clearing. This was apparently the seat of honor, and the happy faces all around her beckoned for her to sit. *"Welcome Mother Alaina! Let us rejoice! The Mother Alaina has come home!"*

Now definitely uncomfortable, a vague, sick feeling took hold deep inside. "No. I don't want to sit. I want to know where my family is!" Isaboe's gaze darted around the crowd, and she pulled away from the golden-haired woman, looking for any recognizable face. "Who are you people? Why do you insist on calling me Alaina? My name is Isaboe McKinnon. My husband is Nathan and…," she quickly panned the crowd, "I don't know where he is, or my children." Beginning to panic, she turned toward the path that led back to her home.

But the golden-haired woman caught her before she had gotten far. Gently, but firmly taking Isaboe by the hand, she led her back to the circle. "My name is Lorien. I am your guide, and your friend. It's alright. Everything will be fine." The woman's voice was soft and soothing. Her demeanor was so welcoming that she seemed almost angelic, and Lorien's transparent hazel eyes were captivating. "All is well. You are among friends here. Relax, rejoice, for today is a day of celebration," she said with an air of confidence and that same hypnotizing smile.

When Isaboe was again led back to the platform, for a lack of options, she resigned herself into taking the appointed seat. Lorien took her place next to Isaboe and swept her hand over the congregation, causing all the children to immediately cease their dance and song. No sooner were the two women seated when a number of young girls and boys appeared with trays of food and drink. One tray was full of cheeses and small brittle crackers. Another had slices of meat, venison or lamb, along with small wooden cups filled with a variety of sauces for dipping. A large stone bowl filled with fresh fruits and a platter piled high with various breads rounded off the appetizing spread. As Isaboe's senses took it all in, hunger pangs rattled in her stomach.

The trays were all placed directly in front of Isaboe, as if the entire feast were meant for her alone. Abruptly, a goblet was placed in her hand, and a young man holding a pitcher poured a dark red liquid into her vessel. Whispering that it would help her to relax, Lorien guided the goblet to Isaboe's lips. Before she could protest, the bittersweet wine found its way down her throat. Though she had no intention of taking another sip, Lorien again encouraged her to do so. With each sip, the wine began to taste sweeter and went down easier.

After the day had faded to dusk, the pile of wood in the center of the clearing was lit, adding a bright glowing fire to the festivities. Holding hands, the children danced in a circle around the blaze, while their contorted shadows followed behind them. As the music grew louder, the dancing, singing, and chanting also intensified. Bodies flew around the fire in a blur, almost as if their feet weren't touching the ground.

Even though something still gnawed at her, a feeling she couldn't quite identify, Isaboe felt a sense of calm wrapping around her like a soft blanket. Food and drink were offered to her by pretty young girls who encouraged her to relax and enjoy. Everything tasted wonderful, and she was swept up in the abundance of it all—food and drink, song and dance.

Watching the display and listening to the children's lilting song was hypnotic, but the thought that she didn't belong here kept nagging at Isaboe. She needed to get back, but back to what? Back to who? As she struggled to recall what she'd been doing before joining this little party, Isaboe realized that she had lost all track of time. *How long have I been here? I was doing something before, and I'm missing something. What is it? But most disturbing, who am I? Alaina?*

The name Alaina didn't feel right, but that was what the people were calling her. Each time she tried to question Lorien, it was as if the woman could read her thoughts and would reply before the question could be asked. "Just relax and enjoy the celebration. It is for you that we rejoice. It is a night of renewal, of rebirth. So eat and drink freely. Tonight you will be honored as The Mother, and this bonding will bring new life. Tonight, we will reunite our people with your world, and everything will be as it should be," Lorien said with a smile of commanding eloquence.

Though it sounded important, Isaboe had no idea what the woman was saying, nor did she care. The bittersweet wine had gone down like water, and at that moment, she didn't care about anything else. As the children danced around her, chanting; "*Alaina of the Moor*", the acceptance that somehow, she was the mysterious Alaina began to take seed.

In the next moment, Lorien stood up and took Isaboe's hand, helping her to her feet. Isaboe's head felt disconnected from the rest of her body, and she giggled as she floated in a wine-induced fog. Lorien motioned toward three young ladies who appeared to be just on the verge of womanhood. All very lovely, they wore the same beautiful, flowing dresses. Purple and pink ribbons were woven through their hair, and they smelled of fresh lavender.

As her attendants surrounded their Mother Alaina and led her through an entrance in the hillside, she could feel the soft, delicate smoothness of their small hands in hers. Pushing back a vine-woven curtain, they entered into a candlelit room whose darkened interior was heavy with the smell of rosemary and thyme. Unstable from the wine, she didn't resist as the young women undressed her, washed her body in fragrant lavender water, and massaged scented oils into her skin. She was then dressed in a flowing white gown, held by only two small straps tied at her shoulders. It was so light and airy, she felt almost naked. That thought made her giggle again.

After they had guided Mother Alaina to sit on a small stool in the center of the room, Lorien led the girls in a chant while they performed an eerie ritual with bundles of burning sage. As the smoke enveloped and surrounded the anointed one, the chanting continued, and her attendants began brushing her skin with long, white feather plumes.

The three younger women stepped aside after completing their ritual. Dropping their heads, they folded their hands and continued the chant as Lorien stepped closer, hovering over the wobbly woman perched on the stool. Placing a firm hand under Mother Alaina's chin, Lorien lifted her head, and stood looking down at her unsuspecting victim.

Behind closed eyes, Alaina heard the strange woman muttering odd words she didn't comprehend. Her mind wondered why Lorien's gentle fingers were caressing her neck and chest so seductively. But then Lorien pressed gently down on her lower jaw, leaving her mouth slightly agape. In the next moment, the woman's mouth was upon hers, their lips locked as Lorien breathed her own essence into her dazed captive. Almost casually, she ran a hand down the front of the Mother's gown in between her breasts and continued until it reached the spot between her legs. Being touched so intimately caused the jolted reaction Lorien must have been expecting, and she nodded to her attendants.

The younger women gently helped Mother Alaina to her feet and led her further back into the hillside. Pulling aside a fabric curtain, they guided her to a bed that sat in the middle of a dimly-lit room. A single candle cast a soft glow, and it took a few moments before her eyes could adjust to the dim light in the small enclosure. Once again, the pungent smell of rosemary assaulted her senses, rising seductively from bundles of the evergreen herb placed in vases around the room.

Lorien stood at the opening, watching as her attendants escorted Mother Alaina to the bed, and helped her to lie down. Soon the bonding ritual would begin. All they had to do now was wait for nature to take its course.

When first she lay down, the nausea and spinning instantly returned, but as Alaina's head settled into the soft pillow, a warm, relaxed feeling embraced her, its intoxicating effects allowing her to slip away on a cloud of contentment.

Just before sleep completely pulled her under, the sensation that she was being watched jerked Alaina back to wakefulness. Suddenly aware that someone was standing beside the bed, she opened her eyes just wide enough to see a man looking down at her. Though something deep inside told her to be on the alert, she wasn't afraid.

As the man stood next to the bed, she felt his eyes examining her. From her wine-induced fog, she couldn't make out his features. But she did notice his well-chiseled body and strong muscle definition. Other than a small piece of animal skin tied around his hips, he wore no clothes. Without saying a word, the man reached out, and she instinctively placed her smaller hand in his. He closed his fingers around hers and brought her to her feet, facing him. As she struggled to gain her balance, he quickly caught her around the waist until she could stand on her own.

About a head shorter than him, she stood staring at his powerful chest and wide shoulders. Her gaze slowly moved up to meet his vivid blue eyes, and she felt trapped by what she saw. There was a war of hunger and softness in his eyes, intense desire, but with a promise of trust. Lost in the depths of those eyes—eyes she thought resembled intricate glass beads—she detected a musky scent that wafted from the heat of his skin. When he caught a lock of her hair and gently wrapped the auburn tress around his finger, she closed her eyes as a shiver ran down her spine. An awaking was taking place in her body.

Placing his hands on both sides of her face, the man slowly turned it up towards his. In the next moment Mother Alaina felt his mouth on hers. The kiss was sweet, moist, and short-lived. He pulled back to look down at her again, but before she could recover from the first kiss, his mouth was again on hers, but this time with more passion and hunger. She felt a stirring deep within that spread and intensified as his tongue eagerly sought hers. Holding her tight against him, his arms enclosed her body in a hot, needy embrace.

As the passion between them rose to a fever pitch, he reached up to untie her gown, and it slid down to her feet. Standing before him naked and vulnerable, she heard a small muted voice deep within scream out a warning, but her intense desire snuffed out any inhibitions for her virtue, or even her wellbeing. Unable to hide his need, the small cloth tied around the man's waist was quickly tossed aside. For a few moments, they stood, observing the other's body while the heat steadily grew between them. Moving onto the bed, he took her hand and coaxed her to lie next to him. Firmly, yet gently, he eased her legs apart.

Their encounter was fervent, and the sensations she felt were explosive, full of desire and longing. She responded to his body with equally passionate movements as an avalanche of feelings collided within her. At the height of their climax, a small cry of pleasure escaped from her lips. Whoever she was outside of this room, in that moment, she was the Mother Alaina.

After a few more pounding, writhing movements, it was over. Sweat beading off their bodies and breathing heavily, they lay together. Completely exhausted, all she wanted to do was sleep. When his hand reached behind her neck, she couldn't even open her eyes as he lifted her head slightly up from the bed, but she heard his voice for the first time: "So I may find ye again, my love."

She had no idea what he meant, but her eyes popped open when she felt a quick sting on the back of her neck. In the dim candle light, she saw him turn and walk quickly from the small room. The sting had already passed and sleep was now her only priority. Pulling the soft deerskin hide over her shoulders, she curled up on the bed and fell asleep.

CHAPTER 7

A BAD AWAKENING

Summer eventually has to give way to the bitter cold of winter, whether we are ready or not. If we are blinded with the idea that we can live only in the golden days of the sun, then we are in for a cruel hard reality.

—Author unknown

There was only one similarity between Isaboe's first awakening and her second—she still lay on a bed of moss. Sitting up, she looked around for her basket, which was nowhere in sight. Dusk had arrived, filling the sky with clouds, and the sun had dropped below the horizon. Isaboe silently chastised herself for falling asleep in the forest. Margaret and Nathan would be worried, and she didn't even have the mushrooms she'd come for.

Isaboe took a few wobbly steps back toward the house, but a sense of unease settled over her as she walked. The trail she had taken earlier now seemed overgrown and was difficult to find. Feeling disoriented and confused, she wondered if she had accidently gone in the wrong direction. Finally recognizing a landmark, an old twisted oak, she followed the path toward the village. But when she reached her house, Isaboe couldn't believe what her eyes told her.

Her once tidy home was now in a horrible state of decay. All the doors and windows were all boarded shut and looked like they had been for years. The roof was partially caved in, and the structure was covered with long trails of vines and overgrowth. "This isn't my home." She spoke her thought aloud, but the place where it stood was where her house should have been. Taking in her surroundings, she recognized, yet didn't recognize it, all at the same time. This made no sense! What she knew and what she saw in front of her didn't mesh. Not only baffled, Isaboe felt panic brewing within her belly.

She tried to open the door, but it was boarded shut and refused to budge. Pounding on it, she called out for Nathan and her children. But there was no reply. Frantically searching for something that made sense, she screamed out their names as she ran to the back of the house. But thick ivy brambles, that hadn't been there that morning, now blocked her way.

As the last trace of light vanished from the gloomy sky, rain began to splash on her forehead and shoulders. Picking up her dress, Isaboe pushed the hair from her face and ran frantically back to the front of the house. Again she called out, but still there was no response. Her pounding heart matched the pounding of the rain, now heavy and drenching. Her body trembled with shock and cold as she tried desperately to understand, but only confusion filled her mind.

"WHAT IS HAPPENING?!" Isaboe screamed into the night as she ran down the dirt road toward the MacDougal home, hoping they would have an answer, but when she arrived, their home looked exactly like hers; abandoned, boarded up, and deteriorating. There were no signs of life, or the people she was hoping to find.

Utter fear now took hold. Its constrictive grip caught in her throat as she ran down the dark, empty road. The rain soaked through her clothes, which clung tightly to her body, making it difficult to run. She tripped and fell into the mud, scraping her knee and elbow. But she ignored the pain and pushed herself back up. Running blindly through the night, she called out for anyone to answer. But every house she passed looked empty and abandoned, as if they had been that way for years. Panic and confusion filled her mind. *How can this be? People live in these homes. I saw them here only this morning!* So many unanswered questions only magnified her dread and terror. Tears ran down her mud-splattered face, mixing in with the rain.

Isaboe's heart pounded in her ears as she stumbled through the dark with no idea where she was going. Slipping in the mud, she tumbled down the side of a small knoll, ripping her dress. The cut on her elbow was now bleeding down her arm, but she hardly noticed as she struggled back up the side of the muddy slope. Finally seeing a light in the distance, Isaboe ran toward it. Rain was blurring her vision when she reached the small home and stumbled up the steps. Pounding on the door, she called out for help as the rain fell in torrents behind her.

When Clara Robertson slowly opened the door and peeked out, what she saw was a pitiful sight. Isaboe stood on the porch, muddy, wet, bleeding, and hysterically rambling. Clara called to her husband, but before he could come to the door, Isaboe dropped to her knees and frantically grabbed the woman's skirt with her muddy hands. "I don't know what's happening! I don't know where my family is! Please, help me."

Liam and Clara Robertson took Isaboe into their home, but she kept begging to know where her family was. Clara helped her out of her muddy dress, wiped the splattered mud from her face and hands, and gave her a clean smock to wear. She tried to attend to the hysterical woman's injured arm, but Isaboe was so wildly animated she wouldn't hold still long enough for Clara to do more than wipe the blood away.

Attempting to calm her, the couple gave Isaboe a strong sedative tea and promised to help find her family come morning. Emotionally exhausted, but with a faint hope of soon being reunited with her family, Isaboe finally nodded off on the small bed her hosts had offered for the night.

"Where d'ye think she came from? Do ye think she be mad?" Liam asked his wife as they walked out of the room, closing the door behind them.

"Shhh, keep yer voice down," Clara whispered, giving her husband a reprimanding glare.

"But the home she's carrying on about, the one she says she *lives* in, that house has been boarded up for years!"

"I know. But she insists she still lives there, with her missing family. Aye, I think she must be crazy, so I'd rather she wasn't here by morning," Clara said as she retrieved Liam's cloak and hat, holding them out to her husband. "Go to the constable's office and have her taken in."

"Now? It's dark. And it's raining," he whined. But his wife's expression made it clear he would have no peace if he did not abide by her wishes. Since he had to be out anyway, why not stop off at the local pub? A mad woman had shown up on his doorstep on this dark and stormy night. It was just too good a story not to share over a pint of ale.

"So, ye say she's at yer house now? Do ye think it's wise to leave the missus alone with a mad woman?" Stewart Thornton asked as he sat next to Liam, leaning on the counter with a mug in his hand, taking in all the embellished details.

"Clara? *Pfff! I'm* afraid of Clara. I dinnae think I need to worry about that one. She can handle herself."

"But where did this woman come from? Did she give ye a name?" Rosie Mactavish sat on the other side of Liam, also absorbed in his late night story.

"I dinnae catch it. She was babbling on hysterically. Crazy she is. Hell, she thinks she lives in one of those boarded-up houses on the ol' side of town! Says she lives there with her husband and two children, but they've gone missing. Don't quite know what to think of it." Liam shook his head as he took another swig off his mug.

Staying out of the conversation, but listening intently, the pub owner was an unusual fixture behind the bar. There were few enough women who owned their own business, and even fewer willful enough to control a pub, but Margaret had taken on the challenge with gusto. She had been on her own for so long, she'd become accustomed to self-sufficiency. When she took over the pub, the outspoken redhead had made it clear that she could run the business better than any man. With a tongue that lashed faster than a whip and arms that could easily throw out a patron or heft a barrel of ale, she quickly earned the respect of the small community of New Faireshire.

"What does she look like?" Margaret's curiosity was piqued as she wiped her hands on a towel.

"Ah, well, she's a younger woman, probably not more than twenty or so. Has reddish-brown hair and a slender figure. If she hadn't been so frantic, I'd say she has a pretty face. But the one thing I did notice was her wild green eyes! Terrified, they were. I'd say something *bad* has happened to that lass."

"All right you two, you're done for the night. Go home," Margaret said, swiping her patrons' mugs off the counter.

"What the hell, Marg?" Rosie complained, staring at her unfinished drink.

But Margaret ignored Rosie and Stewart's scowling faces. "Liam, you're taking me to your home. Now."

"But, I cannae go home without the constable. My wife'll have my head!"

"Then I'll go to your home alone, without your sorry ass, and the whole town will know that your wife married a sniveling little coward."

"Fine!" Liam snapped as he grabbed his hat and cloak. "But, first, couldna we stop at the…"

"No! There'll be no need for a constable," Margaret said, pulling on her overcoat while ushering her other patrons out. After locking up the pub, she followed Liam home.

When they arrived, Margaret was led to the small room at the back of the cottage. Walking over to the bed, she looked down at the sleeping woman. "Holy Mother of God, she's come back," Margaret whispered. "May I sit with her? She'll need someone here when she wakes up."

Even Clara knew better than to argue.

Early the following morning, sleep gradually lost its hold. As Isaboe slowly opened her eyes, she looked around a strange room. It was not her room, nor was it the bed that she shared with Nathan. Instantly the events of the previous evening crashed down upon her like a rogue wave. Her eyes filled with tears of confusion, she sat up abruptly. When her gaze fell upon a woman sitting in a chair across the room, Isaboe stared at her with anxiety written across her face.

"Isaboe, it's alright, you're safe here. You're among friends." The woman seemed to have anticipated her response, and the words were laced with comfort.

"Who are you? Where am I? Where's Nathan? Where are Benjamin and Anna?" The questions came rapidly and frantically, without waiting for answers.

"I'll answer all your questions, but you have to remain calm. You must be very scared and confused right now, but…"

"WHERE ARE MY CHILDREN?" Isaboe screamed.

The stranger stood and took a tentative step toward the bed. "Throwing a fit won't get your questions answered, lass. I'll tell you everything you want to know, but you'll have to calm down."

Glaring at her, Isaboe swung her feet to the floor and threw back the covers. "I don't know who you are, or how you know me, but you better tell me where my husband and children are, *now*! And why is my home all boarded up?"

Her fear mounting, Isaboe watched as the woman took a deep breath and let it out slowly before answering. "Isaboe, I'm your friend, Margaret MacDougal. I'm here to help you, but you need to stay calm and listen to what I'm going to say. It'll be hard to hear, but you need to know the truth."

Isaboe scowled. "Margaret MacDougal is a twelve-year-old girl. I have no intention of listening to your lies, or anything else you have to say until I know where my family is!" she spat as she stood and headed for the door.

Margaret leapt into her path and grabbed Isaboe by the forearms, looking her square in the eyes. "I *am* Margaret MacDougal, and you're gonna have to trust me, because there is nobody else here to help you. Now sit back down and I'll try to answer your questions."

Pulling away from Margaret's grasp, Isaboe stepped back, trembling as she looked into the eyes of the woman standing before her. "I, I don't understand what's happening," she said, feeling pathetically lost. "You can't be Margaret. I saw her yesterday at my…home." Not knowing what else to do, she sat back down on the bed and dropped her head into her hands as her tears began to fall.

Margaret opened the door and mumbled something to Clara in the other room before sitting down on the bed next to Isaboe. "I know this is hard for you. Right now, you're scared and confused. But I promise I'll help you every step of the way. You won't have to go through any of this alone."

Confused and distraught, Isaboe raised her head and looked at the woman who claimed to be Margaret, "I don't understand what you mean. I won't have to go through any of what alone?" Isaboe could feel her anxiety rising. "Where is Nathan? Where are my children?"

Just then the door opened and Clara Robertson entered with a plate of biscuits and two cups of tea. The confused woman just stared at Isaboe, shook her head, and quietly left the room.

"Here lass, you need to eat something. First, have a sip." Margaret's attempt to help her friend take nourishment was cut short when Isaboe swung her arm, sending the tea flying and the cups crashing to the floor.

"I DON'T WANT A DRINK! I NEED TO KNOW WHERE MY FAMILY IS!" The words came out vile and demanding as Isaboe launched herself upright, glaring at Margaret.

"Alright, fine then. Don't drink. I'll come back when you can be civil." Margaret picked up the pieces of the broken cups and headed for the door.

"Stop, wait!" Isaboe exclaimed. She had no idea what was happening, but this woman who claimed to be the twelve-year-old neighbor girl, now seemed to be her only possible link to find out. She was the only thread of hope at the moment, and letting her walk out did not seem a wise idea. "Please, don't go."

Margaret stopped and turned around. "Alright, but you need to drink some tea, eat a few biscuits, and try to calm down."

Stepping back, Isaboe gave a weak nod and sat on the bed. After leaving the room, Margaret returned in minutes with another cup. Begrudgingly, and with shaking hands, Isaboe took a few quick sips then placed the cup and saucer on the table beside the bed.

Margaret sat down beside her old friend, took a deep breath, and began again. "Alright, do you remember going into the woods to gather mushrooms, after you asked me to watch Anna? We talked about the festival that evening. I warned you not to go into the forest on midsummer's eve, but you just laughed it off as some sort of faerie tale. Ironic, isn't it?"

Eyes wide with fear, Isaboe just stared as Margaret went on. "If I remember correctly, it was a sunny day. You were feeding Anna creamed potatoes, and she had them all over her face. I helped to clean her up and then took her outside to play, and... My God, Isaboe! Look at me. I am

Margaret!" She reached out to take Isaboe's hands. "Of course I'm older, but it's still me. In those days, I had unruly, bright red hair and a face full of freckles. I loved your family, and I watched after young Benjamin and Anna every chance I could. I just about died when you disappeared. If only you would have listened to me!"

Isaboe trembled, her heart filling with dread as each word rang true. But how could this woman be Margaret? She was in her thirties, a little on the plump side, and her short red hair was a far cry from the vibrant locks of the young girl she knew. There had to be another explanation. Perhaps Margaret had shared these things, but then, where was Margaret? Where were Nathan, Benjamin, and Anna? Why was her house boarded up and looking as if it had been abandoned for years?

"Isaboe, look at me. How else would I know these things unless I am who I say I am?" Margaret paused for a moment. "You told me you were adopted by a wealthy family. Your father died when you were young, and you were never close to your mother." She paused again, struggling to recall something else Isaboe would identify with. "I remember when you and Nathan moved here from Glasgow. It was such a novelty to hear your stories from the big city. The day you moved into your home; Mum, Dad and I all helped. Little Benjamin wanted to help too, and he dropped a box of cups. Do you remember that? Most of the cups were broken and he cried so hard, poor little thing. You met Nathan at a school dance. Your family moved here to oversee the building of a bridge, a bridge that never got built."

As Isaboe listened to the unbelievable truth, she felt the life draining out of her, but it was Margaret's next words that hit like a lethal blow. "My sweet woman, you've been gone for twenty years."

CHAPTER 8

THE SAD REALITY

Stunned by Margaret's words, Isaboe just sat on the bed as confusion and disbelief fought against logic and reason. How could this twisted, baffling story possibly be true? This must be some sort of cruel joke. She struggled to control her shaking body as her mind tried to make sense of the unacceptable. "What's happened to me? Where is my family?" Though afraid to hear the answers, she had to know.

Margaret stood up, and by the look on her face, Isaboe knew that whatever she would say, it wasn't going to be good. "When you didn't come home that afternoon, Nathan and I gathered a group of people to go out looking for you. There was no festival that evening. The next day, the entire town started searching the forest for any sign, but all we found was your basket. We looked for days, but found nothing. No one would come right out and say it, but most of the people didn't expect to find you. I remember hearing the rumors, what the people really thought. We all knew you'd been taken by the faeries. But Nathan refused to accept it and kept searching. A few men continued to help, but gradually the number decreased, and eventually it was Nathan alone who continued looking for you."

As Isaboe listened to the horrible truth, tears ran steadily down her face. Margaret tried not to tell her everything at once, but Isaboe wouldn't let her stop until she knew what had happened to Nathan and her children.

"Nathan became so distraught he couldn't do nothing 'cept look for you. He couldn't even care for your children, so Mum and Dad took 'em in. Your disappearance was so unnatural, many of the townspeople felt our once-peaceful little village had been dangerously tainted by faerie magic and would never be the same. The bridge project fell apart when the British went scurrying back to England, taking their money with them. After that, Nathan's life went into a downward spiral of sleepless nights, roaming the streets and the forest. When he wasn't out looking for you, he did his best to drown his pain in the bottom of a bottle. Nathan became so absorbed in his loss that eventually we had the children living with us full time.

"Every night Anna cried for a mother who would never come. Not willing to talk to anyone, Benjamin withdrew completely, and Nathan blamed himself for bringing his family to Faireshire. We never knew for sure if it was the stumble of a drunken man, or if his grief was more than he could live with. But two months after you disappeared, his body was found floating in the loch."

Isaboe's breath caught in her throat, and her body shook uncontrollably. "Where are my children?" she asked in a quivering voice as the tears ran unabated. Her foolishness had ripped her family apart, and she had no idea what, if anything, was left of her tattered life.

"After Nathan's death, Mum sent word back to his parents in Glasgow, and to your mother in Edinburgh. With you both gone, it seemed only right the grandparents should take guardianship of Benjamin and Anna. What we didn't know was that Nathan's mother had suffered a stroke, and the news of her son's death almost did her in. It was everything Nathan's father could do to care for his ailing wife, so there was no way he could raise two children. When your mother showed up, we were surprised she came at all. She just up and took the children back to Edinburgh with her. Didn't give a whit that Anna was sobbin' the whole time, or that Benjamin wouldn't say a word to her. Just *took* 'em."

"Marta? You let Marta take *my children*?" As if the shock of discovering that twenty years of her life had been stolen and her husband was dead wasn't bad enough, knowing her children had been taken by that unloving woman nearly pushed Isaboe over the edge.

"We had no choice," Margaret said sternly. "Marta was their legal grandmother, and you were gone!" She took another long breath and rubbed her hands across her face before sitting back down next to

Isaboe, who was now staring at the floor. "The children didn't want to go," Margaret continued. "They clung to me, crying. Though I tried to prevent it, there was nothing I could do. I was only twelve. After that, I wrote to the children but never heard back. Eventually all my letters were returned, unopened." Margaret's heavy words were laced with sadness as she looked at her friend, who was now shaking uncontrollably from the shock of this new reality.

"And something else you should know—you weren't the first to be taken. After your disappearance, Mum told me a story from her childhood. It was an event she'd all but forgotten until then. When Mum was just a little girl, a young woman showed up one day out of nowhere, raving about her missing family, just like you. No one knew who she was. Everyone thought she was a crazed, mad woman, not right in the head. The authorities took her to an asylum in Edinburgh, and no one knows what happened to her after that." Taking Isaboe's hands, Margaret gave her a sympathetic smile. "When I heard that story, I knew I couldn't let that happen to you. If you had been taken into the realm of the faeries, I vowed to be here for you, if you ever came back."

Isaboe looked into the woman's compassionate eyes, but felt only emptiness. She had lost everything: her husband, her children, her entire life was gone. Collapsing on the bed, she sobbed uncontrollably.

Living in the loft above her pub made it easy for Margaret to stay involved with her customers, even during off hours. On more than one occasion she was known to let a patron sleep off his drink on a cot in the back room. However, the small second bedroom in her dwelling above the pub was rarely used for anything but storage. Now, she was thankful she could offer this extra room with its small bed to Isaboe. And she was pleased when her long-lost friend quietly assented.

Margaret had not expected it would be easy to help Isaboe restart her life, but she was not prepared to deal with the woman's unwillingness to live. For three days and nights, Isaboe refused nourishment, taking nothing but water, tea, and an occasional biscuit. She drifted through her days in a way that reminded Margaret vividly of Nathan's wretched mood following Isaboe's disappearance. There were times when Isaboe's grief was so overwhelming there was nothing Margaret could do but hold her, and rock her as she cried. She convinced herself that if she could just hold on long enough, she could bring Isaboe back. But every night Margaret awoke to the sound of her friend's mournful sobbing, and it was so easy to just stare at the ceiling, letting Isaboe's misery consume her as well.

It had been over a week, and she'd made little progress to help Isaboe when Margaret was startled out of her sleep by the sound of breaking furniture. She wasn't sure she could deal with much more misery and distress, but when she opened the door to Isaboe's room, what she saw tore at her heart. Curled up in the corner, next to the pieces of a broken chair, Isaboe was quietly sobbing. Slowly Margaret made her way across the dark room and sat down next to her friend. The weight of Isaboe's loss felt like a heavy, wet blanket that Margaret couldn't toss off. Though she was weary to the bone from the nearly constant despair, she still attempted to console her hurting friend.

But Isaboe lashed out and pushed her away. "*I WISH I WERE DEAD!*" The words came out so vile and full of pain that Margaret leaned back from the sting of them. She had known this would not be easy, but she wasn't prepared for so much hate and bitterness being directed at *her*. She simply had not anticipated the intensity of Isaboe's pain. It was exhausting. All the same, she sat with her old friend throughout the night, letting her sob, rant, and scream obscenities. Allowing herself to be Isaboe's target, though every insult hurled at her cut deeply, Margaret sat among the splinters of wood, and the splinters of a woman's ruined life.

The following morning and weary-eyed from lack of sleep, Margaret stood in the kitchen making tea, dreading another day of heavy despair. But she reminded herself that she had taken on this burden of her own accord, and it was too late to turn back now. Hoping her houseguest might have an appetite after last night's rage, she placed slices of bread and a cup of strong herbal tea on the tray before starting toward Isaboe's room.

As she approached the door, the sound of breaking glass stopped

Margaret in her tracks. She dropped the tray on a hall table and rushed into the room. Standing over broken pieces of the mirror that had previously sat on the dressing table, Isaboe was holding a piece of jagged glass over the smooth white flesh of her wrist.

Moving across the room faster than she thought possible, Margaret snatched the broken glass out of Isaboe's hand and pushed her down on the bed. "What the bloody hell are you doing? I'm trying to help you, but if you insist on wallowing in this hopelessness, I don't know what I'm gonna do with you. You seem hell-bent on your own destruction. No matter what I do, I can't reach you!" Lashing out from exhausted frustration, Margaret grabbed Isaboe by the shoulders and shook her. "You have to come back to the living! Somehow you have to let go and move on. That was then; this is now. You still have a whole life ahead of you. Can't you see that?" Margaret stood back and looked at the shell of a woman she used to know.

With her red-rimmed eyes staring vacantly ahead, Isaboe showed no sign of having heard anything Margaret said. Leaning up against the wall, Margaret let the weight of her frustration pull her to the floor. Completely drained, her chest was heavy with the burden of caring for someone who didn't want to live. She knew the pain Isaboe was going through, but Margaret now doubted that she would be able to help her. Wrapping her arms around her knees, she stared at this woman she had once known so long ago.

After a long silence, Margaret realized she had to reach deep if there was any chance to bring back the vibrant Isaboe. She had to make one last attempt to save this woman whose spirit had been ripped so violently from her being. "Isaboe, what if we could find your children?" Margaret's quiet words came tentatively. "We could contact someone in Edinburgh and see if we can locate them."

For the first time, there was a faint glimmer of life in those familiar green eyes as Isaboe finally made eye contact. "My children? You think we could find my children?" Though Isaboe's voice quivered, Margaret saw a flicker of hope, and she vowed to do whatever she could to fan that tiny spark back to life. Rising from the floor, she sat on the bed next to her pale friend, whose tear-filled eyes were searching for an answer.

"Do you really think we can find them?" Isaboe stared desperately at Margaret, who shamefully realized that she would say whatever Isaboe wanted to hear, regardless of what she was committing to.

CHAPTER 9

A LONG JOURNEY BACK

For the next three weeks Margaret watched her friend's slow ascent from depression, one hour, one day at a time. To keep Isaboe's mind occupied by something other than her misery, Margaret brought her down to the pub every day and kept her busy washing dishes and doing trivial chores. Though Isaboe still lived in something of a daze, very seldom speaking to anyone, at least Margaret could keep an eye on her. Her friend remained a far cry from the woman Margaret remembered, spirited and full of life, and somehow she had to help Isaboe find that woman again.

Margaret's letter to the City of Edinburgh asking for information about Marta Cameron went unanswered. Almost a month passed, and every day Isaboe would ask, but the answer was always the same—nothing yet. Though she tried to hide the tears, Margaret could still hear Isaboe crying in the night. News of the children had to come, and soon.

The day finally came when a letter arrived from Edinburgh. Uncertain what its contents may reveal, Margaret decided to read it alone. After opening the envelope from the Office of Public Records, she took a deep breath and read the words printed carefully on official city letterhead:

To Miss Margaret MacDougal;
This note is in reply to your inquiry regarding a Mrs. Marta Cameron, or Benjamin and Anna McKinnon, residing in or around the vicinity of Edinburgh. After reviewing our most recent census, we could find no listing with the name of Mrs. Marta Cameron. Nor is there a record of a Benjamin or Anna McKinnon. This does not mean that they may not have been

members of our community at one time, but no current record
was found.
Sincerely,
Jonathan Gibbons
Secretary of Public Records

Knowing she could not pass the letter on, Margaret realized that the
only thing left to do was to travel to Edinburgh with Isaboe, and see
what they could find out on their own. No matter how long it took,
Margaret would do whatever was necessary to help Isaboe find out what
had become of Benjamin and Anna. But the thought of what they might
discover caused a new wave of concern. What if it wasn't good news? It
may not be the best thing for Isaboe to know what had happened to her
children. But what other choice did she have? For the sake of Isaboe's
sanity, there was no other choice. If nothing else, the action of doing
something would give her friend a reason to live.

Margaret left the pub in the care of Dunivan, her only employee, who
nodded along with Margaret's last-minute instructions as he helped her
strap a large satchel to the back of her saddle.

"I don't know how long I'll be gone," Margaret said over her shoulder
as she secured her last bag. Since she only had one horse, one of her
regular customers had loaned her another so both ladies could ride and
still carry all the bags they would need. This was a trip with no planned
ending. Margaret may have taken more than what was necessary, but she
wanted to be prepared for a lengthy stay away from home.

She had been lucky the day young Dunivan walked into her establish-
ment two years earlier. He was passing through New Faireshire on his
way to make his mark in the world. Although he had just stopped in for
a drink, Dunivan talked himself into a job before finishing his first tank
of ale. Margaret had been working the pub by herself since purchasing
the dilapidated building from the city ten years prior, but this gregari-
ous young man turned out to be a valuable asset and a good friend. The

customers liked him, and he had proven himself completely trustworthy. Knowing that she could leave for an unknown length of time and her business would continue on without her made this trip easier to bear.

Giving Dunivan a quick hug, Margaret pulled back and looked him square in the face, "And don't give old man Angus any more free ale, regardless of what he tells you. Unless he lays coins on the counter, you're not to serve him." Releasing Dunivan, she turned toward her horse and secured the last strap. "I've cleaned out the coffers, so whatever you bring in while I'm gone is all you'll have to run the place with. Don't spend it all at once. I still want a pub to come back to," she said over her shoulder.

"Dinnae worry about a thing, Miss Margaret," Dunivan said as he helped her up into the saddle. "I'll mind the pub. It looks like ye'll have a pleasant day for traveling, and ye should make it to Dornach before dark," he added as he stepped back, smiling and nodding reassuringly.

"Yeah, if all goes well, we should. I just hope the weather holds, and that Frieda and Niles won't mind puttin' us up for the night. I'll ask 'em to bring back the horses." Margaret glanced over at Isaboe, who was already mounted on the borrowed horse packed with more bags. The hood of her long, dark riding cape was pulled up over her head, casting her face in shadow. Margaret thought she resembled the monks at the Abby of the Pristine Loch, silently wrapped in their own thoughts as they went about their days. Annoyed with Isaboe's withdrawn demeanor, she shook her head and jerked on the horse's reins harder than necessary. "Wish me luck Dunivan. I'm likely to need it."

"Safe travels to ye both," Dunivan shouted as he waved them off.

The following morning was cool, and fog hugged the countryside when Margaret and Isaboe boarded the coach leaving Dornach. Frieda and Niles had been more than hospitable when they warmly opened their home the night before, and Niles assured Margaret he would promptly return the animals back to Faireshire.

Setting off toward Inverness, the next stop on their route to Edinburgh, the morning was blanketed by fog, but there was the promise of clear skies for their trip, as the driver informed them while loading their bags onto the back of the carriage. He asked if they had brought along food for their travels, as it would be a long while before they reached their destination of Inverness, the next stop on their route to Edinburgh. Margaret assured him they had all the provisions they needed and just wanted to be under way.

On their short ride from New Faireshire to Dornach the day before, the silence hadn't been so unbearable. Each woman had her own horse and found it easy to lose herself in thought. Now, in such close proximity, Isaboe's sullen quietness left Margaret feeling restless and annoyed. They discussed little during the first hour of their journey, and what they did exchange remained simple and unemotional. When Margaret became tired of carrying the conversation, they sat quietly on the carriage bench, looking out their respective windows at the passing scenery. The rhythmic movement of the rocking carriage, along with the steady click-clacking of the horses' hooves on the road had a hypnotic effect, and it wasn't long before Margaret was snoring. With her head propped up against the frame of the window, Margaret's mouth hung slightly ajar as she slept.

Isaboe envied her friend's ability to drift off so quickly, so soundly. A good night's sleep was something she hadn't had since coming back. But back from where, she still didn't know. Not being able to remember where she had gone or what had happened to her created a horrible nightmare, a nightmare from which she couldn't wake. She was drained from the weight of it, the ache of her loss, and the pull of the mystery that caused it. Yet deep inside, Isaboe knew she couldn't stay buried in depression forever. She had to come out from behind the veil of misery; she just didn't know how.

Isaboe had been so consumed by her loss that she hadn't really appreciated how much Margaret had done for her. If it hadn't been for Margaret, she would be lost, if not dead, by now. As she looked at her sleeping friend, Isaboe felt a seed of guilt germinating in her stomach. Margaret had set her own life aside and waited for her return, though they had known each other only briefly when Margaret was but a child. Now she was helping to put her life back together without asking for anything in return. Isaboe's tears began to well up as she contemplated what that friendship meant.

Retrieving the handkerchief Margaret had given her, she dried her tears. As she wiped her nose, Isaboe's eyes drifted to the initials in the corner of the fabric. Turning the fine cloth in her hands, she read the letters *MF* delicately embroidered in fine silk thread. She wondered what it meant to Margaret, if anything, and whose initials they were.

For the first time, Isaboe realized she had no idea what this other woman's life had been like during those missing twenty years. She'd been so absorbed in her own grief that it hadn't even occurred to ask Margaret about her life. All Isaboe knew was that her friend was now thirty-two years old and that she had come back to Faireshire specifically to wait for her return, but had Margaret ever married, or had children of her own? What had enticed her to own a pub in a dying town? Were her parents still alive? Isaboe's ignorance shamed her. In that moment, she decided that when Margaret awoke, she would do her best to start making it right. As difficult as it might be, Isaboe wanted to know all she had missed. She knew she had to step into a new place, in her new life. She had to let go of the past and start over.

But there was more to her realization. If she were lucky enough to find her children, would she have the strength to tell them who she was? She had to recapture the woman she used to be. She could not make the same mistakes Nathan had and let herself waste away. She owed it to her children, to Nathan, and to Margaret, but most of all, to herself.

For the first time in weeks, Isaboe felt a spark of life in her chest, however small, and it gave her a reason to carry on. A slight smile found its way across her pale lips. Tears—though this time from gratitude, and not loss—slid down her cheeks and onto the handkerchief she still held in her hands.

Looking out her window she saw that the fog had cleared, just as the driver had said it would. The sky had taken on beautiful azure tones with only a few puffy clouds to offer contrast. The passing countryside was dotted with stately oak trees, and Maidenhair ferns grew abundantly in their shadows. When she pushed open the window, Isaboe could feel the sun's warmth on her face. Birdsong and the sound of rushing water from a nearby stream blended with nature's ballad, accompanied by the crunching of the carriage wheels as they passed over the dirt road. Everything seemed new, as if she were experiencing the color of life for the first time, and the beauty of it touched her. She took a full breath of fresh air, drawing much needed life back into her being. The air smelled sweet and clean, offering a temporary distraction from the ache in her heart.

"Whoa!" the driver's voice interrupted the moment, and the carriage came to an abrupt stop. Isaboe heard his quiet murmur as he spoke with someone. When the carriage door opened, he assisted a little old woman up the coach steps and onto the bench across from her. The driver gave a slight nod of his head and apologized for the delay before closing the door. The carriage was once again on its way.

The tiny woman was wrapped in an ebony-hooded cloak that was pulled up over her head. Wild strands of flyaway, white hair and a pair of thick, black spectacles stuck out from under her hood. The new arrival made no indication that she was aware of other passengers, and Isaboe wondered if the woman was blind. But if so, what was she doing out in the middle of nowhere, alone?

In the small space Isaboe noticed that a light herbal scent had floated in with the latest passenger. The old woman's small leather satchel was laid on the seat beside her, and a cane engraved with strange carvings of a beastly creature was balanced on her lap.

Oddly, Margaret hadn't awoken for the stop or the new passenger. As Isaboe sat silently across from the old woman, an unease twisted inside her.

"You be on a long journey." The throaty sound of the old woman's voice was startling. At first, Isaboe didn't know if the crone were muttering to herself or attempting conversation.

"Pardon?" Isaboe asked. "Are you speaking to me?"

"Lived ignorant, too. Don' know her own problems. Don' know what's comin. Don' even know 'bout the child. Ye've been used, girl. Ye have the stink of magic and manipulation 'bout ye."

The blood drained from Isaboe's face as she leaned forward toward the woman. The crone *was* talking to her. "So, it's true? I am …," but she couldn't say the words. She had thought this idea only once, earlier in the week, after throwing up for the fourth time in as many mornings. It had been over a month since Margaret found her, and she hadn't seen any sign of her courses. She assumed, hoped, that whatever she'd been through had disrupted her body's cycle. But this was confirmation. "Is the child Nathan's? Do you know what happened to me?"

The crone cackled, but it was wicked and humorless. "Wha' happened? The Fey Queen took ye, used ye. Tha's wha' happened, lil' fool."

"What Fey Queen? Who are you?"

"Who I be ain't important. Who you be is." With a wrinkled hand, the old woman pushed back the hood of her cloak to reveal a head full of bristly, white hair. Then she removed her dark spectacles.

What Isaboe saw sent icy fingers down the back of her spine. The old woman had not the eyes of a human, but the eyes of a bird with large black orbs amidst a pool of amber, and they stared directly at Isaboe. As much as she tried to turn her gaze away, Isaboe stared back, feeling her soul being bared.

"Rest your heart, child. I not be the one ye need to fear," the crone said. "It be she that hides behin' the magic, using it 'gainst ye, that ye need be wary of. Got caught up in her web, ye did. Don' know how to get free. Paid no mind to sound advice, fell into a trap, now too foolish to see yer own way out."

The crone is chastising me? For what? Hunting for mushrooms in the woods? For not believing a child's tale?

"But you be the chosen one," the old hag continued. "With power to take back wha' be lost. No easy task. Must be stronger than faerie magic."

"What do you mean, 'the chosen one?' Do you know what happened to me? Please, I have to know!"

"Good questions, but answers not easy to hear. Best to leave the thorn in, 'lest all the blood drain out. Aye, the prick may be painful, but the remedy is deadly."

"What? I have no idea what any of that means!"

The crone abruptly leaned forward and took Isaboe's hands. Pulling her close, the woman's bird-like eyes once again caught Isaboe's. "There be danger 'round ye, death for some. Fey folk want what's yours. The magic can help ye, or hurt ye. You decide."

These words made Isaboe's heart pound. Her breath came quick and short as she tried in vain to pull her hands from the old woman's vise-like grip. She looked desperately in Margaret's direction for help, but her friend was in a deep sleep, and Isaboe wondered if the woman had caused it.

When the crone finally let go, Isaboe sat back, holding her hands against her chest. Her heart was beating rapidly as she stared at the strange creature across from her.

"Heed my words, child. Listen to the voice in yer heart, not the poison in yer head. *She* be there. Don' know what's true. Don' know what's lie. Fey folk not done with ye; want the child. Seek the protector, the one whose heart be true. A fire burns in that one. Look for the Celtic cross."

While her words were cryptic and made little sense, the woman had at least confirmed what Isaboe already feared. She was with child. The father was still a mystery, but there was something special about her unborn child, and her life was in danger because of it. The small ember of hope Isaboe felt earlier had now been snuffed out. Just when she thought the worst was behind her, this strange old hag rekindled her anxiety.

The rattling of the carriage, the thick, hot air, and a sudden burst of inescapable dread caused nausea to bubble up in Isaboe's stomach and into her throat. She was forced to lie back lest she lose her stomach right there in the coach. As she laid her head back, tears rolled out from behind closed eyes and flowed down her cheeks.

When Isaboe finally felt sure her insides would not turn against her, she slowly lifted her head and opened her eyes. She saw the old hag rifling through her leather bag, apparently looking for something. Isaboe tried to focus on what the woman was mumbling, but the spinning nausea turned into a dull throb at the front of her skull. Attempting to stop the pain, she dropped her head into her hands and closed her eyes, pressing hard against the pounding. Suddenly, she felt something being slipped over her head and down around her neck. When Isaboe looked up, the face of the crone was only inches from her own. Startled, she jerked back.

"Ye've been chosen, child. This here be a gift from the other side. Be wise, listen, and heed their words. Be a fool, lose life and child," the old crone said in a scratchy whisper. She then held up her wrinkled hand and blew what looked like sparkling dust into Isaboe's face. That was the last thing she remembered before Margaret woke her for lunch.

CHAPTER 10

A DREAM, OR
A DIRE WARNING?

When the carriage stopped for lunch, Margaret climbed out of the coach, and with hands on her hips, looked back at Isaboe. "I'm sorry, my dear, but I really don't know what you're talking about. I wasn't asleep for that long. If we'd picked up another passenger, I would've woke up." Margaret was trying not to be frustrated with her friend, but Isaboe wouldn't admit the old woman was just a nightmare.

"I know you didn't see her. You were snoring. Actually, it was more like snorting. I can't believe you never woke up! You slept through it all, even while she was saying all those strange things right here, in this carriage. I'm not making it up!"

"Snorting? You don't have to be insulting just because I didn't see your imaginary old hag. Why couldn't you have dreamt her? When you just woke up, it took a long time for you to come to. You were probably just in a deep sleep."

"I was not dreaming! She was here in this carriage with us. She told me many strange things. She held my hand!"

"Well then, where is she now?"

"I don't know. Maybe she got off while we were both still asleep," Isaboe snapped, climbing out of the carriage. "I'm going to ask the driver; he'll know."

"Crazy woman!" Margaret shook her head as Isaboe walked toward the front of the coach. "What have I gotten myself into?"

Clutching a blanket and the basket that held lunch, Margaret selected a soft patch of grass on the side of the road to have their noontime meal. As she stood, enjoying the warmth of the sun on her face, Margaret could hear Isaboe and the driver talking on the other side of the carriage. Although she couldn't make out the words, Margaret could tell by Isaboe's tone that she wasn't getting the answer she wanted. Pouring two cups of sweet tea, Margaret laid out their lunch of crackers and dried fruit as she waited for her friend to return. When Isaboe rounded the carriage, her face said how frustrated the conversation had left her.

"Well, what did he say?" Margaret asked, munching on a cracker.

Standing silently, Isaboe didn't reply immediately. She seemed to be thinking deeply before finally answering. "He said that he never picked up another passenger. He said we are the only ones who have been on this trip." Isaboe sounded bewildered, almost afraid. Whatever she had experienced, she had done so alone.

Margaret only nodded and continued quietly eating her meal. When the silence between them grew uncomfortable, she offered her friend a piece of fruit. "Let's just sit and have a bite of lunch, and then you can tell me more about what you think happened."

The two ladies ate in silence, watching the finches dart between trees and listening to the songs of the swallows. The carriage had stopped for lunch alongside a small creek, and they could hear the sound of rushing water. The sky was blue, with only a few billowing clouds, and the after-noon breeze carried the sweet scent of pine.

"Alright, maybe I did dream her," Isaboe finally broke the silence. "But Margaret, she seemed so real! She told me things. It was all so…so cryptic and strange, but she knew so much about me. I can't shake this feeling that she was really there, in that carriage with us. She…she told me things that scared me. I can still smell the herbs she brought in with her." Isaboe held her hands up to her nose and tried to breathe in the lingering smell of the old woman.

Margaret looked at her companion. "Like sage?"

"You smelled it too?" Isaboe looked at Margaret, the hope of validation showing on her face.

"I thought I noticed it when we stopped," Margaret replied, "after the driver woke me. I thought it was coming from outside. Sometimes herbs grow in the ditches. I couldn't place it at first, but when you mentioned herbs just now, it came to me."

"So, you do believe me?" Isaboe asked, but Margaret said nothing. "Oh, God, Margaret, I need you to believe me! She was really there in that carriage with us!" Isaboe ran her hands through her hair and let out a long sigh before turning to lock gazes with her friend. "Look, you told me that I have been gone for twenty years, and I believed you. Can't you just take my word there really was a woman in the carriage with us while you were sleeping?"

"Alright, then tell me what she told you," Margaret said, taking a bite of dried apple.

Taking a deep breath, Isaboe began. "Well, most of what she said didn't make sense. And she had the strangest eyes I'd ever seen. Margaret, she said I had been taken by the Fey Queen! She told me that I'm...," Isaboe paused and swallowed her words. She wasn't ready to place the burden she now felt from the acknowledgement of her pregnancy on Margaret's shoulders. She opted to save that bit of information for later. "The old crone said that magic surrounds me, that the fey folk aren't done with me yet, and that I was the 'chosen one!' What do you think all that means?"

"Chosen for what?"

"I don't know!"

"Isaboe, this is too strange. The driver stopping the carriage to load another passenger—something that he doesn't even recall —I mean, you have to admit that makes no sense. And I don't sleep that heavily. I would have heard something."

"But, if she were a sorceress, or a witch, she could have made you sleep through the whole thing, and bewitched the driver, too. Maybe this message was meant just for me."

"Bewitched? Really? Don't you think that's more than just a little odd?"

"Don't you think being gone for twenty years, when it seems like only one day to me, is a little odd? Everything that is going on in my life right now is a little odd, so why not this old woman too? Margaret, I believed you. Why can't you believe me?"

Before Margaret could reply, the driver approached. He had finished his lunch and was ready to be underway. They still had a long journey ahead, and he wanted to travel as far as possible before dark. Isaboe paused, and her eyes dropped to her half-finished lunch. Margaret knew that look; it was the same look Isaboe wore just before the tears would begin to fall. "I believe you, Isaboe, and I am not just saying that."

Isaboe looked up as her friend continued. "What happened to you was magical. That I know. So, who am I not to believe that anything and everything is possible? If all we encounter is a strange old woman babbling about magic, well, then I think we should consider ourselves fortunate. Truth be told, lass, I don't think that'll be the last of it on this journey. Just like the old woman said, you were chosen. For whatever reason, I have no idea. Honestly, I'm a bit apprehensive about what the rest of this journey will be like."

Giving her a soft smile, Margaret reached out and took Isaboe's hands. "But whatever happens, I'm here for you, love. I waited for you for twenty years, and I'll not let you down now. I have been, and always will be your friend, Isaboe McKinnon, no matter what happens. Alright?"

CHAPTER 11

A TIME REMEMBERED

With lunch finished, the travelers were bundled back into the coach for the second half of the day's ride. It took some prodding, but Margaret managed to engage Isaboe in light conversation. "I hope Dunivan doesn't give away the store while I'm gone. He's not very conservative when it comes to dealings with money. More than once I've seen him give out a free mug of ale when he thought I wasn't looking. The lad has a soft spot for a fella down on his luck without two coins to rub together. I don't mind so much if it's a local now and then, but not to strangers passing through, looking for a free hand-out."

"He's a nice young man, Margaret. I was a stranger, and he was nothing but kind to me," Isaboe replied. "You gave me some of his duties, taking money out of his pocket, but he didn't seem to mind. Dunivan might challenge you sometimes, but he respects you. You're fortunate to have him."

"Aye, you're right, he is a good bloke. But when it comes to business, charity doesn't keep the doors open. I just hope I have a pub to come back to."

"How is it that you own your own pub, anyway? You haven't lived in Faireshire all these years, have you?"

"No. I've only been back for seven or eight years now. Before that I was working a pub in Aberdeen. The owner was a loud-mouth jackass, but I learned a lot from him—mostly what not to do. I worked hard, learned the business, and I run a pub much better m'self, if I do say so," Margaret said smugly. "One day I saw a bulletin posted in town, announcing the rebuilding of *New* Faireshire. The Brits were back on the bridge project, and they wanted people to move back. Of course, I immediately thought of you. When I came back to my childhood stomping grounds and found the old pub up for sale, I took that as a sign. If you ever did come back, I'd be waiting for you."

Isaboe's thin smile showed her gratitude. Dropping her gaze, she looked at the handkerchief she'd been twisting in her hands. "Oh, I meant to ask you: whose initials are these?"

Margaret took the handkerchief from Isaboe and held it tentatively in her hands. "MF—Margaret Ferguson. I haven't thought about that name for a long time," she said, looking out at the passing landscape without really seeing it. In her mind's eye, she was somewhere else, in a time long past.

"Is that you? Are you Margaret Ferguson?"

"I was, a long time ago. When I was married, or thought I was."

"You were married? What happened? Why did you take back your maiden name?"

Since Isaboe seemed genuinely interested, Margaret found herself sharing. "Well, like I said, it was a long time ago." She took a deep breath and turned to face Isaboe. "After we left Faireshire, my parents bought a large farm in Aberdeen, and they did pretty well, mostly sold potatoes. Dad had a contract with the British Army, and they were pretty much our only customer. It was a large farm, and we hired help to run it. One day, a drifter who was passing through stopped and asked for a job."

Margaret went quiet for a moment, her mind wandering back before she continued. "He was the most handsome man I had ever seen. Hair any woman would want to run her fingers through, all dark and wavy, and beautiful brown eyes. His name was Robert Ferguson. At least, that's what he told us. He wasn't very tall, but was well built and strong looking. I think that's why Dad hired him. Working a potato farm isn't easy, lots of hours bending and lifting heavy bags, but Robert didn't seem to mind. He was kind of quiet and kept to himself most of the time. I found all sorts of excuses to be where he was, and spent as much time as I could just hanging around, watching him.

"At first, he didn't make much attempt to talk to me, only when I didn't give him a choice. After a while though, that changed, and he started to seek me out, too. Sometimes we would talk for hours, though I did most the talking. He usually just asked questions and listened. The only thing he ever really told me about himself was that he wanted to go to America. He did tell me I had a pretty smile. That always made me blush."

Margaret paused, rubbing the handkerchief between her fingers. "It made me feel special. No man had made me feel that way before. Let's face facts; I've never been a gal you would call pretty, aye? I had a face full of freckles and had never even had a suitor. So to have that kind of attention from a handsome man, well, I thought I was in love. I didn't try to hide the fact that I was sweet on the fella, and I guess I rather made a fool o' myself. My parents picked up on it and did their best to discourage my interest. He was just a drifter, and we knew almost nothin' about him.

"It must have been about a month later when a troop of British soldiers showed up at the farm. I saw Dad talking to the captain, and after the soldiers left, he asked where Robert was. I should have known something was amiss, because Robert had disappeared when the Brits showed up. When I asked Dad what was going on, he turned on me with angry eyes and said I was to have nothing to do with Robert anymore. He was letting him go. God, I was so upset! We got in a big fight and I ran out of the house into the woods. I went to the place I would go when I wanted to hide from the world, and cried for what seemed like forever. I hated my father, and I hated Robert for disappearing."

Margaret paused to collect her thoughts before continuing. "Just before dusk, I was walking back to the barn when I saw Robert and Dad coming out of the house. Robert was carrying his pack. I didn't know what to do, but knew I couldn't just let him go. As he walked past the barn, I waved him over so Dad wouldn't see. I asked him what had happened, why he was leaving. I knew it had something to do with the soldiers, but he said it was just time to go. He had made enough money to buy his way to America. I was so upset. I begged him not to leave me and pleaded with him to take me along. What a foolish girl I was." Margaret shook her head. "At first, he wouldn't hear of it, but I was pretty persuasive, even then." She smiled ruefully. "I was only sixteen, and I thought my whole world was coming to an end. He finally gave in and agreed to take me with him. I knew my parents would never approve, so we devised a plan.

I told Mum and Dad I was going to spend a week with my Aunt Ruth. I had an open invitation to visit my aunt, so it wasn't anything unusual for me to go on a moment's notice. Especially after the fit I threw, they thought it would be a healthy distraction for all of us. I left a letter at the postal office to be delivered to my parents ten days after our boat would have left for America. That would give us plenty of time before they knew I was gone."

"How exciting!" Isaboe leaned forward, enraptured in the story, "Running away to be with the man you love."

"Aye, that's what I thought too. I would have gone anywhere, done anything to be with Robert, and he knew it. After meeting at our pre-arranged location, we bought passage on a ship leaving the next day. As we were leaving the ticket booth, Robert asked me to be his wife. I'll never forget how I felt when I heard him say those four magic words: 'Will you marry me?'" Transported back in time, Margaret sat staring out the window. She could see the top of his head, his glossy hair, and could feel the warmth of his hands as they held hers. She shivered, remembering him dropping the knee of his best pants onto the dusty road. "You know, up to that point I thought I would never be married. It was all so out of character for me, but I jumped at the chance. I probably should have known that Robert didn't really love me, but I was completely in love with him. He wanted to marry me, and I would've had enough love for the both of us. Still, I was so worried about how my parents would feel that I almost didn't go through with it. It was all happening so fast. He even told me that if I wasn't sure, he would understand. He was so damn understanding that it made me want to marry him all the more. So I did. He quickly arranged for the minister and the witnesses. We were married that afternoon; no big fanfare, but we were running away, so I hardly cared. We spent our wedding night in a dingy little hostel just a couple blocks off the dock. It wasn't very romantic, but there was a bed, and so we consummated our marriage that night, for the first and last time," Margaret laughed bitterly.

"Why the last time? Did something happen to Robert?" Isaboe hung on every word of her friend's tale.

"Aye, you could say that. The next morning we were standing at the dock, waiting to board our ship and sail off to America, husband and wife, Mr. and Mrs. Robert Ferguson. I was so excited. I was going off to start a new life, in a new land with the man I loved. But then it all came crashing down around me. As we were preparing to board, a troop of British soldiers suddenly came out of nowhere and grabbed Robert. As they dragged him away, they called him Avery McGarry and said he was under arrest. I ran after them, hitting and screaming at the soldiers to let my husband be. They had him confused with someone else, I said. All the while he never protested or put up a fight. He just let them cuff him and take him away. 'This is my husband, Robert Ferguson!' I screamed. I remember yelling at Robert, 'Tell them who you are! Tell them!' I was trying to grab hold of one of the soldiers when Robert looked at me with the saddest eyes I had ever seen. 'I'm sorry Margaret,' he said. 'I'm so sorry.' That was the last time I ever saw him."

"So, Robert, was he this McGarry fellow? What had he done to be arrested? Why did you never see him again? You were his wife. They should have at least let you see him."

"After the soldiers took him away, I went to the constable's office for help. He did some investigating, and as it turned out, Robert was in fact Avery McGarry, a Jacobite rebel who had been on the run for five years. When the soldiers came to the farm asking about him, Dad didn't give him up, even though he knew it was Robert they were looking for. That is why Dad made him leave before the British found out. The constable told me that since Robert hadn't used his legal name, the marriage contract wasn't valid, so we weren't legally married.

"I was so humiliated. Somehow my parents had realized our plans and informed the authorities. That's how the soldiers knew where to find us. We were so close. If only we had set sail before the Brits arrived, he would have been safe, though I would've been living a lie with a stranger. Who knows what would have happened once we arrived in America? He probably would have left me anyway." Margaret looked down at the handkerchief, and rubbed her thumb slowly across the embroidered monogram.

"So, did Robert give you this handkerchief?"

A small, awkward grin crossed Margaret's face. "He was so sure I would say yes that he had three of these made before I met up with him.

I found them in my bag after he had been taken away. He must have put them in there the morning after." Margaret took a deep sigh and looked out the window. "Well, that was then, and time has a way of healing old wounds." She turned back to her companion and managed a smile. "And it's a bloody good thing, or we'd be miserable and lonely all of our days, aye?"

Margaret immediately wished she hadn't used those words when she saw pain shooting across Isaboe's eyes. "I tell you this. I couldn't even speak to my Mum and Dad for weeks afterwards," she continued, trying to distract Isaboe's thoughts. "I was so angry with them for turning Robert in. But I eventually turned my anger toward Robert, or Avery, or whatever the hell his name was, for making me feel such a fool. I purposely hardened my heart, and while I've had a bed partner now and then to keep me warm on a cold night, I've never again let anyone blind me like that. And now, well, I'm not getting any younger, and I've long lost my girlish figure. It's not like I have to beat the men off with a stick."

"Now, Margaret, don't talk like that. You are still a vibrant woman. I've seen you run a pub, and offer a well-kept home. Any man in his right mind would be lucky to have you as his wife." Isaboe's words were kind, but to Margaret, they felt hollow.

"Well, you see, that right there is the problem, lassie. Not too many men out there my age have much at all in the way of a mind, so I think I'm better off without them." Margaret forced a smile as she squeezed her friend's hand.

The rest of the trip was more pleasant as Isaboe began asking about the world she now lived in. She had twenty years to catch up on and wanted to know it all. Since the journey to Inverness would take another full day, they had plenty of time.

They had avoided talking about the children, and to Margaret it felt daunting to have no idea how to even start looking for them when they do finally reach Edinburgh. That was still another two weeks' journey away, and she hoped the answers would somehow present themselves. But she continued to feel a small tinge of fear, both for her friend and of the unknown events that lay ahead. Every day, she prayed that this journey wouldn't be the biggest mistake of her life. After all, something strange and mystical had happened to Isaboe. Though she'd had no idea what to expect if Isaboe ever came back from the realm of the faeries, Margaret now suspected that it would be no easy road.

CHAPTER 12

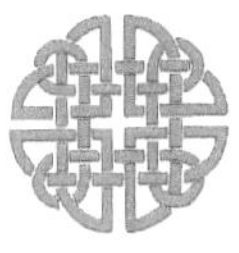

INVERNESS

The sound of passing voices alerted Isaboe that the carriage was nearing its destination. As she looked out the window, the outskirts of Inverness came into view, dotted by campsites along the road. As they continued toward the city, the campsites grew more numerous. Some of the tents seemed to be housing small parties, with plenty of loud talk, laughter, and though the afternoon was still young, a good deal of drink as well.

By the time the carriage rolled onto the main street, the crowd had become a mass. Vendors lined the road, shouting their wares as potential buyers pushed by. When the coach came to a sudden stop and the driver opened the door for his passengers, Isaboe stared at the throngs in amazement. "What's all this about?" she asked, looking back to where the driver was unloading their luggage.

"Tis the Inverness Summer Festival, of course. I thought that was why the two of ye came here," the driver replied. "Today is the last day, so ye've missed most of it."

Isaboe looked around the town square which was filled with people mingling around vendors' booths, eating, drinking, and browsing. Others gathered around stages on which actors and musicians played. Music filled the air, along with the smell of roasted meats and sweet, ripe fruits. The square was alive with activity.

"With all of these people here, do you think we can get a room?" Isaboe asked as she looked over the sea of humanity.

"Unless ye already have a reservation, ye'll be hard pressed to find anything for this evening. By the looks of it, most of these folks won't be leaving here tonight."

"Maybe we'll get lucky, and there'll be an available room, somewhere," Margaret said quickly.

Isaboe shot her a wishful look, and the driver made a guttural noise of disbelief as he climbed back up onto the coach. "Not likely that'll be happenin'. Good luck to ye ladies. If nothing else, enjoy the celebration. Maybe ye'll meet a fella or two that'll take ye in for the night." The driver chuckled as he slapped the reins of his team. The carriage slowly moved away through the crowd and down the street, leaving the two women standing with their bags at their feet.

"Well, I hope it doesn't come to that," Margaret said, stooping to pick up her bags. "But I suppose we may want to keep that option open."

"What?" Isaboe shot her friend a scolding look, but Margaret only chuckled before stepping into the street.

Following suit, Isaboe quickly grabbed her own bags. Pushing their way through the happily drunken crowd, they looked for any sign of an inn or hostel. After two days of isolation in the carriage, the vast amount of people and activity surrounding them was almost overwhelming. Yet there was something thrilling about being at the center of the mob, and Isaboe's heart rushed with the music. She couldn't help but smile as children and lovers danced by, swept up in the party atmosphere.

The enticing smells and sizzling sound of grilling meat seduced Isaboe's senses. Her stomach growled in response as they passed booths where patrons were eating and drinking. When a young boy walked by munching on a steaming leg of lamb, civility prevented her from reaching out and snatching it from his hand. Her hunger was attacking her defenses, and she needed to eat—soon.

But Margaret was determined to first find them a room, and she pushed ahead through the crowd, using her bag as a battering ram. As they wove their way through the throngs of people further into the heart of the town, the thickness of the crowd was oppressive. Jugglers, dancers, musicians, and singers stood on every street corner. Vendors with colorful trinkets and mouthwatering foods hawked their wares.

"Look! There's an inn," Margaret exclaimed over the noise as she led the way towards a building with a sign above the door: *Inverness Inn.*

"But I'm starving. Please! Can't we eat first?" Isaboe whined.

Wheeling around to face her friend, Margaret's glare was intense. "I'm not sleepin' on the ground again tonight if I don't have to. We can get dinner after we have a room. Now, come on!"

Unfortunately, the *Inverness Inn, the Town Square Hotel*, and a sleazy little hole called *The White Knight's Room and Boarding* had no vacancies, leaving the women with no place to stay for the night. However, at the *Town Square Hotel* they did get a very nice offer from a fat and very drunk Englishman who said he would be honored to share his room with them. Though firmly declining his offer, it wasn't only the Englishman's attention that Isaboe drew. Earlier that day, she had let her hair down, and her auburn locks now framed her face perfectly as they flowed loosely around her shoulders. She noticed more than a few heads turning as the two women made their way through the crowds of entertainers, vendors, diners and drinkers. Isaboe let her head drop, and focused on where she set her feet, trying not to attract the gaze of any other men with crude offers.

Dressed simply in a dark frock that Margaret's curves had grown out of, Isaboe felt plain as the eyes of men, even some women, followed her. She'd been told how pretty she was her whole life, but this was scoffed at by her mother. Isaboe knew jealousy, had felt it herself, and had spent her time in Faireshire trying to ignore the way others looked at her.

Outside of Faireshire, outside of what she knew as normal, Isaboe decided not to let herself care. Raising her head, she let the thrum of the crowd and the celebration carry her through the market and vendor booths. The carnival atmosphere made her feel like a child wanting to experience it all. Expectations be damned!

When the ladies reached the center of town, they came upon the *Ambassador Hotel*. With a well-kept entrance and upscale Victorian décor, it looked to be the nicest by far.

"If every other inn is full, this one must be too," Isaboe complained. "Can't we please get something to eat, I'm famished!"

"Room first; then we can eat." Taking Isaboe by the hand, Margaret pulled her into the lobby. With a wide, open-beamed ceiling and intricate architecture which accented the building inside and out, the hotel was quite grand. Large, oriental vases sat atop beautiful carved tables that lined the lobby. The lounges in the waiting area looked as though they would be more than sufficient to sleep on, should it come to that.

Making their way to the front desk, Isaboe noticed the pungent smell of cigar smoke drifting through the open area. Like the ghost of a large serpent, a cloud of grey vapor slithered across the ceiling. The balcony overlooking the lobby provided the source of the tainted air. Strategically placed next to the railing, a number of men were seated at a table, talking, drinking, and of course, smoking. Some were British officers. Others were dressed in civilian clothes, but not in common attire. They looked like businessmen, city officials, or politicians. Those who wore powdered wigs seemed to be looking down over the lesser patrons below. Isaboe watched a young barmaid scamper up the stairs, her service summoned by one of the occupants at the railing.

It was in a darker area towards the back of the lobby where the rest of the people were served. The low murmur of conversation drew Isaboe's attention, and she scanned the poorly lit bar. The sun had dropped low on the horizon, and its rays cut through the smoke-filled lobby like giant white sabers. Looking through the long fingers of sunlight, she could see a group of Scotsmen sitting at one of the tables in the pub. Hovering over their drinks, they chatted low, creating subtle shadows against the sunlight and smoke. Most of the city's population was still outside, enjoying festivities on the last day of the summer games. But there were always the few who shied away from the crowds.

At another table further back in the bar, Isaboe noticed the solitary outline of a hooded figure sipping on a mug. Though the face was completely shadowed from view, she had an odd feeling she was being watched. Dropping her gaze, she caught up with Margaret, now standing at the reception desk interrogating the hotel clerk.

"Oh, is that so? You don't have a room, or you don't have a room that you think *I* can afford?" Margaret's gaze bore into the dark eyes of the tall, greasy-haired clerk, who had bluntly informed her that there were no rooms available.

"There was no judgment on whether or not you can afford a room here," the clerk said defensively, as he looked down his pointed nose. "I merely answered your question. There are no rooms available."

"What did you expect him to say?" Isaboe asked, letting her annoyance show. "I told you this hotel wouldn't have any rooms either. Let's just go."

"No! I was looking forward to sleeping in a bed tonight, Isaboe, and I don't care for this one's attitude!" Margaret's outburst had drawn the attention of the men in the balcony, and Isaboe noticed that two of them had taken an interest in the exchange below. "You didn't even check," Margaret continued interrogating the man. "Every other hotel clerk had the decency to at least look in the book before turning us away. You just glared down your nose at me, like I wasn't good enough to stay in your *fancy* hotel!"

"Please, Margaret. I know you're frustrated, but you're making a scene." As she gently grasped her friend's arm, hoping to calm her, Isaboe glanced up at the faces looking down from above. One set of dark eyes caught hers and held her gaze. Offering a slight smile, he nodded, but Isaboe chose not to engage. "We're done here," she said, taking her companion's hand and pulling her toward the entrance.

"I didn't want to stay at your stinkin', overpriced hotel anyway!" Margaret shouted over her shoulder as Isaboe ushered her out of the building and onto the street, back into the throngs of people.

"Well, that was certainly a waste of time. We still don't have anywhere to sleep tonight, and I still haven't eaten," Isaboe grumbled. As people pushed by, brushing her aside, she screamed when a man stepped on her foot, but he didn't even stop or acknowledge his crudeness. "I'm beginning to hate Inverness!" she nearly shouted. But Isaboe's complaint fell on deaf ears. Margaret was too interested in what was quickly becoming the center of attention. In the middle of the street, effectively blocking foot traffic, a boxing competition was about to get underway. Waving coins in the air and barking out wagers, men and women gathered, eager to place their bets. Under a hanging lantern in a tent over a small table, one man fervently took the offered money while another scribbled on a writing tablet.

After following Margaret into the middle of the congregation, she watched as her friend peered over the shoulder of the man in front of her. "What are you doing?"

"It's a boxing match. It's been a while since I've seen a good fight," Margaret replied with a smile. Her bad mood seemed to have vanished.

"A boxing match? I've always thought they were a touch…barbaric."

"Aye, but there's a bit of satisfaction in watching a couple of blokes beat the piss out of each other. I havta say, I've always found it quite entertaining." The grin on Margaret's face told Isaboe that she wasn't going to have that meal anytime soon.

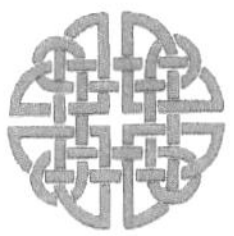

CHAPTER 13

THE LIEUTENANT

"Sounds like your friend here knows what makes for a good show." The sound of an Englishman's voice caused Isaboe to turn away from the boxing match. She found herself face-to-face with a British soldier, the same officer who had stared down at her from the balcony of the hotel. About a head taller than Isaboe, the officer held a pompous, educated look. His brownish hair was slicked back neatly, but his dark, heavy-lidded eyes were bloodshot, and the smell of brandy and cigar smoke wafted off his clothing and his breath. "She's a spunky one," he said, pointing at Margaret, "a Scotswoman who speaks her mind and enjoys a good clashing of *mano a mano*." The man's words were slurred. "I couldn't help but overhear her back in the hotel. No vacancy, I take it?"

Isaboe hesitated, but decided to respond. "No, unfortunately we have not found a room yet for the night, nor had a decent meal," she grumbled.

The man held out his hand. "Allow me to introduce myself; I am Lieutenant Colonel Jonathan Blackwood, of his Highness's Royal British Army."

She regarded his haughty and intoxicated demeanor before tentatively taking his hand. "Isaboe McKinnon. It's a pleasure to meet you, sir. In regards to this exposition, I suppose it might be entertaining, for some," she said, pulling her hand free as she leaned away. "I've never watched a boxing match, and personally, I don't understand the attraction."

Turning away from the crowd that had gathered, Margaret joined the conversation. "Oh, you have to see it for the sport, lass, the competition. It's a test of a man's willpower, strength, and how long the bloody fool can take a beatin'. See that big man over there?"

Isaboe lifted up on her tip toes, trying to peer over the crowd. "Where?"

"I'm sure a tiny thing like you can hardly see," the lieutenant said, looking down at her. "Let's move you up, so you can have a better view, aye?" Before Isaboe could protest, Lieutenant Blackwood took her hand and pushed his way through to the front of the mob. "Move aside! An officer and a lady coming through," he barked out his command in a military tone, but it didn't disguise his drunken haze.

"Make that *two* ladies," Margaret added as she stepped quickly in behind Isaboe, taking advantage of Blackwood's ability to clear the path. Though Isaboe didn't care for the looks she received from the people they pushed aside, Blackwood's authority wasn't questioned.

When they arrived at the edge of the clearing, Margaret reached out her hand in introduction. "Margaret MacDougal."

"Jonathan Blackwood," he replied, taking Margaret's hand.

Pointing to a large, shirtless man, Margaret said, "See that big fella?" Curly red hair covered most of the man's pale, freckled body, and his arms were as thick as tree trunks. "I just heard he's never been beaten. He's taken on every challenger and has knocked out every one."

"Aye, but he hasn't met Brawler," another man added as he nodded in the opposite direction.

Isaboe glanced toward the other side of the clearing that had been created for the boxing event. Not far away stood another bare-chested man who was entirely hairless, from his head to his waist. A dark, zigzagging scar stood out on his thick, sun-browned chest. His arms were equally well-muscled, and the furrowed glare and animalistic growl he shot his opponent sent the crowd into a hooting tizzy.

"Oh, this match-up looks bloody great!" Margaret's excitement was oozing. "Who's your money on?" she asked the lieutenant.

"I haven't decided yet, but I think we should make it interesting."

"What'd ye have in mind?"

Without answering, the lieutenant offered a crooked smile as he sauntered toward the betting table. He had a short discussion with one man, then turned and walked toward the first opponent, Big Red. Slowly circling the man, Blackwood examined him closely. He then crossed the clearing to where the other man stood and repeated his inspection, circling the bald man with a lightning strike on his chest. Isaboe watched carefully as Blackwood scrutinized the man's powerful physic, sizing him up against his massive opponent.

"May I have your attention!" the lieutenant announced, drawing in the crowd. "My name is Lieutenant Colonel Jonathan Blackwood, and I'm placing a very substantial wager on one of these men—five hundred pounds." The crowd gasped and began murmuring at the size of the wager. Even though his speech was affected by the amount of liquor he had consumed, Isaboe could see the officer's training coming through in his approach to the crowd. "And should I win, I will give my suite at the Ambassador Hotel to these two lovely ladies." From inside his coat, Blackwood pulled out the room key and held it out for all to see.

Startled, Isaboe looked at Margaret. She hadn't seen that coming.

"You are all my witnesses." The lieutenant took a step forward to where Isaboe stood with her mouth slightly agape. "No strings attached, the room is yours, as long as you agree to have dinner with me first." Leering wolfishly, he looked down, waiting for a response. But Isaboe was no fool. "No strings attached" was a child's myth when a man was involved—particularly a man who has had too much to drink.

"And if you lose?" Margaret asked.

"You'll be no worse off than you are now."

"Well, then of course we'll have dinner with you!" Margaret answered for both of them. "You're paying, right?"

Blackwood chuckled. "I still haven't heard Miss McKinnon's answer. Will you have dinner with me?"

"Isaboe, he's offering us his suite and a meal. Just say yes!"

But Margaret's eagerness only made Isaboe more cautious. She looked carefully at the officer, who was still waiting for her answer. "You'll just give us your suite if we agree to have dinner with you? Sir, you'll pardon me, but we could hardly take your room for just nothing." Nor did Isaboe think he expected nothing.

"I insist! The room is yours, but only if I win. If I lose, well, I'll have no money to buy anyone's meal, much less afford to give up my room. So, is that a yes?"

Isaboe glanced around at the faces that stared at her, waiting to see what her answer would be. She heard multiple shouts from the crowd willing to take his offer if she didn't want it. Some of the eyes she met held judgment, some jealousy. She kept her eyes moving until her gaze fell upon the face of a silent stranger, a hooded man staring at her from across the clearing.

"Isaboe!" Margaret barked. "Just say yes, already!"

"Alright, yes, I will agree to have dinner with you."

"Splendid!" Blackwood said with an arrogant smile, "So, which one of these brutes should I put my wager on?"

"I'll leave that for you to decide," Isaboe replied, stepping back.

"Well, if you want to know what I think," Margaret offered up, since Isaboe apparently had no opinion, "you should put your money on this fella right here." She nodded towards the challenger with the lightning scar. Blackwood turned and strolled to where the man stood, flexing his massive arms and growling at the champion.

"You better hope we don't regret this," Isaboe hissed at Margaret.

"Don't worry 'bout it. Do you see how smashed he is? He'll probably pass out before dinner is over."

"Then we better get the key first."

The lieutenant circled the large man one more time. "Yes, he has a strong and brutish build, but look at that specimen over there." Blackwood pointed toward Big Red, who was pacing at the other edge of the clearing, just waiting to throw his first punch. "Look at that man! They say he's never been beaten. And for good reason; he's built like a bloody warship! Those arms look like canons."

And the crowd did look, just as Blackwood wanted them to. But Isaboe wasn't looking across the clearing at Big Red, who was flexing his muscles and taking the opportunity to work the crowd. Her eyes were on the lieutenant as he slipped up to the large, bald man, brushing his hand ever so slightly. It was a subtle move, hardly noticeable if she hadn't been watching, and over quickly as Blackwood returned to entertain the masses. "However, after intense scrutiny of both men's attributes, I'm placing my wager on…uh, what's your name?"

"Brawler," the large man said in a husky voice.

"I'm wagering five hundred pounds that Brawler can defeat the champion." Blackwood announced before swaggering over to the betting table. The crowd roared, some in agreement and some in dissent, but the excitement was contagious.

Margaret dug into her bag and pulled out a handful of coins. "I'll take some of that action! Ten schillings on Brawler!" she shouted, heading towards the betting table, along with other gamblers who wanted a piece of the prize.

For the first few minutes of the bout, the fighters exchanged light, equal blows, dancing and bobbing to feel the other man out. Isaboe was caught up in the roar of the spectators as they cheered on the fighters. Grunts, groans, and the sound of flesh hitting flesh was barbaric, but the excitement from the throng fed the fury of the fighters. As sweat and blood flew across the clearing, it all seemed so violent and brutal. Glancing at Margaret shouting her own cheers, Isaboe couldn't deny that the sport held an attraction, at least for some. And it was obvious there was a lot of money to be made—or lost.

Just minutes into the third round, Big Red took a blow to the chin that rocked his head backward, and his enormous body followed suit. With an earth-rattling impact, the huge man hit the ground, out cold.

After a moment of stunned silence, and an official examination of the unconscious man, the announcer proclaimed in a loud voice, "The champ's been defeated! Brawler is the winner!"

Shouts, cheers, and moans filled the air as people flooded the betting table. "We won! We won!" Margaret shouted, jumping up and down.

But Isaboe didn't share her friend's enthusiasm. She watched suspiciously as Blackwood immediately went over to the betting table. He then sauntered over to Isaboe, holding the key out toward her with a self-righteous smile. "Looks like this turned out to be your lucky night, my lady," he said, giving her a slight bow and a cocky grin. "Now that I've collected my winnings, I'll buy you the best meal this town has to offer."

"You cheated." Isaboe looked directly at Blackwood, stopping him in his tracks. "You gave him something just before the match. I saw you put something in his hand."

"What?" Blackwood said with a nervous laugh.

"Isaboe, what are you talking about?" Margaret asked. "The lieutenant just offered to take us out to a nice dinner, give us his suite, and you call him a cheater? What's wrong with you?"

"I saw him. He cheated."

"You don't know what you're talking about," the lieutenant whispered as he leaned in towards Isaboe. "Whatever you think you saw, you were mistaken." The gaze he bore into her eyes held a threat that she didn't care for, so she took several nervous steps back.

"He cheated!" Isaboe said again, but louder. "I saw him put something in Brawler's hand."

Rumblings in the crowd were the first indication that people were paying attention to Isaboe's accusation. "Check his hands!" one voice yelled. "The fight was fixed!" yelled another. It wasn't long before the new champion, who only moments before was being exalted for his victory, was now being interrogated. Though Brawler tried not to draw attention as he tossed a small steel rod behind him, when the metal hit the ground, a young boy blew his cover.

"He's a cheater! The fight was fixed! Give us back our money!" Shouts and curses went up as the crowd pushed, shoved, and scrambled over each other to reach the betting table.

"You stupid little wench!" Blackwood spat, yanking Isaboe by her arm, and effectively pulling her from the chaos of the crowd. "We could've had a wonderful evening tonight, but you had to ruin it," he growled into her face.

"I don't want anything from you!" Isaboe screamed back at him trying to free herself from his grip. "You're a cheater and a drunk! Get your hands off of me! Margaret!" Isaboe looked desperately at the faces flashing by, but Margaret had gotten separated in the mass of people pushing and shouting.

"Don't let that officer get away!" a voice called out. "Where is that cheating Brit?" yelled another.

"Because of you, I could lose a great deal of money," Blackwood snarled, yanking Isaboe into step beside him. "And possibly more than that!" With a vicious glare, he turned away from the crowd, his grip still firmly on Isaboe's arm.

"Let me go!" she yelled, trying to break free. But the lieutenant ignored her pleas, dragging her along as he wove in and out of the throngs of people.

The sun had set below the horizon, bringing out the lamp lighters. The mass of spectators, musicians, entertainers, and vendors barking their wares in a city alive at night gave Blackwood the cover he needed. Dragging Isaboe along, he raced feverishly down the street. Though she screamed out when she could catch her breath, the sounds of the crowd smothered her cries.

When she caught sight of the angry mob searching for them, Isaboe shouted in their direction, but Blackwood ducked into an alley and clamped a hand over her mouth. After the group passed by, the lieutenant took a quick glance to be sure it was clear before releasing his grip on Isaboe's mouth.

"Why are you doing this? Please, sir, let me go!" Isaboe's plea sounded more and more desperate.

"If they catch me, I'll lose a shit-load of money because of you," Blackwood snarled. "You're going to pay for this, one way or another."

They both heard a familiar voice in the distance—"Isaboe! Isaboe, where are you?"

"Margaret! Over here…," but before Isaboe could say anything else, Blackwood bolted down the alley and onto the street. They were back on the run, but the angry group called out, demanding that Blackwood halt. Even his fellow British soldiers were now hunting him.

"You must know you won't get away with this," she said breathlessly, struggling to keep up with the lieutenant's long stride. "They'll surely catch up with us unless you let me go."

"Not if I can help it. Enough with the goddamn fighting!" Blackwood growled, jerking her arm harder than necessary. Pushing people aside he barged back into the crowd, dragging Isaboe behind him. That was until he made a wrong turn down an alley with no exit. When he turned to retreat, the path was blocked by the mob of angry gamblers looking for justice. Two of them held torches whose flickering light danced off the faces of the people.

"It's over lieutenant. Let the woman go," said a soldier of lesser rank.

At least half a dozen uniformed soldiers stood with the civilians, all looking to bring down the man who had rigged the fight.

The sound of steel-on-steel rang out as Blackwood slid his sword from its scabbard. "There's not one among you who's man enough to take me on," he snarled. Pulling Isaboe in front of him with his free hand, he used her as a shield with his arm across her chest.

When Isaboe saw Margaret pushing her way through to the front of the mob, she let out a small whimper. But Margaret could only stare with the rest of the crowd, wondering what their next move would be.

"Looks like yer the one who's not man enough, hiding behind a woman," said a man in a cloak as he pulled his own sword from its scabbard. "Let the woman go, or are ye too afraid to fight—man to man?"

Though terrified, Isaboe saw the hood and knew he was the same man she had made eye contact with earlier. Now, the hood had fallen to reveal an unshaven jaw, shaggy brown hair, and dark, fearless eyes as the stranger locked gazes with the British officer.

Blackwood chuckled, and tossed Isaboe aside, sending her sprawling to the ground. "You're a fool if you think you can take me in. I'm the King's champion swordsman, and you're just a bloody Scot," Blackwood sneered as he moved into position, slicing the air with his sword.

Taking opportunity of the distraction, Isaboe scrambled up and ran into Margaret's arms. "Are you alright?" Margaret asked, closely examining her friend.

Engrossed in the confrontation unfolding before them, Isaboe only nodded as Blackwood lunged forward with a violent slash of his sword. But his opponent stepped aside, easily blocking the officer's attack, and sending him off-balance. Calculating that the officer's intoxication would play in his favor, instead of making a counter move with his own sword, the challenger simply approached the lieutenant and punched him square in the jaw. Tripping over his own drunken feet, Blackwood stumbled backward, dropping his sword in the process.

"The King's champion swordsman, aye?" muttered the Scotsman as he looked down at the fallen officer.

Immediately surrounded by his fellow soldiers, Blackwood was hauled to his feet with his hands restrained. An official-looking man wearing a white powdered wig stepped forward, glaring at him. "Take the lieutenant and lock him up."

"I'm the King's man! You can't lock me up!" Blackwood hissed as the soldiers struggled to control him. He shot an evil glare at the man who had so easily taken him down, embarrassing him in front of his men. "You better hope our paths never cross, Scotsman. If I ever see you again, you're a dead man!" He then turned his eyes on Isaboe with a look that made her shudder. "And you still owe me, bitch. This is not over! You'll pay for this!" Blackwood shouted as he was led off by the mob.

Holding tightly onto Margaret, Isaboe couldn't stop shaking until she saw Blackwood disappear around the corner. Not until he was truly gone did she take her first breath of relief.

"Are you alright? That must've been frightfully scary!" Margaret held Isaboe at arm's length to take a good look.

"I guess I'm alright. Just a little shook up, but I'll be fine." She gave Margaret a reassuring smile before glancing at the man in the white wig. He was talking with the stranger who had stepped up to save her when no one else would.

Now that the mob had dispersed, so did the light from their torches. Isaboe watched as her savior started to walk out with the man in the powered wig, but then he stopped and looked back. Though it was dark and she couldn't see his eyes, Isaboe knew he was looking at her. Without thinking, she walked toward him, and he carefully watched her take every step until she stood in front of him.

"You are a very brave man, sir, and I don't know how to thank you," she said, holding out her hand. "My name is Isaboe McKinnon."

He regarded her for a moment before finally taking her hand, "Connor Grant. No thanks are necessary. I'm glad to see ye're unharmed."

"Yes, thanks to you."

Margaret joined Isaboe and grabbed Connor's hand, shaking it aggressively. "Aye, thank you, Mr. Grant! I'm Margaret MacDougal, and it's rare to see a man who'll stand up to a British officer, even a drunk one. You noticed his soldiers weren't jumping in. They all looked like scared chickens, not willing to take on a commanding officer. But you just stepped up and popped the cheatin' weasel in the face. He didn't even see it coming.

It was a thing of beauty, it was!" Margaret's words were intense, fed by the rush of the wild chase through the streets of Inverness.

"Miss McKinnon, my name is Constable Davies," said the man in the white wig. "If you wish to press charges against Lieutenant Blackwood, please come by my office in the morning."

"I…I don't think I want to do that," Isaboe replied. "When we stopped in Inverness, all I really wanted was a decent meal and good night's sleep. I didn't expect to be accosted and dragged through the streets. I still haven't eaten yet, nor have we found a room for the night. I just want to get out of this town as soon as possible!" Isaboe didn't try to hide her frustration.

The constable gave her a sympathetic nod. "Well, as far as the meal and a room for the night, the township of Inverness will take care of both. Consider it an apology for the bad impression our fair community has left you with. As far as leaving right away, unless you have your own transportation, that may not be possible. I was at the station this afternoon, and every coach out of town is booked for the next three days."

"What? I can't stay here that long!" Isaboe moaned, giving Margaret a desperate look.

"Nor should you," the constable replied. "Lieutenant Blackwood may be a cheater, but he does have connections in high places. He won't stay locked up for long. By the threat he made, it would be best for you to leave town as soon as possible. Let us talk about it over dinner. Perhaps there's another option for you," the constable paused. "What about you, Mr. Grant. Would you care to join us for dinner? On the township, of course."

"No thanks. I'm leaving first thing on the morrow. I think I'll turn in."

"And where will you be going?" the constable asked.

"I'll be leaving for Edinburgh."

"There's a great deal of land to cover between here and Edinburgh, and some of it is very rough country. Safe travels to you then." The constable shook Connor's hand, and they turned to walk out of the alley.

Isaboe shot Margaret a look. "Wait, Mr. Grant," she said. "My friend and I are also traveling to Edinburgh. Since we are all heading to the same destination…"

"I travel by horseback. Do ye have horses?"

"Well, no, but we could buy them, couldn't we Margaret?"

"Uh…well, as long as they don't cost too much," Margaret mumbled. "I s'pose we could do that."

"The ride to Edinburgh will take a week. With the two of ye tagging along, it could take two weeks. Have ye been on the back of a horse that long?" Connor asked, looking closely at Isaboe. "Nothing personal, but ye dinnae look like ye've done much riding. I doubt that ye could handle two weeks on the back of a horse."

"It'll be fine. I've ridden before. Maybe not that long, but I can handle it."

Looking for support, Connor glanced at the constable, who only smiled and shrugged his shoulders.

"We'll pay you!" Isaboe almost shouted when she saw him wavering, knowing he didn't want them along. "We'll hire you for your services; to escort us to Edinburgh."

"Isaboe," Margaret hissed, "we can't afford horses and a bodyguard!"

"It'll be fine. We can sell the horses later, and you'll get your money back." Isaboe turned her attention back to the mysterious man, who seemed to be looking for an escape. "We'll have hot coffee for you in the mornings, and hot meals on the road. I promise that we'll be no trouble." Isaboe offered up an innocent smile, hoping that the attributes God had given her would work, as they had on most men she'd ever met.

"In the couple of hours ye've been in Inverness, ye've already gotten in plenty of trouble. I can just imagine what ye could do in a couple of weeks," he replied.

"Please, Mr. Grant," Isaboe pleaded. "Margaret and I would feel so much safer if we weren't traveling alone. You heard the constable; there's some very rough country between here and Edinburgh. Please, may we travel with you?"

"Paid escort service, hot meals on the road, and two lovely ladies to keep you company. Sounds like an offer you can't refuse," Constable Davies said with a chuckle.

Connor Grant rubbed a hand across his stubbled jaw and took a long, deep breath while shifting from one foot to the other. "I'm leaving right after breakfast," he said, as a look of resignation fell across his shoulders.

"Be at the Town Square Hotel with reliable horses no later than nine o'clock. *Reliable* horses," he emphasized.

"Thank you, Mr. Grant. Thank you!" Isaboe shook his hand enthusiastically. "You won't regret this."

"That's yet to be seen," he grumbled.

CHAPTER 14

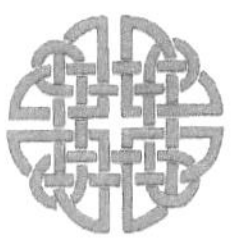

CONFESSION

Margaret was up with the dawn, quietly repacking their clothes in the small one-room loft she shared with Isaboe while her friend still slept. Though it wasn't a suite at the Ambassador Hotel, the accommodations Constable Davies had arranged for them were more than suitable. He had graciously excused himself from joining them for dinner, but as promised, the ladies were finally able to satisfy their hunger, courtesy of Inverness.

Margaret held up the dress that had been ripped while Blackwood dragged Isaboe recklessly through the streets the night before. But her concern for the tear in the garment paled in comparison to the bruising on Isaboe's arm. "Maybe you should reconsider and press charges against Blackwood after all," Margaret had suggested after seeing the dark blue, hand-shaped bruise on her friend's fair skin. But Isaboe had insisted it was nothing and just wanted to leave town, especially if there was a chance Blackwood might be released.

"How long are you gonna sleep?" Margaret asked, giving the heap under the blanket a nudge as she walked past the bed, picking up the last petticoat and stuffing it into her bag. "Mr. Grant said no later than nine this morning, with horses. That means we havta go to the stables right away. The sooner we get there, the better our chances, so get your lazy arse up."

"Hmm…. just let me sleep a little longer," Isaboe mumbled from under the blanket.

"Isaboe, *you* talked Mr. Grant into letting us travel with him. The only way that's gonna happen is if we have horses. You heard the constable; there's no leaving on a coach today. So get up before we can't leave at all,"

Margaret growled as she stood beside the bed with her hands on her hips, waiting for a reply.

"Horses? Did you say something about horses?" Isaboe yawned deeply as she struggled to open her eyes.

"Aye, we discussed this last night, remember? We need to buy the horses here so we can ride out with Mr. Grant this morning. If there's a town along the way where we can catch a coach, we'll sell the horses and let him go his way. At least we'll be getting out of Inverness."

Rubbing her hands across her face, Isaboe slowly pushed back the blankets and sat up on the side of the bed. "Do you know how far it is to the next town? Truth be told, I'm not too keen on riding on the back of a horse for any great distance."

Margaret noticed that Isaboe's words were strained, and she was taking long, deep breaths. "I'm not sure how far it'll be. Maybe we can find out before we leave town. But let's not wait much longer to go buy those horses." She stopped her packing and looked at Isaboe, who hadn't moved from the bed. "Are you feeling alright? You look a little pale, like you could…" But before Margaret could finish, Isaboe was off the bed, vomiting violently into the wash bowl on the dresser.

"Oh my, you aren't feeling well at all, are you?" Margaret cringed as she held Isaboe's hair back, while her friend continued spewing out the remains of the previous evening's meal.

As she fought her own gag reflex, Margaret noticed a mark on the back of Isaboe's neck. At the base of her skull, a group of small, dark intertwined circles stood out against her pale skin. If it were a tattoo, it went against all Margaret knew of Isaboe—to say nothing about how strange its placement was. Margaret made a mental note to ask her about it later.

After Isaboe had finally emptied her stomach, her whole body shook from the effort. Taking several deep breaths, she pulled her face up from the bowl.

"It looks like we won't be going anywhere today after all," Margaret said, handing her friend a fresh towel. "Maybe we can just stay in this room for a couple of days, until you're feeling better."

"NO! I don't want to stay in this town one more day." Isaboe finished wiping her mouth and sat back down on the bed. "I'll be alright before long. I just need a little more rest."

Margaret watched her friend with obvious concern. "I'm not so sure you'll feel like traveling anytime soon. Did this just come on, or have you been feeling ill for a while?' Margaret asked the question, but she already suspected the answer.

"What do you mean by that?" Isaboe snapped. "Last night scared me, and I'm still upset about it." Looking up at her friend, she gave a shrug. "I'm sorry, Margaret. I just need to rest for a little while longer, and I'll be fine." Isaboe laid back on the bed and curled into a ball, pulling the blanket over her head.

Margaret sighed as she looked down at the mass of auburn hair spilling out from the top of the blanket and over Isaboe's pillow. Shaking her head, she picked up the wash bowl, holding it out as far away as possible, and left the room.

When she returned a few minutes later, Margaret placed a clean bowl on the dresser. Walking past the bed, she noticed that not a hair had moved, nor a wrinkle on the blanket been disturbed. "Alright then, you just rest." She softly patted the blanket covering Isaboe and turned toward the door. "I'll go investigate the horses. If it takes too long, I might just head directly over to meet up with Mr. Grant. I don't want him to leave without us." But Margaret's comment created no response. "I'm taking the key and locking the door behind me, so don't plan on leaving this room. If you need, there's a bedpan in the corner." With her hand on the door, Margaret looked back at the lump on the bed that hadn't moved or acknowledged anything she had said. "Isaboe, did you hear me? Are you still alive under that blanket?"

"Yes, I heard you." The reply was muffled and weak. As Margaret started to close the door behind her, Isaboe called out. "Do you think you could bring me something to eat? I'm famished."

Isaboe was up and dressed when the sound of the key in the lock made her jump. Juggling a tray with a teapot, cups, and a loaf of bread, Margaret stepped inside the small room. "Here, let me help you." Isaboe took the tray and placed it on the table.

"You look much better. The wee bit of extra rest was just what you needed, aye?"

Trying her best to look refreshed, Isaboe smiled back, despite the waves of nausea that swept over her like the ebb and flow of the tide. With each wave, small beads of sweat broke out across her forehead and upper lip. Taking slow, deep breaths, she finally overcame the urge to heave into the wash bowl. "Thank you, my dear friend, for letting me rest a bit longer. That extra hour really helped," she whispered. Now able to take a seat at the table, she tore off a hunk of bread and stuffed it into her mouth. "So, did you get the horses?"

"Aye, I got horses, if you can call 'em that. I just hope Mr. Grant approves," Margaret replied with a doubtful look as she took the seat opposite Isaboe. "All the stableman had left was an old sway-back mare and a mule, and he wanted too much for the both of them. I think he saw me for a fool who didn't know any better. But I've been around men like that, so we did a bit of negotiation. The man could hardly argue with the deficiencies of the animals, so he lowered the price and threw in saddles. Oh, and he's having them re-shod for us."

"Did you see Mr. Grant?"

Margaret placed her cup down and nodded. "Oh aye, I saw Mr. Grant after I left the stables."

"Did he approve of what you bought?

"I left 'em there, so he hasn't seen 'em yet. He was having breakfast, and he didn't look all that happy to see me. I think he was hoping we'd changed our minds."

"What did he say?"

"That he'd meet us here after he's done eating." Margaret sat back in her chair, looking directly at Isaboe. "He don't want us along. You do know that, right? He's only doing this 'cause you asked him in front of Constable Davies. Honestly, I'll be surprised if we see him again."

"Don't say that. If he said he would be here, then I'm sure he will."

"What makes you so sure? You don't know a damn thing about the man," Margaret said, crossing her arms as she scrutinized Isaboe.

"No, but I think he's a good, honest man, or he wouldn't have stood up for me last night. I guess we'll find out when he shows up."

Margaret leaned forward with her elbows on the table. "From my perspective, Isaboe; good, honest, and man are three words that don't fit in the same sentence. I know you want to believe the best about the world, but it just don't work that way. People ain't always what they seem. Lieutenant Blackwood is proof of that." Margaret tore off a hunk of bread and leaned back in her chair. "Honesty is a rare virtue these days, especially among men."

Margaret's comment struck a chord, and Isaboe dropped her eyes, trying to hide the guilt she felt about her own dishonesty.

"What's wrong? Are you feeling sick again?" Margaret reached out, and touched her friend's arm.

"No, I feel better, thank you. This bread was just what I needed." After taking another long, deep breath, Isaboe gave Margaret a weak smile. She felt the tears burning to break free, but fought them back. "I…I keep hoping that the pain will decrease, but…" She shook her head as she dropped her gaze. "It's all my fault. If only I had listened to you. If only I hadn't gone into the forest that day, they would still be here. We would all still be together. Nathan would still be…" but the tears she'd been fighting to hold back finally broke free, choking off her words.

"Alright now, you stop that. There's nothin' to be gained by dwellin' over what can't be changed. You can only go forward from here, and you don't have to do it alone, lass. I'll help you, you know that."

"That's just it. You've already done so much for me. You've helped me in ways that I'll never be able to repay." Isaboe let out a shaky breath. "But, there's something I haven't told you. Something you need to know."

"What is it?"

Isaboe placed on the table a smooth, blue, ovoid stone hanging from a braided green cord. "Have you ever seen this before?"

Margaret shook her head. "No. Where'd it come from?"

"I found it around my neck last night when I changed into my bed clothes."

"Where'd you get it? I've never seen you wear it before."

"That's because I never had it before. Not before being with the old woman in the carriage."

"She gave it to you?"

"I can't say for sure, but I believe so. The last thing I remember is feeling something slip over my head, and her voice saying that this was a gift."

"Hmm," Margaret picked up the blue stone and rubbed her thumb across the polished surface. "It's very pretty," she said, turning the pendant over in her hands before placing it back on the table. "Is this it? Is this what you needed to share with me?"

"Only partly." Isaboe took another deep, steadying breath. "Margaret, I think that I may be, well, it appears that, uh, what I'm trying to say is that I believe I'm...um..."

"You're with child?" Margaret finished the sentence that Isaboe couldn't force out.

"You knew?"

"I suspected it the week before we left New Faireshire. And every day since then you haven't felt well in the morning, but eventually you're fine. This may be the first time I've seen you retch, but I knew. How long did you think you could hide it from me? I've not had children of my own, but I didn't just fall off the turnip cart. I know morning sickness when I see it. You were green with it today."

"I wasn't really sure of it myself, Margaret. I had hoped that maybe my courses were askew with all that had happened. But the old woman confirmed it."

"What did she say?"

"I didn't understand it all, but she said I'd been used by the fey."

"What does that mean?"

"I don't know. I don't recall everything she said, but she knew I was with child. She said the fey folk aren't done with me yet." Just saying these words sent Isaboe into a spiral of panic. Would this unknown force, the same entity that had already destroyed her life, make another appearance? The idea that she could have conceived a child in another world and have no memory of it was too hard for her to accept. Yet, she couldn't deny the crone's cryptic words. "I'm not sure, but I think she was trying to tell me that the fey want my baby."

"Isaboe, why didn't you mention this when you first told me about the old woman?"

"I didn't want to burden you with my fears, and I…I'm not sure how I feel about any of this. I'm truly sorry, Margaret." But Isaboe knew it was more than that. Most of it had been cryptic and confusing, but there were strong warnings in the crone's message. She specifically recalled the old hag's graphic words; *"danger surrounds you, death for some."* That part was quite clear.

After a few uncomfortable moments, Margaret finally broke the silence. "What I want to know is whose child is it, and when was it conceived? Don't forget; you've been gone to who knows where for the last twenty years."

"Of course I've wondered about that. Every time I let myself think of what could've happened in all those years, and that I don't recall *any of it*, I start to panic. I have no recollection of anything, Margaret, nothing! God help me. It was just an afternoon, a short nap in the woods!"

As the tears began again, Isaboe paced the room. "I come back to find my whole life pulled out from under me. Everything I loved and lived for, gone!" Her arms gestured wildly in tune with her words. "Then you tell me that I disappeared *twenty years ago*, yet I don't look or feel a day older. And to top it all off, I'm *pregnant!*"

Margaret leaned back, out of the way of Isaboe's flying hands. "You know, there are herbs you can take. I've heard whispers of 'em, when women don't want more mouths to feed. Heard they can make you pretty sick, and you might bleed heavy for a while, but you don't have to have this child."

"I can't do that." A look of pain and confusion crossed her face as Isaboe resumed her place at the table. "What if I was pregnant before I disappeared? I could have been pregnant and not known it, so this could be Nathan's child. If there is any chance of that, it would be the only thing I have left of him."

"But you don't know that for sure. And if you are carrying Nathan's child, why would the old crone say the fey want it? That don't make sense. You don't know when this child was conceived, or even if it's…."

"If it's what, human?" Isaboe suddenly felt defensive for herself and her unborn child. "All I know is that I don't know. And I'm not willing to risk the life of this child, a child that could be my husband's. I can't do that. You understand, don't you?"

Before Margaret could answer, there was a knock and a voice at the door. "There's a visitor here for ye ma'am. A Mr. Grant is in the lobby. Shall I tell him ye'll be right down?"

Isaboe looked at Margaret and smiled bitterly. "See. I was right." But her victory felt empty next to this latest discussion.

Margaret opened the door wide enough to see the hotel clerk standing in the hall. "Yes, please. Tell him we will be right there. Thank you." Closing the door, she turned back to face Isaboe. "We'll have to finish this conversation later. Right now, we'll havta do some fast talking to convince Mr. Grant that our horses are sufficient. Do you feel up to the challenge?"

Tucking her stray hairs back into place, Isaboe stood up and wiped the last few tears from her cheeks. Looking at Margaret with a forced smile, she tried to look more controlled on the outside than she felt on the inside. "Well, it shouldn't be that big a challenge. He's here, isn't he?"

CHAPTER 15

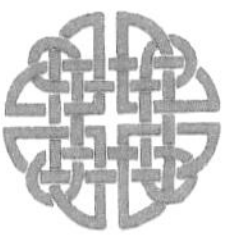

THE JOURNEY CONTINUES

"Salted pork, coffee, beans, crackers, cornmeal, beef jerky, a bag of tatties, bread, two bedrolls, let's see, what else do we need?" As Margaret took inventory of the items they placed on the counter, the store clerk recorded the prices on his writing board.

"I know you've already spent more money than you planned on, but, if it's not too much to ask, I could use some warmer clothes," Isaboe added. Traveling by horseback for a week or longer, with autumn making the nights chilly and the mornings cold and damp, she would need more clothing than just one extra dress.

"Of course you do," Margaret said, giving Isaboe an apologetic look. After paying the clerk, they walked quickly toward the clothing store down the street.

"We don't have much time to meet Mr. Grant," Isaboe said as they hurried toward the clothing store. She recalled Connor Grant's expression in the hotel lobby, looking like a man caught in a trap. "He said he wouldn't wait for us if we were late. Do you think he was serious?"

"Aye. He doesn't strike me as the type to make idle threats. I'm still surprised he even showed up. I just hope he didn't change his mind after seeing the horses I bought. They certainly ain't the pick of the litter by any means," Margaret said, as they entered the mercantile.

They quickly found clothes that would fit Isaboe's slender frame, but would adjust to her changing body. After selecting a pair of riding pants that laced up the front, another simple white dress, two modest shirts, and a pair of practical boots, Isaboe was ready to ride.

Walking briskly, they made their way through streets that had been filled to capacity the night before, passing numerous vacant food stands and stepping over empty bottles and mugs that had been carelessly tossed aside. The street and boardwalk were littered with the remnants of the festivities that had gone on well into the night. Glancing nervously up and down the street, Isaboe was on alert for any red uniforms. Though almost certain Blackwood would still be locked up this morning, the last thing she wanted was to run into him before they escaped the city. The encounter with the lieutenant had left her feeling vulnerable, weak, and pathetic. Obviously, she needed to learn to protect herself, because the stark reality was that Nathan was gone. Even though Margaret was her companion, she was not her protector.

Isaboe's thoughts were distracted by the enticing scents wafting from the diner they were passing by, and instantly her stomach rumbled, but she knew there would be no decent meal before leaving town. Their coerced escort was waiting.

When the women turned the corner and the stables came into view, they both took a deep sigh of relief. Standing in front of the large wooden stable doors was Connor Grant, holding the reins of three saddled horses.

"Unfortunately, ye ladies made good timing. I was just startin' to hope ye might've changed yer minds and I could mount up and be on my way. But since yer here, let me help ye with those," he said, taking a bag of supplies from each woman. He gave them both a courteous nod, but Isaboe saw him drop his eyes, as if looking at her for too long made him uncomfortable.

When she first met him under the cover of darkness the previous evening, and again, in the dim morning light of their hotel lobby, Isaboe hadn't taken the opportunity to really look closely at him. But now, in the light of day, she was pleasantly surprised to see that Connor Grant was quite attractive, in a rather travel-worn and rugged way, even though he wore the stoic expression of a guarded man. He had let his hair grow to his chin, seemed not to have time or inclination to shave, and had thrown his traveling gear together with the nonchalance of long practice. In his comfortable confidence, he somehow managed to make her feel completely ignorant. She might have called him handsome, but too aloof, if not for his eyes. Set back under a heavy brow, they were a sort of sweet blue. Even if she couldn't catch them, Isaboe found herself a bit enamored with his eyes.

"Mr. Grant, these aren't the horses I bought this morning," Margaret said as she set the rest of her bags on the ground and began examining the horses. "These are much better animals. The stable keep must've given you the wrong ones."

"Aye, they're not," the man muttered. Tying the two bags together, he swung them across the back of Margaret's saddle and then secured them into place.

"I don't understand," Margaret said.

After picking up one of the bags at Isaboe's feet, Connor gave her a quick nod before responding. "Well, when I saw what the two of ye were intending to ride out on, and knowing how much ye paid for the sorry lot, the keep and I had a bit of *renegotiation*," he said with a smirk and then resumed packing supplies into the saddle bags.

"That son of a bitch told me he didn't have anything else!" Margaret howled. "Damn bastards think 'cause I'm a woman they can sell me shit. I should have him arrested!"

"Looks like you need to work a little harder on your bargaining skills, aye, Margaret?" Isaboe said, but quickly leaned away from her friend's steely glare.

"Well, I'm going in there to give that cheatin' little weasel a piece of my mind!"

As Margaret turned back towards the stable, Isaboe reached out and stopped her. "Margaret, just thank Mr. Grant for his help, swallow your pride, and let's get out of here. Anything you would say to the stable keep would be redundant. We have good horses. You got your money's worth. Let it be a good lesson, and let's go."

"Isaboe, that man robbed me! He took advantage of me based solely on me being a woman!"

"Maybe it was more that ye didna ken much about buying a good horse than about ye being a woman," Connor said flatly as he finished securing the straps on the last saddlebag.

Now that their guide had pointed out the obvious, Isaboe watched her friend's expression fall from defiance to defeat. As they chose their horses without argument, Isaboe could still hear Margaret grumbling under her breath—something about a no-good, lying bastard.

"Well then, let's be on our way." Connor turned to mount his horse, but stopped and looked back at the two women. "We need to go over a few things before we take our leave. We've a long ride ahead of us and need to cover as much ground as possible each day. I'll be keeping a good pace most of the day, so ye need to keep up. I dinnae wanna stop unless it's important. We'll be following the river, riding along the bank so we can water the horses when need be. If ye need to take care of business, that's the time to do so." He paused, looking at them with a scrutinizing glare. "I take it that neither of ye have been on a horse for any length of time, so ye'll probably be a wee bit sore. Be prepared for that."

Looking first at Margaret, then at Isaboe, he gave a slight shake of his head. "Do ye need help mounting?" he asked, sounding slightly annoyed. Taking that as a signal, Isaboe and Margaret both proceeded to mount their horses. Though Isaboe easily swung up and settled comfortably in the saddle, Margaret had more difficulty. "Here, let me help ye," Connor said as he moved toward her.

But she stopped him with an outstretched hand. "No thank you, Mr. Grant. I can do it myself!"

Backing off, he turned to his horse and mounted as Margaret gave it another effort. With a loud grunt, she swung her leg up and over onto the saddle. Taking a satisfied breath, she smiled. "Many thanks for looking out for our best interest, Mr. Grant. These are far better horses."

He turned in his saddle and looked at the two women with a forced smile. "Well, I wasna 'bout to travel across the country with the two of ye on those pathetic creatures. So it was more for my benefit than yers. And if we're to be riding companions, the name is Conner, not Mr. Grant," he grumbled before heeling his horse onto the street that would lead the small traveling band out of town.

Under a blanket of fog with Connor in the lead, the two women followed without question, both feeling more confident with their new companion. Keeping a slow and steady pace, Isaboe and Margaret rode side-by-side, trying to relax into their horses' gait. Though both had ridden before, neither was an experienced horsewoman. Isaboe noticed Connor looking back periodically over his shoulder to be sure his two riding companions were still in tow. Whether he thought that was a good thing or not, she couldn't tell.

For the first few hours, they rode in silence, the only sound being the rhythmic beat of the horses' hooves on the well-traveled road. As the morning passed, they were frequently overtaken by other riders, and more than once a troop of British soldiers galloped through, pushing the small group off the road. Each time Isaboe saw the crimson uniforms, her heartbeat quickened, and she held her breath until the last rider had passed.

The morning fog began to lift, revealing the makings of a warm, pleasant day, complete with birdsong and a crisp breeze. The land on the outskirts of Inverness was a continuous roll of beautiful green hills and valleys. Clusters of homesteads were tucked neatly between fields of various crops, dressing the land in harvest colors.

After traveling the main road for several hours, they turned off onto a well-trodden path that wound through a grove of oak and maple trees. The first signs of autumn had also brushed the trees, which were just starting to take on the orange and yellow colors of fall. Near a large, hunkered-down elm, their progress was abruptly halted by a herd of sheep being led by two young boys from an upper pasture toward a lower slope of rolling green grass. With no way around, the riders waited for the herd to pass, while their horses took the opportunity to nibble on the grass at their feet.

"I take it that's the direction to the river," Isaboe said as she looked where the sheep were being led. "Is that the way we're going?"

"Aye, the river is that direction, but we'll continue on this road. It'll take us along the river bank, and we can follow it for the next couple of days," Conner said, looking around at the countryside. "We should be at the river shortly. We'll take a break there before continuing on."

The late summer sun was high in the pale blue sky, warming Isaboe enough that she could shed her overcoat. Though it was only midday, she already felt the soreness setting in from the hard, uncomfortable saddle. She hoped tucking her coat under her backside would give her a little more padding. Leaning forward, Isaboe put her hand against the horse's strong neck for support and lifted up out of her saddle by pressing into her stirrups. At the same time, her horse decided to drop its head to nibble on the grass. The downward momentum caught Isaboe off guard and off balance. With a desperate shriek, she tumbled forward, throwing her arms around the horse's neck in a strangle hold. As she struggled to stay on, her feet came free of the stirrups, leaving her with her rump sticking straight up in the air. In the next moment, the horse tossed its head, throwing its rider to the ground with a solid thump.

It all happened so fast that Margaret could do nothing but call out from atop her horse. "Isaboe, are you alright?"

Fortunately, Isaboe managed to break her fall with her backside. Though she had no serious damage, her ego was severely bruised. "*Ouch!* I think I'm alright," she said, rubbing her behind.

When she saw that her friend was unhurt, Margaret started to chuckle. It started out low and muffled, but within moments became out-right laughter.

"Oh, that's nice, Margaret!" Isaboe spat as she pushed up off the ground, still rubbing her derriere. "I'm glad I was able to provide you with some amusement at my discomfort."

"I'm sorry lass, but you should've seen yourself, lying over the horse's neck with your arse up in the air. And the look in your eyes!" But Margaret was laughing so hard she couldn't continue.

Frantically grabbing the reins of her horse, Isaboe shot her friend an irritated look. Margaret was trying, though not very successfully, to choke back the giggles, and it didn't take long before her mirth grew contagious. As Isaboe's lips curled into a grin, her irritation quickly slipped away, and before long she was laughing at herself as well. A good, healthy laugh was something she hadn't had in a long time. "Oh, I can see we're getting off to a *great* start," she said, composing herself as she climbed back into the saddle.

"If you can't stay on the damn horse for even two hours, how are you gonna make it for two weeks?" Margaret teased.

"Hopefully, I won't have to ride this beast for two weeks. I don't think my *arse* can take it." Isaboe chuckled before catching Connor's scowling look. It was obvious he didn't see the humor in her lack of coordination. "Sorry," she said, with an apologetic smile.

The sheep had passed, and the road was now clear, so Connor just shook his head and tugged on his horse's reins. When he heeled the animal into a slow trot, Isaboe gave Margaret an impish smile as they fell in behind.

CHAPTER 16

SADDLE SORE

By the end of the first day's travel, the riders had covered about fifteen miles. When they stopped to set up camp along the river's edge, Margaret and Isaboe busied themselves tending to the campfire and preparing the evening meal, while Connor gave his attention to the horses. Throughout the day, most of the conversation between the women and their guide had been limited to giving directions or answering questions.

"Mr. Chatty he certainly is not," Margaret whispered as she watched Connor rubbing down one of the horses.

"He doesn't want us along; you know that." Isaboe knelt over a large bag, repacking supplies. "Besides, he appears to be more brawn than brain, so I consider his indifference quite fortunate. At least he's a man of his word, and can handle himself in a fight. So what if he doesn't engage in pleasant conversation. That may be a blessing."

"You may be right," Margaret chuckled, as she settled comfortably in front of the fire.

Isaboe rubbed her backside a few more times before taking a seat next to her friend. "I'm not sure if I'm sore from falling off the horse or just from having to ride the damn thing all day," she moaned, pushing her hands into the small of her back. "I have to be honest with you Margaret. I'm afraid that after a week of riding horseback from dusk to dawn, I won't be able to walk."

"If ye think ye're sore now, just wait a few days," Connor said as he walked up from behind. "What's in the kettle? Smells good." He leaned over the pot, taking a deep, full sniff.

"It's lamb and vegetable stew, and we have some bread to go with it."

Margaret smiled while stirring the kettle again. "It's not quite ready. The tatties still need some cooking, but I think you'll like it."

"As long as it's food, I'll like it." Connor dropped his saddle on the ground not far from Isaboe and took a seat. Leaning back against the leather, he stretched out and locked his hands behind his head.

"What did you mean, 'just wait a few days'?" Isaboe asked.

"Those little aches and pains will feel 'bout twice as bad. Ye'll feel as if ye've been trampled by a bloody stampede." He said indifferently.

Isaboe thought Connor seemed much too casual for a man talking about crippling pain. She stared at him, not knowing if he was serious or not, but the contented grin that crossed Connor's face rubbed her the wrong way. "Great. At least now I know what I have to look forward to."

She may have been the kind of woman who preferred traveling in a coach, not on horseback, but Isaboe wasn't about to let Connor Grant think she was too weak to finish this ride. To cover her discontent, and to ease the aching in her spine, she stood and dished herself a bowl of hot stew. Pulling a hunk of bread from the loaf before sitting again, she tried to find the most comfortable position.

"I'm not sure those tatties are done yet, Isaboe." Margaret watched closely as Isaboe dug into her meal.

Connor's apathetic attitude had sent her mood tumbling. "I don't care. I'm starving and I'm tired. I just want to eat and get some sleep."

Before long, Margaret and Connor dished up as well, and the three travelers sat around the fire, lost in their bowls of stew. Margaret tried once or twice to engage Connor in conversation, but his one-word answers left her frustrated. Since Isaboe had gone quiet as well, she finally gave up for the night.

After eating, Isaboe laid out her bedroll not far from the fire and crawled in. The sun had been down for a while, and the cool evening air gave every indication of an even colder night. She dreaded the stiff, aching muscles and heaving stomach she knew the morning would bring. Connor's last comment certainly didn't sugar-coat how sore she would be, or how much discomfort she could expect. He actually seemed to enjoy it. The more she thought about it, the angrier she became. "Bastard," she growled into her pillow. Watching Margaret crawl into her bedroll, she looked around for Connor, who was nowhere in sight.

"Good night, Isaboe," Margaret said softly.

"Good night." Isaboe's reply was short and curt. As soon as the words left her mouth she regretted it instantly. "Margaret?" she whispered as she stared into the dark sky that lay heavy all around her.

"Yes?" Margaret's reply was guarded.

It was another moment before Isaboe broke the silence. "Thank you," she said just above a whisper.

"You're welcome."

The sound of the river gently rolling along its bank only yards away had a soothing effect, and the distant chorus of nocturnal creatures—frogs, owls, and insects—gradually lulled Isaboe into a calmer state. Though the ground was hard and cold, her body was so tired it didn't take long before the edges of sleep danced behind her closed eyes.

But just as she was about to go under, Isaboe heard the sound of the campfire crackling back to life. She opened her eyes to see Conner toss the last log into the flames. Keeping her head down, she silently watched as he stood staring into the fire. His blue eyes looked black in the dark night as the light of the flames danced off his face, giving him a strange, almost haunted look.

Through eyes shadowed by half-closed lids, Isaboe watched as Connor tended the fire, pushing partially burned pieces of wood with the tip of his boot. *What are Margaret and I doing out in the middle of the night, traveling across country with a man we know nothing about?* She wondered as he moved around the flames and took a seat across the fire from her. *Yes, he saved me last night, from who knows what, at the hands of that drunken soldier. But why?* Shivering, she pulled herself into a fetal position as her thoughts spun wildly through her frazzled mind. *He doesn't even know me. Why did he put himself in danger for me? Why would anyone do that? What's his story? Was it really some old-fashioned sense of chivalry? Can the goodness in one man stand against the evil that lies just beneath the surface in all men? And if there is evil in all men, then how deep beneath the facade of honor must this man's evil be lurking?*

As she watched him from across the flames, Isaboe couldn't deny there was something mysterious about Connor Grant. And though she really knew nothing about him, for some unknown reason she didn't feel threatened by him.

Isaboe's thoughts were interrupted by Margaret's snoring. Yawning deeply, she glanced toward her sleeping friend and then looked back across the fire to see Connor pull a small whistle from his pack. He put it to his lips and played a slow, haunting tune as Isaboe closed her eyes and let the sound of his whistle lull her into sleep.

CHAPTER 17

EUPHORIA REVISITED

I am vapor suspended in space. I have no form, no body as I hover weightlessly. Flashes of light, struck by a bolt, tumbling, falling…

On the ground, surrounded by whiteness, void of color or life, a lone door floats in front of me in the fog like a ship rolling on the sea. When I reach for the doorknob, it dissolves in my hand. The door is gone.

A small cottage nests in the middle of a beautiful field of flowers. As I run toward it, the cottage appears to be only steps away. But the more I scramble toward it, the distance seems to increase. I run faster. Finally, I reach the door, but it won't open. Running to the window, I press my face to the glass, but it's covered with filth and grime. I rub my fist in a circle over the dirty pane and look again.

A well-dressed family is gathered around the table. My husband and children sit in chairs across from me, smiling at one another. I look again, but this time all their eye sockets are hallow. Even the children's shriveled and drawn flesh is pulled back from their white teeth in a deathly grin. They're all dead!

"You do not belong here."

I hear the words, but who spoke them? Frightened, I quickly stand. Freefalling backward, flailing arms—there is nothing to grab onto. "Help me! Someone, please help me!"

Warm hands, a kind smile—an angel is standing before me, and my fear begins to dissipate. "It's alright dear, don't be frightened. I am here."

"Where am I? Am I… dead?"

"You certainly are not dead," she says with an alluring laugh. "But this place will soon feel like Heaven. Here, give me your hand."

We are standing in a lovely, forested garden. Tall trees with graceful canopies of branches allow only dabbled sunlight to reach the floor, but wildflowers are dancing everywhere. There's a warm breeze, and the scent of gardenias tease my nose. Toad stools, purple clover, and many colorful, delicate flowers blanket the forest floor. "What a lovely place."

"This is Euphoria, your home.

"My home?

"Yes, this is where you belong, Alaina. Here, sit in the sun, let it warm you. You will remember how wonderful it is to be home again."

"Ah, the sun does feel good. I've been so cold and ill of late."

"But you feel well here, don't you? I'm Lorien, and you will always feel warm and comforted when you are here with me." She takes my hand, and pulls me down to the soft moss. "Just rest and let the sun's rays chase the chill away."

I lay my head on Lorien's lap as she gently strokes my hair. It feels wonderful. "It's so warm here, and I'm so tired of running, of being afraid."

"Soon your struggles will be over. But now, it's time for you to go."

"But why? Why must I leave? You said this is my home."

"This visit is over for now."

"But I don't want to leave! I want to stay here!"

"You can come back anytime you wish, and someday, you will never have to leave."

"Why do I have to go? I'm afraid of being cold and alone again. Please, don't make me leave!"

"Wake up, Isaboe. It's time, time to get up." Margaret's voice found its way into her dream. "C'mon, let's head down to the river to wash."

Isaboe sat up in her bedroll feeling completely disoriented. "I don't want to go!" Her eyes were wide and confused as she found herself staring at a head of curly red hair against the lightening grey sky.

"Well, you have to. Connor wants to be on the road as soon as breakfast is over. If you get up now, we'll have time to dry the bedrolls before we go. Besides, you need time to…uh, get your stomach in line before we're off, aye?" She looked back down at her friend. "Isaboe, did you hear what I said? Let's get down to the river."

As the dream faded away, reality came crashing in on Isaboe like a cold, icy wave. She rubbed her arms, feeling the dampness reaching into her bones. They'd used cow hides to keep the ground moisture from soaking their bedrolls, but they hadn't prepared for the rain. A drizzly mist had fallen throughout the night, and everything was damp and miserable. Shivering in the cold, Isaboe's stomach instantly rebelled when she stood. But wonderful Margaret was prepared with a dry blanket and clean clothes as they hurried off toward the river.

Margaret stood by as Isaboe knelt down at the river's edge, waiting to see if her body was done retching. "I have to go back and start breakfast. Are you gonna be alright?"

"I don't know." Taking long, deep breaths, Isaboe held her head in her hands, unsure if she wanted to move for fear of bringing on another wave of nausea.

"Do you want me to help you change, or can you do it yourself?" Margaret said impatiently.

"I can dress myself, Margaret. I've been doing it for some time now. Just leave my clothes and go." Isaboe snapped back her reply, but she couldn't ignore Margaret's heavy sigh.

"I can't just leave them, Isaboe; the ground is wet. Please, stand up."

Margaret had more patience than Isaboe deserved, and they both knew it. Slowly, taking deep breaths, Isaboe finally rose. After removing her damp clothes, she shivered in the cold morning air, making it difficult to work her hands, or stop them from shaking. "God, I feel terrible this morning. I'm so cold." Isaboe's purple lips quivered as she hurried to put on the dry clothes. Once she was finished, Margaret threw a blanket around her friend's shoulders before picking up her damp clothes.

"When you're ready, come and warm yourself by the fire." Margaret rubbed her hand briskly across Isaboe's back.

Still hunched over, Isaboe clutched tightly to her blanket. "Why do we have to get moving so early? The sun is barely up."

"Connor wants to be on the road as soon as possible. The sun has been up for a while. You just can't see it through this mist. I'm gonna start breakfast. You'll feel better after you eat something."

Isaboe held a hand over her belly. "I don't think I can get anything down right now."

"Well, you'll just have to try, love." Margaret gave a quick, sympathetic smile before heading back to the campfire, leaving her friend standing alone by the river.

The heavy clouds made Isaboe feel claustrophobic. The tree tops disappeared into a heavy layer of fog as the mist intensified. She pulled the blanket up over her head and stood staring out at the river, watching the drizzling rain make ripples on the water.

The dream had all but faded away, but it hung like wispy cobwebs to the edges of her memory. As she tried to remember what she'd dreamt, Isaboe suddenly felt as if she was being watched. She spun around, half expecting to be looking into the eyes of her long-dead husband, but he was not there. The children were not there.

Overwhelmed by the reality of what she'd once had, of what her life had once been like, the pain of that loss dropped Isaboe to her knees, sobbing.

When Isaboe finally made it back to camp, Connor was packing the horses, and Margaret had already repacked the bags. The dried remnants of what had been breakfast sat on a tin plate next to the fire. Margaret hadn't noticed Isaboe's silent arrival, but her forlorn friend caught Connor's attention. He was looking over the saddle bags, tightening straps and checking hoofs, silently watching as Isaboe made her way to the fire. With the blanket wrapped around her shoulders, she took a seat next to what was left of the glowing coals. More than just a little cold and wet, he thought she looked downright pathetic.

When he had first seen Isaboe in daylight, Connor found her strikingly beautiful. Her long auburn hair had been pulled up and her attire was neat and fresh. She was pleasant, and her smile, though somewhat forced, did seem sincere. After what she had been through the night before with Blackwood, she showed strength, and he admired that. Looking at her now, she didn't seem the same woman. He wondered what could possibly have happened to ruin her mood so early in the day. But she wasn't his concern. Even as he told himself that, he couldn't tear his gaze from her direction.

As she wiped her nose with the back of her hand, Isaboe looked up and caught Connor watching her. For a moment their gazes locked, but she quickly broke the connection, pulling the blanket up over her head. The sadness Connor saw in her eyes was intense, and for an instant, he felt a twinge of empathy. But he caught himself and shook it off. He was only taking them to Edinburgh. He didn't want, nor need, to know more than necessary about either of them.

Before long, Margaret returned to the fire, bringing Isaboe something from her saddle bag. Connor watched them sitting together, talking quietly, and wondered what their connection could be. He knew they were friends, but they seemed an unlikely pair. It was obvious that Isaboe was refined, well-bred, and had grown up privileged. She didn't look like the type of woman who had ever known a day's hard work. Margaret, however, seemed just the opposite. He watched as she fussed over Isaboe like a mother hen, and decided that Margaret was too patient a woman for her own good.

"If ye ladies are ready, we need to be on our way," Connor said as he approached them. "We have a long ride ahead of us."

"Can't we just wait a bit longer to see if this rain will let up?" Isaboe asked, as if she actually had a choice in the matter. "It would make traveling much more comfortable if we weren't getting soaked."

"Aye, that it would. And if one of ye ladies happens to have a big feather pillow so I can cushion my arse, that would be more comfortable, too." As Connor shifted his weight, impatience shot across his face. "It doesn't look as if its gonna stop raining, ladies. So, let's get a move on."

Realizing the subject wasn't open to negotiation, Margaret and Isaboe packed up the rest of their belongings and prepared to ride. After kicking dirt on what was left of the fire, Connor mounted his horse. Following his lead, the ladies mounted onto their saddles, though not as fluidly as their reluctant guide.

Isaboe looked pained at the thought of riding all day in the rain. "Mr. Grant," she said, with a sharp edge to her voice. "If it starts raining harder, will we stop to find shelter, or will we just keep riding?"

"Look ladies, ye didnae havta travel this way. It was yer choice." Connor let his irritation bleed through. "I didnae say it was gonna be an easy ride, or a pleasant one. From the looks of it, we'll probably get good and wet before the day is done, and we've a long ride ahead of us. If ye have hats, best put them on."

With a sigh of resignation, Isaboe kicked her horse into motion and fell in behind Connor. As they continued their course along the river bank, the early morning rain turned into an all-day downpour. Just as Connor had promised, they rode on with only the necessary breaks to water the horses, stretch their legs, and grab a quick bite to eat. Other than those few breaks, they rode continually throughout the day.

For the next three days, though Connor managed to find dry shelter each night, the trio awoke to the same dismal weather. The rain soaked not only the riders and everything they carried, but their spirits as well. Since they could find little dry wood, the evening fires were hard, if not impossible, to start. Only sporadic conversation took place between Isaboe and Margaret, and Connor continued his stoic distance.

The terrible conditions were only made worse by the late summer hatching of the midges—tiny beasts that swarmed the Highlands. These nasty, biting flies were everywhere and found their way into everything. As large portions of the ground turned to mud, traveling became increasingly difficult. More than a few times the riders had to dismount and lead their horses through the muddy terrain. By the time they made camp at the end of each day, everything had to be wrung out or washed. All their clothes were muddy, and the rain even leaked into the saddlebags that carried their food. Comfort was a distant memory. Misery had become their constant traveling companion, and found itself well suited to its company.

CHAPTER 18

A DAY WITHOUT RAIN

The smell of freshly brewed coffee brought Isaboe to awareness, but she tried to hold onto the edges of sleep as she pulled the blanket—slightly damp, but still warm—up over her head. Ignoring her full bladder, she opted not to get up and face her rolling stomach, at least for now. However, it didn't take long before the sound of Margaret's grumbling, as she rummaged through their supplies, brought Isaboe to full consciousness.

"What are you doing, Margaret?" Isaboe mumbled from under the blanket.

"I'm looking for something to change into that ain't wet or covered in mud! The damned rain has got into the saddle bags and ruined half our food! The bread and cornmeal are mush. The only things left edible are the eggs and potatoes. I'm so sick of this weather!"

As Isaboe lay quietly, hoping Margaret wouldn't make her get up, she noticed that the rain sounded different this morning. Instead of the constant drumming that drenched body and soul, she heard only dripping. Sitting up, she looked out from underneath the low hanging branches of their shelter. Rather than dark rain clouds, small patches of blue poked their way through the early morning fog and the sky held the promise of a day free from rain.

"Margaret, it's not raining!" Isaboe announced, as if she were the first to notice.

"Aye, I am aware of that, thank you very much. That doesn't help the damage the bloody rain has already done to our supplies. I've not one piece of clothing that's not wet, or muddy, or both!"

Isaboe paid little attention to Margaret's rant as she sat contentedly in a small patch of early morning sunshine. Behind closed eyes, she turned her face up towards the sky to soak up each second of precious warmth, but it was short lived. When the fog moved back in to block the sun, the wonderful moment passed. Briskly rubbing her arms, Isaboe turned back to the fire and filled her cup with hot coffee. Taking a long, satisfied sniff, she let the steaming aroma flow seductively into her senses. With a blanket draped over her shoulders, she watched as Margaret continued to organize their belongings. "Where's Connor?" Isaboe asked, suddenly realizing that their guide was nowhere to be seen.

"He's gone down to the river to wash, which is something you and I both need to do as well. I feel like I've got mud in every nook and cranny. It's in my nose, in my ears, and up my arse," Margaret complained without deviating from her task.

"Well, before we wash, can we eat something first?" Isaboe asked. "I'm starving."

"There is no more cracker bread. What's left is nothing but mush." Margaret looked closely at her friend. "Did you say you were starving? Are you not ill this morning?"

"No, I'm just hungry!" A big smile flashed across Isaboe's face at this realization. "I don't feel sick this morning." Standing to test her newfound wellness, Isaboe twirled and did a little jig, yet still felt no need to vomit.

"Whoa, lassie, don't push it. You may not have been up long enough for it to hit you yet. I wouldn't recommend that you be dancing around like you just found a wee leprechaun's pot of gold." Though Margaret was pleased that Isaboe's mood had improved, there were more pressing issues at the moment. "Since you're feeling so spry, take that bucket down to the river and fetch us some water."

"Oh, Margaret, I think this is going to be a good day. The rain has stopped, the sun is trying to shine, and best of all, I'm not sick! This has the makings of a fine day, a fine day indeed!" Isaboe reached down to pick up the bucket and ducked out from under the tree branches of their shelter, leaving Margaret shaking her head and smiling as she watched her friend skip off.

After answering nature's call, Isaboe continued down to the river. Leaning over to dip the bucket into the water, her attention was drawn by the sound of splashing. She took a few steps up the bank to get a better look and caught a glimpse of something moving in the water. Seeing only ripples across the surface, she turned to resume her task, but abruptly came to a halt when a dark head rose out of the river directly in front of her, followed by its sleek, naked body.

With his body turned away from the shoreline, the man didn't see her standing on the bank, but Isaboe had a good look at the back side of Connor Grant. With a silent giggle, she thought that Connor's ass was as tight as his lips and his sense of humor. She also noticed the faded crisscross scars along the length of his back. When he turned towards the bank, she quickly ducked behind a slender Aspen that barely hid her. Hoping she had gone unnoticed, Isaboe held her breath.

After a few moments the splashing stopped, and Isaboe found the courage to look again. She slowly turned her head to see Connor standing knee deep in the water, only a few feet away. His angle to the riverbank gave Isaboe a side view as Connor rubbed a bar of soap fiercely between his hands, and then over the rest of his body. Though she knew she shouldn't be looking, Isaboe couldn't help herself. If she moved, he might see her, and what possible excuse would she have?

Watching Connor running the soap through his hair, over his arms, and across his chest made her feel naughty. Though it was completely out of character for her to spy on someone bathing, no amount of silent berating stopped her from looking.

As he moved the bar of soap along the inside of his thigh, Isaboe noticed more scars, one in particular that ran down Connor's leg from his hip to his knee. But why was she still watching? Isaboe's sense of decency finally got the best of her. She diverted her eyes until she heard him throw the bar of soap up onto the river bank. Trying to make herself invisible, she took one final glance and noticed a tattoo resembling a cross just below his left shoulder.

After Connor dove headfirst into the river, she stood motionless for a few seconds, wondering if it was safe for her to move. When he didn't come back up right away, Isaboe took it as her opportunity. Turning quickly, she didn't stop running until she was hidden by a group of trees. Safely out of view, she stopped to catch her breath. When she looked down at the empty bucket in her hand, Isaboe suddenly remembered why she had been at the river's edge in the first place. After walking back down and finding Connor nowhere in sight, she dipped the bucket into the water. Uncaught, and with her task completed, she felt a smile spreading across her face. "Yes, I think this is turning out to be fine day, a fine day indeed," she said to herself as she walked back to their shelter.

The encounter at the river went unmentioned. Isaboe chose not to share it with Margaret and kept it to herself. When Connor returned to the camp site, she found it difficult to look at him. Even fully dressed, the images of his wet, naked body were still too fresh. She could feel the blood rising to her face at the memory.

However, with the smell of fried eggs and tatties cooking, it didn't take long before Isaboe's thoughts were soon distracted. As they sat watching the steam rising from the earth in the early morning sunshine, all three travelers were in better spirits than they had been for days. After breakfast, their conversation stayed light and easy as the women repacked the salvageable food. From the depths of a saddlebag, Isaboe triumphantly rescued a dark-colored smock for Margaret and a simple white one for herself. Connor enlarged the circle of coals from the remnants of the campfire and began making a drying rack for all their damp clothes. Meanwhile, the women took their leave to wash in the river.

When Margaret and Isaboe returned, they were happily surprised to see that Connor had built enough drying racks to hold all of the clothes as well as their bedrolls. Steam rolled off as heat from the fire penetrated the damp fabrics. Adding more heat to the drying process, rays from the sun broke through what was left of the morning fog.

"They may be a bit smoky, but they'll be dry, aye?" Connor said with a grin. He appeared less anxious to be on the road then on previous mornings. The sun seemed to have brought out a new side of Connor, or perhaps he had washed away more than just mud in the river.

After finding places to hang their wet clothes on the drying racks, Margaret and Isaboe huddled around the fire to warm themselves from their brisk, early morning dip. The simple white dress that hugged Isaboe's still damp body offered little warmth, so she sat as close to the fire as she could. Behind closed eyes, she leaned over the low burning embers, running her hands through her wet hair as the rising heat chased the chill away. She vaguely heard Margaret ask Connor how much longer it would take to reach MucGhine, the next possible location to catch a coach to Edinburgh.

"I believe it's another day's ride or two. From what I recall, MucGhine is on the other side of the river. We should be coming upon a bridge or ferry before long," Connor answered, but Isaboe thought he sounded distracted.

At first, she didn't realize that the simple white smock did little to hide her curves. That was until she stood up straight, catching Connor's eyes on her. His look was intense and penetrating, but she held his gaze for an instant before quickly turning away. Suddenly feeling over-exposed, Isaboe grabbed a shawl to throw over her shoulders. Conner, too, looked uneasy. Finding an excuse to do anything else at the moment, he turned toward the small field where the horses were grazing.

The women went to work turning clothes on the drying racks and repacking bags, while Conner kept himself busy with the animals. He took them one at a time down to the river to wash and brush out their coats from three days of traveling on muddy roads. As the sun rose in the early autumn sky, the finches darted among the trees, and the land smelled fresh and new. All of nature seemed to enjoy the reprieve from the long, heavy days of rain. With everyone busy, the morning passed quickly.

"I saw some apple trees down by the river," Margaret said. "Be right back."

Isaboe took the opportunity to do some mending. Her cloak had caught on a tree branch the day before, and though she had ducked, it hadn't been low enough. She watched as Connor brought the last horse back from the river and tied it off with the others before disappearing into the trees.

Between the sun and the hot burning embers, the clothes on the drying racks finally dried. As Isaboe was packing them away, Margaret hobbled up from the direction of the river holding the front of her bulging skirt. It was full of freshly-picked apples.

"You think you have enough apples there?" Isaboe asked with an impish grin.

It was obvious by the look on Margaret's face that she felt quite pleased with herself. "Well, I may have picked a few too many, but look at these. Have you ever seen such beauties?" Margaret held up a small, yet perfect specimen, turning it over for examination. "Do you want one?"

"No thanks. Not right now."

After finding a place by the tree to unload her treasure, Margaret took a seat on the log next to where Isaboe had resumed her stitching. "Where's Connor gone off to?" she asked between crisp bites of the delicious fruit.

"I saw him come back from the river with your horse a while ago," Isaboe replied. "Then he walked off into the woods. I don't know where he went, or what he's doing. I'm just glad he's not in a big hurry to get going. That's certainly unusual with the way he's been pushing us these last four days."

"Well, I'm not complaining. 'Tis been a relaxing morning, and it'll be good to have dry clothes. They may smell like a campfire, but at least they'll be free of mud," Margaret said, continuing to snack on her apple.

The morning calm was abruptly interrupted by the sound of gunfire, and both women jumped to their feet. "What in the hell was that?" Margaret shouted.

"It's probably Connor, but what would he be shooting at?" Isaboe asked as they stood staring at the tree line, unsure of what to do. "Do you think we should investigate?"

After a few tense moments, Connor appeared, dangling a large pheasant by its legs. Seeing the women, he held up his prize and smiled. "I thought some fresh meat would be a nice change from potato stew." Walking past the two women, he dropped the bird on a log before returning the pistol to his saddlebag.

"What, you don't like my tasty potato stew?" Margaret tried to sound insulted, but she knew they had all grown bored of her staple meal. "I've been doing the best I can, considering the miserable weather we've had to deal with. And don't scare us like that," she scolded. "You could've told us you were going huntin'. We had no idea what that shot was."

"I didnae realize I had to check with ye first," Connor grunted. Turning his back to them, he pulled a knife from inside his boot and removed the shot from the bird. He then presented the dead pheasant to Margaret and began instructing her on how to clean it.

"I know how to pluck a bird! I don't need you to show me." Margaret growled as she grabbed the pheasant from his hand and stomped off.

"Good, then I'll make a spit to roast it on," Connor said with an innocent smile, seemingly unaffected by Margaret's tirade. As he squatted down in front of the fire setting up the spit, he looked up to see Isaboe watching him.

"You know, you shouldn't provoke her so. She is doing her best, everything considered," Isaboe said as she glanced up from her sewing.

"I didnae mean to offend her. I was just trying to help. I have no idea why she's so upset."

"I think her pride may be a bit bruised. Margaret owns her own business and is not used to having a man tell her how to do *anything*, much less how to prepare a meal."

Connor stood up to check the clothes on the racks. "I'll keep that in mind so I dinnae get another lecture," he said with a half a grin as he began removing the dried clothing. After the garments and bedrolls had been folded and the drying racks removed, he returned to the fire and sat down on the log next to Isaboe. "When ye are done with that one, I've a couple of shirts that could use a stitch or two, if ye dinnae mind."

"No, I don't mind. I'm done with this one anyway," Isaboe said. "This seems to be the day for taking care of such things. It's been nice to take a break from riding, and from the rain."

"Aye, it has at that. I know I've been pushing ye ladies these last four days, and I felt ye deserved a break. I have to admit ye've kept up much better than I thought ye would, considering the conditions we've been traveling through. For not being much on riding, yer both doing pretty well."

"Thank you. But I've been having difficulty getting my horse to cooperate."

"Maybe it isn't the horse that's being uncooperative," Connor said as Isaboe shot him a withering look. "I know it hasn't been easy for ye. When we were trying to pull yer horse out of the mud the other day, the harder ye pulled, the more stuck the poor animal became."

"That's exactly my point. I was trying to get her out, but she kept fighting against me instead of working with me."

"Well, see, that's the problem. Ye cannae get an animal to work with ye when it's afraid, and the horse was scared. Being stuck had her all skittish. When ye pulled so hard on her reins, it only made it worse. She needed to be calmed down first then led out slowly, one leg at a time. Horses have feelings too."

"Oh, do they now? Well, I'll try to remember that next time she attempts to throw me, or knock me off on a low hanging branch."

Connor chuckled as he bent over to pick up a twig. "Aye, they can be ornery at times, but if ye spend enough time with them, ye start to understand how they think. After a while, a good horse will know what ye need without much direction. Ye get back from a horse what ye give. If ye treat them with respect and a little affection, ye'll have a loyal friend for life."

Isaboe only smiled and nodded. "How about you bring me those shirts that need mending?"

After rummaging through his saddlebag, Connor returned with a tunic and a long-sleeved shirt, showing her the ragged tears before taking a seat back on the log. It was then that he noticed the apples. "Where'd those come from?" he asked, nodding in the direction of the piled fruit.

"Margaret gathered them, and she is quite pleased with herself."

Walking over to the bunch, Connor picked up an apple, rubbed it across his shirt, and took a big, crisp bite. Just about that time Margaret walked over holding a pink, plucked bird, ready for roasting.

"That's a fine job ye've done there, Margaret. Well done. And these apples that ye picked are very juicy." Connor said with too much enthusiasm.

"Alright, that's enough," Margaret said. "I'm not mad anymore, so you can quit kissin' my arse. I just picked the apples, I have nothing to do with how good they taste."

"Well, ye picked them well, not a bad one in the bunch," he said with a mouthful and a quirky smile. After tossing the core, he took the pheasant from Margaret and proceeded to skewer it on a spit. Attaching a long handle so it could easily be turned without being too close to the fire, he sat down comfortably next to the coals and tended to the task of roasting the bird.

"I dinnae think I've asked why ye're so bent on gettin' to Edinburgh. Ye got families waitin'?" Connor's words were spoken casually, and though she thought it was kind of him to show interest, Isaboe had no idea how to answer. After a few moments of silence, Connor asked again, "Is Edinburgh home?"

"No, it's not, and there's no one waiting for me—for us." Isaboe couldn't keep the sadness from her reply as she cast her gaze down. "I'm…I'm a widow." It was the first time she had uttered the word, and it was more painful then she expected.

Isaboe's pain was still fresh, and it had not gone unnoticed. Connor regarded her from his position next to the fire. "I'm sorry," he said sincerely.

Isaboe looked back, offering him a weak, sorrowful smile.

"Well, I was married once, a long time ago," Margaret announced. "He turned out to be a liar and a criminal, so I've had no wish to try that again. I think I've done quite well for myself without a man in my life. I run my own business, no one tells me what to do, and I've no man to pick up after. I'm quite content, and I have a lot less headache than most married folk." Margaret's attempt to lighten the mood was followed by an uncomfortable silence.

"So, what takes ye to Edinburgh then?" Connor tried again.

"We're actually traveling to Edinburgh to look for someone," Isaboe finally said.

"And who would that be, if ye dinnae mind me asking?"

"No, I don't' mind. We're going to Edinburgh to look for my…," Isaboe paused as she searched her mind. "…for my lost brother and sister. That's why we are going to Edinburgh." She shot Margaret a sidelong glance.

Margaret returned her look with a nod that said, *Alright, that's good. Let's go with that one.*

"Your lost brother and sister? How did ye lose em?"

Oh great, now he wants details. Isaboe's mind raced as she tried to think of something that sounded believable. "Well, we were separated when we were quite young, close to twenty years ago. I want to see if I can find them. The last place they were known to be was in Edinburgh, so we're starting there."

"How did ye come to be separated? Did something happen to yer parents?"

"Well, it's kind of complicated." Isaboe struggled to find something to say without lying, too much anyway. "I was adopted, and I never got to spend much time with my brother and sister before they were taken away. It's a long story. I really don't want to bore you with it."

"No, sure, that's fine. I wasna trying to be nosey, just curious." Connor turned his attention back to his roasting pheasant.

"I'm sorry. I don't mean to be evasive. It's just, well, there's a lot I don't know. I missed out on growing up with them. I just hope that when we do find them…well, I guess I'll cross that bridge when I get to it."

"Do ye think they'll be happy when ye find 'em?"

"Well, I hope so." Isaboe looked over at Margaret, who gave her a comforting smile.

Done with his line of questioning, Isaboe turned the tables. "So, Connor, what takes you to Edinburgh?"

"Well, I'm not actually going into Edinburgh, just outside of it, up into the Lochmund Hills. I'm seeking a woman who lives there."

"This woman you seek, is she a friend, a relative, someone *special*?" The emphasis on her last word made it obvious Isaboe wanted to know if he was seeking a romantic interest.

"I dinnae ken. I've never met the woman." Connor said, playing words with Isaboe, who just smiled and nodded. "Actually, I made a promise to an old man who saved my life, but I must find this woman first. She supposedly has answers to a lot of questions, answers that I must know if I'm to fulfill my promise."

"That sounds very noble of you."

"No, I'm just a man of my word. If it hadn't been for that old man, I would've been dead a long time ago."

For a moment, Isaboe saw something raw and unsettled flash across Connor's eyes, but in a blink, and it was gone. "So, it would seem we're all on a quest," she said. "I hope you find who you're looking for. You're right, a man is only as good as his word, and so far, you have been honest and forthright with us. Margaret and I are grateful to be traveling with you. You stepped up to help when you didn't have to, and, well, I think that says a lot about your character, the kind of man you are. I wish you luck in your venture." Isaboe suddenly felt as though she'd said too much, and dropped her gaze back down to the shirt she was stitching.

Connor turned the spit with an arm resting on his knee as he hung on her every word. "Thank ye, Miss. Same to you."

After finishing the last stitch, Isaboe bit the thread from the shirt. "Here you go, all patched up." She handed the shirts to Connor, who took them and began inspecting the needle work.

"A fine job, thank ye," he nodded graciously before returning the shirts to his saddlebag.

"You're welcome." Isaboe smiled back.

"Alright, enough with the pleasantries already. Is that bird done yet? It's starting to smell pretty good." Margaret had finished packing her apples and stood over the fire, examining the roasting pheasant.

Standing up to stretch, Isaboe took a deep sniff as her stomach grumbled. "Umm, it smells wonderful. And I'm starving!"

"Now there's a big surprise," Margaret said with a wink.

Consisting of roasted pheasant, cooked potatoes, baked apples, and wild turnips they had dug up along the riverbank, the meal was delicious. The women spent the remainder of the day cleaning the rest of their belongings, while Connor worked with the horses, brushing and rubbing down their coats. He carefully checked their legs and hooves to make sure they had managed to survive the days of traveling through the muddy terrain without any ill effects.

It was obvious that Connor felt most relaxed and comfortable in the company of the horses than he did with the women. This was an attribute Isaboe hadn't missed. Even as it started to get dark, he remained preoccupied with the animals. She and Margaret sat around the campfire talking in hushed voices when Isaboe nodded in Connor's direction. "My Lord, how could anyone spend so much time with a horse?"

"I'm sure it must be necessary. Horses do require a lot of care, especially the way we've been riding these last four days. They need rest too."

"Rest, yes, but look at the way he pampers them; rubbing and brushing, and rubbing some more. It's a little odd if you ask me to spend that much time attending to the needs of an animal."

"Why Isaboe, if I didn't know better I'd say you sound a wee bit jealous."

"Jealous of what?"

"Well, I can think of a lot worse things than being rubbed down by Connor Grant," Margaret replied with a sheepish smile.

"Margaret! I'm surprised at you!" Isaboe tried to sound affronted.

"Oh, come on, Isaboe. I've seen the way you've looked at him." Margaret glanced in Connor's direction. "And why not? He's pleasant enough to look at, aye?"

"I have not looked at him in any way, and I think it is a little presumptuous of you to assume such things." Isaboe tried to defend herself, but not very successfully.

"Aye, right." Margaret rolled her eyes. "Quit acting like such a prude. It's all right if you find him attractive—he is."

The truth was Isaboe did find him attractive, but it wasn't something she was going to admit. She was afraid that the memory of catching him nude in the river might show on her face—best to change the subject. "So, I've been thinking about what we are going to do when we get to Edinburgh."

"Subtle change of topic," Margaret said as she shot Isaboe an approving grin.

"No, really, we need to talk about this. When Connor asked me those questions, I realized I haven't thought this through. We need a plan. I think it's best to start at the Greyfriars Kirk. Marta and Henry attended there. If anyone knows what became of Marta, it will be the clergy at the Kirk."

"You can't walk in and introduce yourself as Isaboe McKinnon. Someone there might remember your supposed death twenty years ago."

"I've thought of that, too. I'm going to be the illegitimate daughter of Isaboe that nobody knew about. I was born out of wedlock, and Isaboe gave me away before she married...Nathan." Saying his name was still painful, and she took a deep breath before continuing. "I'll tell them that I'm looking for my half brother and sister, Anna and Benjamin, and that I know Marta took them to Edinburgh after I...Isaboe, died. What do you think of that idea?"

"Well, it's a start, and maybe they'll believe you. I guess we'll just have to find out. I certainly don't have any better ideas. But tell me, what name are you gonna use?"

"I don't know yet. I'll have to make one up."

"Well you'd better make up a good story to go with it, a family history, that sort of thing."

"Oh God, I don't know. I'll figure it out as I go along." Isaboe sighed before leaning back against the log.

"Alright then, we have a plan, sort of," Margaret said as she casually stirred the coals with a long stick.

Lost in their own thoughts, the women sat silently staring into the campfire, spellbound by the snap and crackle of the burning wood and the dance of the flames.

Dusk soon engulfed the last remnants of daylight, and the evening came to life with the buzz and chirp of nocturnal insects. As the evening air turned cooler, Margaret got up to retrieve a blanket, but when she came back to the fire, Isaboe was gone. Looking out into the nightfall surrounding the campfire, she saw Connor still attending to the horses, but there was no sign of Isaboe. With a small knot of uncertainty growing in her stomach, Margaret called out to her friend in the darkness.

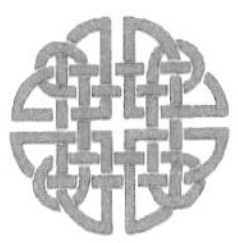

CHAPTER 19

WE'RE ONLY THE MESSENGERS

"Isaboe? Where've you run off to?"

Hearing Margaret's voice, Isaboe detected a tinge of panic in her friend's words. "Over here," she called from beyond the firelight's reach.

"Over where? I can't see you."

"Over here, follow my voice. You have to see this!"

Margaret made her way to a clump of trees where Isaboe stood, looking straight up the trunk of the tallest tree. "What are you doing? What are you looking at?" she asked, as she stood next to her friend and began looking up.

"There, do you see that? Can you hear them? It sounds like wee voices," Isaboe whispered. "I hear faint voices, and they're talking about me. Can't you hear them?" Isaboe badly wanted Margaret to hear them too.

"I only see twinkling stars. Isaboe, are you alright? I don't hear any voices. Let's go back to the fire and sit down."

The concern in Margaret's voice was ignored as Isaboe held her finger to her lips. "Shhh…. listen," she said as her eyes darted along the length of the branch, watching something apparently only she could see.

"Isaboe, this ain't funny. Come away from here." Margaret reached out to take Isaboe's hand, but Isaboe grabbed hers instead.

Holding Margaret's arm firmly, Isaboe never diverted her gaze from the tree. "Who are you? How do you know me?" she asked.

"Who are you talking to? Answer me girl, or I'm calling Connor over here!"

The fear in Margaret's voice was clear, and Isaboe could no longer ignore it. "Why can't Margaret see or hear you?" she said, before turning to face her friend. "They say it's the amulet. If you put it on, you can see and hear them too."

"Who's they?"

"Please, Margaret, just put this on. I'm not crazy, and I'm not losing my mind—just do it." Her eyes wide, Isaboe held the amulet in her shaking hands, waiting for Margaret to concede.

Reluctantly, Margaret finally nodded, allowing Isaboe to place the thin, green cord around her neck. When she turned her face up, at first, Margaret only appeared annoyed, but then her eyes locked onto something in the tree. When Margaret's knees buckled, Isaboe held tight to keep her from falling. "Holy Mother of God! Who...what is that?" she stammered as she looked at Isaboe in astonishment.

"I'm not totally sure. I'm just thankful that I'm not the only one who can see them."

"Can you still see them?"

"No. Not without the amulet."

"Here, maybe if we both hold it, we can see and hear them at the same time," Margaret said, as she slipped the blue stone pendant from around her neck. Holding it between them, the two women stood side-by-side and slowly raised their faces to look back up into the tree.

What appeared at first glance to be a pair of twinkling stars soon began to dive over and around the tree branches. The small lights took form, and right before their eyes, tiny, delicate figures appeared, fluttering weightlessly above the branch on wings as thin as cobwebs. The two tiny figures, almost like miniature dolls, landed on a branch only a few feet above the women's heads. Their delicate, lace-thin wings fluttered slightly when they moved. The beings were wrapped in light, almost ethereal. Isaboe could see the fragile outline of their arms and legs, and though they were very small, their faces were distinguishable. Broad smiles reached from pointed ear to pointed ear, and their bright eyes twinkled with merriment. Small tufts of hair poked out behind tiny ears atop tiny heads.

After a few moments, Isaboe finally spoke. "Who are you? Are you... faeries?"

"Faeries! Do we look like faeries to you?"

Isaboe's eyes widened, hoping she hadn't insulted them. "Well, I…I don't know. I'm not sure what a faerie looks like."

"Well, you should. You've spent enough time with them," said one little figure.

"Finn! She's only a mortal. She doesn't remember, so don't be rude." As the other wee creature spoke, she beamed down at Isaboe. "Allow us to introduce ourselves. I am Teina, and this is Finn. We are *pixies*, not faeries. But since you're only human and don't know any better, we won't hold that against you. Will we Finn?" But Finn didn't reply. He stood on the branch with his tiny arms folded against his chest, a scowl on his miniature face.

Now it felt like *she* had been the one insulted, but Isaboe decided to ignore it. There were more important things she wanted to know. "It is a pleasure to meet you both. Apparently, you already know who I am, and this is my friend Margaret. May I ask how it is that you know me? And what do you know about the time I was gone? I apologize, but I've never seen or spoken with a pixie before, and I have a few questions."

"You have never seen or spoken with us before because you didn't have the amulet. After the seer gave it to you, we were given instructions to find you, watch over you, and make sure nothing bad happens to you," Teina said with a smile. She seemed to take the duty assigned to her very seriously.

"Make sure nothing *bad* happens to her? Teina, we can't control that. Don't lie to her. We're only the messengers!"

"Finn! Stop being so difficult," Teina ribbed him back. "It's not every day that we can speak to a human, and we have a very important message to deliver, so hush!"

As the two little pixies continued their banter, their tiny wings fluttered in time with their heated debate.

"Excuse me, but what's the message?" Isaboe asked anxiously.

The pixies stopped arguing and looked down at Isaboe. Teina rose up in a flutter of light, and hovered in small, excited circles above the branch. "Yes, I have something important to tell you; that's why you have the amulet, so you can hear us!"

But before Teina could recover from her jubilant dance, Finn blurted out as fast as he could, "You're in danger. Don't believe everything you see and hear, 'cause she's a tricky one, a wicked one, too." The little pixie seemed quite pleased with himself.

"What does that mean?" Isaboe's question was laced with concern.

"Finn, I was supposed to tell her that, and you didn't say it right!" Teina scolded him before answering Isaboe. "That's not completely accurate. First, you need to know that not all Underlings are bad. Just as there are good mortals and bad mortals, you mustn't judge all Underlings the same. Secondly, Lorien, Queen of Euphoria threatens you. She is very powerful, so powerful that she does not need an amulet to speak to mortals. She will reach you in other ways. When you sleep, she will come in your dreams. She is sly and clever. If nothing else, remember you must prevent..."

"What are ye ladies doing?"

Both women jumped at the sound of the male voice behind them. "Shit!" Margaret exclaimed, grabbing her chest. She turned to see Connor standing only a few feet away looking up into the tree.

"Damn it, Connor!" Isaboe snapped. "Don't sneak up on us like that. You about scared us half to death!"

"I dinnae mean to scare ye, and I wasn't sneaking." Connor took a step back from the bite in Isaboe's words. "I finished with the horses and discovered the two of ye gone. I came to investigate and heard yer whispering," he said, glaring at both women under a furrowed brow.

"I'm sorry," Isaboe said, breaking the awkward silence. "I didn't mean to snap at you like that. You just startled us," she said. Realizing she was still holding the amulet, she glanced up, but saw no sign of the small figures. They were gone.

"So, what were ye looking at?" Connor asked.

"Fire bugs." Margaret announced, supplying him with an answer. "We were looking at fire bugs up in the tree."

As Isaboe nodded in agreement, Connor gave them an odd look. "Fire bugs? In the Highlands? I can honestly say I've never seen a fire bug anywhere in this entire region."

"Oh, well, maybe that's not what it was. But whatever, it's gone now." Isaboe avoided Connor's questioning look and flashed him a quick smile before rubbing her arms. "Brrrr...it's getting chilly. I think I'll go back and sit by the fire. Margaret, do you want to join me?"

"Yeah, I think I will. My blood feels a bit cold tonight," Margaret replied, leaving Connor standing alone, looking up into the tree with confusion written across his face as the two women walked briskly toward the campfire.

"Fire bugs? That's the best you could come up with?" Isaboe whispered.

"I can't believe what we just saw! That was so incredible!" Margaret had a difficult time keeping her voice down.

"There's something familiar about the name; Lorien. I think I've heard it before. Euphoria sounds familiar, too. The pixies, they called her a queen, didn't they?" Margaret only nodded as Isaboe continued. "Even though I don't clearly recall her, I think she has something to do with my child. There are so many things I don't understand." Isaboe sat down on the log and stared into the fire.

Margaret sat down next to her, wrapping an arm around her friend's shoulder. "Whatever it is, you don't have to go through this alone. I'm here for you," she said, giving Isaboe a little hug.

"I know, thank you." She squeezed Margaret's hand, but regardless of her friend's commitment, Isaboe did feel alone. She was the one who had slipped away for twenty years and lost everything, and now had to deal with the unknown. Both the crone and the pixies had spoken of a threat from a being Isaboe had no memory of, but just because she couldn't distinctly remember Lorien, didn't make the Fey Queen any less real.

Lost in their own thoughts, the women sat together staring into the glowing embers of the campfire when Connor appeared in the circle of firelight with his arms full of wood. He tossed a couple of logs into the fire, and as the flames reignited, hundreds of sparks shot up into the dark night sky. "Are ye two alright?" he asked in a subdued voice.

Margaret looked up at him with an innocent smile, "Oh aye, we're fine, just having a wee bit of girl talk."

Connor only grunted and shook his head before retrieving something from his bag. After finding a comfortable seat in front of the fire, he put his whistle up to his mouth and began to play. It was a pleasant tune, lighter than the one he had played the first night.

Margaret and Isaboe sat silently on the log, almost hypnotized by the flames dancing above the glowing embers. The sound of Connor's music drifting lightly on the evening breeze made it easy for them to become lost in their own uncertain thoughts.

After Connor finished playing his tune, the sounds of the evening once more dominated the night. It seemed to Isaboe that the nocturnal sounds grew darker, more ominous as the evening creatures came to life. She felt the familiar blanket of fear wrapping around her.

"That was nice, Connor. Thank you for the sonata." Margaret obviously noticed Isaboe's anxiety, and in her usual fashion, attempted to coax her friend's mind from her problems with conversation. "Connor, you mentioned earlier that you will be seeking a woman in the Lochmund Hills. If you don't mind me asking, how does this fulfill your promise to this man who saved your life? Is she his long-lost love, and you promised to bring her back?" Margaret teased.

There was an awkward moment of silence before Connor replied, "Well, if she was his long-lost love, it's too late now. He died many years ago."

Isaboe watched his jaw tighten and release as he struggled with his thoughts. Though she figured he was probably only in his late twenties, Connor carried the look of one who had lived hard in his short life.

"I dinnae ken exactly what this woman will tell me, I just havta find her. Even though the old man is gone, a promise is a promise, aye? I owe him my life, and I intend to keep my word, even to a dead man."

"So, was he a friend, or a relative of yours?" Isaboe asked, interested in his story.

"Well, if a man saves yer life that makes him a friend, aye?"

"How did he save your life?"

Connor took a deep breath before looking back into the flames. He was silent for several moments, as if remembering. "He arranged my release from prison."

"You were in prison? What did you do?"

He again looked at her, holding her gaze a few moments before responding. "I was imprisoned for being on the wrong side of a losing battle."

"What were you fighting for?"

"Freedom, and revenge," he muttered intensely. But the realization that he may have said too much showed in Connor's eyes. He quickly smiled as the seriousness left his face. "But that was a long time ago. The only cause I'm involved in now is getting us all to Edinburgh. So, if ye ladies'll excuse me, I'm gonna get some sleep. I suggest ye do the same since we'll be breaking camp early in the morrow. Good night."

Margaret managed to squeak out a quiet response. "Good night, Connor. Thanks again for the music."

The women watched silently as their guide walked over to where he had dropped his saddle. "I don't think I'll sleep at all tonight," Isaboe said, watching Connor crawl into his bedroll, "not after everything we've seen and heard this evening." When she looked at Margaret, she saw that they both wore the same expression.

Who was this man that they were riding with? He obviously placed a great deal of merit on keeping a promise, and would give his life fighting for what he believed in, but prison? Isaboe wasn't sure she wanted to know any more about the mysterious Connor Grant.

CHAPTER 20

A MAN, A WOMAN, AND A HORSE

The morning started with clear skies, and the day's weather promised to be as nice as the previous day had been. The late summer sun warmed the three riders as they set out to continue their journey. Fall was coming in with a brilliant show of color as the sun's rays highlighted the golden hues of the majestic oaks.

But Isaboe saw none of it as she rode silently behind Connor and Margaret. The events of the previous evening and a night full of bad dreams had rekindled her depression. Lost in her own thoughts, she remained quiet throughout the morning. She fought the aching loss, trying to push it from her consciousness, but the bleakness of her current reality would not let her be. Isaboe knew she would never be free of the pain, and could only hope that in time she might become accustomed to it. For now, her loss felt like a canyon waiting to swallow her, and she teetered dangerously on the edge. She chose not to share her demons with Margaret this morning. Lord knew the woman had seen her at her worst and had already heard it all.

After three days of steady rain, the river was completely full. The creeks and streams they had to cross were bursting at their banks, and the largest creek they encountered was a small river in itself. As Connor traveled along the bank searching for the best place to cross over, even he seemed dubious. But after finding what he hoped would be a safe place to cross, he maneuvered his horse carefully down the bank and across the rushing water to the other side. Margaret went next, and though her horse had some difficulty with its footing, she soon joined Connor and waited for Isaboe to do the same.

The rapid current was intimidating, and Isaboe's horse seemed skittish about crossing it, as was she. While the first two riders watched, Isaboe did her best to persuade her mount to enter the water. But the frightened animal would not cooperate, and its rider became increasingly frustrated. "Damn this animal!" she shouted. Each time the horse took a step toward the turbulent waters, it stomped backward nervously and anxiously tossed its head. As its whinnies grew more and more distressed, Isaboe thought the horse would try to throw her, so she pulled the reins tight to her chest, which only agitated the animal more.

After watching the pathetic scene between horse and rider for several agonizing minutes, Connor rode back across the creek. "Give me the reins, Isaboe, I'll lead ye across." Connor held out his hand.

"No! I'm getting this horse across the creek by myself." But with each attempt, both Isaboe and the horse became more agitated, and she struggled just to keep the skittish animal facing in the right direction.

"Not like that, ye won't. Ye've lost any control ye might've had, and now the horse is too frightened for ye to handle. Just give me the lead!"

As the horse stomped around nervously, Isaboe struggled to keep it from bolting. Connor reached out to grab the horse's reins, but Isaboe pushed his hand aside. "No! I can do this myself! I refuse to let this damn animal get the best of me!"

"Isaboe, stop being so bloody stubborn and hand over the reins!" Connor yelled, his patience gone. When she reluctantly gave in and handed him the lead, he immediately took control of the horse and led them both safely across to the opposite bank. Upon reaching the other side, he held the reins out toward her. "Do ye think ye can handle her now?" he asked with a chastising glare.

"I could have crossed the creek myself if you would've just given me a little more time. You didn't have to come rescue me," Isaboe snapped as she grabbed the reins from his hand.

"Oh, I didna, aye? What was yer plan? Wait till the water receded? Ye had no control over the animal. She was too spooked for ye to handle, and ye were only making it worse. If I hadn't come back over, she would've bolted into the woods, probably knocked ye senseless on a low hanging branch, and I'd still have to rescue yer *stubborn ass!*"

"Excuse me!" Isaboe's green eyes sparked with fire as she shot Connor a look of defiance. "Don't ever speak to me like that again! I don't need you to rescue me. I can take care of myself!"

"Oh, will you two just stop it! This is ridiculous!" Margaret interjected. "Isaboe, you are acting like a brat. And Connor, quit provoking her. This whole argument is pointless. Everyone is fine, and we're on the other side of the creek. Can we just be on our way now?" Margaret looked back and forth between Isaboe and Connor like an angry parent.

It was Connor who made the first move. Giving a jerk on his horse's reins, he quickly rode up the side of the bank and over the rise. Margaret watched him disappear from view and then looked back at Isaboe, scowling.

"What? You think this was *my* fault? I can't help it if this...this bloody animal won't cooperate!" Isaboe slapped the reins on the horse's neck, causing it to turn its head back toward her, nipping angrily. She kicked her leg out of the way and pulled hard on the reins. "See, it hates me!"

"The horse doesn't hate you, Isaboe, but she senses that you don't like her," Margaret scolded. "Connor was right. You had no control and you made a big fuss for no good reason. So, I suggest that you change your attitude, lassie. Get over it, and let's go see if Connor is still waiting for us, or if he's left us to find our own way!" Margaret snapped, before turning her horse and riding up the bank.

As she sat on her horse—the damned animal that had caused the whole mess to begin with—Isaboe considered what Margaret had said and felt the sting of truth. Her only option now was to ride up the bank to face Connor, swallow her pride, and apologize. Unpleasant as the idea was, she wasn't sure she had a choice.

"Isaboe, are you coming?" Margaret called from the rise.

Spurring her horse, Isaboe reached the top of the bank where she saw Connor leaning against a tree with his arms folded across his chest and chewing on a blade of grass. Margaret stood next to him still holding the reins of her horse, and both watched as Isaboe slowly rode over. After dismounting, she sighed deeply and then walked around the horses. Stopping in front of Connor, she looked directly at him and stood as tall as possible, with as much dignity as she could muster.

"Connor, I apologize for yelling at you and for...for my attitude," she said, shooting Margaret an apologetic look. "Unfortunately, you were right. I didn't have control, and being frustrated obviously didn't help. I appreciate how helpful you've been and..." She dropped her gaze and muttered, "I'm sorry."

"Ouch. That sounded painful. Did it hurt as much in the telling as it was to hear?" Connor asked with a hint of humor in his voice.

Again, Isaboe tried to regain some composure before responding, "Are we done here now? Shouldn't we be going?"

"Are ye sure ye wanna get back up on that horse? The two of ye haven't exactly had the best go at it, aye?"

"I don't see that I have a lot of choice in the matter, now do I?"

Connor tossed the blade of grass from his mouth as he walked over to stand directly in front of her. Though he was a bit too close for comfort, Isaboe did not step back. "Now, there's where ye're wrong, 'cause ye do have a choice. Ye can choose to ride or ye can choose to walk. And if ye choose to ride, I suggest ye remember what I told ye yesterday. Do ye recall what I said?"

"You mean that sentimental drivel about horses' *feelings*?"

Placing a hand on her arm, Connor gently led Isaboe to stand next to her horse. As they approached, the skittish animal started to back away before Connor grabbed hold of the reins. He stood in front of the horse, slowly running his hand down the side of its neck, and it didn't take long for the horse to respond. Spending so much time with him, all the horses had become accustomed to Connor's touch. He talked softly to the animal, the way a parent might talk to an upset child. After a few moments, a transformation began to take place, in both horse and man.

As Isaboe stood to the side watching Connor interact with the animal, she began to realize why he spent so much time with the horses. There was a connection—a connection of spirits between man and beast—and it showed as the horse began to relax. A bond had been formed, and the animal trusted him. From the expression on Connor's face, this interaction had a soothing effect on him as well. As she watched him connect with the horse, a different Connor was exposed, a softer, more caring side revealed itself. With big lips, the horse gently nibbled his cheek, and the moment brought a smile to Isaboe's face as Connor wiped away the horse's kiss with the back of his hand.

"Ye see, all ye need is a little patience. Just give some affection and she'll calm right down. Come over here and try it," he offered with an outstretched hand.

Isaboe reluctantly took a few steps forward to face her horse. Its nose was only inches from hers, and she tried to step back, but Connor stood directly behind her. When she bumped up against him, he didn't budge, keeping Isaboe between himself and the horse.

"Just do what I was doing. Stroke her neck slowly, and talk to her softly. Ye haven't bonded with her yet, so she has to get comfortable with ye first before she can trust ye. That's why ye were having such difficulty getting her to cooperate." Connor's calm voice had an effect on Isaboe as well. Though she tried to do as instructed, she had no idea of what to say to a horse. Connor standing so close she could feel his chest against her back made it even more difficult for her to concentrate.

"Ye're too stiff. Relax a bit and let me show ye," Connor said as he laid his arm over the top of hers. Slowly gliding their arms together down the horse's neck, the two of them softly stroked its downy coat.

With Connor standing behind her, his arm draped over her own, Isaboe grew increasingly uncomfortable with what she was feeling. She stroked the horse's neck a few more times, but soon the confusing feelings got the most of her, and she quickly pulled out from under his arm.

"Alright. Thank you. I think I understand what you are trying to communicate here...I mean, with the horse." Isaboe took a few steps back. More than a little flustered, she tried desperately to swallow her embarrassment as Connor chuckled to himself.

Interrupting the moment, Margaret spoke up. "If the two of you are done with whatever it is you're doing, can we be on our way? I'd like to make it to MucGhine before nightfall."

"Before we get going again, can we eat something first?" Isaboe pleaded. "I'm starving,"

Walking over to her saddlebag, Margaret pulled out a round, red object and tossed it at Isaboe before turning to mount her horse.

Isaboe looked at the apple in her hand, then back up at Margaret, "An apple? That's all I get?"

"Look, if there is any chance I can sleep in a real bed tonight, I'm not stopping to make any meals. You'll just have to make due." Margaret reached into the pouch that hung at her waist. "Here, take this too. Enjoy." Handing her a few strips of dried meat, Margaret gave Isaboe a quick smile and heeled her horse into movement.

"Ye heard the lady, we're on the move," Connor said as he swung up into his saddle. Quickly biting into the apple, Isaboe tucked the jerky into her pocket and followed suit. Though an apple and a bit of jerky wasn't what she had anticipated for lunch, when one is eating for two, one takes anything one can get.

CHAPTER 21

A CLOSE ENCOUNTER WITH DEATH

The creek crossing ordeal and the subsequent interaction with Connor and her horse left Isaboe pleasantly distracted. For the rest of the afternoon, the small band of riders made good time and even found it easy to chat idly as they rode.

Just before noon, the terrain became densely wooded, and the trio found themselves once again riding single-file on a dirt road through the forest. Isaboe found herself contemplating what Connor had shown her earlier with her horse. Though not completely comfortable with the idea, she tried to show more patience, even a little affection toward the animal. Stroking its long neck, she leaned forward to whisper in its ear. "You're not a stupid horse, are you? You think you made me look bad, kissing up to Connor. But if you try to bite me again, I'll tell you a little story about how they make glue."

The afternoon sun was on its descent when Connor suggested that they were only a few hours from MucGhine. Margaret was true to her word and other than a couple of stops to let the horses drink and to refill their own water flasks, there was no break for an afternoon meal. Lunch on horseback consisted of hardboiled eggs, jerky, and of course, apples.

Riding steadily, they were making good time. But on one particularly narrow portion of the trail, their progress was abruptly interrupted. When the ladies heard Connor's horse cry out in alarm, and then Connor himself cursing viciously, what they saw caused them both to catch their breath.

Standing side-by-side blocking the path were three ugly, filthy men, each holding a weapon. The one on the left was missing most of his teeth and wielded a long, nasty-looking knife. The hideous creature standing in the middle had a long scar that ran across his distorted face from his ear to the corner of his mouth, and his pistol was pointed directly at Connor. The last man was the worst looking. His bulbous face was covered with oozing scabs, and he waved his sword threateningly toward the ladies. The men's clothes were ragged, torn, and covered in filth. Only the one in the middle with the pistol wore boots. The other two were barefoot, and their feet were blackened from layers of dirt and grime.

The hair stood up on the back of Isaboe's neck, and Margaret looked just as frightened as she was.

"We're just passing through gents; no need to give us any trouble." Connor sounded incredibly calm facing three thugs with weapons pointed at him.

"Oh aye, we dinnae want no trouble neither, just da 'orses. So git ye arses down, or we'll take them out from under ye!" said the one with the pistol.

"And we'll take da women too!" Scabface exclaimed with too much enthusiasm. He looked directly at Isaboe with a repulsive grin as the other two laughed and licked their lips.

"Well, the women ye can have, but ye'll havta fight me for the horses." Connor replied to their demand as if he were negotiating the sale of livestock.

Toothless started laughing and turned to his comrades, "Did ye hear that? He dinnae care bout da women! We can have 'dem too!"

"Connor, I don't find this the slightest bit amusing." Isaboe's statement held an edge of stark panic.

It happened so fast that neither Isaboe nor Margaret saw where it came from. In a flash of movement, Connor had pulled a dirk and thrown it directly at Scarface, striking him cleanly in the throat. Blood spurted around the blade as the man gasped and choked. Grabbing at his throat, he stumbled and fell backward. But before he hit the ground, the would-be thief pulled the trigger of his pistol, releasing a loud shot that exploded through the air.

The noise startled everyone, but especially the horses. Both Margaret and Isaboe's mounts reacted violently to the sound. Eyes wide with fear, Isaboe's horse reared up and she was thrown from her saddle. As her horse bolted, running off down the road, Isaboe landed on her back, the wind knocked from her lungs.

Before Scarface even hit the ground, Connor swung off his horse, wheeled his legs around, and landed both feet in the middle of the toothless robber's chest. The man went flying backward and landed in the trees.

"Get the pistol out of my saddlebag!" Connor barked before turning to pull his sword from the scabbard hanging at his side. Margaret only sat on her horse, shocked. Everything was happening so fast, she was unable to move.

"NOW!" Connor shouted as he turned just in time to block the downswing of Scabface's sword. The clash of metal and Connor's urgency moved Margaret into action. Scrambling off her horse, she began digging through Connor's saddlebags. Isaboe jumped up and frantically started searching through the saddlebags on the opposite side. Scabface, it seemed, was a fairly good swordsman. He gave Connor a real battle as their blades clashed, sending the sound of ringing metal echoing through the woods.

"Here it is!" Isaboe shouted.

Margaret rushed over to the other side of the horse. "Is it loaded?"

"I don't know. I know nothing about pistols," Isaboe said, handing over the weapon. Glancing around the horse, she saw Connor duck just in time as Scabface swung his weapon dangerously close. But Connor recovered and lunged toward his opponent's chest, only to have his sword blocked.

Margaret dug around further and found a bag of black powder, wrapped lead balls, and a ram. With the speed and efficiency of an expert, she poured the powder down the barrel, rammed the lead ball on top of it, snapped the frizzen in place, and cocked the hammer.

Connor's attention was focused solely on his fight—on blade and footwork, measuring the determination in his opponent's eyes. He did not see the figure coming up from behind. As Toothless came lumbering out of the trees, knife in hand, he was only a few steps away from plunging it into Connor's back when Margaret held up the pistol, aimed, and fired. Toothless stopped dead in his tracks, dropping to the ground as blood poured out the side of his head. When Scabface turned to watch his companion fall, Connor struck, shoving his sword deep into the man's abdomen. Scabface's body lurched forward, then doubled over and crumbled to the ground.

After pulling out his sword, Connor wiped the blood off on his pants and stepped back. Breathing heavily, he surveyed the scene around him. Three men lay dead on the road, but only two at his hand. He spun around to see Margaret and Isaboe clutching one another with wide, terrified eyes.

"Are ye alright?" he asked, sword still in hand.

"Yes, we're alright. Are you?" Isaboe replied, her heart racing.

"Aye, but he gave me quite a fight." Connor's face was beaded with sweat, his chest heaving from the exertion of the battle. "Which one of ye did that?" he pointed his sword at Toothless, who lay peacefully on the ground with a hole in his head.

"I did," Margaret said timidly, the pistol still in her hand.

"That was one hell of a shot, my lady!" he said, giving her a quick smile. "Now we need to move. There could be more of their lot out there," Connor said, nodding toward the trees. "Give me the pistol and get on yer horse." He took the weapon from Margaret and quickly reloaded it, then placed it in his saddlebag, keeping it within easy reach. Seeing that Isaboe no longer had a ride, he jumped up onto his saddle and reached down to her. "Here, give me yer hand!" Grasping her extended arm, Connor swung Isaboe up in one fluid motion to sit behind him. Margaret wasted no time and was soon on her saddle, kicking her horse into action.

Leaving three dead bodies behind them, they galloped away at a rapid pace. They rode hard and fast for several miles while Isaboe clung tightly to Connor. The tree line flew by them in a blur, and more than once he shouted *"Duck!"* when low hanging branches threatened to sweep them off the horse's back. At one point, Isaboe imagined that she saw someone running alongside them, just inside the tree line. Though logic told her that no one could possibly keep pace with a galloping horse, her heart still leapt into her throat, and she held onto Connor a bit tighter.

After miles of hard riding, the forest opened up, giving way to a vast, green meadow. The grassy field stretched out in front of them, reaching down to the river's bank. With the forest and its threats behind them,

Connor allowed the horse to slow. It was then that Isaboe noticed the blood-soaked sleeve on his left arm.

"Connor, you're injured! Your arm is bleeding. We need to stop and attend to it."

Apparently unaware of his injury until Isaboe brought it to his attention, Connor looked down at the red stained sleeve of his shirt. "It's alright, I'll be fine," he said ignoring his wound and continuing their pace.

"No, it's not fine! You have no idea how bad it might be. We need to stop!"

Connor looked over his shoulder into Isaboe's demanding eyes; she wasn't going to let this drop. Reluctantly, he did as asked. After dismounting, he rolled up his sleeve and walked down to the river. Kneeling to wash, he inspected his injury. Margaret had the foresight to purchase some bandage cloth in Inverness, and after retrieving it, Isaboe knelt beside Connor to do her own inspection. It was a nasty cut that ran from inside his elbow, down his forearm, ending just above the wrist. It was long, but fortunately, not very deep.

"Oh, Conner, that's not good. Does it hurt much?"

"It stings a bit, but I think I'll live."

"Come back up and I'll wrap it for you." As they walked back up to the grassy shore, Isaboe tore the cloth into strips. "Honestly, what kind of men wait in the forest to steal someone's horses?" she asked.

"*Fuckin salach coin!*" It was the first time Isaboe had heard Connor speak Gaelic, and the words rolled off his tongue viciously. "They looked like marauders, probably a band of them hanging out in the forest, just waiting for people to pass through. We were lucky today. Most who run up against the likes of them dinnae live to talk about it." Taking a seat on the grass, he let his injured arm rest on his knee so Isaboe could bandage it.

"I cannae believe I didna have my pistol loaded and ready. Damn it! I ken better and I put ye both at risk." Connor paused, "I promise, it will never happen again." After a few moments he turned to look at an unusually reserved Margaret sitting next to him on the grass. "I'll havta start calling ye *One Shot Margaret*. Where did ye learn to shoot like that?"

"I've never killed anyone before," Margaret said quietly, her gaze never leaving the grass.

"Oh, Margaret, you had no choice," Isaboe said, offering a comforting touch on her friend's arm. "If you hadn't shot that man, he would have stabbed Connor in the back, and he'd probably be dead now. Then who knows what would have happened to us!"

"Isaboe is right, ye had no choice. Ye did what ye had to do. Thank God ye didna hesitate, or I would've been dead. And the two of ye would've been playthings for a whole group of those dogs. Now isn't that a pretty thought? So, where did ye learn to shoot like that?"

"My father taught me. Mum would make bread or biscuits every day, and Dad would save the hard, stale rolls to use as targets. We would go out to the pasture and put 'em on the fence posts. I got quite good at it actually. He figured that I might end up alone and have to protect myself." She laughed ruefully. "It looks like he was right."

"Dinnae worry about it, Margaret, it gets easier after the first one," Connor said teasingly. But neither lady found it funny, and Isaboe intentionally cinched the cloth around his arm tighter than necessary, making him flinch. "Hey, not so tight there, lassie!" he said as he caught her reprimanding glare.

"You'll probably need stitches on this or it will leave a nasty scar," Isaboe said as she put the finishing touches on her first aid. "And Lord knows, you already have enough scars."

It was one of those moments she wished she could take back. No sooner had the words left her mouth when Isaboe knew it was probably too late. She sat in front of Connor and Margaret, hoping that maybe they didn't catch her slip, but no such luck.

Margaret gave Connor a curious glance before addressing her friend, "How do you know how many scars he has?"

But before Isaboe could think of anything to say, a slow, mischievous grin broke out on Connor's face, along with a twinkle of merriment in his eyes.

"What?" she asked, glaring at him.

"Ye were spying on me." The satisfied look of what he had just realized radiated in Connor's smile.

"I was not!" Isaboe cried out defensively. But Connor only smiled wider. He didn't need to say anything; his face said it all.

"You were spying on him, while he was bathing in the river? Isaboe, I'm shocked at you!" Margaret teased.

"I did not spy on him! I would never do such a thing…I mean, not intentionally." Isaboe knew she was caught.

"So, ye admit to spying on me."

"It was an accident! I was down at the river getting water for Margaret and… well, I heard splashing. When I looked…I mean…I was not spying!"

"You just admitted you watched long enough to see his scars. It sounds like spying to me."

"It was unintentional! I didn't mean to. It was an accident. That's not spying!"

"If you weren't spying, why didn't you tell me about it?" Margaret folded her arms across her chest and Isaboe watched her friend's lips twitch as she fought back a smile.

"Cause she was too busy gettin' an eyeful," Connor said with a satisfied grin.

"How dare you imply such impropriety!" Isaboe stated defiantly. "I am a lady. I would never sink so low. And I've had enough of the two of you!" She stood and spun on her heels, walking over to the horses with the furor and dignity of a queen.

"Isaboe!" Connor called out before she got far.

"What?" she called over her shoulder, refusing to turn.

"So, did ye like what ye saw?"

That stopped her. With her face burning red, her fiery, green eyes shooting daggers, Isaboe turned and stomped back toward Connor. Stopping just short from where he sat, she looked down at him with a murderous glare. "You sir are an arrogant, insolent, over-prideful *jackass!*" she spat, before turning and stomping off toward the horses.

With a smile on his lips and a twinkle in his eyes, Connor looked at Margaret. "Aye, she liked what she saw."

Back at the horses, Isaboe tucked away the bandages, muttering under her breath when she heard him call out her name. He called out to her three times, but she opted not to respond and didn't even turn around. When Connor finally stood behind her, Isaboe refused to acknowledge him.

"I didna mean to make ye so upset," he said softly. "Margaret and I were just having a wee bit a fun with ye."

"Yes, at the expense of my dignity!" Isaboe finally turned to face him. "Connor, I wasn't spying on you. Yes, I did see you...naked in the river, but I didn't set out to do that—it just happened. I don't know what else to say. I'm sorry."

"For what?" he asked. When she looked at him like she didn't understand the question, Connor took a deep breath before continuing. "If the truth be told, I kind of knew ye were there," he admitted sheepishly.

"What?"

He gave her a crooked smile. "The whole thing with the soap, ye had to ken, that was all for show, aye? I mean, I had a whole river to bathe in, why did ye think I chose that spot?"

"Are you telling me that you *knew* I was there, and you put on a *show* for me?"

"Hey, I'm a man. It's not every day that a beautiful woman wants to watch me bathe, *unintentionally* of course," he said, looking down at her with a sly smile.

As she looked into his playful blue eyes, Isaboe wasn't sure if she should be flattered or angry. "You really are an arrogant jackass, aren't you?"

Connor only shrugged his shoulders, giving her what appeared to be a charming, incriminating grin. "So, am I forgiven, or are ye still mad at me?"

Unsure of how to reply, Isaboe dropped her gaze as she shuffled her feet. But then Connor placed a hand under her chin, gently lifted her face, and his eyes danced with hers for a moment. "I'm sorry if I embarrassed ye. I would never disrespect you."

Standing so close to him, trapped by his eyes holding hers, Isaboe completely forgot about her anger. But the moment was broken by the sound of an impatient woman clearing her throat. Connor dropped his hand, and they both turned to see Margaret standing only a few yards away holding the reins of their horses.

"If you two are done with this sweet little moment, I think I see chimney smoke over there," she said, gesturing to the south. Over the next rise in front of the setting sun, they could see thin trails of smoke rising up into the late afternoon sky. MucGhine was only a short trip away, and so was that bed Margaret had been counting on.

CHAPTER 22

WAITSBURGH

By the time they rode into the small town, the sun had dipped below the horizon, and there was a noticeable chill in the air. The hills had turned a beautiful shade of purple, and the sky was a brilliant backdrop—white puffy clouds brushed with pink from the setting sun. Four small boys chased one another through the street as a torch lighter walked from one building to the next, lighting the lanterns hanging from porch awnings. The town was small, only about two dozen buildings in all. A one-room school house, a church, and the Beaumont General Store were the first buildings Isaboe noticed. Other than a stable and a blacksmith shop, the rest of the town was comprised of homes and cottages spread around the small community.

As they rode past the stable's open door, an animal caught Isaboe's eye. "Isn't that my horse?" Both riders came to a halt. Tied up inside the stable, its saddle in place and all their bags still attached, stood Isaboe's horse.

"Guten abend!" A man with a thick German accent approached Connor with a big smile. "Ve expected that someone vould come to claim dis fine horse. Vun of da boys found her valking alone, and brought her here. Would dis be your horse?"

Connor dismounted and extended his hand. "Connor Grant," he said, "Thank ye for rounding her up. I dinnae think we'd see her again.

The tall, balding German returned the handshake heartily, "Fredrick Gerhardt, at your service. Velcome to our little town of Vaitsberg. Vhere you bound?"

"I believe there's a ferry not far from here that'll take us across to

MucGhine. We were hopin' to make it there before nightfall, but it doesn't look like that's gonna happen."

"Oh, da ferry to MucGhine vould be right here in Vaitsberg, but unfortunately it is…how to say…out of commission?"

"What do you mean, out of commission?" Margaret asked.

Fredrick stepped around Connor to address the red-haired woman on her horse. "It means, not vorking."

Taking a deep breath, Margaret smiled and tried again, "I know what it means, but why isn't it working?"

"Oh, because a tree fell on de ferry two days ago. Vith all de rain, the river has been very full, de land very soggy. Da rope attached to de udder side broke, and no vay to fix it now." Fredrick explained.

"Great," Margaret grumbled.

"Vhy do you need to go to MucGhine?" Fredrick turned back to Connor.

"I was plannin' on taking the women there so they could catch a coach to Edinburgh. Do ye know where the next ferry crossing is?"

Fredrick's brushy eyebrows furrowed together in deep thought before he replied. "I believe dat vould be in Firth, just across the river from Edinburgh. It's a two-day ride from here."

Connor nodded as he looked back at Margaret and Isaboe, "Well, what do ye think ladies? Are ye up to finishing the trip on horseback with me then?"

"It doesn't sound like we have any other choice," Isaboe responded.

"Vell, you can't go any vhere tonight, so you might as vell stay here. Ve can find a room for you and your frau," Fredrick said, looking at Margaret, then Isaboe, apparently trying to decide which one of them was most likely Connor's wife.

"Oh, we're just traveling companions," Isaboe quickly interjected. "We'll need separate accommodations."

Appearing from around the corner, a girl just on the verge of becoming a young woman walked up next to the tall German and slipped her arm through Fredrick's. With a head full of long golden curls, a smile set off by matching dimples and wide blue eyes, she was a pretty young thing and only a head shorter than her father.

"Hello Papa. Mother sent me to tell you that supper is ready." She turned her bright cornflower-blue eyes on Connor and broke out in a bashful smile.

Fredrick reached over, put his arm around the young girl and kissed her on the forehead. "Dis is my beautiful daughter, Bernadette." After Fredrick had introduced the girl, she daintily held out the end of her blue dress in a formal curtsey. "Bernadette, 'dis is de Herr Grant. He and his traveling companions vill be our guests tonight."

Margaret and Isaboe took that as a signal and dismounted to introduce themselves and thank their host for his help. Just then, a mirror image of the first young girl appeared. Only her dress was different.

"Ah, and here is my udder beautiful daughter, Emma." Once again, the formal little curtsey and bashful smile were directed toward Connor, with little acknowledgement of the women.

"Twins. Double the fun, aye?" Connor said with a mischievous grin. Instantly and in perfect unison, they broke into a giggle.

"Oh, these two can be a handful, ja." Fredrick nodded before he addressed his daughters. "Ve need to find a room for Herr Grant, and for Fraulein McKinnon and Fraulein MacDoughal as vell."

"Papa, since Fritz is gone on harvest, Mr. Grant can stay with us in his room," Bernadette offered, bubbling with excitement.

"Ja, that is a good idea!" Emma squealed with equal excitement.

"Ja, my son Fritz is avay at my brudder's home for harvest, so ve do have one extra bed. I suppose it vould be alright." Fredrick appeared to be contemplating the idea of having a strange man sharing the house with his two excited daughters. The girls spoke with less of an accent than did their father, talking over the top of each other until they convinced him their idea was a good one, and he finally agreed.

"Alright den, and maybe Frau Mitchell will help us out vith a place for de ladies tonight." Fredrick added. But Isaboe wasn't paying attention to the arrangements being made on her behalf. Watching the twins was captivating. The girls could hardly contain their excitement.

"I need to rub down the horses," Connor said. "We rode them pretty hard today. I'd like to take care of them first. Can I put them up here for the night?"

"Oh, ja. I veel have the stable boy take care of dem; you don't need to vorry." Fredrick nodded confidently.

"Thanks, but I'd rather do it myself." Connor politely smiled back.

Thinking that it was just like Connor to put the horses first, Isaboe suddenly recalled his injury. "Oh, I almost forget. Connor needs some medical attention. He has a bad cut that requires a few stitches. Do you have a doctor here, or a healer who can look at it?" Isaboe asked, putting a hand on Connor's arm.

"Ja, Mother can fix him!" Emma suggested with enthusiasm.

"My Frau Hilda is a good medicine vomen, da closest ting ve have to a doctor. She's very good, vill fix him right up." Fredrick gave Isaboe a reassuring smile.

Isaboe nodded, and when she looked up at Connor, he seemed quite pleased with the arrangements being made on his behalf. Apparently, her nod was an indication she approved of this suggestion, so both Bernadette and Emma rushed over and took Connor's arms, pushing Isaboe aside in the process.

"We'll take him to Mother now, alright Papa?" Before Fredrick could reply, the two golden-haired girls escorted Connor out of the stable, arm-in-arm-in-arm.

"I'll be back to tend the horses," Connor said as he looked back over his shoulder. He then turned toward Margaret and Isaboe. "See ye later ladies," he whispered with a large grin and merriment in his eyes.

As they strolled down the road the twins hung on Connor's every word, and it didn't take much to set them giggling again. Isaboe watched them walking away, not sure what to make of it all. "Your daughters are lovely," she said, forcing a smile.

"Danke schoen. Now, let us go see Frau Mitchell about getting you ladies a room for de evening, ja?" Fredrick tied the horses to the post outside the stable door before leading the women down the street.

Regardless of where she ended up tonight, Isaboe was sure that an evening with Frau Mitchell wouldn't be anywhere near as exciting as what the twins had in store for Connor.

CHAPTER 23

EVERYTHING IS MORE FUN WITH DANCING GIRLS AND WHISKEY

She was completely exhausted, but Isaboe had a difficult time falling asleep that night, even though the accommodations Fredrick had arranged for her were quite pleasant. The Mitchells were more than hospitable, but they had only one small spare bed, so Fredrick took Margaret to stay at the home of a Mrs. Grayson.

After Margaret disappeared into the night, Mrs. Mitchell served such a wonderful evening meal that Isaboe ate more than she considered proper. After two days of hardboiled eggs, apples, and tough jerky, the roasted pork and tatties, accompanied by fresh greens, tasted absolutely heavenly. They were fortunate to have stopped in Waitsburgh during harvest, and the fresh vegetables were a rare treat.

As Isaboe tried to sleep, the distorted faces of the three assailants haunted her, as did the image of them lying dead in the road. She saw Connor fighting them, saw him cut a man down with his sword. But instead of the horror and violence, her mind's eye roamed over the flex and grace of his body. These were thoughts a grieving widow most certainly shouldn't be having.

When she rolled over and looked out the window of her little room, the moon was just a hair shy of full. Hanging high in the starlit sky, it was large and bright, with a tinge of orange—a perfect harvest moon if she had ever seen one. She stared at the moon until her eyes became heavy, and eventually gave into sleep....

Strolling barefoot along a moss-covered path, the ground feels spongy and soft under my toes. Glancing up, wispy willow branches dance in the breeze. The scent of rosemary, the sun's warmth on my face—it feels like home, yet foreign all at the same time. A shiver runs down my spine.

"Welcome back, Alaina." The golden-haired woman appears beside me.

"I know you. You're... you're Lorien."

"Yes. It's so good to see you again. I always look forward to your visits."

"I'm just visiting? I thought this was my home. Why can't I stay?"

"Soon, but not this time. Come, walk with me. Tell me, how fares the child?"

"What child?"

"The child you carry, of course."

"How did you know about the child?"

"I know all about you, my dear, and your unborn child. Ah, here are some of your friends."

"I don't see Margaret. Where is she?"

"Margaret doesn't belong here. This is not her home."

"Then where is her home? Is it where I come from? Does that mean this isn't really my home either?"

"My, you ask a lot of questions. I believe a feast has been prepared in your honor. Let's go eat, and enjoy the day together."

"Wait, Lorien. Are you my friend?"

"That's a silly question. I am the only true friend you have."

"What about Margaret? She's my friend."

"Of course she is, my dear. She just doesn't understand how you feel or what you're going through like I do."

"What am I going though, Lorien? I don't understand. I don't." Flashes of memories, dainty wings, rituals and chants, and Margaret's laugh—all mingle together and wrap around my mind, causing confusion. "I don't belong here. I shouldn't trust you, that's what they told me."

"Who told you that?"

"I can't remember. I'm confused now. I always feel confused when I come here."

"I need you to remember who told you not to trust me, Alaina."

"Why is that important? What's happened to me, Lorien? You know, don't you? Tell me!"

"You seem a little out of sorts today, my darling. Maybe you should come back later, when you are feeling more like yourself."

"What does that feel like? Tell me, Lorien, because I really don't know! I'm not sure who I am. You call me Alaina, but Margaret calls me by a different name."

"It's time for you to go now."

"Wait! Where am I going? Why won't you answer my questions?"

"It's time for you to go."

"I don't want to go! Lorien, please help me understand! Lorien, where are you?"

Isaboe jerked up in bed. Her heart was racing, and she struggled to get her breathing under control. As she tried to hold onto the remnants of the dream, she gradually became aware of someone knocking at the door. Shaking off the last of the cobwebs that clouded her mind, she heard Mrs. Mitchell calling to her. Breakfast was ready, and her hostess wanted to know if she would be joining them.

"Thank you, Mrs. Mitchell. I'll be out shortly." Isaboe spoke through the closed door as she wiped the sleep from her eyes, trying to clear her head. But remnants of the dream still remained. She remembered looking up at beautiful willows. There were trees—warm, comforting hands—a longing—a need—confusion—*Lorien?* Though she tried to convince herself that this was only a suggestive thought brought on by what the pixies had said, there was the real possibility Lorien had actually been in her dream. She shuddered from the stifling chill that ran down her spine.

When Isaboe finally came out of her room, Mrs. Mitchell had already placed a large breakfast on the table. Her grey hair was rolled into a loose bun at the top of her head as she scurried around her kitchen in a dirty apron. Creamy oatmeal, eggs, blood sausage, flapjacks with syrup, and fried tatties left over from the previous night were all laid out for an early-morning meal.

"Sit." Mrs. Mitchell motioned to a chair. "Sit down and have some breakfast," she ordered before returning to her kitchen.

Isaboe sat. It would be rude to reject her host's hospitality, and though she wasn't hungry yet, she dished up a small portion—one egg, a piece of toast, and a slice of sausage.

"Are you not eating with us, Mrs. Mitchell?"

"Oh, no, dear, I already ate. You go ahead and enjoy your breakfast," the matron said with a smile. "I'm making some blood pudding for Mrs. Whitmore. She's been down in bed with a bad foot. I saw Jane Beaumont taking a dish over there yesterday and I want to find out the latest news. Leroy and Jane Beaumont own the general store and Clarence Langley's pig up and disappeared last week. He accused Leroy of stealing it, and he's making a big ruckus about it. Leroy admits taking the pig, but he said it was in exchange for all the merchandise Clarence took on credit and hadn't paid for. Most likely the man never would. Clarence might be a freeloader, but taking a man's livestock without his say is stepping over the line. Don't you think?" Mrs. Mitchell paused only long enough to take a breath.

"But the Beaumonts gave him plenty of time to pay up, and since they are the only store in town, there aren't too many folks willing to take sides with old man Langley. However, Della McCrumb told me yesterday that Clarence said Alma Jo Ramey has been having a fling with Leroy Beaumont, so things could get interesting."

Mrs. Mitchell continued her one-sided gossiping on the comings and goings of Waitsburgh as Isaboe watched Mr. Mitchell pour maple syrup over a plate full of food. Flapjacks lined the bottom, topped with two eggs, fried tatties, and sausage. Creamy oatmeal topped it all off and syrup covered the whole pile, filling the bottom of his plate. Picking up his fork and licking his lips in anticipation, the man dug in. Though she knew she was staring, it was hard to believe anyone would actually eat like that. But by the look on his face, he enjoyed every sloppy bite.

Trying to avoid eye contact with Mr. Mitchell, or his concoction, Isaboe took tiny bites of her own breakfast, pushing the food around her plate, while the lady of the house continued her banter…"and when I told that busy-body old hag to stay out of my affairs, well, you should have seen the look on her…" A knock on the front door stopped Mrs. Mitchell in mid-sentence, and she scurried across the room.

When the door opened, Isaboe was pleasantly surprised to see Connor standing in the frame. "Guten morgen," he said lightheartedly.

"Good morning to you, too," Mrs. Mitchell chuckled. "You must be

Mr. Grant. Welcome to our home." She stepped back to allow Connor through the door before closing it behind him.

"Please, call me Connor," he said, grasping Mrs. Mitchell's extended hand in greeting. When he saw Isaboe sitting at the table, Connor smiled. "Sorry if I interrupted yer breakfast."

"I was just finishing," Isaboe said as she eyed Connor—refreshed, clean, and recently shaven. His hair was washed and combed, his clothes free from stains, and he seemed almost relaxed. She wondered if the twins had anything to do with his improved attitude, then silently chastised herself for caring. "You look like you had a good night's rest."

"Aye, I did. And you?"

"Yes, thank you. How is your arm?"

"It's still a bit tender," he said, touching the sleeve of his shirt. "But Hilda did a fine job of stitching me up last night, though we did use a whole bottle o' whiskey," he snickered. "Some on the arm of course, which hurt like a bitch, but most of it Fredrick and I drank, to numb the pain, ye understand. I cannae speak for Fredrick, but I think I'm still a bit numb this morning."

"Yeah, Fredrick Gerhardt likes his drink, no doubt about that," Mrs. Mitchell chuckled. "Can I offer you a cup of tea, Mr. Grant…uh, I mean, Connor?"

"No, thanks, I've already had plenty. I just wanted to stop by and let Isaboe know we'll be leaving shortly." Connor turned toward her. "I'm on my way to the stable now. Can ye be ready to leave within the hour?"

"Yes, I'll be at the stable by then."

"Good. Then I'll say my goodbyes. It was a pleasure to meet you ma'am. Ye all've been very kind for feedin' us and puttin' us up for the night." Connor looked back at the table and nodded, "Mr. Mitchell." The bald man looked up over his prominent nose, but only nodded at Connor in return before resuming his meal. "I'll see ye ladies at the stable then," Connor said, shooting Isaboe a glance before walking out and closing the door.

Isaboe picked up her plate and carried it to the kitchen. "Thank you so much, Mrs. Mitchell, for everything."

"You're welcome, dear." The older woman stepped closer. "That

Connor Grant fellow, have you known him long?"

"Not really. Why do you ask?"

"He's sweet on you. You do know that, right?"

Isaboe tried to look shocked. "What makes you say so?"

"His face lit up as soon as he saw you, and I could see it in his eyes. Men don't get cleaned up like that for the road; they do it for a lady."

"I…I think you're mistaken, Mrs. Mitchell. Connor and I are just traveling together, for convenience. He's escorting Margaret and me to Edinburgh, and then we'll be going our separate ways."

Mrs. Mitchell stared at Isaboe as if trying to determine whether or not she believed her. "Well, that's too bad."

Connor set a quick pace out of Waitsburgh. The rains had held off for the last few days, but there was a storm brewing, and he was determined to outrun it. By mid-day, the trio had covered over ten miles, and the storm clouds had rolled off in the opposite direction.

After a quick lunch of jerky, fresh apples, and some of Mrs. Grayson's fruit bread, that she insisted Margaret take before leaving, Connor fell in line with his two charges on a slower trot across the countryside. The afternoon sun burned off what was left of the morning clouds, and the land opened up to rolling hills, allowing the travelers to ride comfortably abreast of one another.

"The stopover in Waitsburgh was a good idea, ladies," Connor said causally as he leaned forward, resting his arms on the saddle pommel. His body rocked easily in unison with his horse's gait, and Isaboe thought he looked almost too relaxed.

"Aye, it was. Especially for you, I suppose," Margaret said with a smirk. "So, tell us how your evenin' went with those twin blondies," she teased, "as if we didn't already know."

"Aye, I had a very interesting evening, to say the least." Connor sat up in his saddle and shot Margaret a quick grin. "After Hilda stitched me up, Fredrick pulled out his fiddle and played some ol' German tunes. He even sang a few songs, though I couldna understand a single word. But the best part was when the girls danced for us; put on a show, they did. That was fun." Connor's eyes twinkled and his smile grew. "They tried to teach me a jig, but even with one twin on each side, I couldna get my feet to move right. I spent more time just trying to keep from fallin' over, though that may have been from all the whiskey I drank." Looking more relaxed than they had ever seen him, Connor chuckled. "And Hilda is not just a damn good medic, but a cook too. She made something called *sauerbraten*, served up with potato dumplings."

"What's sauerbraten?" Margaret asked.

"Not sure, some kind of meat, but it was good."

"Sauerbraten means *sour roast*," Isaboe added, as she shifted over to ride on the other side of Margaret. "It's usually veal, marinated for a few days in wine vinegar, or so I'm told. I've never made it myself." She didn't bother to hide the slight edge of irritation she felt.

"Sour roast? That sounds terrible," Margaret said, furrowing her brow.

"It was actually quite tasty, and Hilda kept shoveling more onto my plate. One thing about the Gerhardts, they know how to make a fellow feel welcome!"

"Between the music, drinking, and a great meal, sounds like you had the best of the accommodations," Margaret jested.

"Don't forget the entertainment, Margaret," Isaboe said sharply. "He had dancing girls performing for him. Did they tuck you into bed as well, Connor?"

"*Isaboe!* Where'd that come from?" Margaret chided, regarding her friend curiously.

But Isaboe had no reply. She knew her words sounded spiteful, but his overly-enthusiastic description of the previous night's events rubbed her the wrong way. Jutting her chin a bit higher, she ignored both their questioning glares.

That was until Connor broke out in a mischievous chuckle. "If I didna know better, Isaboe, I'd say ye sound a wee bit jealous."

Turning to face him, Isaboe shot Connor a furrowed glare. "Jealous of what?"

"The fact that I spent the evening with two lovely young ladies, and ye dinnae like that, did ye?" Connor made no attempt to hide his pleasure over Isaboe's reaction.

"You don't know what you're talking about. I could care less who you spent your evening with!"

"That's not how it sounded," Margaret offered cautiously.

Isaboe swallowed her bitter jealousy, but not before snapping at Margaret. "It's just that, well, my entertainment last night was a silent, old bald man who kept glaring at me over his large, bulbous nose, and his gossiping wife who has no respect for other people's privacy!"

"Did you have a bed to sleep on? Were you provided food to put in your belly?" Margaret's tone turned chastising. "Just because you didn't have two pretty blondes dancing for you is no excuse to be ungrateful."

"I didn't say I was ungrateful!" Isaboe lashed out. "I just meant…oh, never mind!" she snarled before spurring her horse into a quicker pace and rode off ahead.

"Had I known ye wanted to kick up yer heels last night, Isaboe, I would've come and fetched ye!" Connor's words held a hint of mirth.

But Isaboe ignored his attempt at humor, and the ensuing chuckle from Margaret. "You were wrong, Mrs. Mitchell," she mumbled under her breath. Though Isaboe knew she was being petty, she also knew it was best if Connor kept his interests elsewhere. Silently, she rode ahead, keeping a comfortable distance in front of her riding companions, out of range for easy conversation until the trio stopped to make camp for the night.

CHAPTER 24

UNREQUITED LOVE

Isaboe hadn't said much to either of her traveling companions since they had stopped to set up camp and ate their evening meal. But as she poured hot water over the bowls Margaret had just wiped clean, the lack of conversation felt awkward in the close proximity. "That was a very good meal, Margaret."

"Thank you," Margaret said with a brief smile as she handed Isaboe the last bowl.

"The noodles in the soup were a nice surprise. Did you pick them up in Waitsburgh?"

"Mrs. Grayson gave 'em to me, along with some fresh vegetables and a loaf of her special bread. It was most fortunate that we happened to be passing through at harvest, and Mrs. Grayson had plenty to share. She wouldn't let me leave without filling my bag." Margaret picked up the cleaned bowls and packed them back in her saddlebag. "The woman has a pretty large garden and was most generous. I didn't see a Mr. Grayson around, but there must have been one, at some point in time." Margaret walked over to the fire, and using the folds of her skirt, she lifted the hot metal pot that had been heating on the coals. "She also made us this tea this morning, wouldn't let me leave without taking two jarfuls," Margaret said, pouring the hot liquid into a cup before taking a seat.

Wrapped in her shawl, Isaboe sat down near the fire as Margaret continued her report. "She told me all about a son she doesn't see often, and blames that on his wife—called her daughter-in-law a strumpet, she did." Margaret chuckled. "Said she's manipulative and a bit maddy, but her son doesn't see it. Apparently, Waitsburgh wasn't enough for his young bride, so they moved away. The older Mrs. Grayson wasn't fond of that idea and had words with the new Mrs. Grayson, which apparently didn't go over well with her son."

Though she listened to Margaret's banter, Isaboe found it difficult to stay interested, and soon turned her attention to where Connor attended the horses—*as usual*, she thought. From her vantage point, the firelight cast him in partial shadows of the horses he stood behind. As he tucked his hair behind his ear, the light flickered off his face, revealing the moisture across his brow from his efforts. With his sleeves rolled up, she could see his arm muscles flex as he stroked the brush down the horse's side in fluid movements. She watched closely how his whole body moved, all the way down, but then it suddenly felt wrong. *A woman in mourning shouldn't be looking, or having such thoughts*, she admonished herself. But that didn't stop her.

After her mental chastising, Isaboe realized that Margaret was still talking, but she hadn't been listening. Pulling her shawl tighter around her shoulders, she stood. "I think I'll stretch my legs and go for a walk."

"It's dark, Isaboe. Don't go wandering off," Margaret scolded.

"I won't go far."

"Don't make me come look for you, young lady."

"Alright, Margaret, you don't have to mother me," Isaboe said over her shoulder. As she walked toward Connor and the horses, she heard Margaret grumbling something about *attitude*. But, at that moment, Isaboe didn't care.

Making her steps light and deliberate, Isaboe rounded the horses slowly, so as not to startle them, or so she told herself. When her eyes adjusted to the lack of light, she saw Connor standing next to her horse with his back to her. Bent slightly forward, he was checking out its hoof, cradling the animal's foot against his thigh while he looked it over. Connor's broad shoulders fit perfectly atop the curve of his spine that rolled nicely down toward his hips—tight and defined. Once again, Isaboe caught herself looking at him in a way she considered inappropriate, and she immediately felt uncomfortable. "Hmm…excuse me," she finally said to draw his attention. "Is there something wrong with my horse's foot?"

Connor looked over his shoulder and smiled. Dropping the horse's leg, he stood and faced her. "No, I was just checking for lodged stones, cracks in the nail bed, that sort of thing. But the horses all look good, especially after what they've been through."

"I'm sure it's because you take such good care of them." Suddenly feeling out of her element, Isaboe smiled, but offered nothing else.

Connor dropped the brush and picked up a damp cloth. "I thought ye had turned in for the night," he said wiping his hands.

"Not sleepy yet, so I thought I'd go for a walk." Feeling a bit less awkward, Isaboe stepped closer and watched Connor return his supplies to the saddlebag.

"Maybe that has something to do with the full moon," Connor said playfully. Brushing his hands through his hair, he took a step toward Isaboe. "I've heard it said that the devil is at play during the light of a full moon."

"Oh, is that so?" Isaboe matched his playful tone. Walking over to find an unobstructed view, she turned her face up toward the night sky. It was filled with a moon so big and bright that the stars were dimmed by its brilliance. "Isn't it beautiful?" she whispered, feeling the intensity of Connor's presence as he came to stand next to her.

"Aye, it is." His reply was low and sultry.

When she met Connor's blue eyes, soft and alluring in the moonlight, Isaboe took a step backward. "I've also heard that you can't tell a lie under the light of a full moon."

"Oh, really?" Connor couldn't hold back his grin. "And what happens if ye do?"

Dropping her gaze, Isaboe mumbled. "Uh…from what I remember, if you tell a lie under the light of a full moon, all of your children will be born covered in warts." Trying to cover her reaction to his closeness, she took a few steps toward a nearby path that was lit by moonlight.

"That's a terrible fate—having to bear the punishment of yer parent's lies," Connor made a phony scowl as he quickly stepped in line next to her. "So, if I were to ask ye a question, ye havta tell me the truth, for the sake of yer future children, aye?"

"That depends on what you're going to ask me," she said, lifting her chin defiantly. "And perhaps, you should answer my question first."

"Ask away." Connor opened his arms. "I've got nothin' to hide."

"Fine. What is it you are really looking for? And don't tell me that same noble story about honoring a promise made to a dead man. What is it you *really* want, Connor Grant?"

Taking a step closer, he looked down at her. A sly smile grew on his lips as Connor's eyes danced playfully with hers. "If I tell ye what I really want, ye'd probably slap me across the face."

Though Isaboe should have expected his answer, that didn't stop the look that must have crossed her face, and a larger grin filled Connor's. Trying to avoid his hungry eyes, she took a few steps backward, then turned and continued walking. "That's not what I meant. I'm more interested in what you're looking to find, what you want to accomplish." Isaboe felt a blush rise to her cheeks, but kept her composure.

"I already told ye, and there's nothing new to tell," Connor said as he caught up with her. "Now it's yer turn to answer my question. Yer story of a lost brother and sister ain't so believable either. Who are ye really looking for in Edinburgh?"

"I beg your pardon?" Isaboe stopped and shot him a questioning look. "Are you accusing me of lying?"

Connor casually clasped both of her hands in his. "No, ye're standing under the light of a full moon, so ye wouldna take that chance. But I do think it's not so much who ye're looking for as much as what ye're running from. Am I right?"

As he stood directly in front of her holding her hands and looking down into her eyes for an answer, Isaboe felt that Connor could see right through her. "What do you mean? You don't know anything about me." Suddenly feeling transparent and vulnerable, she tried to walk away, but he clutched her hands tighter, turning her back to face him.

"There are times, Isaboe, I can see the fear in yer eyes. I ken there's something that frightens ye." Closing the distance between them, Connor brought her hands into his chest and stared down at her, holding her gaze. "I just want ye to know that I'm here for ye. Ye can talk to me."

Her words caught in her throat, and Isaboe couldn't speak or tear her gaze away from his penetrating blue eyes. An evening song provided by the crickets filled the air, adding to the nocturnal ambiance and competing with the sound of her heartbeat. A cool breeze gently tossed her hair as the moonlight washed everything around them in a soft luminance. But the coolness of the night did nothing to ease the heat Isaboe felt spreading across her face.

"Isaboe, I know that ye're still in mourning, I understand that, I do." Placing his hands on the sides of her face, Connor took a deep breath before continuing. "And I ken I have nothing to offer except myself. But I could take care of ye, Isaboe. I promise I'll never let anything hurt ye."

The touch of his hands felt cool against her face, and Isaboe's breath caught in her throat seeing the honesty of his promise in his eyes. She wanted to tell him what was in her heart, but she couldn't speak the words. When he softly brushed his thumb against her lips, it sent a shiver down her spine. "Yer skin is so soft." He caressed her cheek and then touched the back of her neck, lifting her face to his. "Ye're the prettiest thing I've ever laid eyes on," Connor whispered the moment before his lips found hers.

All the passion and desire they'd been holding back, all the sexual tension they had tried to ignore, came flooding out. As Isaboe sank into his arms, feelings, both complicated and frightening, were poured feverishly into the kiss. It wasn't perfect; Connor kissed with more enthusiasm than skill. But it was honest and wanton, and for that, she lost herself in his arms. When her lips were coaxed apart and she felt the first brush of his tongue against hers, seeking even more intimacy, Isaboe's panic spiked. Following her heart had led to this moment, but when she thought about what a mess her life was, she knew that bringing him into it wasn't an option.

Though her heart was pounding in her chest, she reluctantly drew away and out of his embrace. Standing in front of him gasping for air, Isaboe could still feel the touch of Connor's lips on hers. As he stared at her in dismay, she covered her mouth, struggling to find her voice. When she did finally manage to speak, the words that came out were stuttered and half-whispered. It wasn't what Connor wanted to hear, but they were the words she had to say.

"Connor, I...I'm sorry, I can't do this. I just can't. I'm so sorry." With that, she turned and ran back up the path toward the campfire, leaving Connor standing alone, confusion written darkly across his face.

CHAPTER 25

THE NIGHT OF THE WOLF

A cloudbank had rolled in during the night, and the morning began under a dismal, grey sky. Isaboe woke with a heart so heavy it felt like she was wearing the low-hanging cloud as a blanket.

Connor kept his distance preparing the horses and had not spoken to Isaboe since she arose. Trying to stay busy repacking the clothes in her bag, she made no attempt to speak to him either. Her heart ached, but she had no words to make it right—best not to say anything at all.

"Did I miss something here?" Margaret finally asked. "When I crawled into my bedroll last night, everything seemed fine. Now it's very apparent that something happened. The tension in the air is rather thick this morning. Did you two have words last night?"

Neither of them acknowledged her question.

"Nothing? Nobody has anything to say?" With her hands on her hips, Margaret glanced first at Connor, then at Isaboe. "Well, this ought to be a lovely ride today," she mumbled.

Once on the road, Connor spoke to the women only when necessary. Determined to make good time to Edinburgh, he pushed them at a steady pace. Except for the few times he took the horses down to the river to give them a break, he kept the trio moving steadily with little conversation.

Though it was painful to see that he wanted to be done with her as soon as possible, Isaboe didn't blame him. She knew it had gone too far. While she suspected they ultimately wanted the same thing, her life was too confusing to add him to it. How could she possibly expect him, or anyone, to understand what she was going through—or what she'd already been through—not to mention the uncertainty of her future? Just trying to understand it herself was more than she could manage on most days. Bringing Connor into the chaos of what was left of her life was simply not an option, at least not to Isaboe's mind. As much as it tore at her heart to know how he now felt about her, logic told her that she had done the right thing.

By the time the three riders stopped to make camp, it was nearly dusk. The clouds had not lifted all day, and the threat of rain hung in the air. About half a mile from the river, they came across a small grove of trees, mostly cypress and a few evergreens. Though it wasn't near the river, they hoped that camping among the trees would provide some protection from the rain, as well as dry wood to build a decent campfire.

As was his usual routine, Connor gathered the wood and built the campfire before making himself scarce to attend the horses. This gave the two women a chance to be alone, and Margaret took advantage of the opportunity. "So, are you ready to tell me what's going on between you and Connor? The tension between the two of you is as thick as a mud bog in spring. What happened?"

"He kissed me, and I…I didn't handle it well. But it's all for the best. There's nothing going on between Connor and me." Isaboe wasn't sure if she said that to reassure herself or to convince Margaret.

"Well, maybe that's the problem, aye?"

Fighting tears all day, Isaboe could now feel them welling up in her eyes, burning at her nose. "Margaret, I don't know what to say to him. I know I let it go too far. I let him think that I…I don't know what to do." The tears finally broke through as she ran her hands through her hair in utter frustration.

"Can you explain to me why you're pushing him away? It's obvious the two of you have feelings for each other, so why are you doing this?"

Isaboe looked at Margaret as if she didn't understand the question. "Why would you ask me that? You know why. There is no way I can be involved with him now. If anyone should know that, it's you."

"No Isaboe, I don't. Do you love him? Ask yourself that question, because he's in love with you. Connor's a good man who could take care of you. So, no, I don't understand why you're rejecting him. Look lass, the way he's pushing us, we'll be in Edinburgh by tomorrow. Is this how you wanna part ways, knowing you may never see him again? You've gotta go talk to him."

"And tell him what? How do I begin to tell him what a *bloody* mess my life is? I don't understand what's happened to me, or what I'm up against. I've lost twenty years of my life and have no idea why. I'm with child, and I'm not sure who the father is. How could I possibly explain any of this to him when I don't even understand it myself? How do I tell him that it isn't my brother and sister I am going to Edinburgh to look for, it's really my grown children—who think I'm dead! What man in his right mind wouldn't go running from that? You tell me, Margaret. Please tell me how I can be with him, because I don't see how it's possible!" As she buried her face in her hands, Isaboe let the tears flow.

"Listen to me." Margaret took hold of her friend's hands, making her look up. "I didn't say it was gonna be easy, but he isn't gonna turn his back on you if you tell him the truth. You might not want to give it to him all at once, but give it a chance. All of those reasons you just gave for not being with him are the exact same reasons why you *need* to be with him. Have you given any thought about how Benjamin and Anna will react if you suddenly show up twenty years after your death? How would you explain where you've been, why you haven't aged? Have you thought about them at all? Maybe the purpose of this trip wasn't to find your old life, but to start a new one. Maybe Connor is the one who can help you do that. You have someone who loves you, lass, and you need that right now. Think about it Isaboe; you are with child. Are you gonna travel all around the country alone with a baby, looking for the ghosts of a past life? What kind of life is that for a child?"

Isaboe only stared at Margaret, not believing what she had just heard. "*Ghosts of a past life!?* Those are my children you're referring to!" She suddenly had a chilling thought, a realization that amplified her anger. "You never thought we could really find them, did you? This whole idea of going to Edinburgh to look for them was all just a ploy—the only way you knew how to bring me back from the edge of insanity—wasn't it? You *used* my children, even though you knew there was no chance of finding them, didn't you Margaret?"

"Isaboe, don't do this. You know I only want what's best for you."

Her lips drawn into a thin line, Isaboe glared at Margaret with furious green eyes. "Margaret, why don't you just go back to New Faireshire? Go back to your life. At least you have one!" The words came out purposely vile as Isaboe turned her back on her friend and stormed off.

"Isaboe, you don't mean that. You're just upset!" Margaret called out, but Isaboe didn't reply as she disappeared into the night, seeking solace in the trees.

When Connor came back to the fire, he found Margaret pacing alone, noticeably upset. Looking around for Isaboe, but not seeing her, he asked where she was.

"She's out there, somewhere." Margaret nodded toward the darkness of the trees. "You need to go after her Connor. She's upset, and I can't talk to her right now."

"What happened? Ye look upset yerself."

"We had words. Please, Connor, just go find her."

Feeling that he didn't have much of a choice, Connor headed off in the direction Margaret had pointed. Though the night was thick with clouds, blocking any light from the moon, he relied on his other senses, and it didn't take long to find her.

With her knees pulled up, her face buried in her arms, Isaboe sat at the base of a tree, sobbing. Connor reached out and touched her arm, but she didn't stir. He wondered if she even wanted him there—likely not. On some level, he knew he had reacted badly to her rejection, though he didn't understand it, especially after the kiss had been so promising. After all he had experienced in life, a little rejection shouldn't have been as earth-shattering as Isaboe's refusal had felt. And yet, it had.

Though the sight and sound of her grief touched him deeply, Connor continued cautiously, speaking her name softly.

Isaboe looked up, and though her tears were flowing hard, she finally found her voice. "Connor...I'm so sorry," she said between sobs.

Kneeling down next to her, Connor took her hands in his. "Talk to me, Isaboe, what's wrong?"

"Last night…I'm sorry about…what happened."

"What about last night are ye sorry for?" Connor's question was guarded. He wasn't sure if she was apologizing for the kiss, or for breaking his heart afterward.

"I'm sorry…for leaving you like that. It was wrong, and I…I don't want you to hate me!" Burying her face in Connor's shoulder, Isaboe threw her arms around his neck.

He held her like that for a long moment, letting her cry before drawing back. "Isaboe, I dinnae hate ye. I could never hate ye. Can ye tell me why ye're so upset? What happened between ye and Margaret?"

Taking a few deep breaths, Isaboe began to calm down. Though the tears were still flowing, she wasn't crying as intensely. "Margaret made me see some things I didn't want to, things I didn't want to face. We said….*I* said something to her I shouldn't have. I don't even know how to tell you how complicated my life is right now. I just know that I need you."

"What are ye trying to say, Isaboe? Just because ye need me ain't good enough. Ye'll havta give me more than that. Tomorrow we'll be in Edinburgh, and our paths will take two different directions unless ye can give me a reason why they shouldn't." Though her eyes were filled with tears, Connor searched them for an answer. "Yer life is not the only one that's complicated, Isaboe. I dinnae ken what my future holds either, or what I can offer except myself. But unless ye can say that ye love me, we'll be going our separate ways."

As Isaboe looked into his eyes, he could see her anguish. "It's not that easy, Connor. I'm afraid that if I tell you about myself, you'll realize…I'm not worth it!"

Connor reached up to wipe away the tears that were now running freely down her face. "There's nothing ye can say that would make me want ye less than I do right now." He knew he was leaving his heart open, but he couldn't help himself. As they sat together in the dark, Connor could feel Isaboe's vulnerability; she was opening herself up as well. He could trust her in this. He wanted to trust her.

When a scream suddenly erupted through the trees, Connor and Isaboe were on their feet instantly, running back to the fire. As soon as they reached the firelight, what they saw brought them to an abrupt halt. Standing with her back to the fire, Margaret was holding a piece of burning wood, waving it frantically in the face of a snarling, black wolf. Connor reached for Isaboe, pushing her behind him. Baring its fangs, the growling creature cautiously stepped forward, its reflective eyes glowing yellow from the light of the fire. With a look of pure panic on her face, Margaret shuffled backwards waving the burning stick at the wolf. Keeping a safe distance from the fire, the animal stalked its prey, looking for the right opportunity to attack.

Connor bolted toward where the wide-eyed horses danced nervously, tugging at their ties. He retrieved the pistol and sword from his saddle, and as promised, this time the pistol was loaded. But before he could turn, the wolf leapt at Margaret, knocking her to the ground.

Both women screamed as the animal's teeth tore at Margaret's clothing and ripped viciously at her flesh. Returning to the fire just as the beast finished its attack, Connor raised his pistol and fired his shot as the wolf fled into the trees. Then, holding his fighting stance, his sword at the ready, he scanned the darkness.

Isaboe ran past him to where Margaret lay curled up on the ground, whimpering and trembling. Her forearms were badly gashed and bleeding heavily from protecting her face during the attack. Long, deep wounds ran the length of her right arm, and blood soaked her clothing, dripping steadily onto the ground. There was so much blood that Connor feared something vital had been severed.

When Margaret's body stiffened from the shock and her jaw went slack, Isaboe wailed, "Oh my God!"

"Isaboe, look at me!" Connor grabbed hold of her arms, forcing her to focus on what now had to be done. "Go get those bandages and whatever clothes ye can find to rip into strips. We gotta stop the bleeding!" As Margaret moaned in pain, Connor propped her up to lean against him. "And grab the bottle o' whiskey from my saddle bag!"

After wiping enough blood away so the jagged gashes on Margaret's arm were exposed, Connor's practiced fingers dabbed and poured alcohol over the wounds. As Margaret's screams filled the night, he and Isaboe set to wrapping her arm.

"Connor, we have to get her to a doctor right away. She's going into shock."

"I know, but we cannae ride out tonight. We'll havta wait till daylight."

"We can't wait til morning," Isaboe sobbed. "She's losing too much blood."

"We dinnae have a choice. With no moonlight to see our way, there's no point in taking that chance." Connor knew if they set out in the dark, they could find themselves lost within an hour, and Margaret would be dead before morning.

Keeping a watchful eye on the perimeter of their campsite, Connor took the opportunity to enlarge the fire, and also to reload his pistol.

Isaboe walked over to where he stood looking out into the darkness. "Do you think it'll come back?"

"I dinnae think so, but I plan on staying awake tonight, just to be sure."

"I didn't know there were wolves around here. Why do you think it attacked Margaret, especially around a fire?" The fear in Isaboe's voice was clear.

"I dinnae ken, unless...unless it was rabid, then they're unpredictable and unafraid. They'll go after anything."

Connor heard Isaboe's breath catch when he said the word *rabid*. Apparently, she also knew that if the wolf in fact had rabies, there was a very good chance Margaret would not survive.

CHAPTER 26

EDINBURGH

Margaret slept little that night, and Isaboe was awakened more than once by her gasping sobs. When Margaret did occasionally slip into a restless slumber, she would wake up screaming, swinging at an invisible attacker. Isaboe did her best to keep her friend calm. Though the bleeding had turned sluggish, and then finally stopped, she was afraid the thrashing would bring it on again.

At the first hint of daylight, the horses were saddled, packed, and ready to ride. Hot with fever and dripping sweat, Margaret screamed as Connor lifted her onto his horse, sitting her in front of him for support. The rain had held off during the night, but a cool drizzle was now falling, and the horizon was obscured by dark, heavy rainclouds. Though it would be a difficult and jarring ride, they had to cover a lot of ground quickly, so Connor pushed them hard and fast throughout the morning.

After three hours of hard riding, Connor knew he had to give the horses a rest, and that Margaret needed a break. She'd been slipping in and out of consciousness during the ride, and when Connor lifted her down, he noticed that the bandage on her arm was again soaked with blood.

Sitting on the bank near the river with Margaret's head in her lap, Isaboe tried to cool the fever with a damp rag on her forehead. "She's burning up and bleeding badly. I don't know how much more of this she can take." Her voice was hushed as she looked up at Connor.

"I know, but what options do we have? Edinburgh is at least another half-day's ride, even at this pace."

Isaboe had no response. Shortly after they set off again, the early-morning drizzle turned into outright rain, which continued throughout the afternoon. After nearly four more hours of hard riding, they finally came across a small farmhouse. White smoke billowed from the chimney, and it stood out like a beacon against the dark, rain-filled sky. A large barn dwarfed the house, and the fenced pasture held a number of grazing cattle, seemingly unaffected by the dismal weather. Isaboe dismounted and rushed to meet the man of the house, who stood in a defensive posture on his porch holding a pistol. After she explained their situation, the man set the pistol on a chair and rushed over to help Margaret off the horse. Minutes later, they were all inside, drying off in front of a warm, welcoming fire.

James McDonald sent his children out into the rain to gather more wood from the shed, while his wife Alma, bustled about the house, boiling water and shredding an old shirt into fresh bandages. As Alma helped Isaboe rewrap Margaret's arm, James led Connor outside to prepare a fresh team of horses for the family's covered carriage.

After having a quick bite to eat, they were off again. James drove the carriage and Connor rode his horse alongside, with the other two horses in tow. Though it was slower going than on horseback, at least it was less jarring. Inside the carriage, Margaret drifted in and out of a fevered sleep, her head on Isaboe's lap as they rode toward the nearest village, Firth.

Fortunately, the ferry at Firth was operative. After making a smooth crossing, they made good time the rest of the way into Edinburgh. They had traveled long and hard, but by the time they reached the outskirts of the city, dusk had fallen. After passing several buildings, they found the first sign of a doctor. Hanging above the entry door of a small office on the corner of a large, brick building was a weathered, wooden sign that read Doctor Edward T. Murray.

A sturdy little man, Dr. Murray was just preparing to close his office for the day when Connor and James bolted through the front door, water dripping from their clothing. As soon as they brought Margaret in and laid her on the bed, the doctor set to cleaning her angry, oozing wounds. It was excruciating, and Margaret gasped and screamed as he worked.

Connor took Isaboe outside to avoid hearing Margaret's pain and to thank James McDonald before he returned home. After they had offered

James grateful handshakes and safe travels, the door to Dr. Murray's office opened, and he signaled for them to come back in.

"I've given Margaret opium for the pain and to help her relax." With deep concern showing on his face, he spoke to them in hushed tones. "The wound on her right arm is severe. Did you say a *wolf* attacked her? Are you sure it wasn't a mad dog? There hasn't been a wolf seen in these Highlands for years. I was sure they'd all been run out or killed off."

"Pretty sure of what I saw, Doc. It was a wolf—a big black one. Apparently they're still around."

"Regardless, the wound is infected and she's burning up with fever. It might be best to amputate the arm so it doesn't take her life."

"No!" Isaboe cried out. "You can't amputate her arm. There has to be another way. Please!"

"Isaboe, Dr. Murray might be right. I've seen wounds like this fester and rot the life out of a man, and it's not a pleasant way to die."

"Margaret is not going to die!" Isaboe shouted fiercely as she faced Connor and Dr. Murray. "And you're not cutting off her arm! Please, please, you have to help her!"

"She should sleep from the sedative, and that will help," the doctor said with a sympathetic smile as he placed a hand on Isaboe's shoulder. "We'll see how she is in the morning before any decisions are made."

Isaboe only nodded, but she knew she would never stop fighting for Margaret, and for Margaret's arm.

"I'm retiring for the evening, but I live upstairs," Dr. Murray said, as he finished cleaning up. "There's a bed in that room over there. Well, a cot, actually, but you're welcome to it." He nodded toward a room adjacent to his office. "If her condition worsens tonight, feel free to come fetch me."

"Thank you so much," Isaboe said as the doctor walked up the stairs, leaving her alone with Connor, and no sense of what to do now. The day had been a wild race to get Margaret medical attention, but the rush of adrenaline was starting to wear off. Taking a seat at Margaret's bedside, she gently wiped the cool, wet cloth over the brow of her unconscious friend. Though Margaret had responded to the opium, and appeared to be in less pain, she still moaned and whimpered in her restless sleep.

Leaning against the office wall, Connor yawned as he rubbed his eyes.

"Connor, you should get some sleep before you fall over where you stand."

"It's been a long couple o' days, and I am tired. But ye must be tired too. I'll sit with her. Go get some sleep."

"I'm alright. I'm going to stay here with her."

Connor started to protest, but Isaboe crossed her arms in defiance. Wisely, he decided he was too tired to argue and simply nodded before walking into the other room.

Sitting alone in the dark with her friend, Isaboe began her vigil, listening to the clock on the desk slowly ticking away the seconds. The last words she'd spoken to Margaret replayed over and over in her mind, feeding her guilt. Isaboe prayed she would still have the opportunity to express how sorry she was. But Margaret looked so fragile, so unlike the strong woman she had been just one day earlier. She had set her life aside to help Isaboe find her way back, and had become her rock, her only consistency. Selfishly, Isaboe now couldn't imagine living without Margaret.

A lone tear ran down Isaboe's cheek as she took her friend's unbandaged hand in hers. "I'm so sorry, Margaret. Please forgive me. Please come back," she whispered through her tears, hoping her words might reach her unconscious friend.

Awakened by the painful cramping in her back, Isaboe jolted upright. Margaret was still hot and feverish, but at least she seemed to be resting easier. As she stretched and rubbed her backside, Isaboe looked at the clock sitting on the desk next to the lantern—12:15. It had only been thirty minutes since the last time she'd looked. She, too, was in need of some real sleep, and could feel the lack of it.

While trying to rub the cramp out of her neck, Isaboe walked over to the adjacent room. Leaning against the door frame, she watched Connor sleeping. He had fallen onto the cot still in his shirt and pants. His boots, tunic, and satchel lay about him in scattered heaps. He looked like he'd passed out as soon as he laid his head down, and she smiled—glad to see that at least he was getting some well-deserved rest. Yawning deeply, she turned to resume her station beside Margaret, but stopped when she heard Connor quietly call her name. He was propped up on one elbow, rubbing his hand across his face. "Is everything alright?" he asked, his voice rough with sleep.

"Yes. I'm sorry. I didn't mean to wake you."

"No, it's alright. How's Margaret?"

"She seems to be resting now."

"Have ye gotten any sleep?"

"I've shut my eyes for a few minutes, but no, not really."

Connor scooted back on the cot and patted the empty space in front of him. "We'll hear her if she wakes. Ye need some sleep too."

Uncertain of his offer, Isaboe took a quick glance at Margaret, but then shook her head. "No, no thank you."

"I promise to behave myself," he whispered, as if he could read her mind. "We both need the sleep."

Not really wanting to go back to the chair, Isaboe finally gave in, and lay down with her back up against his chest. Dropping his arm around her waist, Connor pulled her in tight, closing the space between them, and Isaboe didn't resist. He was warm, and their bodies fit together—almost too perfectly, she thought—but she was too tired to think. As the tension gradually loosened its grip, she didn't resist as he snuggled his face into the nape of her neck. Within seconds, the sound of his breathing gently lulled her into sleep.

CHAPTER 27

MISSED OPPORTUNITY

When Isaboe woke to the sunlight shining on her face, Connor was gone. Dread filled her chest as she jolted from the cot and stepped out into the office. A woman was sitting at the desk, and Margaret still lay sleeping on the bed, but no one else was around.

She walked over to touch Margaret's forehead, still hot with fever as the woman at the desk looked up. "Good Morning. I'm Miss Pritchard, Doctor Murray's nurse," she said, meeting Isaboe at Margaret's bedside. "You all must have had a rough night, I'd say." The nurse placed another cool, wet cloth on Margaret's forehead.

"Yes, it's been a difficult few days. Do you know where Connor is?" Isaboe asked anxiously.

"Oh, you mean Mr. Grant? He and Doctor Murray are out right now. He gave me strict instructions not to disturb you. I hope I didn't wake you?"

Isaboe let out a sigh of relief; he hadn't left her. She smiled back at Miss Pritchard. "No, you didn't wake me." Running her hands through her hair, she looked down at her crumpled riding clothes and realized what a sight she must be. "Is there some place where I can wash up? Maybe get a spot of tea, or a cup of coffee?"

"Oh, aye, you can wash up in here," the nurse said as she led Isaboe to the wash room. "I just put out some clean towels next to the wash basin, and there's hot water on the stove. When you're ready, there's a pot of coffee there too, or I can make you a fresh cup of tea, if you'd prefer. And please, help yourself to a muffin. I picked them up at the bakery on the way in this morning, so they're still fresh." The nurse gave a reassuring smile before returning to her duties.

Clutching her bag and the kettle of hot water off the wood-burning stove, Isaboe disappeared into the wash room and closed the door behind her. Her clothing options were limited, but she found the dark green dress she had worn in Inverness, and was grateful that she had taken the time to mend the tear, courtesy of Lieutenant Blackwood. After she tied the white, lace ribbon at her bodice, Isaboe turned her attention to her unruly hair. Brushing it smooth, she tied it back with a ribbon at the nape of her neck.

Feeling somewhat refreshed, she walked over to the stove and poured herself a cup of coffee. When the front door opened, she saw Connor step through the door frame, his hair and cloak damp from the early morning mist, and his cheeks flushed from the cold air. Though the nurse had said he hadn't left, it wasn't until she actually saw him that Isaboe took a breath of relief.

Connor paused at the door, cupping his hands to his mouth as he caught Isaboe's eyes. He blew into in his hands and rubbed them briskly, never taking his eyes from hers. "It's cold out there! Got any more o' that coffee?" he asked, finally breaking the silence.

"Yes, and it's good and hot."

As Connor walked across the room, Isaboe turned to pour another cup. "Ye look quite lovely this morning," he said softly over her shoulder.

Isaboe felt the heat rise to her cheeks as Connor's eyes examined her closely. When she handed him the cup, though he was standing a bit too close for comfort, she held her ground and smiled up at him. "Thank you."

"I trust ye slept well," he said, giving her a look that brought the blush back to her cheeks.

"Yes, I did. Thank you for that as well."

"Oh, it was entirely my pleasure." Holding her gaze as he sipped his coffee, Connor grinned boyishly, but the moment was short lived. Reality came crashing down around them when they heard Margaret whimpering in the other room. As Miss Pritchard rushed over to assist the patient, Connor motioned for Isaboe to follow him toward a waiting room at the far corner of the building.

Two large windows looked out onto the busy street where they could see residents of Edinburgh bustling about their business. Below the windows, chairs lined the wall, and a table sat to one side. Other than the two of them, the room was empty.

"The doc and I had a discussion this morning," Connor said. "I asked him if he knew of any way to save Margaret's arm."

"And what did he say?"

"He asked around and was told of a new healing method that works without amputation, apparently with good results."

"Does he think it will work?" Isaboe asked, feeling a faint touch of optimism.

"Aye, he's gonna try. He's out gathering supplies now. We'll just have to wait and see." As Connor stepped forward, his face softened, "Isaboe, ye need to be prepared that Margaret may still lose her arm. But better her arm then her life, aye?"

Isaboe's gaze dropped to the floor, and she only nodded. Walking over to the window, Connor placed his boot on a chair and sipped his coffee as he watched the people on the street going about their lives. Isaboe stood a few feet away, also looking out at the humanity racing by, wondering how her life had deviated so far from the norm.

"I found an inn not far from here," Connor said. "It's clean and there are plenty of vacancies, so the two of ye will be close to Doc Murray, and he can tend to her more easily."

"Good," Isaboe said, noticing that he didn't say *we*. She also noticed that Connor seemed distracted, as if his thoughts were elsewhere. Something was bothering him, and her chest suddenly felt tight and restricted. Knowing that she couldn't look directly at him, Isaboe placed her cup down and looked out the window before saying, "You're leaving, aren't you?"

Connor didn't answer immediately, but finally she heard him say it. "Aye, I'll be leaving soon for Lochmund Hills. Margaret will get good care here in the city. It's too early to tell if she's contracted…" he cut himself off, "but she's in good hands."

Isaboe didn't move. She stared at the people walking by, but didn't see any of them. Holding her hands clasped behind her back to keep them from shaking, it took a couple of moments before she was able to speak again. "Are you coming back?" She was not proud of how her words wavered, and she bit her lip to hold herself together.

"I dinnae ken. Is there somethin' for me to come back for?"

When she finally turned toward Connor, Isaboe saw that he was watching her closely, and she walked over to stand directly in front of him. A strand of wet hair hung down just above his brow, and she brushed it back from his face before meeting his blue eyes, searching hers for an answer. "Is my love for you enough to bring you back?" she whispered.

Putting his coffee down, Connor cupped Isaboe's face in his hands and looked into the depths of her eyes. "That's all I needed to hear," he said, just before his mouth found hers. Reaching around her waist, he pulled her into his arms. Held so close, Isaboe clung to him with all the passion and desire she dare let herself feel. His lips were strong and warm, and though she felt the need and hunger in his kiss, she could also feel his tenderness, his love for her.

The sound of a woman clearing her throat drew their attention. Standing at the door, they saw Miss Pritchard, looking apologetic. "I'm sorry to interrupt, but Doctor Murray has returned. I thought you'd like to know."

As he hung his cloak on the coat rack, Doctor Murray said, "You must understand that the rain and the rough ride did her poorly. I'm certain she has an infection, but even if we try bleeding her, that still might not cleanse her of it. Fortunately, this city has the best medical professionals you will find in Scotland, and there are new advances being discovered every year." The doctor clasped and unclasped his hands as he spoke. "I'm going to be trying a new method to draw out the infection; a poultice of goat's milk and yeasty bread. It may save her arm, and her life. I'll be keeping Margaret here for most of the day so I can check on how the wound is responding. But all the same, be prepared that it could be some time before she shows any sign of recovery."

But it was what he didn't say that bothered Isaboe. She knew Margaret was in a bad way, and the possibility she might not survive was very real.

"Let's go have a bite to eat," Connor said. "Margaret's in good hands now." Finally convincing Isaboe to leave her friend's side, they had a quick breakfast before Connor dropped her at the inn and went to the stable to check on the horses.

The second-story room was small but comfortable, and Isaboe could look from the window down onto the street below. As she watched the activity of the city, she reflected on the insanity of her life, and how she had dragged Margaret into it as well. It was all like a bad dream she couldn't wake up from. Even though she had experienced it all first hand, she still had difficulty comprehending it. Now, making it worse, her best friend was lying in a doctor's office fighting for her life. The only thing that gave Isaboe a sense of hope, any chance of bringing her life back into some sort of normalcy, was Connor. And now he was leaving.

As if thinking about him somehow made him appear, Isaboe's attention was drawn by a knock at the door. Connor smiled broadly as he entered, and she returned the greeting. After closing the door behind him, he walked around the room inspecting the accommodations. "It's a wee bit small, but it's close to Doc Murray. Looks comfortable enough, and at least there's a bed," he said glancing at the bed with a sly smile.

Isaboe didn't miss his implication. "Do you know how long you'll be gone?" she asked, attempting to change his focus.

"I dinnae ken. It could be a couple of days, or as long as a week. I'm just not sure," he said as he took a small dirk from his boot and placed it on a table next to the window. He also placed a small bag of coins in the drawer of the same table. "I shouldn't need this while I'm gone. It's all I got, so dinnae spend it all at once," Connor said with a half-grin before an uncomfortable silence filled the room.

Turning away, Isaboe faced her reflection in the mirror above the dressing table. On her face, she saw a slew of emotions, and her desire for Connor only complicated matters. She felt everything at once: confusion, uncertainty, passion. It was all too much.

Connor apparently did not have the same reservations about what he wanted. Within two steps he was standing directly behind her. As they locked gazes in the mirror, Connor reached up and pulled the ribbon holding her hair. Isaboe felt a shiver run down her spine as his fingers traced the outline of her collarbone and up behind her ear, and then dipping to gently touch her hair. The tingling sensation from the wake of his touch left her skin covered with goosebumps.

As Connor gently kissed down the side of her neck, Isaboe felt her desire winning the battle. Easing the dress off her shoulder so he could kiss more of her skin, his other arm slid around her waist. As he pressed in closer, his heat and musky scent was intoxicating. Allowing herself to relax, Isaboe closed her eyes and dropped her head back to rest against his chest. With Connor, she could pretend she was normal, just a woman in love with a man. Losing herself in his touch, she reached up to run her fingers through his hair.

"God I love yer skin," he whispered between kisses. "I've imagined how ye would taste—like sweet cream and fine wine." As he stood behind Isaboe, sucking a small bruise into her skin, the sensation coaxed a soft moan and her legs almost gave way.

"Ye drive me mad," he said, nipping lightly at her shoulder. Connor let his fingers trace along Isaboe's breast bone, down until they teased at where the fabric of her dress pulled at her breasts. As he slipped his hand down the front of her dress, she moaned again.

When Connor's kisses turned more greedy and demanding, she pulled away and turned to face him, opening her lips to meet his. The energy between them was intense and passionate, their wonton desire escalating with each passing moment. Finally, he drew back and took her hand, leading her toward the bed; but Isaboe hesitated.

"It's alright, just sit with me," he said, coaxing her to sit beside him. Cupping Isaboe's face in his hands, Connor looked deeply into her eyes. "Ye're so beautiful; yer eyes are so captivating and yer lips so soft," he whispered, brushing his thumb across her mouth.

"Connor, I..."

"Shhh," he interrupted her with another kiss. Pulling off his tunic, Connor caught Isaboe's shoulders and gently laid her back. As he slid down beside her, his lips found hers again, and his hands began to roam over her body. First to her waist, then to her hips and thighs, but when he began to unlace the bodice of her dress, Isaboe felt a burst of panic. Her heart was pounding in her chest, and the moment suddenly became more than she could take. They were coming to the point of no return, and she knew she wasn't yet ready for this level of intimacy. It was now or never.

With every ounce of her strength, she pushed Connor off. Holding him at bay, she struggled to catch her breath as they locked gazes. "I can't do this. Not now. I'm sorry, Connor, I just can't."

Connor's body language instantly changed, as did his expression. He sat up and flung his legs over the side of the bed. Running his hands through his hair, he crossed the room, breathing heavily as he looked out the window. After retying the laces on the front of her dress, Isaboe sat with her eyes closed.

Sensing that he could finally address her, Connor came back and sat on the bed. "What I need to know is whether it is just not *now,* or is it not ever? Just tell me the truth. I'm smart enough not to pursue something I cannae attain."

"Connor, earlier I asked if my love was enough to bring you back. Now I ask—do you love me enough to wait?"

"Are ye questioning my feelings for ye?" he asked, as a look of shock spread across his face. "Isaboe, I've been smitten by ye since I first saw you walk down the hotel stairs that morning in Inverness." Connor touched the side of her face before running his hand through her hair. "Yer hair was up, yer head held high, and ye looked *breagha.* After what ye'd been through the night before, I was impressed with yer strength. Ye didnae let fear define ye. That only made me want ye more. If ye cannae tell, I've fallen hard. So, again I ask; is it just not now, or not ever?"

Isaboe sat close to Connor and faced him. "Ever since..." she still couldn't speak the words of Nathan's death... "I've felt so lost and alone. I'm still trying to figure out who I am by myself. I feel like I need some time to figure out what my future holds," she said, trying to sound like she really believed her own words.

"Well, I hope yer future has me in it," Connor said with a nervous laugh.

Isaboe smiled at his comment, but the smile quickly slipped off her face. "I'm confused right now, Connor, and I can't add sex into this mess I call my life, not now." Brushing back a lock of hair from his forehead, she ran her hand down the side of his stubble-covered face. "I've fallen in love with you, Connor Grant, even though I tried hard not to." She laughed softly. "Obviously, the heart wants what the heart wants, aye?"

"Aye, and I want yer heart, and every other beautiful part of ye," he said, leaning in for a quick kiss before Isaboe cast her eyes down. Full of emotion, he took another deep breath and lifted her face to again look into her eyes. "But I can wait. For however long it takes, I can wait." He paused, giving her a sly grin. "Do ye have any idea how long that might be?"

Isaboe gave him a shy smile before he stood up. "We better get out of this room," he said, "or I'm apt to ignore your protest, rip off all yer clothes, thrown ye down on that bed, and have my way with ye! *Tha thu gam marbhadh, boireannach!*"

After they were dressed, Connor took Isaboe by the hand and led her out of the room, leaving the missed opportunity behind them. It was before noon, and there was still plenty of daylight for Connor to set out toward Lochmund Hills and make a good distance before nightfall. He held her hand as they walked out of the hotel to where his horse was tied. Delaying his departure, they took seats on a bench outside the hotel entrance. Neither spoke as they watched people passing by, going about their daily lives.

Not knowing when, or even if, she would see him again, Isaboe started to have second thoughts about turning Connor down. Up in the room, she hadn't felt ready, but maybe she had been too hasty. To change her mind now just to keep him around longer didn't seem right either. And just thinking about him going off to find a woman he'd never met bothered her enough that she could keep her silence no longer. "How will you be able to find this woman? The Lochmund Hills stretch across at least thirty miles."

"I have directions, and I know pretty much where I'm going. It shouldn't be more than a day's ride from here. I'll ken for sure when I get closer, aye? Just take care of Margaret, and I'll be back soon." He squeezed her hand reassuringly before walking to the rail and untying his horse.

After he stepped off the porch, Isaboe stood at the rail and watched him check all the straps on his saddle and bags. Sure that everything was ready, he mounted up and looked longingly over at Isaboe, who stood on the porch, her hair blowing gently across her face, tossed by a passing breeze.

"Ye'll be here when I get back?" Connor asked as he turned his horse to side up along the railing, only inches from where she stood.

Holding his gaze, she reached out and touched the side of his face before replying. "Yes, I promise."

Connor took her hand and brought it to his mouth. Kissing her palm, he let his eyes say everything for him. Reluctantly releasing her, he turned his horse and kicked it into a quick trot out of town.

As Isaboe stood on the porch watching him ride out of sight, her tortured mind kept repeating: *You've made a great mistake.* Though he said he'd be back, she felt a rush of fear that it would be a long time before she saw him again. Feeling cold and alone, she hugged her arms as a chilled autumn gust suddenly swirled up around her, eerily lifting her hair and flapping at her clothes.

But it was the voice she heard in the wind calling her name that sent chills down her spine.

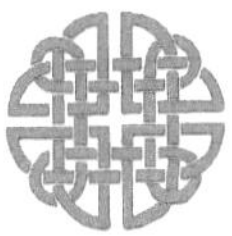

CHAPTER 28

THE SORCERESS

At least half a dozen times Connor contemplated turning back, but by dusk he had already traveled a good distance. Once the sun had made its descent, the cloud-filled sky shed darkness over the land, making riding difficult and potentially treacherous. It was unfamiliar territory and his only directions were a crudely sketched map.

Connor made a small fire and ate his evening meal before tending to his horse. If he had followed his heart, he would have turned around long before and been back at Isaboe's side by nightfall. But logic and honor won out, convincing him that the sooner he took care of this matter, the sooner he could be with her again. After all, he would only be gone a few days, and Isaboe was safe in Edinburgh; he made sure of that. With Margaret unwell, it wasn't likely that she would stray far. He also knew he needed to give her some time to sort things out in her own mind, and in her heart. It was obvious she was still dealing with the loss of her husband. Though he knew nothing of the details, he understood the pain, and saw it in her eyes, those beautiful, captivating eyes—emerald-green with flakes of cracked amber—those eyes that bore into his soul and stole his heart.

In a vain attempt to take his mind off of Isaboe, Connor turned his attention to the fire. Stirring the blaze back into life, he hoped it would keep him warm through the night, though he had his doubts. With the threat of rain hanging heavy in the air, he moved closer to the fire, pulling a blanket up around his shoulders to keep the frigid night from reaching into his bones.

When he poured a cup of coffee to stave off the chill, the scent triggered his memory of standing with Isaboe only that morning. Gazing into the flames, he stared at the image of her face dancing in the embers. How she smelled, how she felt in his arms, the taste of her lips—all teased at his senses. As he recalled their brief encounter, Connor longed for the warmth of her body and felt a deep stirring in his loins. Looking out into the darkness, he shook his head. *What the hell am I doing? What could be so important to leave a woman like that? My God, I'm a bloody fool!*

Connor fought with his own conviction that he must fulfill his promise. Though it was a promise to a dead man, it was a promise all the same. A man is only as good as his word, and as torn as he was, Connor knew he had come too far not to follow through. Determined to finish the task at hand, he resolved to find this woman, seek the answers he needed, and be back at Isaboe's side in no more than two or three days. *She'll wait for me, she promised,* he reassured himself. But the mystery about her, all the things he didn't know gave him doubt. He prayed he was wrong.

Trying to reassure himself that he was doing the right thing, Connor laid down and tried to clear his mind. But the vision of his beloved and the events of the last few days continued to play behind his closed eyes. The last thing he recalled before sleep took him over was the image of Isaboe standing on the hotel porch.

Early the following morning, the rain clouds delivered as promised, and Connor woke to a heavy mist that soaked everything in a damp layer of misery. Sometime during the night, the fire had gone out, and trying to rekindle it with only wet wood proved impossible, denying Connor his chance at a hot cup of coffee to start his morning.

A blanket of fog hugged the hillside, limiting the distance he could see in any direction. The thick cloudbank that draped down from the heavens stretched out over the land, shrouding the valley below. Standing on a small knoll, Connor chewed on a hunk of jerky as he searched the horizon for any recognizable landmarks. He studied his crude map closely, but in this weather, finding his bearings would not be easy.

When he had stopped for camp the night before, Connor sensed that he was close to his destination, so continuing in the same direction seemed the best course of action. He hoped he was right.

Within an hour, the misty rain finally stopped and the fog lifted, making his journey much less challenging. On the lookout for landmarks he had been given, Connor continued up the hillside, hoping to confirm that he was on the right track. According to the map, he would come to a canyon that couldn't be crossed. At that point, he would travel north along the canyon ridge.

As he rode higher, the tree line noticeably thinned. Other than the occasional patches of crowberry and laurel, the land was mostly covered with peat, rock, and dirt. Some of the rocks were quite large—boulders that appeared as if they had been pushed up and out of the earth with extreme force. Others looked like they had fallen from the sky, landing haphazardly on top of one another.

Maneuvering his horse around a pile of boulders, Connor rode under a large outcropping of rock. As he came out on the other side, the canyon stretched out before him. Drifting up from the canyon floor, a cool breeze enveloped him, and he caught the smell of rain in the wind. He brought his horse to a stop and took in the sight. The span of the ravine was wider than it was deep, and the canyon walls were extremely steep. He thanked his good luck that he wouldn't have to make his way down, only travel alongside it.

Continuing his progress, Connor gave a tug on the horse's reins, but was abruptly thrown from his horse when something hard and heavy slammed into his back, knocking the wind out of his lungs. He landed hard, face down in the wet, rocky soil. When he attempted to push himself up, the oppressive weight on his back stopped him; not only unable to move, he could barely breathe.

"Try to move again, an' I'll run ye thru!" a deep, scratchy voice said as the familiar tip of a knife was pressed against the base of Connor's skull. "What's yer business? Who are ye? Why are ye here?"

"Get off and I'll tell ye." As Connor gasped out the words, his chest felt like it would collapse from the pressure. He tried again, but was still unsuccessful in throwing off his attacker.

"If ye calm yeself down, I'll let ye up. But ye best not make any quick moves, or I'll run ye thru!" Slowly, the weight on Connor's back lifted as the threatening voice growled behind him. "Now, git up slowly. No quick moves mind ye, or..."

"Aye, I ken, or ye'll run me through." Finishing his assailant's statement, Connor stood slowly and turned to face him. He was surprised to see a short, but stocky man wielding a nasty-looking dirk in his hand. The fearsome little man was almost as wide as he was tall and built like a bull. He wore clothes made of animal hides, and a sheath strapped across his back held two more long, deadly knifes. Wearing no shoes, his feet were flat and wide, well suited to the rocky terrain. Dark, course hair covered most of the man's body. A thick beard hid most of his features, but his ebony eyes peered wildly from under a furrowed brow, leaving no question of his boldness or his strength.

"Now speak! Who are ye? What's yer business?"

"My name is Connor Grant, and my business is just that, *mine!*" Connor snapped, his ego a bit bruised from being caught off guard by someone who was nearly a dwarf.

"Everyone passen thru Lochmund Hills answers to me! I'll know yer business here, or I'll make yer grave where ye stand!" the dwarf threatened as he reached behind his back and slid another knife from its sheath, pointing both weapons in Connor's direction.

As he locked gazes with the stout, barrel-chested man, Connor stood his ground, debating whether he could make it to his horse and grab a weapon. Figuring the odds were not in his favor, he finally conceded and answered the dwarf's question. "I'm here to find someone who supposedly lives in these hills. She a sorceress, or so I'm told."

"There be no sorceress found here. Ye were told wrong. Now, if ye value yer life, git on yer horse, an' go back from where ye came!"

The dwarf's answer came too quick. Connor knew he was in the right place. "Well, I'm afraid I cannae do that. I dinnae intend to leave without finding what I came for. So, if ye dinnae mind," he said, making a sudden move toward his horse. But the little man quickly leapt into his path and jabbed the tip of his dirk into Connor's groin.

Jumping back from the impact of the knife, Connor shot the dwarf a threatening glare. "What the hell?" he shouted. Though the dirk hadn't reached his skin, it cut a hole in his pants, and the dwarf's intent was clear.

The fierce little man held his ground and his fighting stance. "I'll not tell ye agin, an' this'll be yer last chance. Git on yer horse an' ride back down or I'll cut ye open an' leave ye for the buzzards!" he spat viciously.

By the tone of his voice and the look in his eyes, Connor believed his aggressor. He also knew that riding back down without finding what he came for wasn't an option. As he tried to determine his next move, a voice came from behind—a woman's voice. "Alright, Turock. That will be enough. Sheathe your weapons. I shall speak to this man." The woman's voice held authority, but even so, the dwarf maintained his stance with both dirks pointing threateningly towards his captive. "Turock, drop your blades! I will deal with this now."

Begrudgingly, the dwarf sheathed his knives and stepped back, but never took his eyes from the intruder.

Relaxing his guard, Connor shot the little man a vile glare before turning to face the woman who may have just spared his life.

"You'll have to forgive Turock. He means well, but can be a touch overprotective." The stately woman stood on a rock, frowning down at the dwarf. Her long hair, streaked with faded shades of copper and gray, was blowing in the wind, along with the simple gray cloak pinned at her neck. Standing in a place of vantage over him, her presence was regal. He couldn't tell her age, but the wisdom of a long life showed in her face, even as it held the traces of her youth's beauty.

"I do hope that Turock has not caused you too much damage," she said, casting her gaze down at Connor. "But it would be wise on your part not to agitate him. Now, who are you, and why are you here?"

"My name is Connor Grant. I'm seeking a woman, a sorceress who goes by the name of Rosalyn. Supposedly she lives in these hills."

"What makes you think there is a sorceress to be found here?"

"I was given instructions and this map. I was told it will lead me to her." Connor reached up and handed the woman the scrap of fabric. "Do ye know if such a sorceress exists? Can ye help me find her?"

After examining the crudely-sketched map, the woman looked back down at Connor. "Even if I knew of such, why do you seek her?"

Oddly, Connor felt compelled to answer her questions, and he suspected he would soon discover why. At least she wasn't holding a knife to him or sitting on his back. "I made a promise to a man who saved my life. Fulfilling that promise requires gettin' some answers, and apparently this sorceress is the only one who can do that."

"Who is this man you made a promise to? Why not get the answers you seek from him?"

"He no longer lives. His name was Demetrick. He was a great wizard."

"You are right. Demetrick has passed on. He has been dead for more than fifteen years. You couldn't have been more than a young boy on your mama's lap when he died. Why would he ask a small boy to make a promise that required a journey here, all these years later, to seek a sorceress who may or may not exist? What misfortune was bestowed on you at such an innocent age that it was necessary for your life to be saved by a wizard?"

Ignoring her questions, Connor decided it was his turn to get some answers. "Look, I would appreciate it if ye can just tell me. Does a sorceress live in these hills? Does such a woman exist? Or, am I already addressing her?" Based on her knowledge of Demetrick, he suspected she was the woman he was seeking.

"Do not get arrogant with me, young man! I could easily let Turock have his way with you and leave your guts strewn about for the scavengers. You will answer my question!" Her presence and tone were unquestioningly demanding.

Turock anxiously twitched with anticipation of finishing his task, just waiting for a signal from his mistress.

Seeing that he had little in the way of options, Connor chose to do as directed and tried to answer the best he could. "Demetrick was still alive the last time I saw him, which was 'bout two months ago. That is, two months for me. Apparently, I've been gone for the last twenty years, but I haven't aged. As to where I've been, I cannae say. I only know that the last time I saw Demetrick, he gave me a mission to save a woman's life. He said that she holds the future of mankind in her hands. But then he died, so I have no more than this map and an old man's message. Ye probably dinnae believe me, but...."

"Have you been known by another name, Connor Grant?" The stately woman asked, looking down at him with renewed interest.

"My birth name was Braden MacPherson."

"Braden MacPherson." The name rolled off her lips as her face took on the look of a long-forgotten memory. "Has it really been twenty years?" she mused. Stepping down from the rock, she stood in front of Connor and looked up at him. "I am Rosalyn, the sorceress you seek, and I've been expecting you."

CHAPTER 29

A LIFE CHANGING COVENANT

Rosalyn's simple, yet well-furnished home sat atop the highest ridge overlooking the great canyon. *If I didn't know this was here*, Connor mused, *I would walk right by without even seeing it.* Indeed, the entrance was completely camouflaged by shrubbery and rocks. The home itself was nestled into the heart of a cave that appeared to have been dug out over a period of many years. Two heavy wooden doors framed the opening to the cave, blocking out the strong winds that blew up from the canyon floor. On this cool autumn day, the doors were open. A solid floor built of heavy wooden planks lined the main quarters, as well as the large deck that overlooked the canyon.

Connor stood at the railing taking in the awesome expanse. The vastness that spread out for miles in all directions was breathtaking, and he suddenly felt very small in comparison, yet privileged to view it. Unless you were a bird, it was a sight that could only be seen from this vantage point.

Coming up behind him, Rosalyn suddenly appeared with a tray carrying a teapot, cups, and a plate of food that she placed on a small table sitting between two chairs overlooking the vista. Her long hair was pulled up and pinned at the back of her head. She took the white shawl that was draped casually over one arm and tossed it around her shoulders. "Incredible, isn't it?" she asked, as she came over to stand next to him. Handing Connor a cup, she looked out over the canyon. "I liken it to how God must see the world when He looks down, and I feel both honored and humbled."

Connor took a sip before responding. "Aye, it is breathtaking. And I understand why one would want to wake up every day to see this, but why so secluded? What are ye hiding from?"

"The world, and everyone in it. You have to understand, Braden… or, shall I call you Connor?"

"I prefer Connor. Safer that way," he said, leaning on the railing as he sipped his cup.

"Well then, Connor, I have found that being a sorceress, if that is what you wish to call me, hasn't always been well-accepted by society. I've been called a witch, the daughter of Satan, and worse. It is all based on ignorance and fear, because people fear what they do not understand. Anything that is different than what they know and believe to be true must be evil, and should not be allowed to exist. Because of that, I have been banished, imprisoned, and almost killed. So I live my life here, in seclusion." Turning from the railing, she took a seat.

"That explains Turock. He's quite mighty for his size, and very protective of ye." Connor joined Rosalyn at the table and began helping himself to the food.

"Yes," Rosalyn chuckled. "Turock takes his position very seriously. Little happens in these hills that he is unaware of. He saw your fire last night. That's how he knew you were here."

"So, why am I here? What is it ye have to tell me? Why cannae I remember anything that has happened for the last twenty years, and why haven't I aged? Can ye answer these questions for me?"

The sorceress didn't respond immediately, but held his gaze. "Yes, I can answer your questions, when the time is right."

"And when will that be? I dinnae mean to be rude, but I'd like to get on with it."

Rosalyn stared at Connor for a long, uncomfortable moment before she finally spoke. "You've been gone for twenty years, yet you still carry the crude impatience of a young man. You are correct—you haven't aged at all."

As he sat across from the woman, Connor wondered if coming here was such a good idea. He had come for answers, not to be judged.

Apparently, she could tell by the look on his face that Connor didn't appreciate her comment. "My apologies. I get so few welcomed visitors

I was hoping we could spend some time together, just talking. But of course, you probably have someone waiting for you, so I'll not keep you too long."

Connor found it interesting that she would use those words, as if she could read his mind.

"But first, please tell me about Demetrick. I do miss him so. Any tale of him, even news twenty years old, I would love to hear. So, tell me, Conner Grant, what is your story, and how did you become acquainted with the great Demetrick?"

After downing the last of his tea, Connor settled back in his chair to get comfortable. As he began his story, it was hard to believe it had taken place twenty years ago. It seemed like only yesterday—and to him, it was.

One afternoon Demetrick took Braden on a walk off the grounds to the back side of the hill that stood behind his home. It was an area Alex had never taken him before, and it looked quite different from the rest of the compound. Large ferns grew between the aspens, and there was a well-trodden path winding through the trees. As the two men strolled silently, Braden kept in step with Demetrick, but he felt an uneasiness building in his gut.

"These last few weeks of summer have been warm," Demetrick finally broke the silence. "I have to admit, I'm not looking forward to winter. These old joints complain loudly when the rains come back," he said with a painful grin.

"This is a new area for me," Braden commented. "Alex hasn't taken me this way before."

"Alexander is a good boy, and so is Samuel. Neither of them would function well without this place—or without me, for that matter," Demetrick chuckled. "But this place would not function the same without them either. Of course, I would never tell them such. I've found it useful to keep my subordinates believing they are indebted. It keeps matters in my favor."

"Is that what ye have done with me, then? Keeping me indebted to ye?" Braden asked.

"You might say that," Demetrick replied, but offered nothing more.

They continued walking, covering a good deal of ground in a short time.

With each step, anxiety grew in Braden's chest until he could no longer keep his silence. "Demetrick, when are ye gonna tell me what it is I'm to do for ye? I've been patient, have not pried, but I think I've the right to know," he said, coming to a stop.

Demetrick stopped as well and turned around. "I was wondering how long it would take for you to ask. You're a patient man, Braden. That's a good virtue to have. Be thankful for it," he said with a smile before continuing his way up another small hill whose crest was covered with tall trees.

Confused and frustrated, Braden quickly caught up to the older man just as they entered the coolness of the trees. "Demetrick!" Braden shouted. "Where are we going? When do ye plan on telling me what this is all about? I ken ye do things in yer own way, and I've respected that. But, my God man, dinnae lead me off into the unknown without some idea of what I'm getting into!"

Demetrick placed a hand on Braden's shoulder and gave him a look that spoke of sympathy and understanding. "I'm sorry I've been so vague, but I have my reasons—reasons that are not easy to explain. Come, walk with me. It's time you know what you can expect this day."

Suddenly wishing he hadn't asked, Braden reluctantly followed Demetrick into the shadow of the trees. As the sun's light filtered down through the canopy of branches overhead, the two men entered a small clearing deep in the forest. A number of large oak trees encircled the clearing, and the area where they stood was well-manicured, as if it had been recently attended. Around the perimeter were strategically placed stones, all evenly spaced and roughly the same size.

"What is this place?" Braden asked.

"This is a portal, the place where your journey begins."

"Journey? Journey to where?"

"Braden, there are things of this Earth that cannot be perceived by the senses, things one cannot see, hear, or touch. These things are not easily explained, at least not in a way understood by most men. Because of my ability to reach beyond this world, I have come to understand many things. You may not believe what I am about to share with you, but I assure you it is true." The great wizard paused as he regarded Braden closely. "You are a God-fearing man, are you not? You believe there is a greater power, a Divine spirit? Though you cannot confirm God's existence, you still believe in such an entity, do you not?"

"Aye," Braden answered cautiously.

"Well, that is called faith. It is the act of believing in something you cannot see, touch, or hear, but you still believe it exists. The same is true of other worlds, and the planes on which they reside. These planes run parallel with our world, and though we can't see them, they are real, just as real as this tree, or the ground we're standing on. When one of these planes comes into contact with our world, the inhabitants of other worlds can cross over, and for the most part, they are harmless. One such plane is home to the Underlings, most of whom are curious creatures who exist in a realm we cannot see, though we share the same Mother Earth. It has been this way between the worlds since the beginning of life. It is a delicate balance of different entities who live on the same Earth, but in different worlds. How are you with all of this so far?"

"It's an interesting faerie tale, Demetrick, but what does this have to do with me?"

"I find it ironic, Braden, that you should say faerie tale, because that is exactly what Underlings are; faeries, at least some of them. There are also pixies, sprites, elves, gnomes, brownies, nixies, and muses; we have given the Fey Folk all sorts of names over the years. But what is important to know is that, just like mortals, there are both good and bad Underlings. And it is because of one nefarious and powerful fey that I have brought you here today."

"Wait a minute," Braden said skeptically. "First ye tell me we share Earth with another world that I cannae see, and now ye tell me that faeries live in this other world. Good faeries and bad faeries. What, no dragons?"

"I know how hard this is to believe, Braden, I do. That is why I haven't told you this before. But I swear that what I tell you is true. I've seen these Underlings, talked with them, and I know what they are capable of. I also know what one particular fey has planned. It is because of what I know that I share this with you." Clasping his hands behind his back, Demetrick took a few steps forward before continuing. "There is a reason for all things, and a time for all events to unfold. The time of Underlings interacting with the mortal world is slowly coming to an end. The world is changing, Braden, and with change comes less belief in the myths of old. Our waning belief of their existence has caused a rebellion in the world of the Underlings. One powerful fey from the Unseelie court is determined to alter the natural course of events. If she succeeds, it could drastically alter the lives of the inhabitants of both worlds. This is

where you come in. This portal is a gateway to their world, and as we speak, events have already been set into motion that will change the natural flow of the universe, unless you stop it from happening."

"What in the hell are ye talking about old man?" Braden shouted. "This is nonsense! Ye've lost yer bloody mind!" He turned to leave the circle, but didn't get far.

"Braden, listen to me." Demetrick placed a hand on the rebel's shoulder, halting his progress. But it was the dramatic change in the wizard's appearance that held Braden where he stood. Demetrick emitted an aura of light that filled the air around them with a vibrant energy. Leaves on the forest floor began to lift, spinning into a swirling, powerful vortex, joining the mass of energy that surrounded them. As the dynamic wizard lifted his hands, the words that came from his mouth vibrated with power.

"You will cross over into the world of the Underlings, and in that world, you shall meet a mortal woman. You will be intimate with her. You will mark her so you may find her again after you both return to this world. That is the only way to prevent the plans of this powerful and wicked fey from coming to fruition. I freed you from your prison cell and gave you a second chance on life. Now you must complete this task and fulfill your covenant, not only to me, but to all beings of Earth!"

Demetrick's words echoed with authority and the ground shook at the sound of his voice. The air around him was charged with an unnatural and unseen force that seemed to have a life of its own. Reaching into his pouch, Demetrick pulled out an object and placed it in Braden's hand. It was a silver band. The top was flat and wide, its surface engraved with three entwined circles. "With this ring you shall mark the woman so you can find her upon your return. And when you do return, you will be unable to recall anything about your time in the realm of the Underlings."

Shocked and stunned as Demetrick slowly faded back to his elderly self, Braden could hardly believe what he had seen and heard. "How long will I be gone?" he asked apprehensively. Now that he understood his fate, he couldn't help but fear it.

"I cannot say, but you will not know a day has passed. When you do return, come back to my home. If, God willing, I am still here, I will help you recall

*what has taken place. If not, I will leave a message that will help you begin
your journey in this world to seek the woman you will meet in the realm of the
Underlings. She, too, will have returned."*

*The wizard paused to let Braden absorb the enormity of it all. "The passing
between worlds is quick. You will feel nothing more than a moment of dizziness
before you fall into a deep sleep. I have placed a spell of protection on this ring to
keep the Underlings from knowing that you passed into their world by my hand.
It will bring you back to this very place, whole and intact. Though I cannot say
how you will find the state of our world upon your return."*

*Demetrick led Braden to the middle of the clearing before resting his hand on
the younger man's shoulder. "You are a brave lad and a good soldier. I know you
will not let me down. God's speed, and with His blessings, I will see you again,
if not in this lifetime, in the next." Demetrick turned and slowly walked away.*

*As he watched Demetrick step out of the circle of stones, Braden felt a strange
lightheadedness, and the forest around him started to spin. The last thing he
remembered before blacking out was seeing Demetrick's long white hair and
blue robe being tossed in the swirling wind of energy that still surrounded him.*

CHAPTER 30

A NEW NAME AND
A BAG FULL OF COINS

"And when you returned from the realm of the Underlings, how did you deal with all the changes in this world?" Rosalyn asked, still mulling over Connor's story.

"At first, I didna think I'd gone anywhere, and that the old man was in fact mad after all. I just thought I'd taken a wee nap. But when I returned to the house, I realized that things were very different."

When Braden arrived at Demetrick's complex, the first thing he noticed was the garden. It was gone. The beautiful courtyard that had been so well-manicured was now overgrown and unkept. The rod-iron gate that he and Samuel had created was the only part of the fence that still stood among the dilapidated and rotting wood posts.

The door to the house was unlocked, and when he entered, everything was different. The arrangement, the furnishings, even the smell of the place had changed. As he walked through the house trying to understand what made no sense, the sound of heavy footfalls caught his attention, and he spun around to see a man he didn't recognize.

The tall, stout man stepped into the room glaring at Braden with dark eyes set in a round, bearded face, and both his beard and thinning hair were dusted with gray. His dirty pants held up by suspenders only came down to the top of his ankles above his well-worn boots, and the hems of the pant legs were tattered and torn. His once-white shirt, which did nothing to hide the muscular build of his upper torso, also looked as if it hadn't been washed in years. "Who are you?" the large man bellowed. "Why are you in my house?"

As the big man started taking steps in his direction, Braden felt a sense of recognition, but at the same time, it didn't fit. However, the size of him, the voice, the face—familiar yet different—all told Braden that he did know. "Samuel?" he finally said, though he didn't understand how it could be possible.

The man came to an abrupt halt and cocked his head to the side, giving Braden a confused and curious stare. But suddenly a look of recognition lit up his face, "Braden?" he said, appearing astounded.

"What happened to ye, man?" Braden took a step closer, examining the wrinkles embedded around Samuel's eyes and mouth, along with the gray bushy eyebrows set above his aging eyes. He looked completely different than he had only hours earlier. "Did one of Alex's spells go wrong on ye?"

Taking another step closer, Samuel smiled as he reached out with a meaty hand and tapped Braden on the face, a little harder than necessary. "It's really you!" Samuel exclaimed, again tapping and touching Braden as if he needed to reassure himself of what he was seeing was real.

Stepping back from the intimacy, Braden scowled. "Of course, it's me. But what happened to you? Why do ye look so...old?"

Samuel looked a bit surprised at the question, but then turned and walked toward an old, dirty mirror hanging on the wall. Turning his head one way, then the other, he examined his reflection for a moment. "I don't look any older today than I did yesterday," he finally said, before turning back around. "Where have you been, Braden? You've been gone a long time."

Shaking off his confusion, Braden again started through the house. "Where's Demetrick? Even Alex will do."

Samuel followed Braden through the home like an over-sized house pet. "Master Alexander is away at King's court and Demetrick is dead."

Braden spun around, causing the bigger man to stumble to a halt so as not to run him over. "What? Demetrick canne be dead! I just saw him a couple of hours ago!"

Samuel only gave Braden a curious look before responding. "No you didn't. You've been gone a very long time, Braden, longer than Demetrick. I thought you were dead, too. Where've you been all this time?"

As the gravity of what Samuel was telling him settled in his gut, Braden had to sit down before his legs gave out. "That's a good question, Samuel," he *said, feeling confused and disoriented as he stared at the floor. Demetrick was dead? How could that be? But suddenly the wizard's last words to Braden flashed across his mind; 'You will not know that a day has passed, and you will have no recollection of your time in the other world.' It was too incredible to be true, but all the same, it was just as Demetrick said it would be.*

"Samuel, what year is this?" Braden asked hestinantly.

"Uh…I don't know."

Standing, he glanced around the room. "Does Alex have a desk, or someplace he keeps important documents?"

Samuel turned and gestured for Braden to follow. "I'm not supposed to be in here," Samuel said as he opened the door to a small room with a desk in the middle. "Master Alexander gave me strict orders to stay out of his office."

"Master Alexander?" Braden questioned. "Since when do ye call him Master?"

"Since he took over after Demetrick died and said I had to call him that." Samuel chuckled. "But I only say it when I have to." The smile left his face as he stepped back to let Braden enter. "I don't think he's as good a wizard as he thinks he is," he almost whispered. "But you won't tell him I said that, will you?"

Braden didn't answer as he set to rummaging through the desk looking for anything with a date on it. He found a number of scribbled notes, quills, ink bottles, some small stones with carvings on them, a box of severed bird's feet, and a small burlap bag with engraved pieces of wood, polished and smooth. Pulling open the only drawer, Braden found more odd objects inside, as well as a large, leather-bound book. Lifting it out of the drawer, he placed it on top of the desk and began flipping through the pages. It was Alexander's journal with entries for events that he had attended, and as Braden continued pursing the book, he found future dates for upcoming scheduled appointments. But it was the dates on all of them, even the ones that according to Alex's recordings had already passed, that puzzled Braden the most. He stopped at the last page where Alex had recorded, "Away at King's Court", and what was written next to it confirmed his fear, "July through September, 1766."

"1766? Twenty years have passed!" Braden sat down in the desk chair to avoid falling over.

"Is that how long you have been gone, Braden?" Samuel asked, still standing at the office door.

"It appears that way, Samuel." Shaking off his initial shock, Braden again started going through the desk drawer when his hand butted up against a small, plain-looking wood box tucked away at the back. Sliding it out, he placed it on the desk and lifted the lid. Inside was a folded piece of paper, yellowed with age, as if it had been in the box for a very long time, but he could clearly read his name written across the top.

Braden tentatively lifted it from the box, and as he held the crisp, delicate parchment, he felt anxiety building in the pit of his stomach. He exchanged an uncomfortable look with Samuel before opening it.

January 18, 1752

Dear Braden,

If you are reading this letter that means I have passed on from this life. I must apologize for not being here for your return, but God's agenda is not necessarily our own. It has been five years since I last saw you, and though I was hopeful to see you again, I fear it will not be in this lifetime.

I know you must be confused, and again, I am sorry I cannot be here to help you through this. I sent you forth on a great mission, and even though I am unable to help you complete your task, I have not abandoned you. I have made arrangements for you to seek counsel from a very wise and gifted woman. Some know her as a sorceress, but I know her as Rosalyn, a friend and confidant. She will help you to understand all that has taken place during your journey to the world of the Underlings. She will also help you find the woman you met there, the woman you must now seek in this world.

I sincerely pray that when you return, Alexander or Samuel will be here to help you. As I mentioned when we parted, I do not know how you will find the state of the world when you return. I pray to all the spirits of the universe that you will find it a better place. I have left instructions with Alexander, and Lord willing, this letter will end up in your hands upon your return, whenever that may be. Remember Braden, this is a mission of great importance. Do not underestimate the necessity of its

completion. May the right hand of God be at your side.
Your friend, Demetrick

Braden sat holding the paper and staring at the date written across the top. Demetrick's letter said it had been five years since they had last seen each other. How was that possible? It made no sense. "Twenty years have passed. Twenty years!" Braden exclaimed as stared at the letter, unable to understand how it could be possible. Confused and afraid, he looked up at Samuel, unsure what to do next.

"Are you going to stay now, Braden?" The large man asked. "It'd be nice to have some company again. Since Master Demetrick died, it's not been the same 'round here."

In shock, it took Braden a moment before he realized there were other items in the box which he hadn't yet examined. Unrolling a piece of fabric, he discovered a roughly drawn map with the words: To Rosalyn's Home written across the top. Under the map was another piece of paper with all the information necessary for him to start a new life, a new beginning. In the span of a single summer afternoon, Braden MacPherson died, and Connor Grant was born. A new identity, just as Demetrick had promised.

Taking one more look, Braden saw a key in the bottom of the box. "Do you know what this key might unlock?" he asked, holding it up for Samuel to see.

At first, Samuel only looked confused, but then a sense of recall crossed his face. "Uh…I might know." He started to turn, but then stopped to readdress Braden. "You're not gonna disappear again, are you?" Braden only shook his head. "Stay right here then. Don't go anywhere!" The large man said, and Braden saw the concern in his face. It was as if Samuel was afraid if he stepped away, his reunited friend would vanish on him again.

"Dinnae worry, Samuel. I'm not going anywhere," Braden heard the heaviness in his own words.

Apparently satisfied with his answer, Samuel again smiled wide before he walked down the hall. Pushing away from the desk, Braden followed him to a corner of the house where a large, ornate rug covered the floor under a table. After easily moving the furniture, Samuel pulled the rug back to reveal a lock on the floor. "I've seen Master Alexander…I mean, Alex," Samuel chuckled, "put things in here when he didn't think I was watching. Maybe the key fits here."

Stepping next to Samuel, Braden bent down and inserted the key into the lock. Turning it, he heard a distinctive click, then pulled open a trap door and looked down into the opening. At first, all Braden could see was a few small boxes, manuals, and a couple of bags that had been stored under the floor. But when his eyes landed on a large cloth bag tucked toward the back and covered with dust, the small piece of light-colored wood attached to the string closure had his name clearly burnt into it. Reaching down, he lifted up the heavy bag. When he opened it, Braden found a handful of coins, mostly shillings and crowns. It seemed Demetrick had thought of everything.

"May I see the letter?" Rosalyn asked.

Connor pulled the letter from his jacket pocket and offered it to her. After reading it quite carefully, she gave it back. "Do you still have the ring Demetrick gave you?"

He nodded, and again reached into his jacket. Opening the small pouch, he dropped the ring into Rosalyn's hand.

She held the silver band delicately, turning it in her hand and examining it closely before handing it back. "So, upon receiving Demetrick's directions, you traveled here alone?"

"Aye, but that changed when I reached Inverness," he said as he returned the ring and the pouch, along with the letter, to the safety of his jacket pocket. "I was coerced by two women into escorting them to Edinburgh. So I had some company on the last part of my journey."

"Two women, aye? That must have been either very pleasurable for you or a terrible annoyance." Rosalyn gave him a slight grin, but he didn't respond to her attempt at humor.

"Alright, I've told ye my story. How 'bout ye tell me yers?" Connor leaned back in his chair and crossed his arms. "It seems to me that Demetrick must have trusted ye a great deal to leave such a heavy responsibility in yer hands. What was yer relationship with him? How can ye help me?"

Nodding her head, Rosalyn smiled. "Alright, fair is fair. It's my turn now." After drinking the last sip of her tea, she set her cup on the table before beginning her story. "Demetrick was like a father to me, the only mentor I ever knew. When he realized that he wouldn't live to see your return, he contacted me. I have a gift, a special talent that allows me to see and hear things others cannot. Mind you, I've not always thought of this talent as a *gift*. As I already told you, it has nearly cost me my life more than once.

"One time in particular, I was to be burned at the stake by a village of terrified fanatics. They were certain I had been spewed up from the bowels of hell, and those righteous folks were going to save my soul with a sacrificial burning. Somehow, the burning of my flesh would *'cleanse me of the evil one that consumed me'*, and I would be *'guaranteed a place in heaven for all eternity'*." Rosalyn didn't try to hide her scorn. "I wasn't very old, barely a woman. How some people can be so cruel in the name of their god baffles me. I cannot comprehend how they could think that killing an innocent young woman is right and holy, in the eyes of their god, or anyone's god." Rosalyn's tone spoke of an old wound not completely healed. Lost in her own thoughts, she paused for a moment before continuing.

"When I saw the oil lamps they were bringing toward me, I was terrified. Then I heard a booming voice screaming, *'Stop!'* An old man pushed himself through the crowd, struck the leader of the mob with his staff, sending him rolling to the ground with his lamp shattered alongside him. Instantly, the oil and fire covered the man's hair, beard, and clothing, causing him to scream in anguish as he twisted and rolled on the ground. When Demetrick came to stand alongside me, right there atop the wood, he raised his staff in the air and a bolt of lightning shot out from it, flashing out over of the crowd. I thought God himself had come to rescue me. Everyone cowered as he denounced them for their heresy. I will never forget his intensity or the fire in his eyes when he shouted out to the astonished group; 'None of you are even as half as pure as this girl that you were about to burn! If any of you threatens another misunderstood soul, my wrath shall come down upon you all, and what this man is experiencing will seem like nothing!'" Rosalyn paused, as if she saw the moment in her mind. "I, too, was frightened at being so close to this God-like person, in all of his righteous anger. It made me nearly as afraid as I had been of being burned alive.

"He cut the binds that held me, lifted me up into his arms, and placed me on his horse before we rode off, scattering the crowd." Rosalyn gave Connor a meek smile. "Of course, it wasn't God. But on that day, he might as well have been. Demetrick saved my life. I owe him everything."

"It seems Demetrick had a thing 'bout saving poor souls sentenced to death," Connor said, with a humorless chuckle, "And lucky for us."

Rosalyn smiled, but Connor could see that she had dealt with a lifetime of her own demons, and he couldn't help but respect her strength.

"Demetrick helped me to understand why I am different," Rosalyn continued, "how to use my *gift* to help others, and how to stay out of trouble. After years of learning at his side, I've become a woman sought after for counsel by those of an open mind. That is why he has sent you to me, so many years after his death. With help of my guiding spirits, I can help you recall the time you cannot remember. Once your memories have been restored, you will find this woman you seek. I believe your words were, 'the one who holds the future of mankind in her hands.' But for now, we'll eat, drink, and enjoy our day. Tomorrow will be taxing for both of us, and we'll need our rest tonight."

Rosalyn stood up and straightened her dress. "So, now that I've answered your questions, come along. You can help me gather vegetables from the garden, and then we'll go pick out a bird for our evening meal," she said lively. After gathering the plate and teapot, she walked back toward the cave entrance, talking over her shoulder without breaking her stride. "If we want to eat, we have to work for it, so come along. I'm sure there's a pheasant nearby in need of beheading."

As Connor rose to his feet, he resigned himself to the probability that this would not be as quick a trip as he had hoped. If he wanted answers, he would have to play her game, on her time. Sighing, he followed his host back into the cave, into the heart of her strange home. He did his best to be cordial, but in the back of his mind a question kept nagging at him, *what have I gotten myself into?*

CHAPTER 31

THE QUEEN OF EUPHORIA

After Connor finally rode away to fulfill his pledge, Isaboe spent the rest of the day sitting at Margaret's bedside, though her friend had been completely incoherent since they arrived in Edinburgh, and there had been no chance to communicate with her. Even when the doctor made arrangements to have her carefully moved to the room at the inn, his patient only moaned behind closed eyes, never completely regaining consciousness. Isaboe wasn't sure if Margaret was aware of her surroundings, or even knew how serious her wounds were.

After the wounds were re-bandaged and the nurse had left to attend another patient, Isaboe continued her own bedside nursing. With a cool, damp cloth, she stroked Margaret's forehead as her friend remained in a place where Isaboe could not reach her. Every time she let herself recall the attack, it brought on a shudder of horror. The last words she had spoken to Margaret were said in anger, fueled by months of heartache, confusion, and fear. The thought that there might be no redemption for her selfish tirade felt like a heavy weight around her heart. It was agonizing, and she yearned for Margaret's forgiveness.

"If only I had listened to you twenty years ago, neither of us would be in this place. I'm so sorry, Margaret," she whispered in the ear of her silent patient as she stroked her hair. With Connor gone and her only friend fighting for her life, Isaboe had no one but her own demons to keep her company—a company of sadness and despair.

A knock at the door announced nurse Pritchard and her last visit of the night. After examining Margaret's bandages, she turned to Isaboe. "Has she been awake enough to take any nourishment?"

Isaboe only shook her head.

"What about you? Have you eaten today?"

"Not since breakfast," Isaboe heard the exhaustion in her voice.

"I thought as much." The nurse opened the large cloth bag hanging over her shoulder. "Here, I brought you some bread from the bakery. Even though your friend isn't eating, you should."

"Thank you." Isaboe graciously took the bread.

"Doctor Murray will be here in the morning to check on our patient. Get some sleep tonight, and try not to worry, aye?" Nurse Pritchard placed a hand on Isaboe's arm and gave her a comforting smile as she walked briskly out of the room and closed the door behind her.

Fighting back the tears, Isaboe placed the loaf of bread on the table before lighting the oil lamp on the wall. Though she tried to eat, the knot in her stomach wouldn't allow more than a few bites. As she attempted to unlace her dress, all the emotions she'd been holding at bay became unleashed. Instead of eating, she collapsed on the bed next to Margaret, sobbing uncontrollably.

Curled up on her side with her head buried in her arms, Isaboe cried for her pain, and for Margaret's. She cried for letting Connor leave. She cried for her lost children and for her lost life with Nathan. After sobbing until her body could give no more, she finally fell into a restless, dream-filled sleep. A good night's rest was what Isaboe desperately needed. Unfortunately, it was not to be.

Struggling to breathe, I try to pump my legs, but they barely move, as if my shoes are filled with sand. No matter how hard I try, I can move no faster. When I look back at Margaret, she is also struggling and keeps falling further and further behind. I reach for her. "Here, Margaret, take my hand. We have to keep going; they're right behind us! Hurry!"

"I can't! I can't run anymore!" Struggling to keep up, Margaret gasps for air.

"You have to! Here, give me your hand!"

Margaret slips further away from me, and even as I reach for her, the distance continues to grow. I turn to run back, but the heaviness of my shoes won't let me move. The ground starts crumbling beneath me—I'm sinking. Franticly, I claw at the sand as I try to gain purchase, but it twists and moves around me, slipping through my fingers. I see Margaret trying to run, but it's too late. The wolves leap onto her back, tearing and ripping her flesh. As her bloodcurdling screams assault my ears, I'm unable to do anything but watch in horror.

After the wolves have finished their savage attack, Margaret somehow stands and limps over to where the Earth is trying to swallow me whole. Reaching out a bloody hand, she pulls me out of the quicksand with a jerk. Standing before what is left of my friend's flesh-torn, ravaged body, I can barely look at the gruesome sight. As Margaret's blood oozes down her arm and onto my hand, I try to pull free. But her grip is too tight. With what is left of her face, Margaret smiles a blood-dripping grin before speaking, "It's alright Isaboe. At least I was able to save you."

I watch helplessly as what is left of Margaret's body starts to disintegrate before my eyes. As the remains of my friend crumble into a bloody lump of flesh and bone, I look down at my hands, now stained red from her blood, and scream!

I feel a touch on my shoulder and spin around. Connor is standing behind me! Relief floods over me as I throw my arms around his neck, but I am stopped. Protruding from his belly is the handle of a sword. Blood oozes down the front of his body, wrapping around his legs in crimson ribbons. I look down at this horrific sight, then back up into his eyes—they, too, are filled with blood. When I reach up to touch his face, blood spills out of his eyes and covers my hands.

"Oh, my love, what has happened to you?" I ask as my tears run freely. "Who did this to you?" But before he can reply, Connor's face morphs, blurring and twisting into a completely different face: Nathan's.

Trying to stand on shaky legs, I hear both of their voices: "You did this to me, my beloved Isaboe. My love for you was my death sentence."

"No! No! Oh God, please NO!" As I back away, the blood on my hands— Margaret's, Connor's, and Nathan's blood—spreads up my arms. Vigorously, I wipe it away, but the blood only spreads, creeping across my chest, my neck, and over my lips. I drop to my knees and scream for help, but there is no one left; everyone is gone.

"NO! OH GOD NO! PLEASE HELP ME!" The blood is now all over my face, flowing into my nose and eyes, and its taste fills my mouth. I cough and am struggling to breathe; the fluid is choking me as it makes its way down my throat...

With a racing heart, Isaboe struggled, desperately trying to wipe away the blood. With her breath burning at her throat, it took several terrifying moments before she finally realized that her hands were not red. The moisture she was wiping from her face was not blood, but sweat and tears. Isaboe's whole body was soaked as she sat up on the bed, and her dress had become so twisted she could barely move. Her hair was not only stuck to her face, but had found its way into her mouth as well. As the room slowly came into focus, she looked over and saw Margaret still laying on the bed unconscious, but whole and in one piece.

Realizing it had been a horrible nightmare, Isaboe struggled to calm her rapidly-beating heart. She tried to shake off the still vivid images that continued playing over and over in her mind, but they were too fresh, too real. Brushing the hair from her face, she could feel herself trembling on the inside, and she took a few deep breaths before rising from the bed.

Knock, knock, knock. Isaboe jumped at the sound of a voice calling from the other side of the door. "Are ye alright in there? I heard screaming. Miss, are ye alright?"

She opened the door wide enough to see the crinkled face of an old man whose eyes were squinty, partly from age and partly from having been pulled from sleep.

"Oh, I'm sorry if I disturbed you," she said. "Yes, I'm fine."

"Well, then, what was all the yellin' about?" The old man's look of concern melted into irritation.

"I had a bad dream, that's all. Again, I'm sorry if I woke you." As Isaboe gave the man a weak smile, he grunted, then turned and shuffled back to his adjacent room.

After closing the door, Isaboe walked to the dressing table and stood over the wash bowl for a long moment before splashing cool water over her face and neck. It was still dark outside, and the only light in the room was emitted from the wall sconce, casting strange shadows around the small space. She held a towel over her face and shuddered as the visions of the dream replayed vividly behind her closed eyes, still swollen from crying. Fighting to push the visions away, she dropped the towel back on the table and stared at her reflection in the dressing mirror. Her hair was matted, her eyes were puffy, and her wrinkled dress was bunched and twisted around her waist. After straightening her clothing, she ran her hands over her face and through her hair, taking long, deep breaths behind closed eyes.

When Isaboe looked back into the mirror, it took a moment for her mind to register what she saw—a woman was standing behind and to the left of her own reflection. She spun around, knocking the bowl off the table and crashing it to the floor. Ignoring the water and shattered pottery, she stood stunned as she faced a dainty, fair-haired woman who was standing in the room as if she had always been there.

"Oh, I'm sorry, my dear. I didn't mean to frighten you." The stranger spoke with a soft, velvety voice, and had a warm, inviting smile.

But Isaboe could only stare. Rigid with fear, she remained motionless, her gaze darting around the room, her mind racing to find sense. When she finally spoke, her voice betrayed an edge of panic. "Who…who are you? How did you get in here?"

The intruder frowned and sighed as if she were disappointed. "Oh, Isaboe, we've spent enough time together, you should recognize me. And, I have to say, I'm a little disappointed." Bending down to pick up the pieces of the broken water bowl, the woman carefully placed the remnants back on the table.

Isaboe quickly stepped aside, putting distance between herself and the mysterious visitor.

"Oh, please, Isaboe. Quit acting like a scared child. If you just think on it, I'm sure you will figure this out." The woman gave her shaken host a chastising look before spinning around, her long, white dress flowing behind her like water, and her golden hair hanging down her back like fine silk. After making her way to the bed, the intruder turned and sat down, fanning out her dress. She looked over her shoulder at Margaret before glancing around to examine Isaboe's accommodations. By the expression on her face, she was unimpressed.

Isaboe stood beside the dressing table, still unsure what she was seeing, but more importantly, what she'd just heard. "*We've spent enough time together; if you just think on it, you will figure this out.*" An uneasy feeling began to grow in the pit of her stomach—she did know. As Isaboe watched the strange woman sitting on her bed, seemingly waiting for her to make the next move, flashes of people and places she had once known danced on the edges of her mind. Staring at the woman with wondering eyes, she walked slowly and cautiously around the bed and stopped just short of her reach. With a questioning whisper, not quite sure how it was possible, one word, one powerful name crossed her lips: "Lorien?"

"Ah, I knew you'd figure it out!" The Fey Queen said as she looked at Isaboe with a satisfied grin.

"But...am I dreaming? I must still be asleep."

"No, you're not dreaming."

"I don't understand how this is possible? You can't...*actually* exist." Isaboe looked down at the small woman, still unsure if she was real or a hallucination.

"Come, sit, and I'll try to explain." Lorien patted the bed next to her, but Isaboe didn't move. As she stared at Lorien, every instinct screamed not to get closer, not to touch, or even to listen. "Oh, come now, I won't bite. I have been nothing but kind to you. Why should now be any different? Come, sit down." This time Lorien's words came as an order.

Isaboe slowly took a seat on the bed as far from Lorien as she could. "Why are you here? *How* are you here?" she asked, her hands pressed into the mattress and ready to run if necessary.

Lorien regarded her for a moment before speaking. "Isaboe, when you visit me in Euphoria, you come in your sleep. These are not dreams; they are a way to travel between realms." Lorien stood and took a few steps before turning to face Isaboe. "Mortal minds can be simple, but there is more to Heaven and Earth than what you believe. I come from another world, the realm of the Underlings. Because you are mortal, when you cross over, only small glimpses remain with you, so then you can convince yourself that it was only a dream. But Euphoria is very real, just as real as this world is. And you are very important to Euphoria's very existence. That is why I am here, to help you understand your destiny, and to be your guide."

Lorien took a seat on the bed and grasped Isaboe's hands in her own. When Isaboe tried to lean back and escape the intimacy, Lorien pulled her closer. "I know this is difficult for you to understand, but if you search your soul, you know I speak the truth. You've been to Euphoria with me. We have walked the paths under the great oaks together, danced under the full moon, ate and drank till we could eat and drink no more. We've already shared a lifetime together. Now it is time for you to fulfill your purpose. I have come to help you do that."

Quickly snatching her hands out of Lorien's grip, Isaboe stood, never taking her eyes off of the other woman. "I am familiar with what you call Euphoria. I do have memories of such a place, whether they are real or in a dream. I also recall that when I have been there, in this…this other realm, I am not called Isaboe. You call me by another name."

"Alaina. Yes, you are the Mother Alaina when you are in Euphoria. But here, in this world, I will address you using your mortal name."

"But, how is it that are you here? If you really are from another world, how are we having this conversation, here in this room?"

"It's a bit of faerie magic, but what's important to know is that I'm here to help you. That's all you really need to know."

"Help me with what?" Isaboe asked, glaring at Lorien as the unnerving situation started to become clearer. "You talk about purpose and destiny. What is my destiny, Lorien? Was it to lose twenty years of my life, and my family? Did Euphoria take that time? Did *you* take that time? Why?"

"Now, Isaboe, there is no point in upsetting yourself. I will try to answer your questions, but you must know that none of this is relevant. What has passed is past, and you must not dwell on what cannot be altered."

Isaboe stared at the Fey Queen in disbelief. "*Not relevant?* I lost everything I held dear in my life, and you tell me it's *not relevant!* What do you want with me? Why would you steal from me everything that I loved in this world? What could possibly be so important that it cost me so much?"

Isaboe's voice shook with anger and fear. She was finally going to learn what had happened to her—and the thought was terrifying.

"I did nothing to you," Lorien said defensively. "I am not the cause of any of this. The simple truth is that you were chosen. Sometimes the path that has been chosen for us can be difficult to bear. I understand that you mortals have a strong sense of family, so the loss of that union must be very painful for you." Lorien didn't bother to inject sympathy into her voice. "For that, I am truly sorry. But what you don't seem to understand is how important you are. Not just to a handful of mortals, but to an entire race, an entire way of life. You are the instrument, Isaboe. You are the Mother Alaina, and you carry a very precious cargo. You should feel honored to have been chosen for such a state of grace." Lorien gave a comforting smile as if sharing this would somehow make Isaboe feel better.

She was mistaken. Isaboe's fear swiftly morphed into anger. Sitting back down next to Lorien, she leaned in toward the small fey woman, her fiery green eyes flickering with rage. *"Honored? I should feel honored? My husband and my children were my entire life. All I ever wanted was a family, a family I could love, and who would love me back. That is what is important, or what was important, until you took it away from me!"* Shaking with emotion, Isaboe leaned forward with each word, and Lorien leaned back from their sting. "I DIDN'T ASK TO BE CHOSEN! AND I HATE YOU FOR DOING THIS TO ME!"

Knock, knock, knock came through the wall, followed by the old man's cranky voice reminding her that people were still trying to sleep.

"See what you've done?" Lorien said condescendingly. "You've disturbed the neighbors. Do you feel better now that you've gotten that off your chest?"

As much as she didn't want them to come, Isaboe could feel tears burning at the corners of her eyes. Barely able to comprehend what she was hearing, she felt her world once again spinning out of control. It was too bizarre to be real. This strange woman had summarily discounted everything she held dear, as if her life held no importance. As she sat there staring at Lorien, an enormous pain filled Isaboe's chest, the likes of which she had never felt before. How could this new information possibly make things better? How did it fit into her already devastated life, or bring back any happiness? How much more could she take before she simply fell over the edge?

Falling back on the bed, Isaboe let the tears flow freely down the sides of her face. Overwhelmed with sorrow, she curled into a fetal position and sobbed, oblivious to the fey woman who sat by her side, or the unconscious friend who shared her bed. *Oblivion,* a dark inner voice whispered to her. *Leave this world—stop feeling.* The words felt like a welcome reprieve.

As Lorien observed Isaboe's grief, she shook her head, and sighed. "Mortals can be so irrational."

CHAPTER 32

SISTERS OF GREYSFRIARS KIRK

Isaboe's second awakening was not much different than the first, though now the morning light filled the room. She was sitting up on the bed, rubbing her hands briskly across her face when the cramping hit. She leapt from the bed to find the wash bowl, but since she hadn't eaten much the day before, it was just dry heaves that wracked her body. Taking long, deep breaths, she stood before the dressing mirror in the same place she had been standing the previous night when Lorien had appeared.

Slowly Isaboe turned around. Other than Margaret, who still lay unconscious on the bed, the room was void of anyone else. When she noticed that the bowl on the dresser was now whole and unbroken, she couldn't help but let out a sigh of relief. Obviously, the strange little woman had just been part of the nightmare that had robbed her of a good night's sleep. Though she hadn't gotten the rest she so desperately needed, Isaboe knew she had to pull herself together. Margaret's wounds—the wounds that left her hanging between life and death—needed tending, and the doctor would be arriving soon.

After removing the wrinkled dress she had slept in and pulling up her hair, she poured water into the bowl, grateful that her stomach had been empty. She splashed the cold, brisk water over her face and shivering body, making every muscle flinch. As she quickly washed in front of the dressing mirror, running the wet cloth over her naked body, she couldn't help but notice that her breasts were fuller, and her nipples, erect from the cold water, appeared to be darker. As she continued running the cloth across her abdomen, she felt a definite roundness that hadn't been there before. Her body was changing, preparing for the unborn child she carried. Thinking about her strange dream, Isaboe remembered the fey woman saying something about this child holding great importance, though she had no idea what that meant. Pushing it aside, she reminded herself that it was just part of her nightmare.

An hour later, now dressed and pinning up her hair, Isaboe heard a knock at the door. "Who's there?"

"Nurse Pritchard, Miss," Isaboe heard the familar voice from the other side. "I'm here to make my rounds."

Opening the door, Isaboe stepped back as the nurse entered. "Good morning, Miss Pritchard."

"So, how is our patient this morning?" the nurse asked, offering a smile before glancing at Margaret.

"She hasn't moved all night and has barely made a whimper. Shouldn't she be waking up by now?"

"Doctor Murray has her on some strong medications, but I'm sure she'll wake up soon. He will be here shortly to change her bandages, so we'll know more then." Nurse Pritchard gave her a reassuring smile, but Isaboe only nodded and took her place in the chair next to the bed. Looking down into Isaboe's puffy, bloodshot eyes, the nurse put a hand on her shoulder. "I don't mean to be unkind love, but you don't look like you slept a wink. Have you had a bite to eat yet this morning?"

Isaboe rubbed her hands across her face and grimaced. "No, I haven't. My stomach has been so upset I don't think I could keep anything down."

"Well, if you don't want to end up beside your friend here, I suggest you try. I'll take care of Margaret. You go take care of yourself," the nurse demanded. "That is not a request. Now go."

Knowing the nurse was right, and not having the strength to argue with her, Isaboe conceded and left the room. At a small café three doors down from the inn, she ordered a light breakfast. Feeling somewhat better after her meal, she sat quietly at the table drinking her last cup of tea. She contemplated going back to her hotel room in an attempt to get some rest, though she doubted that sleep would come. Instead, she stayed, watching the restaurant's other patrons enjoying a pleasant breakfast. Some, like her, were alone. But the café was filled mostly with couples and young families.

*What I wouldn't give to trade places with any of those people right now.
Even that old man sitting alone, who probably lost his wife years ago, and his
children never visit any more. Maybe he has a dog to keep him company. At least
he has lived a full life, so the cruelty of an unfair world is only a memory, a past
wound that doesn't hurt as much anymore. Only the scars remain. How grand
it would be to be old, and not feel the pain of the present anymore, knowing
that it's all in the past, just a wrinkled, yellowed page in a book of forgotten
moments.* Isaboe's wishful thinking was interrupted by a piece of paper
that abruptly appeared on the edge of her table.

"We are all equal in the eyes of God. We are all his children. Come
join us in worshipping the Lord!" shouted a man dressed as clergy and
passing out flyers as he swished through the restaurant. While he worked
the room, giving out smiles and blessings, Isaboe picked up the paper he
dropped on her table:

Sisters of the Greyfriars Kirk
Sunday morning worship with
Pastor Patrick
10:00 am—main cathedral
The Lord is my light and my salvation.
Whom shall I fear?
The Lord is the strength of my life.
Of whom shall I be afraid?
(Psalms 27:1)

Isaboe stared at the flyer; *Greyfriars Kirk.* The printed words flooded
through her memory, taking her back to another time, another life, but
more importantly, the reason she had come to Edinburgh. She'd been
so distraught with guilt and anguish over Margaret, and lost in her own
self-pity, she had totally forgotten about seeking the information she'd
come for in the first place.

After quickly paying for her meal, Isaboe headed out the door, but she
wasn't going back to the inn. Though she didn't know what she would
say when she got there, she headed in the direction of the Kirk. It had

been many years since she'd walked these streets, but she hadn't forgotten the way.

Isaboe had no idea what day it was as she made her way up the brick steps of the old church, but she knew she had to come. As she stepped into the dimly lit entryway, the heavy wooden door prompted a flood of memories. The smell of old wood hit first, triggering scenes and flashes from a life long ago. The bowl of holy water at the entrance to the sanctuary was exactly where it had always been. By instinct and ritual, she dipped her finger and drew a cross over her chest before entering.

The large hall was quiet and empty. No ceremonies were being held, and other than the few candles burning on the altar, there were no signs of life. Slowly, Isaboe made her way toward the front of the sanctuary, wondering if this was an appropriate time to let herself in. When she reached the front, she knelt before the Crucifix of Jesus before taking a seat in the front pew.

Staring at the image of Christ nailed to the cross, it struck her that He seemed such a foreign concept. How was the death of one man supposed to save mankind from its own self-destruction? Why would Jesus allow himself to be put to death if He had the power to stop it? Maybe He didn't have the power. Maybe He was only human after all, just a mortal man. Isaboe tried to pray, but felt so hollow inside that she found nothing to draw from. No memorized prayers or scriptures came to mind, only loneliness and a black hole full of pain and fear. A single tear ran down her cheek as she realized how lost and alone she felt. She tried to find something in the midst of the darkness to cling to, something remembered from a lifetime ago.

Isaboe had no idea how long she'd been sitting there when she felt a hand on her shoulder. "Apologies, my child, I didn't mean to startle you. Can I help you? Do you wish to speak with the pastor?" A young woman dressed in clergy stood next to her, looking down with a caring face and concerned eyes, and it took a moment before Isaboe found her voice.

"No, I'm not here for the pastor." For half a second Isaboe thought that was exactly what she needed. She certainly had plenty to rid her soul of, but the pastor would probably think she was insane, and he wouldn't be too far off. "I could use some help though. I'm looking for some information on someone who was once a member of your congregation. Is there anyone here who could help me?"

The sister sat down next to Isaboe before replying. "Who is it you're looking for?"

"Marta Cameron. Or anyone in her family."

"Marta Cameron?" The woman paused in thought. "I don't know that name. When did she attend services here? Are you a relative of hers?"

Isaboe knew she had to be careful in her answers. "Yes. She was my... grandmother. It's probably been many years since she attended here. I'm just trying to find out what became of her, and her family."

The woman studied Isaboe for a few moments before responding. "What is your name, my dear?"

Knowing there might be a chance that someone would remember her as a young girl, giving her real name would only cause confusion. "My name is...Kaitlyn, Kaitlyn Grant." It was the first name that came to mind, and it surprised her that she used Connor's surname, but doubted he would mind.

"Hello Kaitlyn. I'm Sister Jean. I don't think I can be of any help, but I know someone who could be. Tell me, how is it that you don't know the whereabouts of your grandmother and your family? Were you separated from them?"

Having already thought about this line of questioning, Isaboe had fabricated a response ahead of time, and took a deep breath before answering. "My grandmother never knew me. My mother was Isaboe McKinnon. She gave birth to me out of wedlock—before she was married—and gave me away. I know that Isaboe had two other children, a boy and girl, and I'm hoping to find them. They're the only blood family I have, but I don't know where to start looking. All I know is that after Isaboe died, her mother, Marta Cameron, brought the children back here to Edinburgh. So, that's why I am looking for any information on Marta, hoping it will lead to my...half brother and sister." Isaboe held her breath as she watched Sister Jean digesting the information, hoping that it sounded like a legitimate story. She prayed that God would forgive her for lying, especially in church.

"So, I assume it must have been a long time ago when the children were brought here, is that right?"

"Yes, twenty years ago."

The young sister pressed a finger to her lips in thought for a moment. "I think Sister Miriam was here twenty years ago. Maybe she will know something about Marta Cameron."

The moment Isaboe heard the name Miriam, her heart jumped. *Sister Miriam is still alive?* She caught herself to avoid showing recognition. Miriam was a common name, and surely there would've been other women serving the church with that same name during the last twenty years. But could it be the same one? At the thought of the sister she once knew, a flood of memories came flowing along with it. Sister Miriam had always been kind to her, always seemed interested in her wellbeing. She was one of the few women in the church who Isaboe had really made a connection with, and she might be recognized. But the last time she had seen this sister, Isaboe had been only twelve years old. Now, as a twenty-two-year-old woman, her features had matured and her body had changed, but might she still be recognized? She hoped that Sister Miriam's eyesight had aged with her.

"But we must check with the deaconess first to make sure it will be acceptable for you to speak with Sister Miriam. She tends to be a stickler on protocol. Come, the deaconess is in her office. Let's go talk with her, shall we?"

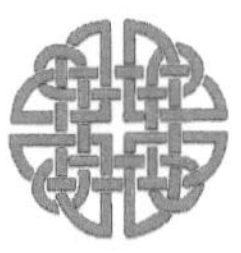

CHAPTER 33

SISTER MIRIAM

Isaboe was sitting on the bench outside the deaconess's office when she heard the door open and Sister Jean stepped out. "The deaconess would like to speak with you first. She may seem a little gruff, but I assure you, her bark is worse than her bite," she whispered before gesturing toward the office door.

Taking a deep breath, Isaboe followed the sister into a small office. The commanding woman who stood behind the desk gave Isaboe pause. She was tall, and the pull of her lips was stern, as was her gaze. The deaconess had a presence about her that was immediately intimidating, but Isaboe walked confidently across the room to take her appointed seat. "Thank you for seeing me."

The deaconess took her seat on the opposite side of the desk. "Sister Jean says that you claim to be the bastard child of one of Marta Cameron's daughters. Is that correct?" Her question was direct, and the tension was thick as she waited for Isaboe's reply.

Offended by the degrading term, Isaboe wasn't prepared with an immediate response. But that was exactly how she had presented herself, so she had no choice but to confirm the statement. "Yes, that is correct," she answered meekly.

"What is it you hope to gain by seeking information regarding the Cameron family?"

"I...I'm not looking to gain anything," she replied defensively. "I'm just hoping to find out what became of Isaboe's children."

The tight, guarded look from the deaconess told Isaboe she didn't accept her answer. "Why?"

"Because, they're my only blood family, my brother and sister, and I would like to know them. I would like to know that they are well, and I would hope to have a relationship with them."

"What makes you think that they would want to know you? After all, you claim to be their mother's illegitimate child, obviously someone they knew nothing of. Why do you think, after all these years, they would want to know that their mother was indecent in her behavior, resulting in an unwanted child? Do you really think it's fair to burden them with this information, tainting the memory of their beloved and departed mother?"

Isaboe struggled to maintain a sense of outward calm, though fury was growing in her chest. She hadn't expected this line of questioning. "I believe that should be up to them. I think they would want to know about me, regardless of the circumstances of... my existence."

The deaconess didn't respond, but studied Isaboe with a scrutiny that made her squirm in her chair. "If you are who you say you are, I must inform you that you have no claim to the Cameron money. If your desire to be united with your kin is somehow an attempt to assert any rights to an inheritance, you will be disappointed, I assure you."

Isaboe felt the heat rising on her face. "I can assure you, ma'am, that I have no interest in the Cameron money. I could care less about an inheritance. That is not why I am here. My only desire is to locate the whereabouts of my...Isaboe's children," she said, gripping her hands together on her lap to keep them from shaking.

The deaconess studied Isaboe, considering her response. After a few moments of tense silence, her posture changed, becoming less guarded, as if she no longer saw Isaboe as a threat. "I knew Marta Cameron for only a few short years. When I came to take my place in service here, she lived alone. She had no family here in Edinburgh, though I do believe one or two of her daughters did contact the Kirk upon hearing of Marta's illness, and then her subsequent death. I don't know their names or where they may be now. However, as Sister Jean has already informed you, Sister Miriam may have some information on this matter. If she is willing to speak with you, I have no objection in you asking a few questions. Mind you, she is elderly and sleeps a good deal of the day. If you do find her awake and willing, you have my permission to speak with her. Sister Jean will take you to her room."

Without another word, the deaconess rose and walked out the door. Apparently, the conversation was over. Most women in her position were distant and stoic, but Isaboe thought this one was definitely more than a little cold.

After escorting Isaboe out of the office, Sister Jean spoke in hushed tones as soon as they were in the hallway, "I must apologize for the deaconess. She was quite harsh to you. I really don't know what to make of that."

Though still upset from the encounter, Isaboe assured the sister that it was of no importance, but she suspected the reason for the deaconess's guarded words—the Camerons had money, and a lot of it. Isaboe was sure that Marta didn't take it to her grave, and had likely left most of it to the church.

As the two women made their way through a series of hallways and staircases, Jean chatted on about Sister Miriam. Even though the woman was in her eighties, her mind was as sharp as it had been in her youth. If one needed to know anything about the past, Sister Miriam was the one to seek. Isaboe found that comforting, yet at the same time, disquieting. She found herself hoping that the elderly woman's eyes were not as sharp as her memory.

It took a while before the heavy door opened. When the small, elderly sister looked up at the two women standing at her doorway, Isaboe looked into the familiar, yet aged face of her old friend, and felt the urge to embrace her. But she maintained her distant composure. An air of unfamiliarity was her first defense against Sister Miriam's memory.

"Good morning, Sister. I hope we didn't wake you," Jean said pleasantly before making introductions. "This is Miss Grant, and she has a few questions for you regarding a former member of the church."

Sister Miriam didn't respond at first. She looked at Isaboe with dark, penetrating eyes that seemed to see right through her. By the way the old woman examined her, Isaboe was sure she could see through her façade, and know she was lying. It wasn't until Miriam stepped back and invited them into her room that Isaboe realized she'd been holding her breath.

Having shrunk a bit since Isaboe had last seen her, Sister Miriam's hunched frame made her appear fragile. Though her hair was covered with a scarf, a few gray hairs found their way out, framing her aged face—a kind face full of wisdom and knowledge. Her hands, knotted and drawn, shook slightly as she made her way over to a chair and sat down. Beside her was a table where a small oil lamp burned next to an open Bible.

"I hope we're not interrupting your reading," said the younger Sister.

"No, that's alright. Come, come take a seat." Sister Miriam's voice crackled with age, but was kind and welcoming as Isaboe took a seat on the bed. "So, tell me again, what is your name?" she asked, looking over at Isaboe, who sat on the bed with her hands in her lap.

"Kaitlyn Grant."

"So, Kaitlyn Grant, what is it you wish to ask me?"

Isaboe sat up straight, and relayed the same story she had told the deaconess, hoping for a more favorable response. The old sister concentrated as she pondered Isaboe's story. Slowly, remembrance crossed her face, and a soft smile began to grow, creating deep lines around the corners of her mouth.

"Isaboe, oh yes, I remember her. The last time I saw her, Isaboe was a very young woman, not much more than a child actually. Marta sent her off to boarding school after her father died, and I never saw her again." A look of sadness melted the smile on Miriam's face as she continued the journey through her memory. "What a tragedy. From what I recall, Isaboe and her husband—I didn't know his name—both died young and left two small children. Sad, it was." As Sister Miriam seemed to lose herself in her thoughts, going quiet for a moment, Isaboe fought back the all too familiar pain at the mention of Nathan's death.

"Marta brought the children back to Edinburgh, but shortly after they arrived here, she made arrangements to have them fostered. I don't recall ever seeing them. That doesn't mean I didn't, I just don't remember. It all happened quite suddenly, you see."

Hearing that her children had been fostered, Isaboe felt a sinking feeling in her heart. Though she tried not to let it show, the fear of never finding them brought on a new anxiety. "Do you know if they were fostered together, or separately?" she asked cautiously.

"I'm sorry, my child. I don't know how much help I'll be to you." Sister Miriam answered compassionately.

"What about Marta's other daughters? The deaconess mentioned that they contacted the church upon their mother's death. Do you know what became of them? Maybe they know where Isaboe's children are." Feeling a sense of desperation rising, she tried to keep her composure.

"Yes, Marta had three other daughters. I believe their names were, hmm…Deidra, Cecilia and…what was the other one…oh yes, Saschel. Let's see, if my memory serves me correctly, Cecilia died in a riding incident shortly after the oldest one married. Yes, that's right. Deidra married, and then moved away, though I can't remember if that was before or after the children arrived. Now Saschel, she was the youngest, and she stayed with her mother for some time. She wasn't very fair of face, not what you would consider pretty, for a suitor's interest anyway. Now Isaboe, she was a beautiful young girl with long chestnut hair and green eyes—the face of an angel." Sister Miriam stopped talking, and took the time to really examine Isaboe. "You do look like how I would imagine she would look, had I known her at your age. There's quite a resemblance between you and your mother, my dear. She was probably about your age when she passed." She crossed herself and sighed quietly.

Feeling the tears stinging her eyes, Isaboe wanted to throw herself into Miriam's arms, open her aching heart, and say, *it's me! I am the Isaboe you remember!* But she fought back the tears and held her poise, knowing that wasn't possible.

"Now where was I? Oh, yes, Saschel, let's see. She did marry, but from what I recall, that marriage ended badly. Shortly after the nuptials there were rumors of his infidelity. I believe Saschel even caught him with another woman on more than one occasion. It appeared he was only interested in the Cameron money. Before Marta realized what had happened, he had managed to tap into some of her holdings, stole a good deal of money, and then just disappeared. Poor Saschel was so humiliated, and of course, Marta was furious. She immediately demanded that Saschel get an annulment before he got away with any more of her estate. Marta blamed Saschel, though the poor girl had her mother's blessings.

Of course, Saschel had the annulment, and it wasn't much later that she left town as well. I believe she went to live with her sister, as she wrote a few times inquiring of her mother's health. The letters came from Orkney. I remember that because I received a letter from the girls when Marta took a turn for the worse. Shortly after their mother's passing, they came back to Edinburgh.

"But Marta left most of her estate to the church. She made few concessions for her daughters, other than her worldly possessions. The girls sold the house and whatever else they could, but it was a far cry from what the Cameron estate was worth. They left here with not much more than a few boxes of legal papers, some family heirlooms, and their memories. Marta was a hard, stoic woman, and she only got worse as she got older. I don't know what happened to make her heart so cold."

"Did you ever hear from Deidra or Saschel again? Do you know if they still live on Orkney?" Isaboe asked anxiously.

"It seems that a few years later, there was another letter from one of the girls. I believe that it did come from Kirkwall, on Orkney. If I remember correctly, Deidra and her husband, I wish I could remember his name..." Sister Miriam wrinkled her brow in concentration as she tried to recall names and events from a life time ago. Licking her wrinkled lips, she shook her head in silent frustration. "Oh well, no mind. But I do remember the letter mentioning they had a small fishing business that had fallen on hard times. They made a request that the church release some of their mother's money. My understanding was that the deacon took charge of that request, but it may have fallen into the hands of the deaconess, as she knew the family better. I don't know the outcome."

Isaboe was now certain why the deaconess was so suspicious of her request for information.

"That's really all I can remember. I'm sorry, my child. I fear I've not been much help to you," Sister Miriam said, rising out of her chair to signal the end of their visit.

"Oh, no, you have been very helpful; thank you so much." Standing as she took the woman's aged hand, Isaboe kissed it gently.

Sister Miriam took both of Isaboe's hands in hers. "Blessings on you my child, and may the Lord watch over you on your journey. I hope you find what you are looking for, whatever that may be," she whispered with a twinkle in her eye, as if the she *knew* something.

As she followed Sister Jean out the open door, Isaboe paused for a moment and returned the older sister's smile. Then slowly turned and closed the door behind her.

CHAPTER 34

A SORCERESS,
A DWARF, AND A GIANT

In Connor's mind, the venture in the garden began as nothing more than woman's work. While following Rosalyn about the tidy rows, he initially found the task trivial and a waste of time. But as she talked about the attributes of the plants she'd been able to grow on the ridge, and the obstacles she had overcome, he was surprised to find himself becoming interested.

"I've spent years attempting to grow anything in this rocky soil," Rosalyn said. "It's been no easy task, and the vicious winds haven't helped either. But I've learned how to amend the soil, and after a lot of hard work, I have a garden to be proud of." Bent over a leafy green bush, she plucked a ripe tomato and turned it over in her hands. Seeming pleased with its form, she carefully laid it in the basket.

The vegetable garden was abundant, full of autumn's harvest with a vast assortment of herbs, tubers, and roots—both for cooking and medicinal use, as Connor soon learned. Lining one garden wall were rows of flowers and shrubs. A white, flowering vine with delicate fingers stretched out in every direction up the side of the wall, which had been built to block the wild wind.

"But why have such a large garden?" Connor asked as he glanced across the rows. "There's a lot to harvest for someone who lives alone."

"I'm not alone now," Rosalyn said with a mischievous smile. "Would you please dig up some potatoes over there?" She pointed to a patch of garden near the vine-covered wall, and then went back to pushing through leafy bushes, searching for the ripest vegetables.

After digging for a short while and finding six good-sized potatoes, Connor stood, admiring his bounty. Digging in the dirt for the tubers sent him back to his childhood and the farm he'd grown up on. But the memory quickly fizzled when a large shadow suddenly stretched over the ground, blocking the afternoon sun. Shooting a glance skyward, Connor looked up at the tallest man he had ever seen, and he stumbled backward at the sight of the giant.

"Who are you?" The voice was as deep as might be expected from a man with such a massive mouth, and on such an immensely large face.

As Connor stared up at the incredible sight, Rosalyn poked her head around the giant's leg. A smile broke across her face when she saw the look on Connor's. "This is Leonardo, my friend and companion. Leo, this is our guest, Connor Grant. He will be staying the night."

The giant's scowl never changed as his dark, beady eyes bore into Connor's. After a tense moment, he slowly reached out his immensely long arm, whose hand was as big as Connor's head, offering it in greeting.

Cautiously, Connor reached up and placed his hand in Leo's, preparing to feel his bones crush in the handshake. Surprisingly enough, the enormous man had a gentle touch, though Connor was certain that those same hands could do serious damage, should they choose to.

"It's a pleasure to make yer acquaintance." Having a hard time grasping the enormity of the giant man, Connor looked back at Rosalyn. "Ye do keep some very odd company!"

As the afternoon wore on, Connor shadowed his host through the garden, carrying baskets that became filled with herbs, fruits, and vegetables. Rosalyn was taking advantage of his strong back, and he felt a bit like a mule, but didn't complain. It didn't take long before they had gathered as much as she wished and were back inside.

"So, how did ye end up living here? How did ye find this cave?" Connor asked, placing the baskets of harvest on the large wooden table.

"I had heard rumors of a giant living in this canyon," Rosalyn said, sorting through her freshly-picked bounty. "Exaggerated rumors that he had terrorized a village and eaten a child, which I didn't believe. But I wanted to see for myself. So I looked until I found Leonardo—scared, injured, and hungry—hiding in one of these caves. But he wasn't a child-eater. He was a frightened and misunderstood outcast, a simple, tortured soul hiding from the world, and we instantly connected. I tended to his wounds, helped him find food, and we've been dependent on each other ever since. I couldn't live here without him, and he couldn't live here without me. It works well for both of us."

"Now I know why ye have such a large garden," Connor chuckled. "But how does the dwarf fit in? Where'd he come from?"

"Turock just showed up one day. I caught him stealing food from my garden. When I told him he had to pay for what he took, he ran off. But the next the day I found a beautifully carved stone bowl at my door, and he's been around ever since. Though I don't exactly know where he lays his head at night, he always seems to show up when he's needed."

As promised, a pheasant had been cleaned and was ready to be dressed, thanks to Leo. When he saw such a wide array of fresh fruits and vegetables scattered across the cooking table, Connor realized Rosalyn was making an elaborate meal, and he felt honored she had gone to so much effort on his behalf.

Pulling a mug from her cupboard, she poured Connor a drink, and placed it in front of him on the table. "Here, sit and relax. I made this spiced ale last year. It's been fermenting nicely in the back. Please, tell me what you think of it."

As instructed, Connor took a seat and quickly drained his mug. After enjoying his second round of Rosalyn's tasty brew, he did begin to relax. Feeling the effects of the stout drink, he watched closely as she scurried around her kitchen preparing dinner. After stepping outside for a quick moment, she returned and poured her own mug of ale. "Leo has just placed the pheasant over the fire," she said while refilling Connor's mug. "Would you like to join me in the reading room? It will be a while before dinner's ready." Picking up her mug, she walked out of the kitchen with Connor in tow.

Leaving the main cave, the hub of her home, Rosalyn led Connor to a small alcove. It was a cozy room with two overstuffed chairs, a bookshelf that ran from ceiling to floor, and a few narrow ledges that jutted out from the wall, supporting oil lamps. The burning lamps created an easy glow and wafted a gentle fragrance around the room. In the center was a low table, and upon it sat a large, black stone bowl holding a number of strange objects. Among the brightly colored stones in the bowl, Connor noticed the severed foot of a large bird, the jaw bone of a small animal, and a bundle of dried herbs blackened with soot at one end. As he felt the ease the room offered, a soothing and relaxing retreat at the end of a hard day, Connor studied the hundreds of titles that filled the bookshelf. "Have ye read all these books?"

"Aye, most of them, some more than once." The enchanting sorceress took a long, satisfying breath as she sunk down into her overstuffed chair. Letting her head fall back, she closed her eyes. Connor watched her sit like that for several minutes. It was one of the longest stretches of time since his arrival that she hadn't spoken, and he wondered if his host had fallen asleep. Taking a seat, he was contemplating whether he should say something when Rosalyn finally raised her head and looked at him. "This is where we shall do it," she said, breaking the silence.

"We shall do *what*?" Connor's initial sense of comfort started to wane.

"Take you back. I will take you back through the last twenty years you cannot recall. We'll go back through the veil of forgetfulness, which is the faerie magic that keeps you from remembering. It is a very powerful magic that the fey place on mortals when they cross over, so it will take equally powerful magic to get through, but not tonight. Tomorrow, after breakfast and after I have prepared, we will meet back here." She paused and sat up, looking directly into his eyes. "Connor, you need to be aware that it may take a while to get through. The veil of forgetfulness is thick and laden with magic. It will be trying and exhausting for both of us, but we will get through it. However, you must completely trust me for this to happen. You need to let go and give yourself over to my powers. Can you allow me into your most inner thoughts? Do you think you can do that? Do you trust me?"

Connor sat back in his chair, not quite sure how to respond. "Ye've shared a good deal about yerself with me today, but I ain't stupid. I ken there are things ye still haven't told me. If I'm to be completely honest with ye, no, I dinnae want ye diggin' around in my head. But I also dinnae think I have a choice." Taking another drink, he sat up before continuing. "Demetrick made good on his promise to me, and he trusted ye. There are two things I know for sure. One is that somehow I've lost time, the how and the why I dinnae ken. The second is that I have to find this woman I supposedly met in another world. But that's all I know, and the unknown makes me feel like half a man. Demetrick saved my life for whatever this great cause is, and whether or not I am the right man for the job, I have an obligation to see it through. I've come this far, and I willnae leave without answers. So, if this is the only way to get those answers, then so be it. Ye seem to be a wise and compassionate woman, albeit strange, but then, everything about my life is a bit strange right now, so why not ye too?" Connor wasn't sure if it was the ale that made him so unguarded, or if there was something about Rosalyn that made people open up to her. "So my answer is, yes, because I *need* to trust ye."

As Rosalyn's gaze bore into Connor's soul, somehow he knew she was reading him, judging him as well. But then her demeanor quickly changed, and a soft smile broke across her face. "Alright then, it's settled," she said before strolling out of the room. "Let's go check on that pheasant. We're going to need a hearty meal tonight."

"And maybe another refill o' this wonderful ale," Connor suggested, as he picked up his empty mug and followed her out.

CHAPTER 35

A NEW FRIEND
OR AN OLD FOE?

Isaboe made it half-way down the steps of the church before she was forced to either sit down or fall over. She hadn't known what to expect when she walked into Sister Miriam's room, but she wasn't prepared for what she'd heard. Not only had her children been fostered, but now her only lead in finding them lay clear across the country.

"Orkney Island!" she whispered with resignation, knowing what she now had to do. Even with winter close at hand, there was no option other than to continue on and travel to the country's most northern coastline, an excursion that would take months.

You're on a long journey. The words of the strange old woman who had appeared in the carriage crossed her mind. Isaboe hadn't given much thought as to what she would discover upon arriving in Edinburgh, but she certainly hadn't prepared for having to travel so far with so little information.

Wrapped up in her new-found knowledge, Isaboe felt a quick stab of guilt when she realized that Margaret's plight had completely slipped her mind. Her best friend was still fighting for her life. Pulling herself together as best she could, she made her way back to the inn.

As she sat next to the bed, Isaboe gently rubbed Margaret's fingers, the only part of her hand that wasn't wrapped in bandages. Her friend still had not regained consciousness, and though the doctor encouraged Isaboe to talk to her, she struggled to find anything pleasant to say. Consumed by the idea of having to go to Orkney, she found herself whispering the story to Margaret.

"I went to the church today, Margaret. I spoke with a sister I knew as a young girl, so I gave her a false name. I made up a story about who I am, and why I was looking for information. I felt terrible lying to her, but what choice did I have? She's quite old now, and even though she seemed to have a good memory, I don't think she realized who I am. But then why would she? As far as she knows, Isaboe McKinnon is dead." Sighing deeply, she paused before continuing. "She told me that Marta had the children fostered, but that's all she knew about them. Deidra and Saschel were living on Orkney Island when she last heard from them. Orkney Island, Margaret! That's my only lead. Apparently, Deidra's husband had a small fishing business there, but that was years ago. She didn't even have the husband's name or anything else to go on. Margaret, I need you to be well again. I feel so alone, and I'm so afraid I'll lose you." Weary from the heaviness in her heart, Isaboe's head dropped from exhaustion. "I just don't know what to do," she mumbled to the floor.

"Sounds like you need to go to Orkney Island."

Isaboe sat up quickly at the sound of a strange, yet familiar voice. A woman dressed in a nurse's uniform stood on the other side of the bed looking down at Margaret, smiling. Though it took a few moments, the face soon registered. Confused and disoriented, Isaboe was looking at a woman she had desperately hoped would prove to be a figment of her nightmares.

Looking quite professional in her assumed role, Lorien shot Isaboe a smug grin. "You know dear, with your mouth agape and your eyes bulging, you look a bit like a toad unable to catch its dinner."

After a shocked moment, Isaboe picked her jaw up off the floor and found her voice. "Lorien? I thought you were…just a bad dream!"

The Fey Queen smiled at being recognized. "Well, I am sorry to hear that. Unfortunately, you're not dreaming, and I must say, your friend here doesn't look at all well," Lorien said as she placed a hand on Margaret's head, causing her to moan slightly.

"Get your hands off her!" Isaboe slapped Lorien's hand away. "Don't you touch her!" Taking a protective stance over her unconscious friend, she glared at the Fey Queen.

A knock at the door announced the arrival of Doctor Murray. As he entered the room, Isaboe stepped into his path. "I don't want this woman anywhere near Margaret!" Isaboe glared at Lorien as she barked out her order.

"The nurse is only doing her job. She must be allowed to treat the patient," the doctor said before looking at Lorien for the first time. "I was expecting to see Miss Pritchard. You must be filling in for her. I don't think we've met before, nurse..?"

"You may call me nurse Fey." Lorien smiled as she reached out her hand in greeting.

But Isaboe interceded, cuffing Lorien's hand back. "She's no nurse! She's lying!"

"Really?" Doctor Murray glanced at Lorien before turning back to Isaboe. "If she is not a nurse, then who is she? And why is she here?"

"Yes, dear, tell him who you think I am," Lorien said with a satisfied grin.

"She's a…a…" Blurting out that Lorien was a faerie suddenly didn't seem like a good idea, so Isaboe abruptly walked around the bed and grabbed Lorien by the arm. "We need to talk," she said, escorting Lorien into the hall and away from the doctor's curious expression before closing the door. "What in the bloody hell are you doing here? What do you want from me?" Isaboe almost shouted.

"Isaboe, my dear, why are you so upset?" Lorien asked, as she struggled to detach herself from Isaboe's grasp.

"What?" Isaboe was shocked that Lorien could ask her such a thing. "I don't know what's happening here, or if you're even real. You're probably just a figment of my imagination, a hallucination created by my insanity. Perhaps I've finally been pushed too far!"

"Well, if I am a figment of your imagination, that doctor has the same imagination you do."

Isaboe couldn't deny that Doctor Murray had acknowledged Lorien, even spoken to her. This rather minimized the likelihood of Isaboe's insanity, but it was the last thread of hope she had been clinging to. The fey woman standing in front of her was as real as she was, and Isaboe was wide awake. Her nightmare had just become undeniably tangible, and the weight of it hit like a punch in the gut. "What do you want from me?" she sobbed, as a heavy wave of defeat washed over her.

"I only want to be your friend, Isaboe. I know what I told you in the wee hours of the morning was hard for you to hear. You were quite upset, crying so hard that there seemed no point in trying to continue our discussion. So I thought it best if I let you sleep for a while. I assumed you would want to wash upon rising, so I replaced the broken bowl before I left. Don't you see? I do care about you, Isaboe, truly I do. And I'm very sorry for your pain. I just want to help you. That's why I'm here."

Lorien's sympathy felt like a cruel joke, and Isaboe didn't believe it. "I don't want your help. I just want you to leave me alone."

"I can't do that, Isaboe. And let me remind you—you have no one else."

"I have Margaret and Connor. I don't need you."

"Oh, well, let's talk about those two. Poor, dear Margaret, lying there on her death bed. Who knows when, or if, she will ever recover? And Connor, where is he? Oh yes, he's off attending his own agenda, obviously something more important than you."

"Don't you say that! Margaret is *not* going to die, and Connor *is* coming back for me. I know he will!" Isaboe couldn't deny the desperation in her voice.

"I didn't mean to upset you, my dear. I just wanted to point out that, right now, I'm the only one here for you. I thought you could use someone to lean on, someone who cares about you." Lorien's voice was overly laced with compassion.

Feeling confused and alone, Isaboe wasn't sure what to think. And this woman, as strange as she was, did offer something she desperately needed—someone to talk to. With frightened eyes, she looked around, taking deep breaths before turning back to the smiling face of the small faerie woman. "I do feel awfully alone right now."

"Well, see, there you are. I'm here for you. Come, let's take a walk. Some fresh air will do you good."

After saying a hasty goodbye to Dr. Murray, the two ladies went down the stairs and left the inn. As they strolled along the boardwalk through the streets of Edinburgh, Isaboe shared her new knowledge with the dainty fey woman.

"So, you don't know Deidra's husband's name, or the name of his business?" Lorien asked, sounding almost bored.

"No, I don't. So even if I do go to Orkney, I have no idea how to start looking for them."

"Hmm, if only there were some way you could find out his name. Were they married here in Edinburgh before they left for Orkney?"

Isaboe abruptly stopped and looked closely at Lorien. "Yes, I believe Sister Miriam said they were married at the Kirk. They would have had to file for a marriage license here in Edinburgh. I could go to the courthouse, or maybe the city hall, to look for that marriage certificate. It would have both her maiden name and his name on the license," Isaboe heard the hope in her voice.

"Oh, splendid! You should go right away." Lorien mimicked Isaboe's enthusiasm.

"Will you go with me?"

"No, I can't. It's very draining for me to maintain this mortal form. I can only stay in this world for a short time before I require a reprieve back to my own world, to regenerate, you might say."

"Oh, alright. I can't believe I'm asking you this, but, will I see you again?"

"Oh, most definitely," Lorien said with a gracious nod. "Good luck with your investigation. I'll see you soon."

Isaboe's attention was drawn by the sound of someone shouting, and when she turned back around, Lorien was gone. In the blink of an eye, the fey woman had vanished just as quickly and mysteriously as she had appeared.

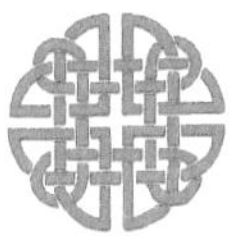

CHAPTER 36

BACK THROUGH THE VEIL OF FORGETFULNESS

An early morning mist dampened Connor's hair as he stood at the railing, surveying the great canyon. The view was exhilarating. Dawn cast the deep ravine in shadow as the rising sun caressed the ridge's peak, making the rusted reds and deep greens of the stone come to life. But Connor saw none of it. His thoughts drifted like the wispy fog that rose up from the canyon floor, and he was barely able to acknowledge the natural beauty of the morning. It was merely a scenic backdrop to his worry.

His last thought before sleep, and his first thought upon rising was of Isaboe. But he felt confident he was giving her the time she needed, time to sort out her feelings about him, and about her late husband. Though he had no idea of Margaret's condition, he hoped she was recovering. Isaboe would of course be at her friend's side, her heart heavy with worry. At that moment, he fervently wished he could be holding her, giving her comfort, keeping her safe.

Connor tried to shake off his concerns by rationalizing that he would be back with her soon enough. But it didn't lessen his longing, or make the wait any easier. He had known her for only a short while, but something about Isaboe had burrowed deeply into his soul. She was beautiful, yes, but it was more than that. She had an inner beauty, earnest and heartfelt. He knew she was stubborn, but vulnerable and naïve at the same time. And there was an undeniable pain hiding behind her emerald-green eyes, eyes he could not get out of his mind. She was dealing with more than just the loss of her husband, and there was a mystery about her he couldn't identify. He wanted badly to understand her, to help shoulder her pain, and hopefully one day, help free her from it.

After indulging in a few more moments watching the sun rise, Connor came back from his thoughts with a sigh. Knowing that Rosalyn was making preparations for his *remembering*, as she called it, he was reluctant to go back inside. Even though that was why he was here, now that it was at hand, he wasn't sure he was ready. She had shared briefly over breakfast what he could expect, and it didn't sound pleasant.

Connor's thoughts were interrupted by the woman herself, who appeared at the door. "Whenever you're ready, I have everything set up."

He turned and gave her a formal nod before taking another long look across the great canyon. Whether he was ready or not, this was something he had to do. He had made a covenant with Demetrick after the great wizard chose him for this task, saving him from a most certain death. Connor was an honorable man, a man who knew the meaning of loyalty and commitment. Even in moments of uncertainty, where a part of him wanted to run, he knew he wouldn't. He was bound by the ties of honor, and it was now time to face his memories and complete the task Demetrick had assigned him decades ago. Taking one long, last breath, he turned and began walking back toward the heavy wooden door when a sudden sound stopped him.

Only feet away, a golden eagle gracefully hovered over the deck, screeching its presence in a reverent song. The elegant bird's wings caught the updraft from the canyon floor, and it floated effortlessly, suspended in air by an invisible current. When the eagle suddenly swooped down and disappeared from view, the moment brought a brief smile to Connor's lips before he turned and entered the cave.

He found Rosalyn in the reading room, sitting in one of the overstuffed chairs. Her eyes were closed and her hands were placed lightly on her knees as she took long, deep, controlled breaths. She wore a dark robe, which reminded him of the ones that Demetrick had worn, and hair hung loosely down around her shoulders.

There were fewer candles lit than the night before, so it took a few moments for Connor's eyes to adjust. Rolling smoke that smelled of musk and spice burned at his nose as it curled upward from oil burners on the shelves that lined the walls. On the table in front of Rosalyn, the black stone bowl was filled with water. Evenly spaced around the bowl's perimeter sat small cups. Some were filled with white powder, some with what appeared to be dried herbs. Other items on the table included a large eagle feather, colored stones, and a necklace made of animal teeth and claws.

Upon Connor's entrance, Rosalyn looked up and motioned for him to join her. As he took his seat, she handed him a cup. "Drink," she instructed.

The liquid was bitter and nasty. It burned all the way down his throat. "What the hell was that?" he grimaced as he put the empty cup back on the table.

"It was a mixture of some very potent herbs that will help you to relax so your mind can stay open and receptive to my instructions." Picking up the necklace made of animal bones, she handed it to Connor and instructed him to place one end in his hand as she held the other. "This is a spirit loop that will connect our thoughts and our minds. What you see, hear, and feel, I will see, hear, and feel. Our souls will be linked during this ceremony, and you will have no secrets that I will not know. Do you accept these conditions?" Rosalyn's demeanor was focused, and she spoke with an eerie, unnatural tone.

"What, no magic wand? No faerie dust?" Connor tried to lighten his anxiety, but Rosalyn shot him a look that was almost angry.

"This is not child's play, Connor. This is very powerful magic. If you are not going to take this seriously, then there is no point in going forward."

"I'm sorry." Connor instantly regretted his taunt as he felt the sting of Rosalyn's reprimand. "It just seems so hard to accept that ye can really do this. Have ye ever done it before?"

"Just once, but it was I who went through the remembering, and Demetrick who performed the ceremony. Not to worry, the master taught me everything I need to know."

"Why did ye need to go through a remembering? Had ye been to the world of the Underlings as well?"

"This is not about me. This is about you, and why you are here. This process will be difficult enough, so what I need from you is your trust and cooperation. If you think you can't go through with this, say so now. Otherwise, no more questions." Rosalyn's words rang with authority.

Since she had been through this, and it appeared that her mind was still intact, questionable or not, he supposed he could as well. "Let's be about it then." He made the statement with commitment, deciding to turn his life, or at least his mind, over to the sorceress.

"Very well, I need you to relax. The potion you drank should start to take effect very soon. Lay your head back, try to clear your mind, and listen to the sound of my voice." Rosalyn took some powder from one of the small cups and threw it into the bowl of water in front of her. The surface of the water instantly clouded and began to swirl. What looked like smoke slowly drifted up, and when it lifted, the surface of the liquid turned clear as glass. A strange light radiated from the water, almost as if it was coming from within the bowl.

As the potion took effect, Connor laid his head back. His eyes became heavy, and the sense of floating made him feel a bit nauseated. Behind closed eyes, he saw flashes of light spinning and exploding. Soon, the flashes melted into swirling colors, drawing together until they formed a vortex of color and light. A sense of freefall sent him tumbling, and Connor felt pulled towards its center. It was as if his soul had left his body and launched itself down a tunnel that had formed in his mind.

"I call upon all the powers of the universe. I pray to the Mother Goddess for protection, and ask that God the Father be at our side. All the spirits be with us now, direct us, guide us, protect us. Open the connection between these two souls. Let us become one!" Connor sensed Rosalyn's words more than he heard them, as if they were coming from somewhere deep within him.

"Go back. Go back, Braden MacPherson, to a time and place where Underlings live, where fairies dance and sing, chant and cast their spells on unsuspecting mortals. Go back, go back to a time where you lived among them, and remember what took place in their world while you were there. Push through the veil of forgetfulness and return to that place, to that time, and be there now. Go back, go back and remember. Go back…and remember."

Stepping out of the trees, Braden saw fleeting shapes and shadows, but who or what they were, he had no idea. The effigies that sped by gave no hint of recognition in the dim light of dusk. As he realized he didn't know where he was, anxiety settled like an evil curse in his gut.

Confused and disoriented, Braden turned in circles to take in his environment, but the forest that surrounded him only added to the mystery—the trees were moving! Not only were the branches swaying, but he could see motion at the base of the trees, shadows that jumped and slithered along the ground. Instinctively, he reached for his weapon, but the dirk was missing.

Feeling a slight breeze brush by, Braden spun again, but he could make out only quick flashes of light before they disappeared into the darkness of the trees. "Who's there? Show yerself!" he shouted. But the only responses he received were giggles and hissing, coming from somewhere out of sight in the cold obscurity.

Something suddenly bit into the side of his neck. Startled by the impact, Braden reached up and felt a small protruding shaft. Grasping it firmly, he ripped the dart from his skin, tearing flesh along with it. Though it felt no more painful than a pin prick, the small weapon he held in his hand was far from harmless. As Braden's knees buckled, his eyes rolled back in his head.

Though his mind was cloudy, Braden became cognizant of others around him. How many, he didn't know, but he was acutely aware of the physical sensations he felt from their touches. He struggled to understand whether his erotic dream was still playing out, or if he was awake. As he fought to open his eyes, his head felt heavy, but floating at the same time. He was able to make out several beautiful women who moved provocatively around the bed he found himself lying upon. With the exception of a small cloth tied around his hips, he was completely naked. The women had long, willowy fingers, which they skillfully used to trace the energy up his inner leg to his thigh, and along the joint of his hips. As the delicate hands caressed his body, Braden heard a moan escape his lips. He rolled his head to one side to get a better view and noticed a ring on the finger of his right hand; it was dimly glowing.

But the ring instantly lost Braden's attention when he felt lips nibbling at his ears. Soft, dainty fingers glided across his chest and down the length of his body, sending ripples of goosebumps over his skin. When he attempted to lift his head, the room tilted out of focus. It was dark, with only a few candles, and the flickering lights only added to the sensuous atmosphere.

Suddenly his vision became clear, and he found himself staring into the face of an angel. The woman's eyes were almost iridescent, shimmering in the candlelight. Her full, dark lips brushed up against the corner of his mouth before lightly nipping at his chin. Braden felt his breath catch in his throat as she suckled his nipple while running one hand down the front of his abdomen. After barely touching her lips to his, just enough to feel the brush of a kiss, the woman smiled seductively at his reaction, then quickly turned and melted back into the twisting shadows.

The sound of drums beating somewhere in the distance made its way through Braden's foggy senses, as the rhythmic repetition began to move the women into a slow and sensual dance. With each beat, he could feel his heart pushing the blood that pulsed through his veins. When he propped himself up on one elbow, the room still lilted and moved, but he stayed focused on the women who seemed to be floating around him. Dancing to the beat of the drums, they swept their bodies through the air as if moved by primal instinct. Even in the dark, their dresses were so light and airy they did little to cover what was underneath.

Somewhere in the distance, a chant began, low and repetitive, but Braden couldn't make out the words. As the vibrant energy escalated around him, so did the intensity of the women's movements. They took turns thrusting toward him, touching him intimately, and rubbing their bodies against his, before swishing away out of his reach to again rejoin the alluring dance.

Braden's mind struggled to understand what was happening, but his body responded strongly to the sensuous stimulus that surrounded him. When he reached for the women teasing him, they tauntingly slipped away from his grasp. He was feeling so light-headed that it took a moment for him to realize that he was being lifted off the bed. With a woman on each arm, he was able to stand. They led him to a chair with a high back and wide armrests. After taking the appointed seat, a goblet was placed in Braden's hand. A beautiful, dark-skinned woman with elaborately-braided hair and full lips appeared beside him with a carafe and poured red wine into his goblet. After carefully placing the carafe on the floor, she led the goblet to his mouth and encouraged him to drink. Kneeling down at his knees, she rubbed her hands up his thighs as the other women joined in, licking and kissing his chest and face, all in order to arouse him.

When the kneeling woman stood up in front of him, her transparent white gown shimmering in contrast to her ebony skin, his eyes swept appreciatively over her slender form. She took his hands and lifted him to his feet, her dark eyes dancing with his as a slight smile crossed her lips.

"It is time, my Lord," she said in a sultry tone. As she led him by the hand, he felt his blood rising in anticipation. When they reached a cloth-covered opening, she pulled the fabric back, and the smell of rosemary wafted out. In the middle of the enclosure was an ornate bed, and though his focus had not completely returned, it appeared to be occupied.

"The Mother Alaina awaits you, my Lord," the woman said softly. Pressing her hand against the small of his back, she encouraged him forward before dropping the cloth. One lone candle cast a soft glow about the room, and he waited until his eyes adjusted. Taking a few cautious steps, he could see a beautiful woman reclining on the bed in front of him. As he looked down at her with intense desire, she slowly opened her eyes....

CHAPTER 37

THE NIGHTMARE BECOMES REALITY

After feverishly scouring Edinburgh, Isaboe finally found someone willing to help her. She waited in the courthouse for hours, only to be told how difficult it would be to dig through the records to access such ancient information. She finally felt forced to pass over a few coins, so the greasy little man, now with money in his hand, would stop whining over how laborious this task would be. It was amazing how a little money made his discomfort suddenly disappear.

"Come back in a week," he said. "I'll have the document by then."

"A week? That's not good enough. I'll pay you two more schillings if you can locate the marriage certificate by tomorrow morning."

"I understand yer anxious, little one, but these things take time, and my back ain't what it used to be." He grinned, revealing a row of red gums, his front teeth nowhere to be seen.

Isaboe sighed and held up a third shilling, the little coin glittering in the half-light. "Fine. I'll give you three if you can deliver by tomorrow morning, but only after I have the document."

"Three shillings will hardly pay fer a man's supper." He held up his hands in surrender when Isaboe scowled, "but yer charity is beyon' kind. I'll do my best."

Isaboe left the clerk's office feeling rather bad about spending Connor's money, but she rationalized that if Margaret had been by her side, she would have done the same thing. But then, Margaret most likely would have tried intimidation before agreeing to give the greasy little man any more coins. As a businesswoman, Margaret prided herself on her dealings with men, despite her negotiation with the stable keep in Inverness.

Isaboe recalled fondly how Connor looked out for Margaret's investment when he really didn't have to. Procuring good horses in place of those she had purchased must have been a sour note for the stable keep who thought he had gotten the better part of a bad deal.

The days spent with Connor made her heart ache as she realized just how much she missed him. He had only been gone for three days, but it seemed so much longer than that. Though still physically present, Isaboe missed Margaret too: it was as if she had gone away and left as well. Margaret had not been coherent for days, drank little water, and ate nothing. She was lost in her own world, unreachable by Isaboe, Doctor Murray, or the kind nurses who attended her. If Margaret didn't soon come out of the deep sleep she was lost in, Isaboe feared she might die.

As she stepped out of the courthouse into the damp, early-evening air, Isaboe noticed that the sky was full of dark clouds holding the promise of rain. Cinching the cloak tightly around her shoulders, she pulled the hood up over her head as she made her way back to the inn. On her way, she passed a small diner, and the aroma that wafted through the open window made her stomach growl. She hadn't eaten since morning, and the smell of food made her realize how hungry she was. Though she felt guilty for having spent most of the day away from Margaret's side, Isaboe decided that a few extra minutes wouldn't hurt, so she stopped for supper. After all, she was eating for two.

The next morning, there was a new gait in Isaboe's step as she walked toward the courthouse. She wasn't sure if it was due to the cool, brisk wind that pushed her along, or if it was the good news she had just received about Margaret. When the doctor had stopped by the inn that morning, he informed Isaboe that the patient's fever had broken during the night, and that her wounds were finally showing signs of healing. He couldn't explain why Margaret wasn't waking up yet, but this was the first good news Isaboe had received regarding her friend's condition.

Isaboe made her way quickly up the steps of the courthouse and entered the clerk's office. Pleased to see that the greasy little man was in, she presented him with a pleasant greeting. "Good morning, sir. I've come to collect the document we discussed yesterday. Do you have it for me?"

The man looked up from his desk and put his pen down. "Oh, it's you. I'll have ye know, I was up all night, rummaging through mounds of boxes, trying to locate this marriage certificate. Now my back is so bad, I can't even stand up straight." Moaning as he stood, the little man rubbed the small of his back as he hobbled over to the counter, holding a piece of paper. A terrible look of pain crossed this face. "I had to do extensive searching. The toll it took on my poor back, *oohh!* That will be five schillings," he said, holding tightly onto the paper.

"Five? I told you I would pay you three, and I'll not give you a penny more!"

Gripping the paper with both hands, he started backing away. "Well, then I ain't so sure this is what ye were looking for. I wouldn't want to give ye the wrong document, would I?"

"Look, you little weasel! I already paid two schillings last night, and that was over and above what I paid to the office of records out front. So don't you try to finagle any more money out of me, or I'll go out there and turn you in! I'm sure there are plenty of other people, people who don't have bad backs and would love to have your job. Now hand over that certificate!" Glaring fiercely at the clerk, Isaboe pulled out her three schillings and held them tightly.

"Oh, well, I guess this is the right document after all," he mumbled as he put the paper on the counter.

Slapping the coins down, Isaboe grabbed the certificate and began scanning through the legal wording and dates. She stopped upon seeing Deidra Cameron listed as wife, and Tomas MacFarland recorded as husband. This was exactly what she was looking for. Letting out a sigh of relief, she looked back at the clerk and gave him half a smile. "Good day to you sir," she said, closing the door behind her.

As she walked with quickened steps back to the inn, Isaboe's mind raced with anticipation as she considered what her next move would be. Now that she knew Deidra's husband's name and where they had last lived, how and when she could get there was the next question. Connor should be back soon, and Margaret was finally showing signs of improvement, though it would probably be many days before she could travel. But that didn't matter, because for the first time in months, Isaboe finally had something to give her hope, hope that she might find out what had become of her children. Even if Marta had them fostered, her two sisters should have all of their mother's legal documents, and there must be information about the fostering parents. She just hoped that if she actually found her sisters, and if they still have the legal documents, she could somehow convince them to believe her. There were a lot of ifs, but it was better than having nothing at all.

"So, what did you find?"

Jumping at the sound of Lorien's voice, Isaboe turned to see the fey woman walking beside her. "Lorien! Do you have to do that?"

"Do what?"

"Just appear and disappear whenever you wish with no warning."

"What would you have me do? Circle around you like a twinkling star so you know I'm here?"

"Can you do that?"

"Well, of course I can, but I won't. It's a bit beneath me. I am a queen after all."

"But, how do you do it? I mean, how do you travel from your world into this one?" Isaboe shot Lorien a questioning glare. "And if you really are fey, why don't you have wings?"

"It's called faerie magic, my dear, and how I travel in between worlds is no concern to you," The Fey Queen's answer was curt. "Did you find the information you were looking for?"

"Oh, yes. Deidra's husband's name was Tomas MacFarland. I now have a place to start looking, and a name to look for. I just need to wait for Connor to return and Margaret to be well."

"Oh. Is that your plan? Wait for Connor and Margaret?"

"Well of course. What else would I do?"

"Go without them."

Stopping abruptly, Isaboe turned toward Lorien. "Go without them? Why would I do that?"

"Oh dear, I was so hoping it wouldn't come to this," Lorien said, glancing across the street as she clutched Isaboe's hand. "Come. Let's go sit for a moment. We need to talk."

Reluctantly, Isaboe followed the Fey Queen and sat next to her on a wooden bench. A familiar anxiety began to grow in the pit of her stomach knowing that Lorien had something to tell her—something she was sure she didn't want to know. "What is it, Lorien?"

"I really wanted to spare you this, but if you do intend to wait for your friends, well, I feel I must tell you."

"Tell me what?" Isaboe felt her guard rising.

"Isaboe, when I was in your room the other morning, I told you that you were chosen to be the Mother Alaina long before you were born. I have been aware of you since the moment of your birth. I know everything about you and everyone who has been in your life, even your birth mother."

"You knew my mother?" Isaboe asked, her interest suddenly piqued.

"I only knew of her, and that she gave you up when you were born. You weren't wanted, Isaboe. She didn't love you."

Taken aback, Isaboe was even more surprised that the words hurt. She'd always believed that was exactly why her birth mother had given her up, but she wasn't prepared for how it would feel to actually have someone confirm it.

"You were given a new mother and father, an adopted family. However, your adopted mother also chose not to love you, and I know that was painful for you. But your father loved you, didn't he? Sadly, fate intervened, and you lost his love when he died. Then your mother sent you away, but you met Nathan, your husband, and he loved you very much. Together you had your own children who loved you, too. Unfortunately, their love was also taken from you. Nathan died because of his love for you, Isaboe. And the children, well, we don't know what became of them, do we?"

A mixture of fear, anger, and the familiar feeling of loss began to build in Isaboe's chest, and she let it show on her face. "Why are you telling me this? Nathan died because *you* took me away from him!"

"Isaboe, I didn't cause you to be taken. I've already told you that you were chosen long before you were born." Lorien's answer seemed almost smug. "I am only your guide and companion, here to help you."

"I didn't ask to be chosen! I didn't ask for any of this. Why me? And what does any of this have to do with waiting for Connor and Margaret? What are you trying to tell me?" Isaboe felt her fear mounting with each passing moment.

"Isaboe, you are the Mother Alaina. That is your destiny, and only that. You were never meant to have or know mortal love. Anyone who loves you…well, this is hard for me to say, but, anyone who loves you will….die."

"*What?*" Isaboe stood up and stared down at Lorien. "What are you telling me?" She suddenly felt trapped in a blinding whirlwind as a variety of upsetting images flashed through her mind.

"Think about it, Isaboe. You know what I tell you is true. The first person who showed you any love was your adopted father, and he died. Nathan loved you, and he died. Wasn't Connor injured trying to protect you? He was lucky that day, but he may not be so lucky next time. And Margaret, poor Margaret is still very ill. Death hangs over her bed, waiting. And they both love you, don't they?"

"*Stop it!* Don't say that! Margaret is not going to die! Her fever broke and her wounds are starting to heal. She *is* getting better!" Isaboe fought back the tears that were burning to break free.

"Even if she does recover, it is just a matter of time for her, Isaboe. As long as you are with her, she is destined for the same fate, as is Connor. If you truly care about them, you must leave them. You must leave here before Connor returns, and before Margaret is well, if she does in fact ever recover. Their love for you is their death sentence. Can't you see that? "

"I will not leave Margaret. Do you hear me? I will not leave her! I hate you for telling me this! I wish you would just disappear, and LEAVE ME ALONE!" Screaming out in her pain, Isaboe turned and ran, leaving Lorien behind.

But she was not far enough away to avoid hearing the fey woman's last words; "Then their blood will be on your hands!"

CHAPTER 38

REMEMBERED

Connor's head was laid back and his eyes closed. He could hear Rosalyn calling to him from somewhere deep within the darkness, as if her voice was coming across a great abyss.

"Connor, wake up. It is time to return. Can you hear me?" Sitting at his side, still holding the spirit loop, Rosalyn looked anxious as she dribbled warm oil on his forehead, rubbing it in with small circles. "Connor, can you hear me? It's time to come back through the veil; come back to the present." For long moments, Rosalyn continued with her rituals, trying to bring him back from another world, from another place and time.

Slowly, he started to stir, mumbling indistinctly with rapid eye movement behind closed lids. Gasping for breath, he jolted upright, his eyes wide, darting from side to side. The sweat that beaded on Connor's forehead mixed with the oil, and began dripping down the sides of his face.

Prepared for such an awakening, Rosalyn stood over him, holding out a mug of water, which he grabbed with both hands and pulled greedily to his mouth. "Slowly now, not so fast," she said, keeping her fingers wrapped around the mug as Connor slurped the water down, drinking it dry. She then sat down and removed the spirit loop, giving him time to recover.

Finally able to calm his heavy breathing, his eyes still glazed over, Connor gasped, *"Isaboe! It was Isaboe!"* He was startled by his own words. Rubbing his hands over his face, he tried to bring his mind back to the present, though his thoughts were very clear.

"Isaboe? That's the name of the woman you were with?"

"My God, it was Isaboe!"

"Did you know this woman before?"

"No. I met her in Inverness, and we traveled to Edinburgh together." He still couldn't believe that the woman he was chosen to find—the woman he had encountered in the realm of another world—was the same woman he had fallen in love with, right here in his own world. "Isaboe," her name slipped across his lips in a whisper.

"This woman, Isaboe, you were more than just traveling companions I take it."

"Aye. Though I cannae say why, we became very close. It was so easy to care for her, to…"

"Fall in love with her?" Rosalyn finished his sentence.

Resting his elbows on his knees, Connor leaned forward with his face in his hands, trying to rub the last remaining cobwebs from his mind. His breathing had slowed, but his heartbeat was still rapid, and Isaboe's face burned in his memory like a rekindled fire.

"By all the Gods!" Rosalyn sat back in her chair, taking her own cleansing breaths. "The very woman that Demetrick sent you to look for ends up being the same woman you met and traveled with, yet you didn't even suspect it! Sometimes the universe lays things out right in front of us so close we can't even see it." Shaking her head in amazement, Rosalyn chuckled. "You see now why it was so easy to fall in love with her, don't you? You knew her in another time, another place. Even though you couldn't recall that time or place, you felt a connection with her, deep in your soul. My guess is she felt it too."

As if on cue, they both fell into silence, drained and exhausted. After a few moments, Rosalyn placed her hand on his shoulder. "Are you feeling any better yet?"

"To be truthful, I feel like I've been kicked in the head and could use a wee nap," Connor said behind closed eyes as he sank into the chair and dropped his head back.

"Well, the kick in the head is from the potion I gave you, and that will pass. Sleep is definitely in order. This ceremony took all day, so you'll need a good night's sleep. We will talk more on the morrow."

Connor lifted his head. "All day? Are ye telling me that the whole day has passed?"

"Yes. It took a good while for you to get through the veil. That's why we are both so exhausted. Would you like something to eat first?"

"No." Connor stood up slowly, steadying himself before trying to move. When he felt he could walk without falling over, he gave Rosalyn a weak smile. "I'll say good evening to ye then. We'll talk in the morning."

Rosalyn nodded and watched as he walked out of the reading room. With concern etched on her face, she remained sitting in her overstuffed chair. "Isaboe," she whispered the name slowly before casting her eyes to the ceiling.

"It has started, Demetrick. I hope you knew what you were doing."

CHAPTER 39

MOTHER ALAINA

As Isaboe hurried back to the inn, tears ran freely down her face, blurring her vision, and she neither saw nor heard anyone. Dodging around the people on the street, oblivious to their worried looks and offers of assistance, she could only hear Lorien's words: *"You were never meant to know mortal love. Their love for you is their death sentence; their blood will be on your hands…their blood will be on your hands!"*

Visions of the horrible nightmare she'd had only two nights before returned to haunt her—Margaret savagely ripped apart by wolves, the blood running up her arms, blood spilling out of Nathan's eyes, and a sword protruding from Connor's belly. As she remembered Lorien's words, the gruesome images kept repeating themselves, falling on top of one another, over and over in her mind. As Lorien's voice echoed in her ears, she couldn't ignore the creeping suspicion that the Fey Queen was telling the dreadful truth.

After reaching her room, Isaboe had to fumble with the key before the door finally opened. She immediately threw herself on the bed next to her unconscious friend and began sobbing into her pillow, knowing that her wailing fell on deaf ears. "Margaret, how much more of this can I take? God, oh God, I can't do this anymore. I just want it all to go away!" Isaboe sat up and wiped away the tears before looking down at Margaret, who had shown no sign of hearing her rant. "I wish you were here. I feel so alone," she whispered, squeezing Margaret's hand.

The enormity was just too much. Margaret still lay unconscious, and Isaboe had no idea if her friend would ever wake up again. Connor had run off somewhere, and there was no guarantee that he would return either. And even if he did, if what Lorien said was true, then she would only hurt him. *The tip of a sword split its way through the skin of his chest, protruding obscenely.*

If she had to live her life alone, Isaboe didn't want to live. She sat up on the bed and looked at the dirk Connor had left on the table. Wiping the last remaining tears from her cheeks, she walked across the room and picked it up. This was the way out. She watched the light glint off the sharp line of the blade. It would be quick, and the pain couldn't be any worse than what she was currently feeling. A quick thought for her unborn child flashed through her mind, but she pushed it away.

Why have a child I cannot love? Balancing the blade in her hand, she gave a thought to Margaret. Glancing at her unconscious friend, she hoped that someone other than Margaret would discover her cold, stiff, and lifeless body. She turned her back to the bed and touched the blade to her wrist, where the dark veins pulsed beneath her transparent skin. *Don't think, just get it over with,* she told herself, as she felt her heartbeat quickening.

But before she could apply pressure, the dirk was torn out of her hand. She looked up to see Lorien standing next to her. "What are you doing?" the Fey Queen asked, a look of horror on her face.

"Why do you care? Give it back. Let me be done with this." Her voice low and lifeless, Isaboe had no energy to fight. She was exhausted. If death was the only way to escape her fate, then so be it.

"I certainly will not! Isaboe, you are being ridiculous! This is not the end of the world for you, it is only the beginning. Think of your unborn child. Even if you cannot find a reason to live for yourself, the baby is innocent. You're not being rational!"

"Rational? Of course I'm not being rational. I'm trying to kill myself. There is no rationality in that." There was something hysterical to that statement, and Isaboe wasn't sure if she was coping or panicking.

"But why would you take your own life?"

"Because, I don't *want* to live my life if I can't have love!" Isaboe furrowed her brow and turned her angry eyes on the Fey Queen. "All I have ever wanted was to have a family and to *love* them. All I have ever wanted was to *be loved* by them. What good is my life if I can't have the very thing I've fought for since I was a child?"

"I didn't say that you would never know love, Isaboe. What I said is that you were never meant to know *mortal* love."

"As usual, Lorien, you make no sense. So just give me the knife and go away."

"Mortals make everything so complicated," Lorien snapped. "I don't know why I waste so much energy on you." Sighing deeply, she began pacing the room, tapping the dirk in the palm of her hand. "Isaboe, I'm trying to be understanding, truly I am, but you are testing my patience. Had you not been so hysterical and ran off the way you did, I could have told you the rest."

"The rest of what?" Isaboe snapped, not wanting to hear anymore from the Fey Queen.

"That because you are the Mother Alaina, you will *always* be loved, loved by all the people of Euphoria. You are held in a position of great honor and are adored by each of them. You are Mother Alaina; the mother of the child. If you think on it, you must remember the love you felt from the fey when you were in Euphoria."

"It's not the same. The people of Euphoria are not my people. I'm not one of you. I'm a mortal woman who needs human love, not the love of a bunch of...*faeries!* I can't believe I'm even having this conversation!" Isaboe ran her hands through her hair before turning to sit on the bed. Leaning over with her elbows on her knees, she buried her face in her hands.

"Oh, but you're wrong, my dear. You *are* one of us. You just haven't accepted it yet." Lorien sat next to Isaboe, putting a hand on her shoulder.

With exhausted eyes, Isaboe sat up and looked at the fey woman sitting next to her. "Why Lorien? Why me? You keep talking about my destiny. What is my destiny? What does this child have to do with the people of Euphoria? And what do you know about the father of my child? Is the father a..." Isaboe hesitated.

"A fey? Of course not. The father of your child is mortal. He was chosen, just as you were. But his identity is of no importance."

"*No importance?* How can you sit there and be so smug about ruining people's lives? Not only have you stolen *everything* from me, but you have also destroyed the life of a man for your own perverse goals. What happened to him? Where is he now? Did you rob him of his life as you did mine?" Though Isaboe felt she had no options, the thought that someone else may be suffering her same fate only added to the fire that burned in her breast.

"Concerning yourself with him is a waste of energy. You don't even remember him. He had only one purpose—to plant the seed of the child who was conceived in the land of the fey—a child who must be very closely guarded. Therefore, *you* must be very closely guarded."

"Why? From whom do I need to be guarded?"

"There are forces that do not want to see this child born, powerful forces that have been following you all of your life, just as I have. Though I have managed to keep you protected, I cannot protect those around you, especially those closest to you."

"Like…Nathan?"

"Yes, as well as Margaret and Connor. I have placed a shield of protection around you, but I cannot for them. Their lives are at risk just for being with you, for loving you."

"But why is this child so important, and who doesn't want my baby to be born? Explain why I have to live a life without my friends for a race of people that are not my own." Isaboe couldn't hide the desperation in her voice. "Help me to understand, Lorien. Please!"

Lorien stood up and again paced the room before turning to face Isaboe. "Thousands of your mortal years ago, the realm of the Underlings and the mortal world existed on the same plane, here together on this Earth. Mortals and all manner of Underlings—faeries, elves, pixies, and muses—lived side by side, cohabitating. Even trolls and goblins roamed about, causing their fair share of trouble. This was the way life was intended to be. Mortals called upon the Underlings for different needs. The Green Ladies sprinkled blessed water over newly planted fields to insure bountiful crops. Argea, the Guardian of Health would be called upon when there was an illness; she loved good wine, so when a mortal tied a wine-soaked rag to a tree behind his home, as the wine dried up, so did the illness.

"The Primrose Faeries inspired music and poetry, while the river nixes created fine clothing. Tree sprites brought the promise of new life to a woman's barren womb, and the selkies of the ocean brought good fortune to fishermen. Some fey folk fostered spiritual empowerment, and some took it away. But for every deed that was performed by an Underling, there was always a payment made in return. There was a give and take between our species, a unity of balance. It was a time of acceptance that all creatures, mortal or fey, had a rightful place on Earth.

"But then a new religion began to spread over the land, and things began to change. It was like a plague. One single, supreme leader outlawed the Underlings. It was alright to believe in angels, but not in pixies. It was however, acceptable and encouraged to believe in *Heaven*," Lorien scoffed, "which is a place you mortals cannot see and have no way to confirm its existence. But you will not accept that Underlings have shared this Earth with you since time began. The balance was broken, and now our interaction with humans is considered to be the work of Satan.

"Mortals began to fear us and reject us. Now they no longer believe in us! As this gap between our two ways of life expanded, the realm of the Underlings split away from the mortal world, and our two worlds have been moving further and further apart with each passing of the seasons.

"Now, it is only a rare occasion when the planes of our two worlds ever connect, and someday they may never again. You mortals live such short lives, and the memory of the days when we lived together in harmony has long been forgotten. Only a few stories, believed to be simply myths or lore, have survived. So, there is no recollection of how it used to be. The balance in nature, the harmony and flow of life between our two worlds has all been lost.

"That is why you are so important, Isaboe. This child you carry, this mortal babe that was conceived in the realm of the Underlings, will be of both worlds. She will be able to cross over whenever she wishes, and she will have a chance to reunite our worlds once again. She is the hope of a new generation where we can all live together on the same Earth, co-existing for the good of both, as nature intended it to be.

"But there are some Underlings—the narrow minded and inflexible— who do not have the insight to see the crucial opportunities this union would bring. They do not wish for us to interfere with the lives of humans, or to question what you mortals choose to believe. It is those Underlings who do not want this child to be born, and they will try to prevent the birth." Lorien sat down next to Isaboe and took her hands. The dainty fey woman looked into Isaboe's wide, frightened eyes. "The best way to prevent the birth of an unborn child is to take the life of the mother." Lorien paused, and her expression softened. "But I promise you, Isaboe, I will not let that happen. As long as I'm here, I will protect you."

"This is all too much, Lorien. It's…it's too overwhelming. I can't do this. I can't be the mother of a child who will change the world! It's just all too…too incredible to accept!"

"Yes, Isaboe, you *can* do this, because you will not be alone. I will be with you through your journey, and when I can't, I will place a veil of protection around you to keep you safe. No harm will come to you, or the child, I promise you that."

Unsure of what her next move should be, Isaboe sat on the bed trying to wrap her mind around the enormity of what Lorien had told her. "So, what do I do now? What is this journey I'm supposed to take?" Isaboe's voice was rimmed with resignation.

"Well, what was your intent upon coming to Edinburgh?" Lorien asked with a look of relief.

"You know very well what my intent was. It was to find my…children," she answered meekly.

"Then find your children we shall. That is your journey, to seek and find the whereabouts of Anna and Benjamin."

"But, you said I cannot…I mean, no mortal can…love me." Isaboe sounded like a frightened child, accepting whatever fate was bestowed upon her. Whatever willpower she did have was quickly vanishing. As if it had been caught by a wave and taken to the depths of the ocean, she felt the last trace of hope being sucked away, lost forever.

"Yes, but you still want to know what became of them, that they are well, don't you? You don't need to tell them who you are, they wouldn't believe you anyway," Lorien said smugly. "It may take many months to locate them, but we shall, and we shall do it before we return to Euphoria. That way you will leave here knowing that Anna and Benjamin went on to live full lives, and you can have peace with that knowledge."

With a satisfied smile, Lorien patted Isaboe's hand, stood up and smoothed out her dress before strolling across the room. "Well, I must be going. I've stayed too long and have used more faerie glamour than I should have, but I do believe that we've made great progress. Don't you?"

Isaboe only looked at Lorien with a blank stare, and she felt the heavy weight of surrender settle into her chest.

"Alright, well, you look like you could use some rest. Why don't you get some sleep, and I'll see you tomorrow. We'll discuss our route to Orkney." Lorien tried to sound cheerful, but her words fell on deaf ears.

"Wait!" Isaboe stood up quickly. "Is there anything else that you haven't told me? Anything else I need to know?" She searched Lorien's eyes, hoping that she knew the whole terrible truth.

Lorien just smiled and placed a hand over hers. "No dear, that's it. There isn't anything else that you need to know. Now, you get some rest, and we'll talk tomorrow."

In a quick flash of light, Lorien disappeared. The room suddenly felt cold, and filled with a dark emptiness fed by what Isaboe now knew. For the rest of her life, she would be the Mother Alaina in a land called Euphoria.

CHAPTER 40

THE THREAT REVEALED

Rosalyn pulled her cloak tightly around her shoulders as she stepped out into the cool dawn air and made her way over to Connor, who was preparing his horse to leave. "Gentlemen of character usually say goodbye. Or at least wish me a safe trip to hell. I'm rather disappointed." She stood behind Connor shivering as she watched him cinch the saddle around the horse's flank.

After finishing his adjustments, Connor turned around. "I was coming back in to give ye a proper farewell. I just wanted to make sure everything was ready so I could be on my way."

"Connor, there are things you need to know. I saw things in the Remembering yesterday that were… disturbing. I don't think you know what you're up against."

"I ken I need to get back to Isaboe as soon as possible. I'll deal with everything else as it comes," he said, turning back to his horse and preparing to mount.

"Running off to save your woman without knowing what you're up against will only get you both killed. You are dealing with powers you've never experienced before. Faerie magic is strong, Connor. It can be deadly if you don't approach it with the respect it deserves."

Connor reeled around. "Isaboe is in danger, and I need to get back to her as soon as possible. I appreciate everything ye've done for me. So, if ye have any last bits of wisdom, now is the time, cause I'm leaving."

Rosalyn ran her hands through her hair before taking a deep sigh. "Yesterday, I received more than just your memories. I saw a very powerful force surrounding Isaboe. A Fey Queen from the land of Euphoria named

Lorien has become her constant companion, manipulating and twisting her mind. I believe she's been telling lies to make Isaboe believe her, to trust her. This is a very strong and powerful fey. She will do whatever it takes to accomplish her task—to take possession of Isaboe's child—*your* child.

"I have no idea what she's telling Isaboe to keep her under control, but the truth is she is just the vessel in which the child grows. Once the Fey Queen has the baby, she will no longer need Isaboe. I fear that as soon as the baby is born in the land of Euphoria, Lorien will dispose of Isaboe. She will send her out from the world of the fey, back into the mortal world alone, and any number of years will have passed. Lorien cannot allow Isaboe to stay and be a mortal mother to this child. The queen must raise the child as her own. A half-mortal, half-fey child to be groomed for her ultimate goal—to return the Earth back into the hands of the Underlings, regardless of the changes it will bring to mortals."

Rosalyn paused to let that sink in. "You must prevent this, Connor. If Lorien takes Isaboe back into the realm of the Underlings, all is lost. Everything you and I know in this world could be changed forever, and not for the better. But know this; Lorien will stop at nothing to succeed in her goal. She will use whatever means she deems necessary. She is deceptive, misleading, and powerful. That is a very dangerous mix. She will not give up easily, so be very wary not to be caught up in her web of deception."

Confusion written across his face, Connor stood staring at Rosalyn. "If this Lorien wants the child so badly, why did she ever let Isaboe leave there in the first place?"

"Remember what Demetrick said about the diversity between our two worlds, the different levels of energy and time? It must have something to do with their measurement of time being different than ours. If Isaboe had remained in their world, it might have been as long as a hundred of our human years before the child would be born. Maybe even for faeries, that's just too long."

Connor mounted his horse before looking down at Rosalyn, "Anything else?"

"Yes. Isaboe has suffered a great loss. Her psyche has to be very fragile right now, especially if she is alone with Lorien. With the lies that are being told to her, she has to be very confused and frightened. Be careful what you say to her, especially concerning the child, as she may see you as a threat."

"Demetrick was right in sending me to ye. Ye're a wise and compassionate woman. Thank ye for yer hospitality, for everything."

Rosalyn smiled up at him before reaching out to touch his leg. "Before you go—Isaboe's last name—do you know what it is?"

"McKinnon. Why?"

"No reason, only curious. Now go, and be safe." Rosalyn nodded as Connor spurred his horse forward, and soon he was riding back down the side of the ridge. She watched until he was no longer visible before turning back into her cave to make arrangements for her own departure.

CHAPTER 41

ACCEPTANCE

Visited again by her nightmare, Isaboe spent another restless evening. Broken bits and pieces replayed themselves throughout the night; blood on her hands, Margaret's cadaverous body, and the sword protruding from Connor's chest.

My love for you was my death sentence.

At least I was able to save you.

Now my blood will be on your hands.

Isaboe's eyes snapped open, and her breath caught in her throat as she stared up at the ceiling. Though awake, she was not free of her dream; she was living her nightmare. She clutched at her blankets as the frightening images continued to echo around in her mind. Her hands were shaking, and her heart felt like it would beat its way out of her chest.

After forcing herself to rise, Isaboe quickly dressed and brushed her hair before looking at her reflection in the mirror. Her eyes were swollen from crying and there were dark bags beneath them. She just wanted this to be over. Why did she allow Lorien to stop her?

Isaboe scarcely noticed the people, animals, and vehicles on the street as she walked toward the small restaurant. Though it was a struggle, she managed to eat at least part of her breakfast. As she sat staring at what was left on her plate, moving it from side to side with her fork, she tried not to think about leaving Margaret. It felt as if she were abandoning her friend, something she knew Margaret would never do. But Margaret would never accept, let alone believe, what Lorien had told her. Nor would Connor. For that reason, Isaboe knew she couldn't tell either of them why she had to go alone.

Though it went directly against what she knew was right—to walk out on a friend and to break her word—what choice did she have? She had made a promise to a man who loved her. Just four days earlier, she thought she could be happy with Connor forever, but not anymore. Lorien had showed her that fate had different plans for her future.

"Mind if I join you?"

Pulled from her thoughts by a familiar voice, Isaboe looked up to see Lorien taking the seat opposite her. The Fey Queen's dress was as red as her lips, dark and crimson. Her blond hair fell to one side as she gave Isaboe a haughty smile.

Feeling no need to reply, Isaboe looked at Lorien with a vacant stare.

"My, don't we look glum today? It doesn't look like you've eaten much of your breakfast. You know, you do have the child to consider."

"What do you want, Lorien?"

"I see your manners have not improved this morning."

Isaboe had no response to Lorien's quip, offering her only a steely glare.

"In no mood for conversation today either, hmm? How is Margaret this morning? Any better?"

Isaboe doubted the Fey Queen's show of concern. "She's still asleep. She hasn't ever really woke up. I find that a little odd, don't you?" She watched Lorien jut her chin a bit higher, nor did she miss the disdain she saw in the Fey Queen's haughty expression. After glaring at her for a long uncomfortable moment, Isaboe continued, "But according to the doctor, her wounds are healing, and the infection seems to be gone."

"Well, that's splendid news! So now that you know Margaret is on her way to recovering, we can be on our way."

"Now? *Today?*" Isaboe wasn't prepared, she wasn't ready. But how could she ever prepare for what she was facing.

"We would be wise to move quickly."

"But I...I can't go yet. I know that the nurses and Doctor Murray will continue to take care of her, but what if Margaret takes a turn for the worse? I need to be here for her. I have to know she'll be alright."

"Isaboe, when Margaret recovers, she'll have questions. What are you going to tell her? Not the truth. She won't believe you. You don't want to have to lie to her, so it would be best not to have to address it at all. Now is the time to leave, before she realizes what our…what *your* plans are."

As much as she had tried to prepare herself for leaving Margaret, realizing that the time had arrived brought on such intense anxiety that Isaboe had to run out the back door of the café and vomit what little breakfast she had eaten. It took more than a few deep breaths before she could regain her composure and return to the table where Lorien waited patiently.

Feeling like a helpless child, Isaboe was unsure of what else to do but follow instructions. She sat and waited for Lorien to dictate the how and when of their departure.

"You still have a horse, do you not?" Lorien finally asked.

"Yes." Void of any hope, Isaboe's reply was timid and withdrawn.

"Well then, we'll put some supplies together and send you on your way north. You should make fairly good progress today. The weather seems to be decent, though a bit chilly. Do you have any warmer clothing?"

"What do you mean, send *me* on my way? I thought you were coming with me?" There was an edge of fear in Isaboe's voice, and though her relationship with Lorien was built on mistrust and anger, the fear of riding out on her own presently outweighed the resentment she felt for the fey woman.

"Of course, I am. I just won't be with you every moment. I'll make sure that you have everything you need before you depart the city, and I'll come to you each evening before dark. I'll make sure you'll have plenty of food and water, and help you find shelter. During the time I won't be with you, I'll keep a veil of protection surrounding you, just as I always have. I told you that you would not be alone, and I meant that. I will take care of you, Isaboe, I promise." With something that may have been compassion glittering in her eyes, Lorien reached out to take her hand, but Isaboe quickly pulled it away.

Pushing back her chair, Isaboe stood up. "I have something to do before I leave."

"What is that?" Lorien asked suspiciously.

"I may not be able to tell Margaret or Connor why I'm leaving alone, but I am not walking out on them without leaving proper goodbyes. I owe them both at least that," she said sharply before turning and walking out of the café.

Margaret was awake and sitting up when Isaboe entered the room, and a nurse sat by her side, spoon-feeding her broth. Though still very weak, Margaret managed to give Isaboe a smile and a little wave. After the broth was finished, the nurse left, saying she would be back later.

"I can't even begin to tell you how great it is to see you awake, and eating too!" Isaboe said, giving Margaret a hug before taking the seat vacated by the nurse.

"Well, I can't actually say that was edible, but the nurse said it would be…good for me." After struggling to get the words out, Margaret laid back on the bed, closed her eyes, and began breathing heavily.

"My dear, dear friend, how are you feeling?" It took so long for Margaret to answer that Isaboe thought she had fallen back to sleep.

"I'm…doing alright, been better though."

"Do the wounds still hurt much?"

"Only when I'm awake."

Isaboe didn't know what to say. Though there was so much she wanted to tell Margaret, she couldn't find the words.

"Is Connor here?" Margaret asked.

"No, Connor left a few days ago. He should be back soon."

"So, you…you've been alone?"

Isaboe didn't answer right away. The truth was she hadn't been alone. Lorien had kept her company—a company she hadn't wanted or welcomed—but company never the less. "Yes. I've been here, watching over you." She paused, taking a deep breath. "Margaret, I'm so sorry for what I said to you just before you were injured. I had no right to be so bold, so cruel to you! All that you have done for me, I…I'll never be able to repay you. What I said to you was so wrong. Can you ever forgive me?" Isaboe struggled to fight back the tears.

"I have no idea…what you're talking about. Whatever it was, I can't recall. So…there's nothing to forgive, wee one," Margaret said, giving Isaboe a weak smile.

Though convinced that Margaret did in fact remember, even in her current condition, Isaboe silently thanked her friend for still being strong for her, just as she had been for months.

"Have you…been taking care of yourself?" Margaret's words came slowly, her eyes closed.

"Well, sort of, though I probably haven't eaten as well as I should. I haven't been sleeping well. I've had some…bad dreams," she said quietly.

Margaret didn't respond right away. Slowly turning her head, she looked at Isaboe through sleepy eyes. "I'm sorry, what were you saying?"

"It wasn't important." Isaboe answered with a lie and a smile.

"So, have you…eaten today?" Margaret had difficulty keeping her eyes open. It was obvious she would soon be slipping back into that place where she could not be reached, and Isaboe didn't want to let her go.

"I tried, but it didn't stay down."

"Well, try again. Go eat something. I'll still be here. I'm not going… anywhere." Her voice was so weak that Isaboe barely heard her words.

"No, but I am," Isaboe whispered as she watched Margaret slip back into the healing rest her body needed. Standing over the bed, she etched the memory of her friend's face firmly in her mind.

Connor pushed his horse hard throughout the morning, hoping to make it to Edinburgh by nightfall. Rosalyn's words and warnings kept repeating in his mind as he tried to figure out what he would tell Isaboe when they were finally together again. But that was secondary. His fear for her, imagining what she must have been going through since he left, is what pushed him anxiously onward.

The memory of Isaboe standing on the porch of the hotel, promising to wait for him, felt distant and faded, as if it were the remnant of a vanishing dream. He felt nearly overwhelmed by the need to wrap himself around her, protect her, and keep her safe. It gnawed at his gut and tore at his heart as he silently berated himself for leaving her in the first place.

Hold on Isaboe, I'm coming. Be strong, my love, I'm coming for ye.

Promises made can easily become promises broken. When two hearts are destined to be one, they both suffer when torn apart. And when the separation is caused by a broken promise, the outcome can only be pain.

ACKNOWLEDGEMENTS

When I think about all the people who have played a role in the fact that you are now reading this book, it goes without saying that my editors Sara Kraft and John Thompson deserve top billing. Not only did they see a gem in my roughly written manuscript that needed polishing—*a lot of polishing*—they challenged me to become a better writer. At different times throughout this process, it has been my editors who have lifted me up, kept me focused on the goal, held my hand, and given me the courage to keep moving forward, one step at a time. I cannot praise my editors enough, nor over-emphasize the depth of my gratitude for what they have meant to me on this journey. Thank you, John and Sara. As you know, I couldn't have done this without you.

I also want to thank my family, and apologize to them at the same time, for forcing them to read those first drafts so many years ago. You were all very gracious in not telling me the truth about how bad they were. Fortunately, that's what editors are for.

But years before the universe brought my fabulous editors into my path, I needed to know that I had a product that was worth the effort. Even though it was still very rough, I asked two women whose opinion I respect to be my draft readers: Gina Pafundi and Kay Howell. After graciously doing so, they both told me, "You've got something here, girl. Go for it." Thank you, Kay and Gina, for that push of faith.

There have been many others who have inspired me on this journey. Friends, family, and writing professionals have offered meaningful nuggets along the way, and many of them don't even realize how they've contributed. Staying focused and positive when writing a series of books that you're preparing to publish is not always easy. But, thanks to people like Kristen Lamb, an author/social media guru and founder of W.A.N.A.— We Are Not Alone—I haven't felt so alone. Thank you, Kristen, for all of those wonderful blogs—for the ones that kept me laughing and for the ones that kept it real. You always offered support and words of wisdom.

Another professional the universe graciously brought into my path is Erik Jacobson of LongFeather Book Design. Thank you, Erik, for tapping into my artistic mind and creating a work of art, exactly what I was going for.

And I would be remiss if I did not mention the greatest of those who have inspired me to write fantasy. JRR Tolkien, author of *The Hobbit* and *Lord of the Rings*, believed in a world where fey magic was very real and very powerful, where magical creatures from other realms interact with beings in our primary world. Tolkien knew the power of literary imagination to bring those mystical characters to life, and he paved the way for all future fantasy writers.

Lastly, I have to thank my husband and best friend, Tom. Without his love, support, and belief in me all these years, I wouldn't have been able to accomplish this.

ABOUT THE AUTHOR

As far back as I can remember, I've been enchanted by the magic of the fey and fascinated by anything Scottish. My love for literary fantasy and storytelling began at an early age, and I knew I was destined to share this incredible tale with the world someday. I just hadn't expected "someday" to take so long. But as life will do, it threw some obstacles in my path as an author.

Being a career-oriented woman, I've owned and operated two successful businesses, raised two wonderful sons, and have managed to stay happily married to my best friend for over forty years. But my desire to share this story—a story that has been twenty years in the making—has always remained my golden ring.

www.ingramcontent.com/pod-product-compliance
Lightning Source LLC
Chambersburg PA
CBHW021133110726
47900CB00002B/336